This story has been written as a memorial to the search party from Englee who went far beyond the call of duty to search for the lost Ranger, fighting all the elements that nature could unleash. Let this be a report on behalf of the people of Englee and the surrounding area, to the Federal Government, requesting that the four people who made up this search party – Pleman Gillard (Deceased), Arthur Compton (Deceased), Jack Thomas (Deceased) and Jack Brown (Living) be awarded their long overdue recognition.

First published 1986
Reprinted 1987

Will Anyone Search for Danny?

Earl B. Pilgrim

Typesetting and Production
by
Typecraft & Design
Cover design by - C.C. Keats Advertising, Ltd.

Printed
by
Robinson-Blackmore

As this manuscript took shape, I received helpful comments and criticisms from many colleagues. I wish to thank: Honourable J. R. Smallwood, Bernim Gill, Rex & Barb Boyd, Freeman Cull Jr., Eric Kinden, Bert Weir, Alvonne Sutton, Chesley Pittman, Herb Pittman, the late Chesley Cassell, David Owens, Winston Ropson, Samuel Compton Sr., Rev. Roy Rogers, Robert Gillard Sr., Wayne Canning, William Clarke, the late James Trok, Bernard Bromley, Sheila Maynard, the late Edward Corcoran, Ward Cooper, William Greene, Eugene Mercer, James Hancock, Frank Bearsford, Wilson Canning Sr., Samuel Compton Jr., the late Noah Pittman, William Noseworthy, John Goodyear.

Special thanks to Ada Beaudain, Gayle Chaulk, Joe Sheen, Ivy Kearny (Cull), Ina Simms, Ross Pilgrim, Dr. Peter Roberts, John Newell, Kevin Simms, Bill Carpenter Jr.

Prologue

Who's got the grit to listen to a story that's untold
About the dying Newfie Ranger, lying in the ice and snow
With his feet and hands all frozen, his food and shelter gone
He is dying, yes he's dying, lying in the chilly dawn.

Danny Corcoran 21, has St. John's down in his heart,
He hasn't met the northern blizzards that can tear your soul apart.
He ignored old timers' warnings "Only travel in the trees,
If you walk the open country, you are guaranteed to freeze.

A report has reached the Ranger, they're killing all the caribou.
"Then I'll patrol the open country, it's the proper thing to do
I'll catch those crooks and lock them up over in Port Saunders jail
And return in four to Harbour Deep in time to catch the mail."

He never returned in just four days to catch the Northern mail.
They found him dying in the snow next to a logger's trail.
It took seven days to the hospital from his icy bed of snow
"Too late, too late," said the doctor, "to live he can't. We know."

Now it's in the poachers cabins as they sit around at night
When the wind blows through the mountains and they gaze at the lamp light.
You can hear the sound of crying, of sobs, of moans, and yells,
It's Danny, the Newfie Ranger, the Red Head Newfie Ranger
He's frozen, limping, crawling, and lost on the open hills.

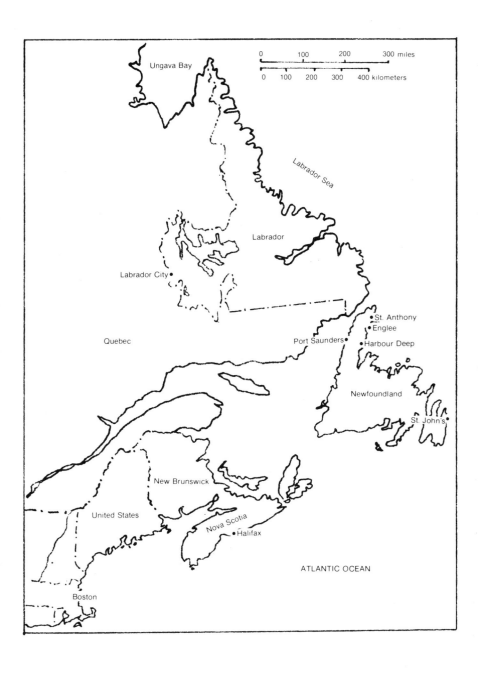

Ungava Bay

Labrador Sea

Labrador

Labrador City

Quebec

St. Anthony
Englee
Port Saunders
Harbour Deep

Newfoundland

St. John's

New Brunswick

United States

Nova Scotia
Halifax

ATLANTIC OCEAN

Boston

0   100   200   300 miles

0   100   200   300   400 kilometers

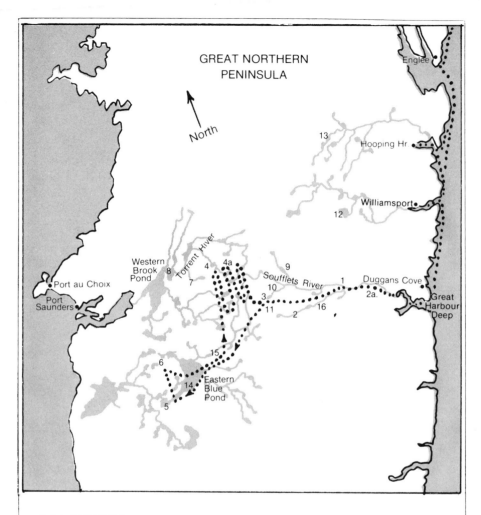

GREAT NORTHERN PENINSULA

North

Englee

Hooping Hr.

13

Williamsport

12

Western Brook Pond

Torrent River

8
4
4a
9
Soufflets River
1
Duggans Cove

Port au Choix

7
10
3
2a.
Great Harbour Deep

Port Saunders

11
2
16

15

6

Eastern Blue Pond

14

5

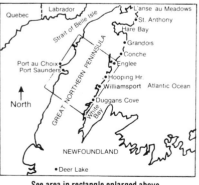

Labrador

Quebec

Strait of Belle Isle

L'anse au Meadows

St. Anthony

Hare Bay

Grandois

Conche

Englee

Port au Choix
Port Saunders

Hooping Hr.

Williamsport

Atlantic Ocean

North

Duggans Cove

White Bay

GREAT NORTHERN PENINSULA

NEWFOUNDLAND

Deer Lake

See area in rectangle enlarged above.

1. Hancock's Camp, near where Danny spent his 15th and 16th nights and was found by search party.

2. Ben Hynes Brook.

2a. Elige Newman's Camp, where Danny spent first night.

3. Spent second night and froze feet.

4. Devil's Lookout

4a. Area where Danny was on country and could not get off.

5. Belburn's Camp, fourth night.

6. Where Danny fell in water, lost compass.

7. Lady Worster Hill.

8. Middle Pond

9. Rocky Stent

10. Wolfe Barren

11. Copper Barren, spent 12th and 13th nights here.

12. Red Sea Pond named so because of slaughter of caribou years ago.

13. Blue Skirt

14. Spent three nights here.

15. Spent the night.

16. Spent 14th night here.

*Winter
1935 – 36*

Chapter 1

The early morning sun shone brightly on the copper coloured hair of the Newfoundland Ranger as he very smartly paced along the narrow dirt road of the little town known as Harbour Deep, located on the Northeast coast of Newfoundland. His ears very quickly caught the thudding sound of an axe on wood which brought his attention to a workshop about 100 feet away. A few quick strides brought him to the open door. He found himself looking down at the back of a man dressed in a mackinaw oil jacket, chopping a knee for a boat that was in the workshop under construction. The chopping ceased and the man with the axe quickly turned towards the visitor. The sweating face lit up when he saw the red-headed stranger, and the uniform the man was wearing quickly made the introduction. This was the young Newfoundland Ranger who would be posted in this little town this winter.

"I am Danny Corcoran. Glad to meet you."

"I'm Noah Pittman, but they call me Uncle Noah around here."

"Okay Uncle Noah," he said with a sense of belonging, "what will you do with that piece of wood?"

"I'm going to fit this piece in the stern section. Watch!"

"By yourself?"

"Yes."

"No need to do that. I'll give you a hand."

"Okay, thanks."

Danny reached down, picked up the big end and easily lifted the block of timber while Uncle Noah lifted the small end.. Together they very quickly put the stern knee into place. This started a great friendship between the 21 year old Newfoundland Ranger and Noah, the 36 year old fisherman.

As they walked along the narrow road, they chatted getting to know each other better.

"Danny, I heard you have Joe Norcutt's house."

"Yes, the Government has borrowed the use of it for the winter."

"We are neighbours," Noah said. "Come in for a cup of tea. Times are bad here you know. We had a bad summer. No fish. The water was too warm."

The two men stepped into the porch. "Hey Nellie, got the teapot on?"

A pause, then a clear voice said, "Are you alone?"

The pantry door opened and a middle-aged woman looking older than she actually was, stepped into the kitchen. "Sir," she said, "I am glad to meet you and especially at such an early hour."

He held out his hand and said, "Call me Danny."

She shook hands and said, "I'm Nellie." Her gaze settled on the red hair. "What a fine young man" she thought. Then she said, "On what side of the family did the red hair come from?"

"From my father. They tell me he had red hair but it turned grey overnight. He died just a few years ago. My mother is still living and I've got three brothers and one sister." He looked at the floor.

She said, "Danny, I'm sorry!"

He said, "You can hear a lot more about my father this winter." It made him feel better.

The conversation regarding the weather during the winter was not very encouraging. "Did you say, Uncle Noah, that the snow could get up to 8 feet deep?"

"Yes, and some places maybe even more! Last year we had a storm which lasted almost 30 days. It was almost blizzard conditions all the time, cold enough to freeze ya." He looked out the window. "Do you see that river? That is Soufflett's River. We call it Northeast Bottom Brook. You go in a ways, straight up, then straight down, all hills." His eyes rolled, he put his hand to his forehead to wipe off the sweat.

Danny said, "What kind of people live in Williamsport?" He looked at Uncle Noah. "Do they hunt out of season?"

Uncle Noah quickly answered, "I don't know. You"ll have to ask them."

"I'm sorry, Uncle Noah. I didn't mean it that way. What I meant was are they countrymen?"

Uncle Noah looked him in the eye and replied, "We're all countrymen, Danny, and we're that way because we have mouths to feed, no pleasure involved at all. I'll tell you more about that later. Let's eat."

Aunt Nellie placed baked beans and toutons in front of the two. It was a meal for hungry working men. After two cups of strong tea, the young Ranger thanked Aunt Nellie and walked out.

As he stepped out on the road, he noticed faces in almost every window and then he realized that he was one of a group of men that the people of the Northern Peninsula looked up to and thought a lot about. He very quickly picked up the pace and let his military training take over. He made approximately 100 paces when he noticed someone coming towards him. He forgot the faces in the windows and for a moment his gaze settled on a girl that made his heart leap. The girl in front of him was wearing a knitted two piece, wine coloured suit that hugged her 120 pounds. As he got closer, he noticed the long black hair under the bandana she was wearing. He stepped to the side of the road and said, "Good morning. I'm Danny Corcoran, the ranger."

"Good morning. I'm Barbara Gale. How do you do?"

"Fine," was his reply. "By the books you're carrying, you must be the school teacher."

"Yes, I am, Danny," she replied with a smile.

He started to blush knowing this was no ordinary girl. She must be the most beautiful girl in the world. Her smile could turn the dirt road into streets of gold. "I want to walk you to the school," he stated.

"Yes. Please do."

"May I carry your books?"

"Yes. But first, call me Barbara."

"Thank you, Barbara." He took her books and started to walk towards the school. "Barbara, how long have you been here in Harbour Deep?"

"Just two months. I came here August 24th and this is October 26th. Time has gone fast."

"Well," he said, "I came here last night on the Prosproe. I was seasick for two days."

She laughed. "You'll get your sea legs."

Very seriously he said, "This country looks strange to me. Maybe it's because of the hills and all the forest." He paused, then said laughingly, "It's not like St. John's."

"You'll love it here," was her reply.

"Have you got the people all sized up yet?" Then he added, "I mean, what kind of people live here?"

She thought for a moment, then replied, "Danny, the people that live here are great. They are hard working and kind. For instance, there's not one morning yet they have let me go into a cold school. Someone is always there to light the fire at least one hour before I arrive. And since I've been here, I've seen everybody drop their work and run to Ezekiah Cassell's house upon hearing his little girl had something in her throat. If for instance, someone isn't in from fishing at dark, everybody in the place is alert and ready to go. In fact, the people here are ready for any emergency. This is my personal view."

"A good report, Barbara. These are my kind of people," he said. "How many people do you teach?"

"Twenty-four, from grade one to grade eleven, and my hours are 9 A. M. 'til 4:30 P. M. and from 7 P. M. 'til 10 P. M."

"Well," he replied, "You are a busy girl."

"Not every night," she quickly replied. She started to blush. She stumbled on a rock and almost fell, but he quickly reached and prevented her from falling. "Barbara, you have to be more careful."

She thanked him and he replied, "It's the duty of every Newfoundland Ranger to prevent..."

She interrupted, "We are at the school. My books please."

He handed her the school books. His eyes met hers. He opened his mouth to say something, but no words came.

"See you later, Danny."

She quickly turned and went into the school. He turned to walk back the road. His heart was pounding. What a girl! He looked at the windows in the houses. Only one face was visible. It was Uncle Noah, smiling. He waved for him to come near the window. He walked over. Uncle Noah opened the window and said, "Danny, I'm going up to Northwest Bottom. There's freight up there for me. Would you like to come along? I want you to meet Gill Ellsworth. He's the wireless operator."

"You got yourself a passenger."

He went to his house and got his cap and plain coat and the two men started out for Northwest Bottom. Noah didn't start any conversation but he knew what the young Ranger was thinking about.

Chapter 2

It was almost Christmas when Danny sat down to dinner at Jim Pollard's house. At the table sat Gill Ellsworth, a boarder at Jim's. They were talking about the hard times the people were experiencing along the coast as a result of the failure of the fishing season just past.

"I was looking at statistics last night," said Danny. "I have issued more dole-orders in two and half months than what was issued here in the past two years, and we haven't even gotten into winter yet."

Gill replied that he didn't know how people could live on dole-orders. (The dole-orders were forms of relief. It was 6 cents per day per person. For instance: if there were ten in a family, that family would receive 60 cents per day or $18.00 per month.) But like Gill said, there wasn't any other choice. The conversation changed very quickly.

"Danny, do you still intend to go over to Port Saunders for Christmas or has Barbara changed your mind?" asked Gill.

Danny laughed, "Nobody changes the mind of a Corcoran!"

Gill smiled, "But...?"

Danny replied, "But I have decided not to go. I may go to Englee instead."

Gill quickly replied. "You'll go nowhere for Christmas my son. You wouldn't leave Harbour Deep for all the world."

Everyone at the table laughed. Then Gill added, "Now people hear this. I am madly in love with Grace Loder and I want everyone to know that it is my intention to marry her."

Everybody laughed. Then there was a knock at the door, so Mrs. Pollard went to see who it was. A little girl with curly hair entered the kitchen. "Aunt Milly," she said, "Mom wants to know if you got any dinner cooked. She was wondering if you got any pot liquor left so we can soak our bread in it."

"All eyes were on the girl. Her clothes were clean but full of patches. Gill told Mrs. Pollard to leave his dinner in the pot when she gave it to the girl. Danny could hardly believe his ears. Mrs. Pollard said, "This is Helen, my sisters's little girl. Her father, Gord Ropson, died last summer with T.B. There are seven kids besides her. I don't know how they'll make it through this winter. I guess we'll have to take them in."

Danny rose from the table. "Helen, come with me."

When they were outside, she showed him where she lived. It was a big two-storey house all beautifully painted. Together they walked up to the house, Danny holding the little girl's hand. When they reached the door, the girl opened it and the Ranger stepped inside. In the kitchen he saw a table at which eight places were very neatly set. The only sign of food on the table was bread. Standing near the table was a neatly dressed woman of about forty. She wore her hair in a roll. Danny noticed the tidiness of the house. The snow white tablecloth and the white apron that she wore told Danny that this was a special woman, but due to her present circumstances she was put in a very tight spot.

"Ma'am, I'm Danny Corcoran, the ranger stationed here for the winter."

I'm Vera Ropson. Please sit down."

She pulled out a chair from the table and Danny sat down. She then asked Helen to leave the room so the adults could talk.

"Mr. Corcoran, my husband was a hard working man, who always provided us with full and plenty, but for the last two years we've seen hard times. Ever since he took sick and had to give up fishing we haven't had very much. I've had many hunger pains in the last month, and the only food we've had is what people have given us and God knows everyone is having it tough. You see this table? The only thing we have in this house in the line of food is bread. Just before the children come home at noon, I send Helen out to ask the neighbours for anything they could give me to help us get down bread. Helen should not have gone to Milly's when she had visitors." She sighed.

Danny looked at her with tears in his eyes and said, "Mrs. Ropson, why haven't you come to me? At least I can help some. I am permitted to give you $18.00 per month. It would be a help.

She admitted her pride could not feed her children. He gave her a note for $18.00 and called Helen. "Helen, you and I are going to the store." They walked to the store, bought a can of beans, tea, butter, milk, and two candies. "Give one candy to your mother," he said, "and tell her it's from me."

He took the youngster in his arms and prayed a silent prayer and wept out loud as his mind went back to when he grew up in St. John's and his mother had to work every day to keep food in the mouths of him and his sister after his father had died. "Tell your mother that God will take care of her."

The little girl ran home with the armful of parcels.

It was a blusterous day with the wind Northwest and a lone figure was seen coming from the mouth of Soufflett's River. The man was not running and yet he was not walking. The pace looked to be what Danny saw at the races around St. John's, where men would walk in the ten mile race and at the end would have to be given oxygen, but his pace seemed to be a little faster. Danny knew this from being an athlete and from running in the six mile races on Regatta Day. Danny decided to put on his snowshoes and run up to meet the stranger. He strapped on his snowshoes and started to run. The distance was about one mile. He was running in a dog team track, and as he drew near the oncoming man, he noticed he was walking outside the track. When they met he asked, "Is there an emergency, sir?"

"I don't know," was the reply.

"Are there?..." Danny noticed the bag on the man's back, on which was written "Royal Mail". "Ah, ah", he thought. This is the mailman from Englee, that all the people have been talking about. Danny noticed this man did not slow down, but he still had to run to stay abreast of him. "I'm Danny Corcoran."

"You're what?" was the stranger's reply.

"I'm Danny Corcoran, the Newfoundland Ranger stationed here in Harbour Deep."

"Do you have any mail for me? If you do, I want it right away. Have it ready. I'll be stopping for five minutes. Got to be back in Englee by supper. How is the ice? Is Edgar Pollard's dogs off? Is anyone here sick?" The man said all of this in one breath.

"Sir, would you mind telling me your name?"

"Nat Johnson."

"Sure", thought Danny. This is the man he had heard so much about.

"Sir, how far is it to Englee from here?"

"Forty-two miles up and forty-two miles down."

Eighty-four miles return in one day at that pace. Danny looked at him dumbfounded. "A man of steel. What an athlete he would have made."

"What'd you say?"

"I was just thinking out loud."

"I thought you said I was out to steal."

Danny saluted him as if he was his commanding officer. "How heavy is that bag on your back?"

The man replied in rapid speed. "Eighty pounds. I think someone must be having nails come." The man talked like he walked, full speed ahead.

Danny turned off at the Ranger's house all out of breath. Nat went to Sam Cassell's house. Sam's wife looked after the mail. He took off the load. Mrs. Cassell had his dinner already on the table. He looked at his watch. Almost every man in town crowded around him. Some were loading the return mail into his pack sack while others were repairing his snowshoes. Between mouthfuls he was answering one man's question. The question was, "Do you know if the nurse from Roddickton is coming up?"

"Hit Hillier is bringing her up next week," was his reply. He was asked many more questions but his replies were too fast to be understood, so everybody became silent. Then as quick as the mailman came, he left, and was out of sight, disappearing into the snowy jungle. Danny watched him when he left, then said to himself, "If he can leave Englee 42 miles away and return the same day, then surely I should be able to go across the Northern Peninsula to Port Saunders in 2 days. Yes, I think that's what I'll do. Its only 45 miles."

Chapter 3

It was January 16, 1936. Danny finished putting the supper dishes back in the pantry and sat down at the kitchen table looking over the list of dole orders he had issued so far between October and the end of December, 1935. He had already issued most of his budget and the winter had only begun. He would have to send a wireless to his commanding officer tomorrow. The wind outside howled but it looked like there was a break in the storm which had been raging for four days. He had never seen such a storm around St. John's. It was amazing how people could even keep their houses heated, especially burning all wood. The frost on his windows was close to half an inch thick.

As he studied his books, he heard dogs barking outside and he heard someone talking very loudly to the dogs. He hauled over the blinds, but he could see nothing. He was almost startled at the loud knock on the door and the first thing that came to his mind was a fire. He very quickly started for the porch. When the porch door opened in front of him, a man stood in the doorway wearing snowshoes, he was covered in snow and ice.

Icicles hung from his moustache and eyebrows. The homemade parka he was wearing looked like it was made from brin bags (burlap) all ragged at the elbows. He took off one cuff and was struggling to get the other off, but it was frozen to his wrist. "You," he said, very deeply, "I want to see the Ranger. Where is he?"

Danny looked very keenly at the man. There was something about him that appeared to be very special. "I'm the Ranger," Danny replied.

"Mr. Ranger, I have a letter for you."

"Shut the door and come inside."

The man started to slide and almost fell down, but caught his balance and then took off his well worn snowshoes. He stepped into the kitchen and took off his cap. Inside his coat a safety pin kept the top of his pocket closed to protect the letter. His large fingers fumbled at the pin. Then he produced a brown envelope addressed to the Newfoundland Ranger, Harbour Deep. Danny took the letter and stepped over to the light. He sat down and opened the letter and motioned for the man to sit down. The letter read:

> To Ranger Corcoran:
>
> Sir, I take my pen in hand to inform you that things here in Williamsport are not very good. A lot of people are hungry. I own a store, but I am unable to give out any more credit, and I would like for you, if at all possible, to come to Williamsport with Mr. Javis Pollard (Jave), the bearer of this letter.
> Thank you.
>
> Signed, Mr. Herb Randell, J.P.

Danny put down the letter and looked at the man who was about to light his crooked stem pipe. "Mr. Pollard, would you like to have a cup of tea?"

The man looked at him startled. "How do you know me?"

"I read it in the letter," replied Danny, then asked, "Would you like a lunch?"

"Yes. I had nothing to eat since me breakfast. Too cold."

Danny moved the kettle to the hottest part of the stove. "In fact Mr. Pollard, you can stay here in this house all night."

Jave put down his pipe and asked, "Is dar a hatch where you could get up in under the house?"

Danny looked at him startled. "No. No sir, you don't have to sleep up under the house. I got beds in this place with no one in them and one of them is yours for tonight."

He looked at the man with a sad look in his eye. Jave started to grin and looked at the Ranger with humor in his eyes and asked, "How many beds you got in this place, you?"

Danny stopped, then replied, "There are three extra beds, sir." He waited.

"Fine enough you. One for me and me eight dogs. They don't worry about sleepin' along with another four in each bed." His eyes gleamed like fire and biting on his pipe stem he waited for a reply.

Danny leaned over the table and said without a smile, "Sir, what I should do is put your dogs in bed and you out in the toilet."

Jave laughed and Danny knew that Jave had gotten the joke off on him. Then he thought that by the time this was told three or four times, what a story this would be. However, the best thing now he could do was to treat Jave a little bit extra.

"Okay," he said, "under that window outside you'll find a hatch. Let your dogs go in under there, but if they go fighting, I'll shoot the eight of them."

Jave just laughed and went outside. Danny heard a bit of loud noise as he made supper for Jave. He was just pouring up the tea when Jave came in with his arms full of dogs' harnesses and traces.

"Can I hang them up behind your stove, you?"

Danny looked at the man. "Would you like to put them in the pantry?"

"No, it's too cold in dar. Behind the stove is good enough."

"Yes," Danny replied.

Jave hung up the harnesses and traces behind the Waterloo Stove and took off his jacket and sat down at the table. "I'm some hungry, you, and, Ranger, call me Jave."

Danny looked at the man and said, "Call me Danny." He looked at him again, "or Dan."

Jave made a loud noise stirring his tea and said, "No, I will call ya Ranger." He quickly ate the soup and bread and lit his pipe again.

Danny then asked, "How are you off for food this winter, Jave?"

Jave lifted his head and replied "I got plenty of grub. I worked in Roddickton in the woods with Saunders and Howell and made $64.00 last month - a fortune."

Danny had to agree. He was making $1.50 per day. Then he thought, this is the first lumberjack he had met. He had heard talk of the hearty breed who worked around Canada Bay. He then asked, "What are the conditions up there? Many people hungry?"

"Dar's no dole orders up dar. Everybody works in the woods. The Company store got plenty of grub. They even got baloney."

Danny thought for a moment then asked, "Do they sell bacon?"

Jave looked at him in wonderment. "I don't know what that is. What is it?"

Danny replied, "That's pork smoked and you cut it in strips and fry it. It tastes delicious."

Jave started to laugh. "Someone said that Bill Stokes, the head man up in Roddickton, fries eggs and eats 'um. No difference in that?"

Danny kept silent.

Later that night the alarm clock brought Danny out of bed with a sudden jolt. He sat up, put his hands to his head, elbows on his knees. He felt warm air in the room. A voice called, "Hey, you, Ranger, breakfast is ready."

The lamp light flickered. He looked at the clock. 4:30 A.M. How good the warm air felt. It reminded him of the Newfoundland Hotel the night he had spent there waiting to catch the Prosproe to come to Harbour Deep.

"Listen, you, you're not going to spend all day in bed." Jave walked into the room. "Have a guess what I've made for breakfast for you."

"I don't know," was Danny's reply.

Jave put his pipe back in his mouth. "Munge," was his reply. "And if you soon don't come, I'll give it to the dogs."

Danny pulled on his pants and shirt and walked into the kitchen. It felt good to walk in a warm house this early in the morning.

"Sit down, Ranger. Everything is ready to eat."

He looked into the bowl on the table, then sat down. "Jave," he said squinting his eyes from the lamp light, "What in the world have you got cooked?"

"This is munge, Ranger, one of the best feeds going."

Danny took the spoon and gave the substance a few stirs. "Do I add sugar?"

"No," was Jave's reply. "The lassy makes it sweet enough."

Danny stirred some more, then crossed himself and tasted what he had in the bowl. He looked at Jave.

"How is it Ranger?"

"Flat!" Danny quickly replied. "What's it made from?"

"Some flour in cool water. Then you boil it and add lassy. Don't you think that's not good?"

Danny put down the spoon, reached over and turned up the light, got up from the table, walked into the pantry and came back with a bottle of squashberry jam. He said, "Jave, you give your munge to your dogs. I'll settle for bread and jam."

Jave picked up the dipper and spoon and started eating. "Any man who don't like munge is sick." He smiled as he ate.

It was a clear morning. The dogs under the house were moaning. They could smell the food. Jave stamped the floor and yelled, "Brandy, be quiet." The lamp flickered from the vibration.

Danny said "Take it easy, Jave. You might put your foot through the floor."

"Brandy is constantly barkin' but don't think he's not a good hinder. Hurry up we gets on the move."

Danny started to get his things together. "Jave, you get the dogs ready." He put on his heavy clothes, caught hold of the latch and pushed the door open. It was so frosty that it made a loud scruppling noise.

"Must be forty below," Jave said as he stepped out into the early morning air. The stars were twinkling in the sky. In a matter of minutes Jave had the dogs in harness and was ready to roll. Just as Danny was ready to put out the light, Noah Pittman appeared in the doorway. "Danny, where are you going?" he asked.

"To Williamsport," Danny replied.

"You're going to have a big break from Northeast Bottom Brook to the open country. Do you need any help?"

Danny thought for a moment. "If you want to come along, I would be pleased, and if you went then Jave wouldn't have to come back."

"Sure thing," replied Noah. "You tell Jave to go ahead and break the road and you get on the komatik with me."

"Great," said Danny.

Uncle Noah disappeared. Danny walked out into the morning. His first gulps of air almost took his breath away due to his lungs being filled up with cool air.

He never thought, being a Ranger, he would ever have to do this, but he was told in Whitbourne, (the headquarters of the Rangers) that he would be required to do everything and go everywhere to help people in need.

"Jave," he called, barely heard above the barking of the dogs, "you go on and break the road. I will be coming with Uncle Noah."

Jave looked very pleased that this was going to happen. "Ranger, that's some wonderful!" he replied.

Sometime later Danny stood on the hill and looked down at the smoke stacks that extended up from the whale plant and across the narrow fiords. A mile away hugging the foothills was a cluster of houses and stages. The smoke from the stove pipes went straight up in the air.

"Jump on, Danny. We could get a fast ride down to the shoreline."

And almost instantly they came down the 800 feet from the top of the hill along a narrow trail. They quickly crossed the ice to Williamsport and stopped in front of Herb Randell's store. Almost instantly people started to gather. Danny walked into the store, stood in the middle of it and looked around. The shelves looked very empty. As he turned towards the counter a voice cackled to him from the corner of the store. "Mr., who's you?"

The voice had a ring combined with a squeaking tone. "Who is ya? Yeah, I knows who you is. You're the Ranger from Harbour Deep."

Danny saw the woman. Her look gave him the impression of an able-bodied man. She lifted a giant hand and pointed her finger towards the man behind the counter. "Look," she said loudly without any hesitation. "Do you see him? Do you know what he's doin'? And listen to me Ranger, if you don't make 'em stop you can say goodbye to the vried lassy here in Williamsport. Yes, that's right Ranger. You can say goodbye to vried lassy in Williamsport. I feel like gettin' onto 'em myself only I'm not a man, but if I was a man, he'd sell no more shine lassy."

Danny looked at Noah who started to grin. Danny then decided to increase the show. He stepped in front of the woman. "Carry on Ma'am. The evening is still young." Danny took off his cap.

"Well pawn my socks!!" she replied. "Who knitted the red hair and smacked it on yer skull?"

People were beginning to congregate and laughter was heard. Danny hushed the crowd and asked, diverting his question towards the woman, "Ma'am tell me. What is vried lassy? Do you get drunk on it or is it good for a hangover?"

She looked at him curiously. "Vried lassy is vried lassy and you can't make anything else of it."

Herb Randell spoke up, "Sir." Everyone fell silent. "She's talking about fried molasses and the reason she's mad is..."

"Shut up, you!" yelled the woman and she shook two clenched fists at Herb.

Just then Danny noticed something slide from under her coat. With speed like lightening he dropped on one knee, reached out about six inches from the floor and caught the package. He stood up, opened the paper bag and brought out a bottle of moonshine. "Ah!" he said. "Is this vried lassy or is it shine lassy?"

The smiles left the audience. Danny looked at the woman very sternly and said, "Ma'am, there is only one thing that keeps me from putting you in prison, and that's your children and there is not a jail handy, but," he said, "you're not going to get off that light."

The crowd roared as Molly walked stark raving mad out the door. "This man even had a sense of humor," Uncle Noah thought to himself. "Molly Randell will not make any more moonshine in Williamsport."

Chapter 4

The mailman stepped into town, threw off the mailbag, ate his lunch and disappeared. Mr. Cassell opened the mail and gave Danny a letter. It was postmarked "Port Saunders". He became very excited. A letter from his buddy who went through recruit training with him in Whitbourne, Roy Hiscock. He rushed home and got his pocket knife out of his pocket and quickly opened the envelope. The letter was written January 26, 1936. It read:

Hello Danny,

I received your letter just after Christmas. I should have answered before. However, I'm a very busy man and we are having a very stormy winter so far. I was glad when you said you found a girl. It helps break up the long nights. I was looking at the mountains a few days ago and said, "Just think, over these mountains is Danny Corcoran at Harbour Deep. I think I'll go over one of these days and see him and maybe take away that school teacher from him." Ha Ha!

But, Danny, I'll tell you what. If you come over I'll get you a date with a girl here. She's the wireless operator, Shirley Simms. She's beautiful and a very nice girl. You will like her. If you decide to come, let me know before you start out. Some of the boys from here might be going in that way, especially people going in poaching. Is there much of that going on over your way? A lot is going on here. We expect to step up some extra patrols soon. If so, I will be in contact with you soon.

Your old buddy,
Roy Hiscock

Danny looked out the window at the hills and said, "Yes, I think I will start to plan a trip soon. It's only 45 miles. I'll go over and see Roy, especially before the rain comes."

Danny had a package arrive in the mail as well. What could it be? He quickly held it up to the lamp and noticed the postmark read,"Whitbourne". "Oh," thought Danny, "something from Headquarters." This was not a common thing. Maybe it was a nice cap and gloves or a new shirt. Then he felt it again. The word, "Fragile" was written on it. Must be something breakable. He felt it again. "Ah," he thought, "I know, a new pair of dress shoes. Yes, that's it! But then, "Fragile" would not be on the package."

The door came open and in walked young Ches Pittman, 15 years old, and Noah's oldest son. "Ches, have a guess what I've got in this package. It's from Headquarters in Whitbourne."

Ches looked at Danny with a grin. "A 'We miss you' cake."

Danny shook his fist at Ches. "One more smart remark like that and I'll bar you from this house."

Ches grinned. "I'll tell you what. I'll go get Barbara and let her open the package."

"Good." said Danny. In a few minutes Ches and Barbara came through the door. Danny was more excited than ever. The package lay on the table. Barbara asked, "Danny, can I open it?"

"Not yet!" he said. "You can have three guesses first."

"Good," she said. "No, it's not papers. Oh, I know, it's a lamp."

Ches said, "Maybe it's a rag doll."

Danny pointed to the door. "Out!" he ordered.

Ches just laughed. "Okay, no more, no more. I give you my word."

Danny looked at Barbara and said, "Open it!"

She took the knife, cut the string and took the paper off. She opened the box and their eyes caught the two words, "Phillips Radio."

"A radio!" the three of them said together.

Ches's eyes bulged out. It was the first one he ever saw. He quickly looked at it again and walked out without a word.

Danny looked at Barbara and said, "Ches is so excited, I think he's scared."

Barbara laughed. "The wires and aerial are here but one thing is missing." She looked at Danny.

"I know," he said, "the battery."

She looked up with a very anxious look. "We have to get it going. I want to hear about the rest of the world." She paused. "I know where I can get a battery!"

Danny laughed, "I bet you're thinking about the same place as I am."

Barbara quickly said. "Yes, from Gill Ellsworth."

"Right," said Danny. "Get Ches to harness his dogs. We're going up to the Bottom."

Barbara quickly left the house. Borrowing a radio battery was not a small matter in those days, especially from the Newfoundland Government and especially from Gill Ellsworth who 'went by the books'. However, Danny decided to give it a try. The four miles on dog team at night in thirty below temperatures was travelled quickly. He knocked at

Jim Pollard's door. A boy came out, looked at Danny and called back, "It's the Ranger."

"Well, come in sir!" Jim said as he came out to the porch.

"No thanks," replied Danny. "I would like to talk to Gill Ellsworth, if possible."

"Come in from the cold," Jim said. Danny stepped into the porch. Gill quickly stepped into the kitchen. "Danny, who's dead?"

"The radio!" said Danny quickly.

"The radio?" questioned Gill with eyes wide. "What in the world are you talking about? A radio?"

Danny looked at Gill with a kind of gleam in his eye. "Gill, a radio just arrived in the mail for me from Whitbourne Headquarters, but they didn't send a battery. I got the aerial and ground that came with it."

Gill quickly replied, "My son, to hear the Gerald S. Doyles news tonight I would take the last bit of power the wireless got."

"Come on then," said Danny. "Let's go to the office."

"We got a full case of battery connectors and everything," said Gill. "Jim, how about you harnessing up your dogs and you and I will go to Norde East Bottom and help get the radio going?"

"I'm with you!" replied Jim. Then the show was on the road two dog teams, four men and one radio battery.

So it was back at home again and the aerial and ground were quickly put up. The battery was connected and in the middle of the table stood the radio. Noah Pittman walked in and stood back. "So das a raddyo! I bet she'll never go!"

Danny laughed. "Barbara," he said, "I want to give you the honour of being the first person to turn on a radio in Harbour Deep. If you please?"

Barbara laughed. "I wonder how Marconi felt when he read the first wireless message on Signal Hill from Europe."

"Well, then turn her on!" said Noah.

Barbara reached for the switch, turned the button and the power came on. "Not too loud," said Gill, "you could blow the tubes."

Danny turned the dial. "Good evening, ladies and gentlemen and welcome. This is Albert Perlin bringing you the Gerald S. Doyle news from all over Newfoundland."

Everyone clapped. History was made in Harbour Deep.

Danny called from the doorway. "Hey, Ches, in a couple of weeks time I am going to Port Saunders for a three to four day trip. Do you want to come with me?"

"Yes sir! You bet!" replied Ches.

"Okay. I'm leaving around the 12th of March. I want to be back here by the 17th of March. That's Paddy's Day, you know. There's a program, "Jack Walsh", coming on the radio. I will be back to hear that. I'll invite a whole lot of folks to my house to hear the songs."

Ches said, "I'll talk to the old man about it. He's sure to let me go though."

"Good," said Danny.

Chapter 5

The wind was blowing the snow low over the country and the sun hung still in the afternoon sky. It gave the toughest of men a very uneasy feeling that he had better stick to the rules and not get caught out at night. The man steering the komatik noticed that the two hind dogs were beginning to freeze. He stopped his team and quickly turned to the man sitting on the komatik box. There were icicles hanging from his eyebrows and eyelashes. "Ple, I think the dogs are beginning to freeze. We got to head for the Blue Skirt and get a fire going."

Pleman Gillard stepped from the sleigh and shook himself. "Do you know something Gus? I bet 'tis 40 below and the wind is about 35 knots."

Gus laughed. "What a time for a swim!" He started to beat his arms to keep warm.

Ple's eyes started to stare at something in the distance. The dogs lifted their ears and noses. Gus Compton, the man known for sharp shooting around Englee, reached into the komatik box and took out the rifle, a 32 Special Winchester (12 shooter).

"Gus, we need eight, two apiece," Ple said.

Approximately 400 yards away caribou were running at a tremendous speed on the hard drifted snow.

"You'd better hurry," said Ple. Gus loaded the rifle, stood up and took aim. One shot was fired. The dogs started to bark all at once. The lead caribou fell and the rest of the caribou stopped. Another shot was fired. Another caribou fell. The animals started to run. Two more shots were fired and two more caribou fell on the run. Gus took the gun down. Ple blinked his eyes, then very quickly asked, "What's happening? What happened to the rifle?"

"Nothing," replied Gus.

"Well, knock down four more!" Ple said. "Hurry, they're going to shut in!"

Gus unloaded his rifle, lifted his hand and said, "One each is plenty."

"No," replied Ple. "Get two more for giving away." Ple started to shout with a squeaky voice. "There's poor old Aunt Louey Ellsworth. There's

Uncle Ned Compton and father."

Gus added, "And there's my son just born, and his son, and his grandson."

Both men looked at each other. "Maybe you're right, Gussy. Maybe you're right."

The dogs went wild. Gus waved to the drivers of the other dog team, Arthur Compton and Jack Brown. They quickly came over to where they were.

"Boys, you got some? How many?"

"Four," said Gus.

"Old man," said Art through tobacco juice, "you should have shot the works. Give me the gun. I want to shoot one for Peters." (Peters was the Ranger stationed in Englee.)

"Don't push your luck," said Jack Brown. "Not because you hate the man you want to dare him."

Ple interrupted, "I wouldn't give him fresh air."

Gus answered quickly, "Take it easy, Ple. Some day you might have to travel this country with him."

"Never," said Ple, "after watching his activities in Englee."

They heard 12 rifle shots just over the hill nearby in the direction where the caribou had gone. They saw two men and dogs coming towards them. They identified themselves as the Strait's fellows.

"How many did you get?" asked Gus.

"Seven!" they replied. "That's all was there. We want two more."

There was a pause.

"There are six of us. We killed fifteen yesterday. That makes twenty-two we got now. Two more will make up four apiece."

Gus became furious. There would be nothing left unless something was done. But how could they report this to the authority?

Jack Brown said, "Boys, this is no place to row. Let's get the caribou cleaned. We had better get off this country this evening because we are going to have rain before daylight."

Art pulled his eyes down, "Old man, where do you think you're at? Out on Grand Toss Rock in August? Or has something gone wrong with your head?"

Gus said, "Boys, Jack is right. Look at the ring around the sun. And we're sure to get a mild spell in February."

Chapter 6

It was the twenty-fifth of February just after two days of rain. It had turned cold and the snow's crust was hard enough to walk on. Danny and Ches Pittman decided to go and look at Grandfather Pittman's rabbit snares. It was 7:00 P.M., a beautiful morning. They packed a lunch and started out. After a couple of hours checking snares, Danny decided to boil the kettle.

"Okay," said Ches. "you get a fire going and I will go up in this drook to check five or six snares that are set up there."

Danny agreed.

"Have you got any matches?" Ches asked Danny.

"No, I don't think so." He felt his pockets. "No, I don't have any."

Ches put his hand in his pocket and threw a box to him. "Danny, you never leave the house in this country without matches, especially in the winter. Things can happen pretty fast."

Danny looked at Ches. He knew he was serious.

"You're right, Ches, I think I'll take that as a motto."

Ches turned and walked away and Danny started to make a fire. He cut branches and twigs but was unable to light them. He tried to light green boughs with no success when Ches returned no fire was going. He looked at Danny and asked, "What's the trouble?"

Danny looked at him with hurt in his eyes. "I can't get the wood to burn. I guess it's too wet."

Ches took the axe. "I think I'll get some birch rind."

He came back in a few minutes. He lit it and put the kindling on the fire.

"Ches, that's the first time I ever saw a fire lit with birch rind."

Ches looked surprised but said nothing.

"On the Avalon," Danny said, "There's no problem getting a fire going without using birch rind."

Ches laughed. "Would that be due to the dry climate?"

Danny pulled down his eyes. "No. Maybe it's the fog!"

They both laughed.

It was later that night Danny heard someone tapping on the window, then someone talking, and a voice call, "Ranger! Ranger!"

Danny quickly jumped out of bed. He called, "Hello!"

"Go to the door."

He pulled on his pants. His socks were on his feet. He slept in them. He lit the lamp and went to the porch. He had to strike the door with his knee to open it. It was frozen shut. The door made a squeaking noise because of the frost.

"Yes, gentlemen. Come inside."

Three men stepped into the porch covered in icicles. It was a terribly cold morning, the 29th of February and Sunday morning.

"Men, you must be driven out or the cause must be very great."

Neither man spoke. Danny got the kerosene can and lit the fire in the stove. He pulled on a working shirt over his underwear.

"Now, sirs, where are you from?"

One man spoke up. "My name is Henry Cassell. I'm from Little Harbour Deep."

Danny looked at the men. It was 6:00 A.M. and he knew at one glance that these three men were not ordinary men. They were the pick of the town.

"Sirs," Danny replied, "What can I do for you?"

Mr. Cassell was quick to speak. "Sir, there is an emergency. A maternity case in Little Harbour Deep, Elizer Newman. We left home yesterday at 6:00 P.M. and just reached here now. We are going to Duggan's Cove to get Granny Randell. Would you be able to give us a hand?"

Danny felt the blood surge through his veins. He stood straight in the kitchen and looked at the three men. "I want to go with you. Even if I wasn't a Ranger, I would want to go." He paused.

"The kettle is boiled, sir," said another man.

"But I tell you, it's tough going. It's only three miles to Duggan's Cove from here.

"It might seem alright to say go," replied Henry Cassell, "But it's pretty bad up on the hills."

Danny put some tea in to steep and started to put dishes on the table. "Boys, I am going to boil some fish."

"Great!" said Henry, "but hurry!"

Within half an hour the fish had been cooked and breakfast had been eaten. Danny put on his warmer clothes and got ready to go outside. "Do you think we need some more men? I only have to say the word."

The other man spoke very softly. "Sir, we should go on, but tell Noah Pittman to round up four or five men and come behind us." He looked Danny in the eye. "We've got no time to lose. The woman could be dead by now even."

Danny held out his hand. "I'm Danny."

"I'm Jobie Randell."

Danny said, "Yes, sir," and they got on the move.

It was a hard beat, but 11:10 they reached Duggan's Cove. They stepped into the snowshoe tracks where someone had broken the road to the well. The sun was shining and the wind had ceased. Duggan's Cove was a small village nestled in a small cove that was on the Atlantic Ocean, but 12 miles away one could see land on either side of White Bay. Some dogs started to bark and this drew attention. A storm door swung open and a man with a long beard came out and bawled at the dogs. Then he looked at the men coming along Well Road. He wiped his beard and partly held up his hand. Danny, who was at the lead, motioned for him to come near. He came closer, he saw the badge, the Ranger cap, and the uniform. "Good morning, Ranger."

Danny noticed his keenness. "Good morning," he replied.

As he came closer, Danny noticed the man was younger than he looked.

"All the same, brother! 'Tis the bunch from Little Harbour Deep and Uncle Jobie Randell at dat. I would say somebody up dar is gonna 'ave a baby." He grinned. "I bet you're looking for Granny Randell."

Danny replied, "Yes, we are."

"Well Ranger, do you see dat house down dar, das where she is and listen. You can hear her."

The sound caught his ears. He could hardly believe himself. It was the sound of a piano. "A piano!" he said loudly. "Here in this rock hole! I didn't think there was one on the Northern Peninsula, and on top of that a player."

The man looked at Danny. "She can sing, too. The piano was given to her by Dr. Grenfell two years ago to celebrate the 500th baby she born." He paused. "She born me, I'm 39, and my wife too and my eight youngsters. I wanted to give her something but she made me promise her I would go to prayers. I kept my promise." He looked at Uncle Jobie Randell and blushed.

The group started to move towards Granny's house. The man joined them. All of a sudden Jobie Randell started to sing and in the morning frosty air with the sun gleaming down, he joined the piano rhythm and a voice inside the house singing, "Blessed assurance, Jesus is mine. Oh what a foretaste of Glory divine."

Danny looked out over the frozen ocean and thought about his mother in St. John's. Oh how he loved his mother and longed to see her. Then he looked at Jobie who lifted his hand, covered by a frozen seal skin mitt, over his head and prayed out loud.

"Oh God, my soul is hungry for more of you, for a taste of Heaven, for something real. As we stand here this moment I can feel your mighty presence. I know you're busy in your Heavan making stars and probably hanging a World in Space, but I want you to stop for a moment and protect Elizer and her baby and Granny Randell. Also, help the Ranger do his job. In your Name, we ask everything. Amen."

Danny put his cap back on and felt something more than the frosty air. These men were different, he thought.

They moved to the house where the piano was playing. About twenty people were gathered around. The man with the beard said, "I'll stay outside, sir."

Danny looked at him. "No, you come in with us."

The man felt uneasy but moved inside. Just as they sat down the door came open and ten men, led by Noah Pitman, came in. Most had to stand because no seats were available. Danny then turned his attention to the player who was just beginning to sing.

"My Jesus, I love thee. I know thou art mine."

Danny sat spellbound. He had never heard anything like it. The singer sat very upright. She was heavy set with gray hair, a round face, big hands and a long light blue dress trimmed with white. She looked like a saint. So this is Granny Randell. When she had finished singing, she turned to the audience. "My dear friends, I know there must be an emergency somewhere and it looks like it's in Little Harbour Deep. But there's an emergency here also. There are souls here not saved and that makes a pretty serious situation. I welcome everyone to this meeting."

A pause.

"However, I want to invite Uncle Jobie Randell to give us a little sermon. If you please?"

Jobie stood to his feet and walked to the front of the room. Danny knew there was something different about this man.

"My dear comrades," he said in a soft clear voice. "The reason I am here today in Duggan's Cove is I am a volunteer. I volunteered to come here as part of a group to bring a message to Granny Randell that she is needed in Little Harbour Deep. I didn't know I would have the privilege to say a few words on behalf of our dear Lord. Twenty years ago I became a volunteer for God and He has brought me through rough places and has protected me at all times, and I am glad for what he has put in my soul." He continued to speak for ten minutes, then ended,, "We have to move on with Granny and may the Great Lord protect us."

Granny Randell stood up. "Let's go," she said, "Anne, get tea for the men and someone launch the boat. I believe in miracles. By 1:00 P.M. we will be able to go to Little Harbour Deep by boat."

Danny looked surprised. The ocean is frozen over he thought, but kept quiet. As he walked outside the house, the man with the beard motioned to him to step away from the group. Danny did and the man quickly moved over by him.

"Ranger," he said in a kind of a broad drawled voice. "My name is Sunny Hancock. I'm from Hooping Harbour but my wife is from yer, so I's been livin' yer fer the past two years. I work in the woods in Roddickton. I come home two weeks ago. When I was comin' through Englee on my way home, I was talkin' to my buddie dar and he was tellin' me about all the caribou das bein' shot in on the open country. He said the fellows from the Straits and Main Brook, das up in Belvy Bay, is shootin' hundreds, and dey're right over to Canada Bay shootin' 'em. He said if dar not stopped, by April dar won't be nar one left."

Danny looked at him. He knew he was telling the truth. Then he asked, "What's your buddy's name?"

Sunny hesitated. Then he said, "His name is Gus Compton. He told me he was in. He could hear the roar of guns everywhere and dogs all over the place."

Danny looked worried. "Why didn't he go tell the Ranger in Englee? Peters is his name. There has never been a report come back to me. This is the first I've heard of it."

The man spoke quickly. "He said dey wouldn't go to him because dey was afraid he would turn on 'em. Gus said the Ranger down dar was afraid to go in the woods." He paused. "Gus said it was the common crowd, like all the small youngsters dat not even born that he's worried about. There'll be no fresh left fer dem at all."

Danny thought for a moment. From what this man was saying,, the Ranger at Englee, Peters, was not doing his job. Could it be that the same thing was going on in Harbour Deep and people were saying the same thing about him or maybe Peters was not very much liked for the same reason in Englee. He then asked, "Sunny, when this trip is finished, how about you and I leaving here and walking to Englee? We'll get Ranger Peters and go in the country. We could walk all the way down in the middle of the island and come out to Harbour Deep."

The man scratched his beard. "All the same brother, I know das not a tidy old tramp. I wouldn't mind goin'. Don't think I'm afraid, but the reason I'm home is me wife will be needin' Granny any time, but if you want to go, I'll get someone to go with ye." He looked excited.

Danny thanked him for the information and guaranteed him that something would be done.

He just sat down to tea when a man came in. "We got Nat Ropson's trap punt ready," he said. "But I don't see where you're going to use her. The ocean has been frozen over a week now."

Danny looked at Jobie Randell. Their eyes met. Danny snapped his fingers and Jobie hit the table with his fist. "Right," they both said together. "Why didn't we think of it before?"

Uncle Jobie added, "I bet Granny did. I guess that's why she's born over 500 babies and has never lost a patient by taking chances. Anyway, it has worked."

Danny turned to the man. "Tie the punt on a komatik and put lots of rope in her."

Jobie turned to the man. "Then, try and round up a couple of slob haulers. We could be needin' them before dark."

"Yes, sir," was his reply, and he went outside.

Everything was ready. Danny and the three men from Little Harbour Deep shoved off with the punt on the komatic with Granny sitting in the middle. She signalled for them to stop. They did. Every man, woman and child in Duggan's Cove were on the ice to see them off. Granny stood up. "People," she said, "I am going to pray for a safe trip. We are on a mercy trip and if we don't make it, we'll die trying."

All eyes were on Danny. He felt proud. If his father could only see him. All the "yes, sir's" and "no, sirs" and marching and discipline in training camp at Whitbourne was now paying off. He was about to do something for his fellow man.

Granny prayed a prayer that almost made their hair stand on end. When she finished she said, "Okay boys. Let's go."

It was nine miles from Duggan's Cove West Point to the eastern point of Little Harbour in-draft. There were times when the men broke through. Each man stood his post and at 4:00 P.M. they went around the point looking into Little Harbour Deep. They were met by all the men in the town, Henry Newman was the first man to meet them. "Granny," he cried, "I am so glad to see you. I don't think Elizer is going to last much longer. I think she's dying. Please hurry."

Granny was taken quickly to the house. Three women were there. Granny Newman was just coming out of the room. "Well, Mary," she said, "am I ever glad to see you. How in the world did you get here?"

Granny Randell quickly replied, "By faith. It's not only Peter that walked on the water. Today God let four other men and let it be known, God let them carry an old woman in a punt."

They both grinned.

"This is Ranger Corcoran."

"God bless you, my son. You're an angel. And welcome to Little Harbour Deep."

Danny felt as if he was in the company of Gods.

"I got everything ready, Mary. But she can't have her baby."

Other words were spoken, but the room door was quickly shut. The young girl in the kitchen looked at Danny and smiled.

"My name is Ruth."

"I'm Danny," he replied. He noticed how the girl was dressed. She was wearing a polka dot dress of red and white with a large red collar. On her feet she wore a pair of men's woolen socks folded down for slippers. She had long blonde hair kept up with two combs on each side. Her eyelashes and eyebrows were black and her cheeks were rosy.

Danny looked at her and held his breath. "This must be the most beautiful girl I've ever seen," he thought. Then he asked himself. "Have I been out of St. John's too long, or has the trip over the bad ice taken its toll on me? No. It's true. This is the most beautiful girl I've ever seen."

He finished talking to himself when she said, "Your tea is ready, Danny."

"Thank you," he said. He moved to the table. The door opened and Henry came in.

"Ranger," he said, "the boys said it's all clear water now off Harbour Deep where we came over. I guess it was more than luck."

Danny nodded.

"Have you met the Ranger?"

Before Ruth could reply, Henry said, "Ranger Corcoran, this is my wife, Ruth."

"We have already met."

Then all of a sudden they heard a baby cry. All eyes were on the bedroom door. Tears started to run down Danny's face. He looked out the window and said, "Thank you God, for letting me be among these people." And for the first time in months he felt like kneeling and praying. When he looked back, he saw Henry standing with his arm around Ruth with tears in their eyes. Danny stepped to where they were and the three of them started to cry, Danny with his arms around the others. Danny said. "I believe in miracles."

"So do I," said a voice from the bedroom door and Granny Randell stood with a baby in her arms and all smiles. All three looked her way.

"It's a boy!" she said, "and his mom is doing fine. We have given him his name already."

She looked at Danny. "Over two hours ago, before he was born, when Henry had to pull you out of the water three miles off Harbour Deep, I gave the baby his name. I give you Danny Newman."

She handed the baby to Danny. He took it in his arms and kissed it. "Only time will erase this moment." He handed the baby back.

Granny looked at Henry. "Get ready to take me back by land." She looked pleased.

"Yes, Ma'am. I told Sunny Hancock to get some men and meet us in the country between here and Harbour Deep."

"Good!" said Granny. She disappeared for a moment in the bedroom and then came out. She noticed the tea on the table. It was hardly touched. She sat down. "Get me a cup of tea please, Ruth dear."

"Yes, Ma'am," was her reply.

"I'm sorry the excitement got me carried away." She looked at Ruth, then at Danny. "I born her, Danny. Maybe that's the reason why she's so beautiful!"

Everyone laughed. Ruth spoke up. "Did you born Danny?"

Danny blushed. His face was the same colour as his hair.

"No," replied Granny Randell. "I'm sure that when he was born, the great God of Heaven was glad. He's a beautiful flower and maybe he could sow seed in this area."

They all laughed. Granny Newman spoke up. "Maybe you'd better be careful, son. The Master always gathers the beautiful flowers for his bouquet."

All was silent.

Three hours from the time they left Little Harbour Deep, Danny was back at his house. "What an experience!" he said out loud and to think it was the 29th of February. Leap Year Luck was not supposed to be good on such a date. However this time he had proven the old timers wrong, or were they wrong? Maybe this event was to be continued, he thought.

It was March 1st, a beautiful morning. Danny jumped with the sound of a knock on the door. "Ah!" he thought, a country knock. He put on his pants and shirt and went to the door. It was Albert Hynes.

"Good morning, Ranger!"

"Good morning," was Danny's reply. "What can I do for you this morning?"

"Nothing," said Albert. "I just dropped by to tell you that the dogs got in and killed all of Jennie Cassell's hens last night. She kept them in her kitchen in the coop. I don't know why they didn't hear them. They must have all died. Ned Pittman said they even broke the lamp."

"My! My!" said Danny. "I'll have to check this out."

Albert nodded and left. Danny lit the fire and made breakfast. Then he thought, I had better do something about the caribou in the country. He pondered over what Sunny Hancock had told him, then added, "I'll have to do something." He said out loud, "What can I do? I think I'll send a wireless to Ranger Peters at Englee, but what can I say? If I say caribou are being killed in his area, he might say it's none of my business. Maybe he's hearing stories that something is going on in behind here. I think I'll just get ready and walk over to Port Saunders and check the area on the way over."

Just then he heard someone come in. He waited for the door to open and Barbara stepped into the kitchen. She did not smile but looked him straight in the eye. He stood up, held out his hand but she did not come close. "Barbara, darling. What's the matter? Is something wrong?" She continued to stare. "Yes, Danny Corcoran. There is something wrong."

"Well, tell me about it?"

"You already know. Imagine you travelling to White Bay on ice. I mean walking on ice yesterday afternoon. Do you know that 5:00 P.M. it was all clear water? There is big talk all along the coast, but let me tell you something Ranger, there is a saying that heroes die young, and you might not be so lucky next time." She paused. "Can you imagine what the Daily News would say? "Ranger led parties to deaths. One of the most famous citizens drowned Sunday evening, Mrs. Mary Randell, the famous Midwife who was a passenger. Reports say it was carelessness. An investigation is underway. No bids received." She paused. "It could have been that way if you fell in and had to be pulled out with a mile of water under you."

"Barbara," he said, "we were the cause of saving two lives-a mother of thirteen children who brought another baby into the world. Suppose I had refused. Those men would still have gone." He paused. "Maybe the news would have read: 'Party drowns near Harbour Deep because Ranger Danny Corcoran refused to lead the party or even lend a hand.' Can you imagine what my mother, brothers and friends would say? What would I do? Hide for the rest of my life?" He stopped.

"I'm sorry Danny. We all went through something yesterday and last night. Please, from now on be more careful."

Danny grinned. "I would do it again, even today. You should have seen that baby boy."

Barbara blushed.

"I am going to Port Saunders next week," he said. "I have a report that a great slaughter of caribou is taking place in the country and something has to be done about it."

She looked at him. "Don't go alone. At least you'll be on dry land."

"Take it easy, honey. The Ranger always gets his man."

She left smiling.

Danny decided to take some action. Yes. He could wire a telegram to Peters. But he wondered what kind of man he was. Would he take it as if he was telling him how to do his job? Would it be that he would ignore his report? However, he would take the chance and send him a wireless. He then wrote a telegram:

Ranger Peters
Nfld. Ranger Station
Englee, Newfoundland

Ranger Peters:

Information caribou slaughtered country west Englee. Would like combined patrol.

Yours in the Force
Ranger D. Corcoran
Harbour Deep, Newfoundland

Danny put the telegram in the envelope and sent it by dog team over to the operator, Gill Ellsworth, to have it sent immediately. I am expecting, he thought, that tomorrow I'll be going to Hooping Harbour to meet Peters. He called out to Noah Pittman who was out on the road. Noah quickly came in.

"Good morning, Uncle Noah."

"Good morning, Danny," he said very cheerfully. "What can I do for you this morning?"

"Uncle Noah, what kind of man is Sunny Hancock?"

"Good man, hard worker. Works in the woods wintertime. If he tells you something you can count on it. Why? Is there something wrong?"

"Not with him," said Danny. "But he told me that his buddy at Englee reported that a lot of caribou are being slaughtered in the country by the hundreds."

Uncle Noah said,, "I wonder who he heard it from?"

"His buddy at Englee told him a fellow by the name of Gus Compton."

Uncle Noah's eyes came open. "Well," he said, "I guess you had better do something. It's guaranteed to be true because he lives in the country."

"That's what Sunny said," Danny replied. "Gus seemed pretty concerned."

"Yes," said Noah. "I'd say in behind here, everything is being wiped out."

"I have decided to do a patrol inland. I am beginning to put things together. I just sent a wireless to Ranger Peters at Englee. I suggested we meet in Hooping Harbour to establish a working plan and even tie it in with Ranger Hiscock at Port Saunders. I know him quite well. He was my buddy when we were in training in Whitbourne. A good man. I'm sure he will be glad to get involved, but before I contact him, I will wait to hear from Peters."

"I agree," said Noah. "But, Danny, make sure you have some good men with you if you tackle the open country. If you get in there and the rain comes on, you can get in a lot of trouble. The fog in there gets just as thick as smoke. We got caught in there on foot for twenty-two days. We were lucky we all stayed in a camp. This was in Red Sea Pond and das the same time dey had to look fer the Williamsport crowd." He paused. "Dey had a hard time. Dey lived in a side camp for five days. Only fer Sam Brenton, dev all would have perished like sheep. Dey said he stayed awake for five days and kept a fire in all the time. One feller had to be lugged out and dey were four miles North of us. The big trouble was dat all the brooks busted out and flooded the country. So if you decide to go in dar, make sure you have good men with you."

Danny grinned. "I guess I can always depend on you."

"Not to go in the country you can't, unless there was somebody lost. That was my last time. I don't even want to hear talk of the country." He looked at Danny. "But I can line you up with fellows that will be raring to go and good men."

"That will be fine," said Danny. "Have a cup of tea with me. I can't offer you any munge like Jave offered me."

They both laughed. "Now der's what you call a tough man," said Noah. "Der are a lot of good men in Williamsport."

"You know something, Uncle Noah? I think this coast has the best breed of men that can be found anywhere else in the world."

Noah finished stirring his tea very noisily, "And women."

Danny shook his head. "I will never get that girl out of my eyes. Yesterday at Little Harbour Deep. I think if she had not been married, I would have been satisfied to even marry her right then and there in that house yesterday."

Noah laughed.

"Yesterday," said Danny, "was an experience I will always remember. Not so much the trip over the bad ice or the baby being born, but when I heard that piano playing and Granny singing, a feeling gripped me. Then when I heard Uncle Jobie Randell praying, I don't think I've heard anything like it before. I mean it shook me up and I'm a Catholic. We don't pray like that. He was crying when he prayed. I guess that made a difference."

Noah tapped his spoon in his saucer. "They're very religious people in Little Harbour Deep and in Duggan's Cove. They've got no other choice but be good because they're afraid of Granny."

They laughed. "I am starting tomorrow to cut my firewood for the summer. I suppose a thousand turn will do me. I'll get Ches to haul it on his Easter holidays." He said, "See you later," and left.

Danny sat and thought maybe tonight he would be in Hooping Harbour.

Chapter 7

It was March 5th, 1936. Danny sat near the table waiting for the eight teenagers to arrive for the radio party. They would be listening for the Gerald S. Doyle news, followed by some accordian and guitar music and of course, Irish songs, would be sung by Johnny Walsh, all on the Newfoundland Radio Band. It was going to be an exciting evening.

Barbara came out of the pantry with a large cake. "Well, Danny, how do you feel about having the high grade kids get together?"

"Great!" said Danny. "And I bet they're going to like the radio.

She looked at him and smiled. He heard someone coming. "I like your cake." he said. "It looks beautiful."

The first to enter was Ches Pittman.

"Good evening, Ches."

"Good evening, Ranger Corcoran." Ches stepped in. He was an able looking youngster for fifteen. In fact, he was a grown man. "I think you have met everybody, but anyway, this is Nat, Jim, Key, Andrew, Olive, Maude, and Shirley. Folks, this is Ranger Corcoran."

They all nodded.

"And ladies and gentlemen," said Ches, "this is the greatest creature ever to come off the Avalon Peninsula, the prettiest, the most handsome voice and the most beautifully shaped thing that we have ever seen in Harbour Deep."

All the eyes were on Barbara who was blushing.

"I would like you all to meet our Phillip's Radio."

Barbara's mouth fell open and everyone roared. "Listen Ches, I'm the one who's got to give you the test in two weeks time and correct it." She laughed.

"Miss Gale, we love you, but the radio is different."

Danny said, "Let's get the show on the road."

After they had listened to the Newfoundland news, they sat at the table and had a bowl of delicious rice soup. Then tea and cake was served by the girls. Danny told them how he decided to join the Rangers. He said, "I was always involved in the outdoors. I would leave home early in the morning with our Irish Setter, Rover, and would travel all over the Avalon Peninsula, sometimes not returning until midnight. I used to hear the old-timers tell about the caribou herds on the Avalon Peninsula and would dream of one day seeing them in herds of hundreds, but in all my travel, I never saw one." he paused. "Have any of you ever seen a caribou?"

Key spoke up. "The ones I've seen were all dead, ready for the pot." They all laughed.

"I mean alive," Danny said with a serious tone in his voice.

No one spoke.

"This is the main reason why I am going to Port Saunders after next week. They say they are killing all the caribou in the open country. Who would like to come along?"

Ches spoke up. "I plan to go with you. Anyway, we already talked about that."

"Yes," said Danny, "but I don't know if anyone else wanted to come."

They all agreed that their old man would need them to help get the summer firewood."

"Well," said Danny, "two is a crowd anyway."

They laughed.

He said, "Anyway, gang, I will be back for the 17th of March, Paddy's Day. Aubrey Mack is having a St. Patrick's night party on the radio, so I'll plan a get together then."

They all clapped.

"Time to turn the radio on, boys."

"Good evening, Newfoundlanders. This is Johnny Walsh. Here's 'Take this message to my mother.' This is especially for all you young men away from home."

Everyone looked at Danny. He hung his head and his thoughts were back home. The voice started to sing. Everybody was speechless. The evening quickly passed and everyone left except Danny and Barbara. The two sat very quietly by the stove.

"Danny," Barbara spoke very softly, "please don't go to Port Saunders. I will miss you too much."

Danny looked her in the eyes. "I won't be gone long, just a few days. I can keep in touch. Gill said he would put through some messages for me that won't cost me anything. He has ways."

She sighed. "Be sure and take some men with you. It's a long way."

Danny smiled. "Don't worry, honey. I can take care of myself."

She sighed. Danny walked her to the door.

She looked up at him and said, "I love you!" and turned quickly and stepped out.

Danny looked at the reflection of the moon on the snow, and for a moment he was almost startled. He thought he heard a piano. Then he thought he heard a voice singing. It was Granny Randell. But no. He quickly realized it was his imagination. But how real! This lady had really left her mark on him. He quickly shut the door and made his daily entry into his log: "Had a great day. Tonight we had a party for high grade school pupils. Really enjoyed their company. I am very much in love with Barbara." He paused, I had better erase this last sentence. This is a government log. Then he added instead. "I am falling in love." It could always mean with Harbour Deep or the country.

The word quickly spread around Harbour Deep that Danny was going on the high country to do wildlife patrol and that he was even going on to Port Saunders and young Ches Pittman was going with him and to make things more exciting, they were going to walk.

Nellie Pittman was making bread when Noah walked in with an armful of firewood. "How are you this morning, my dear?"

She looked at him and tried to smile. The dough on her hands prevented her from putting her hand to her back when she tried to straighten up. "I don't feel very good, Noah. I had to force myself out of bed this morning. Then I heard some news that made me feel even sicker."

Noah stopped. "What was that, Nellie?"

"I heard the Ranger is going to walk to Port Saunders and is taking Ches with him."

"Yes," said Noah, "but Ches can't go. He's got his Easter test and even if he had no test, I can't spare him. Too much work."

She looked relieved.

"If the Ranger decides to go, we will send some men with him, not boys. Anyway, we're soon going to have a breakup and maybe no one will get in the country."

She started to smile. Noah Pittman loved his wife, but she was sick. The doctor told him she might not live all winter. He said she had a T.B. spine. Although Noah never told her, he sensed that she knew because she was slowly getting worse, and he could not bear the thought of her not being able to get out of bed. What would he do without her, he thought.

She looked at him. "What are you thinking about, Noah?"

He quickly looked up. "What? Oh yes. No, Ches won't be going in the country."

She finished cleaning her doughy hands. "Let's have a cup of tea. It's 10 o'clock."

"Nellie, I think I'm going to send for a radio for you for Easter. They tell me John Reeves in Englee got them for sale."

She poured the tea, then put her arms around his neck and kissed him.

She knew Noah knew of her sickness but was trying to cheer her up. "Noah, I would love for you to do that."

It made him feel good. "Okay. I will send for it right away."

She smiled. "Thanks!"

Noah drank his tea.

Chapter 8

It was March 7th. Barbara sat at her desk in school. It was a one room school with grades one to eleven. She put her chalk down near the writing pad and stood up. "Pupils," she said in a clear voice, "we will be starting our Easter exams on Tuesday morning, March 13, and they will run until Thursday noon. You will have Thursday afternoon off. Friday the 16th we will be having a spelling match in the afternoon, and on the 17th, which is St. Patrick's Day, the Ranger has agreed to bring his radio here to the school Saturday night for all the class to listen to the Irish music and songs. We also plan to have a lunch. So study hard."

Everyone clapped except Ches. She looked at him, but said nothing. She knew this would change his plans of going to Port Saunders, but that's all she could do. The school must go on. "You're finished for the day," she said. Everyone left.

Ches walked slowly out the door. "I'm sorry," she said. Ches looked at her with a twinkle in his eye."

"Miss Gale, I like you." She blushed. "I like you because Danny likes you. I guess he's an idol of mine. You see, Miss Gale, Danny has done more for us morally than anyone else ever did that came to Harbour Deep and to show our appreciation, we even love you."

She looked at Ches and was unable to say a word. He stepped out and shut the door. "Well," he said, "I guess that ends my dream of going to Port Saunders."

It seemed like only a few steps and he was home. He stepped into the kitchen where his father sat at the table. He was making dog's harnesses. He looked up at Ches. "You're out early."

"Yes. Got to study for an Easter test next week."

"Well," replied Noah lifting an eyebrow, "I guess you won't be going to Port Saunders now."

"No," said Ches quickly. "Test comes first."

Noah was glad he would not have to tell him his mother didn't want him to go. He might even ask the question why. He didn't want to tell his children how sick their mother was. He gave a sigh of relief.

That afternoon Noah Pittman walked into the telegraph office. He brushed the snow from his boots with his mitts, then walked towards the 18 inch square hole. He could hear the dot-dot, dash-dash of the wireless set before he could see the man at the desk sitting almost back on to him. This was Gill Ellsworth. He sat with a pair of headphones on. They seemed to be squeezing his head. Noah waited for ten minutes, then made a coughing noise.

"One minute, please," Gill said holding up one hand. After a few minutes he stopped the movement of the keys and removed the headphones. There were red marks around his ears. He turned around quickly. "Well, hello, Uncle Noah. Looks like snow."

Gill Ellsworth was 22 years old. He was a tall medium structured man with black hair and well grown. He was a man who could spot quality.

Noah took a deep breath. "I say, Gill, it's going to rain according to the heat you've got in here. My son, you're gonna dry up and blow away."

Gill laughed. "The trouble is , Uncle Noah, you're all fussed up. What's wrong?"

Noah shifted from one foot to the other. "I've got a problem and I don't know if it's any of my, our business." He stopped and looked at Gill to get his reaction.

Gill noticed his concern, then asked. "Is it a secret?"

"No, not exactly," was his reply. "Now it's like this, if the ice was bad in the harbour and you were about to go across, don't you think it's our concern to tell you it's bad?"

"Yes," said Gill.

"But," said Noah, "if you wouldn't listen and were going to cross and there was a danger you were going to fall in, I think it's only right for us to grab you and stop you.. What do you think?"

"I think you'd do the proper thing, then turn around and send me to the insane asylum." He looked at Noah who was silent. "Uncle Noah, what's up?" Gill asked.

"Well, Gill, Danny is leaving in two days to do a wildlife patrol from here to Port Saunders and we are up against him. Now I know he's an able man, strong, and a good worker, but that's not the problem. If it rains and all the brooks burst out, he will have a lot of trouble getting out of the country, especially when he doesn't know the trails. It looks like we're gonna have a big batch of snow within the next day or so."

Gill turned sideways to the wicket and looked at the floor very sternly. "This could be serious," said Gill. "What do you want me to do about it?"

Noah looked at Gill. "Try to persuade him not to go. Tell him there's no need of it."

"Well , put it this way, Uncle Noah, Danny's the Ranger and when he gets a report on anything, he has to investigate. But I'll try. What angle can I use?"

"I don't know, Gill. We've begged him not to go. Barbara has begged him, but he says the poor caribou, they will be all wiped out. There's not much left for us to do." He stopped.

"Can't you talk someone into going?"

"No, not one soul. Everybody is scared it will rain."

Gill snapped his fingers. "Let's put together a dog team for him."

"Now, that's impossible. There's no trail. He will have to go through a lot of woods. He will never be able to follow the old country trails."

"Anyway, I'll have a talk with him, I might come over tonight," said Gill. "We might be able to discourage him."

"I hope so," said Uncle Noah.

As he went through the door, he noticed it was starting to snow. "It's startin' to snow Gill and it's pretty mild too."

"Yes. Tell Danny I'm coming over in a while."

"Okay!" said Uncle Noah and left.

Gill thought for a moment. Then said, "It's only fifty miles across there. Maybe it's not all that bad. Danny seems to be a pretty capable fellow." He looked at his watch. It was 4:30 P.M., time to go to work. He grabbed the headphones -- dot-dot, dash-dash.

Chapter 9

Danny was writing in his daily diary. He sat near the kerosene oil lamp which was on the kitchen table. He looked up from his book and turned down the radio. He thought he heard someone on the bridge. Then he saw the lamp flicker for someone had stepped into the porch. He went to the door. When he opened it, he saw a beaming face. "Well, well!" he said, "if it isn't Gill Ellsworth. Come in."

Gill stepped into the kitchen. "I guess I'm just in time for the Gerald S. Doyle news."

Danny shut the door. "In a few minutes. Have a seat!"

"Thanks." Gill sat down at the table.

Danny went into the pantry and brought out a bottle and placed it on the table. "Do you want a drink?"

Gill laughed, picked up the bottle, and looked at the label. "Lime juice?"

"Yes," said Danny, "my favorite drink."

"Do you drink, Danny?" asked Gill very soberly.

"No. I am going to tell you something Gill. I am twenty-one, will be twenty-two in July and I have never tasted beer or any kind of alcohol, to my knowledge in my life, and" he said, "I have never seen my father or mother take a drink of anything stronger than lime juice."

Gill nodded. "You're a very lucky man, Danny. I don't drink either, but now I'll have a double lime juice, please. But don't put any ice in it."

Danny laughed. "Well then, I'd better get the water out of the kettle because the water buckets are sished over."

They both laughed. "The news! The news! Turn it up." Danny then quickly reached and turned the dial.

"This is the Gerald S. Doyle news, bringing you the news from all over Newfoundland."

"That's Aubrey Mack," said Danny. "Usually it's Albert Perlin."

They listened to the news without saying a word. After it was finished they listened to the forecast.

"Seems like it's going to be a good day Monday," Danny said, "light winds, southwest."

"Yes," said Gill. "But sou-west winds mean mild weather."

"Yes," said Danny, "just right for what I've got in mind."

"What's that?" Gill quickly asked.

"I am getting ready to go on a wildlife patrol to Port Saunders. How about coming along?"

"No thanks," said Gill. "I am too busy with the headphones."

"You need a break anyway, Gill. A man can only sit to a desk for so long. I think you should come to Port Saunders with me. Really."

"There is nothing I would like better, but Harbour Deep is a Relay Station and it must operate six days a week from 9 A.M. to 6 P.M., except holidays. I'm not like you, operate seven days a week and even walk on bad ice."

Danny laughed.

Then Gill asked. "What are your plans for the trip?"

Danny got up from the table and went to the shelf. He took down a roll of maps and rolled them out on the table. "Now," he said, "this is a map of the route I am going to take. I plan to leave here 8 A.M. Monday, March 12. I plan to have a boil up at Elige Newman's old logging camp at 10:00 A.M. That's three miles in right here."

They both looked at the spot near the river. The map had the old logging road marked on it.

"Then at 2:00 P.M. I plan to boil up in Stanley Hancock's camp. Here, this is the end of the old road. This is the camp here. It's right where a small brook runs into the Soufflett's (Ben Hynes Brook). I may have to walk in by the side of the brook a ways to get across."

They looked at the map with great interest.

"Uncle Noah tells me I can pick up an old trail on the other side of the brook. That will take me right to the open country." He marked it lightly with his pencil.

Gill looked at the map with keen interest. "How far in is it?" he asked.

Danny picked up his ruler and slid it over the map. "It's approximately, let's see now, eleven miles to Hancock's camp." He moved his ruler ahead. "I'd say it's about seventeen miles to the open country." He put his foot up on the chair and rubbed his hand on his chin. "That's from here."

Gill looked at the map again. "Where are you going to spend the night?"

"Well, Gill," he said. "As you will notice, there's approximately two miles of open country. Then I will get in a valley. This is called the Sou-West Feeder. This valley is full of timber. This is where I hope to meet up with the poachers. They say this is where the poaching is going on. If I don't see any, I will build a side camp here." He pointed to a spot near the river. "I am used to building those. I have been at that ever since I was a small boy, and when I strike the open country, I will be at home, because,

of course, I cut my eye teeth on open country on the Avalon Peninsula."
They both laughed. "I'll then be about fourteen miles from the edge of
the hills right here." He pointed to the contours. "Roy Hiscock tells me
that when I get to the top of the hills, I can look down on Port Saunders. He
said there's trails everywhere, but I plan to go across Bluey Pond and cut
on out to Hawkes Bay. It's all flat land out there."

Gill stared at the lamp. "Well, Danny," he said, "I don't know much
about maps and compasses. I suppose you know what you're doing."

Danny replied, "I wouldn't be in Harbour Deep if I didn't know what I
was doing. Our Ranger training involved a bit of this kind of work."

"I guess so," said Gill, "but what bothers me is you're going alone, and I
hope you'll excuse me for being concerned. I'm not doubting your ability.
I'm sure you know what you can do, but Uncle Noah says that we're going
to have a mild spell. Suppose the brooks burst out?"

Danny smiled. "Thanks Gill, for the concern, but it's only a two-day trip
at the most, and the moment I get over, I'll let you know."

Gill sat down on his chair. "Okay," he said. "When you get to Port
Saunders, go to the wireless operator and tell the girl, I know her quite
well, that's Lavers." Gill paused. "Tell her to say hello to Gill Ellsworth in
Harbour Deep for you. That way you won't have to pay for the wireless.
Then I'll know you're over there."

"Good enough," said Danny with a smile.

"I'll give you four days. That will be Thursday evening, and make sure
she gets the word through, because if I don't get word by six o'clock on
Thursday, I'll have a search party out," said Gill.

Danny smiled. "You don't have to worry about that." He folded up the
maps and put them back up on the shelf. "Have a cup of tea now."

Gill stood up. "I think I'll check the weather first." He went out in the
porch. "Boy, oh boy," he said. "I know it's not snowing, but look old man,
you can hardly see a thing." He shut the door. "Now I got to get going. I
came over with Jim Pollard. He went up to Sam Cassell's. That's not far
up, is it?"

"No. You can see Sam's light from here, but I guess it's too thick now,"
said Danny.

Gill was putting on his big coat and mitts. "We have to go, Danny. And
for goodness sake, be careful and make sure you take lots of matches.
Make sure you take Eddies matches, cause them old Sea Dog matches is
not fit fer nothing. The tops even come off in your pocket. And if you
sweat either bit at all, you can't get them to light."

"No problem," said Danny. "I have a survival kit."

"Great!" said Gill. "Got to go. See you when you get back."

"Good enough," said Danny. Then he shut the door. He was glad Gill
was gone because Barbara was expecting him in a few minutes.

It was Sunday evening, 5:00 P.M. Danny stepped into the kitchen of Skipper Edward Pittman. He was sixty-four years old but very straight and nimble. He smiled as Danny shut the door. "How are you, young feller?"

Danny smiled. "I'm fine, Uncle Edward. And how are you?"

Uncle Edward removed his pipe and lodged it on the fender of the Comfort Stove. "I'm alright except for my thumb. Last night I was batin' the ice out of the water barrel and hit my thumb on the top hoop and almost broke it. You talk about pain." He turned very quickly. He looked at Barbara who was just coming out of the pantry with her hands full of cups and saucers. She was grinning from ear to ear. "You know, young Ranger, I seen the day when I'd..." He reached for his pipe. "You know she was there when I squat my thumb, and you know what she did?" He paused. "She laughed." He stopped.

"Tell the Ranger what you did," said a voice from inside the pantry.

"Now, Blanche, get the supper."

Mrs. Pittman came out into the kitchen. She was smiling and in her hands she carried a cake in one and a pie in the other. "You know Danny, he cried and not only did he cry with his ugly face, he shed tears, real tears."

They all laughed. Uncle Edward was not embarrassed. He was a tower of strength. "I guess I'm getting soft in my old days. My father was an Englishman. They say he sat down for a doctor to cut off two of his fingers. They say that when he had one off and started at the other one, he got them to stop. Then he reached back with his good fingers, got his pocket handkerchief out of his pocket, blew his nose and put his handkerchief back and told the doctor to continue."

They all laughed again. "But," said Uncle Edward, "I guess I turn after me mom."

"That's enough, Ned," said Mrs. Pittman. "Hemp the tea pot for me, will ya?"

"Okay, honey!" He looked at Danny and winked. He came back in the kitchen. "What a batch of snow we had last night. This is the stuff for the white coats. A good feed of seal shoulders would be something. I think I'd eat them raw now if I had them."

Danny grinned and asked, "How much snow do you think we had?"

Uncle Ned looked at Barbara who was just about to pour up the tea. "We had a good batch. The kind of snow that fell is pretty clammy. Should be good for snowshoeing. I'd say we got about fourteen inches."

"Even in on the open country?" Danny knew this man would tell him the truth.

"Yes. Almost every winter, sometimes twice after caribou and trapping, we would usually wait 'til March fer the good going, the hard crust."

He paused. "This has been a funny year fer the country. We have had two breakups this winter, and it looks like an early spring, but we'll know on the 21st when the sun crosses the line."

"What do you think the going is like inside now?" Danny asked.

The old man looked uneasy. He picked up his pipe. "I'd say the walking should be pretty good. The only problem is there's no ice on the brooks. I'd say the weight of this snow has flooded the brooks and ponds. Now, if we get a few frosty nights, it should be as hard as flint."

"Supper's ready!" said Mrs. Pittman.

They moved to the table. Mr. Pittman sat at one end and Danny at the other. Mrs. Pittman said grace, and when she finished, Danny crossed himself. Supper was eaten without too much conversation. The food was well prepared. They had roast pork for supper with partridge berries. When they had finished the main course, Mrs. Pittman said, "I got jelly and blanc mange for dessert. Would you like some?"

Mr. Pittman answered for Danny. "I guess we would, if you please."

The dessert was served by Barbara. Danny ate his quickly and commented on the meal. He was asked if he wanted seconds, but refused. When the supper ended, Mr. Pittman invited Danny into the Parlor. He motioned for Danny to sit in the big arm chair while he sat on the couch. "Now son, I hear you are going in the country chasing poachers." He paused. "Well, I'm glad somebody has the nerve to make a move. If something is not done, nothing will be left. There's a crowd here that's agame to shoot everything on the country. Not only the Straits crowd. To me, they're all alike. Only thing is, there's more of them over on the other side, and it's time they got caught."

Danny knew this man was serious. "Yes. I plan to leave tomorrow morning if all's well. I plan to be back by Friday. I am going to go on to Port Saunders. I've got my route plotted on the map. The way I'm going, I won't have to cross much open country. I plan to follow the rivers."

He studied the face of the elderly man sitting across from him. Mr. Pittman lit his pipe. "The weather is not going to be all that good for the next few days. I think we're going to have rain and that's bad because with that, we get fog, and up there, it gets awfully thick. Going in there is not going to be bad, but on the other side, the brooks are hard to follow. There's a lot of steep hills and turns. I went across there once with a bunch doing a survey. They were from A.N.D. Co. but we went in between here and Little Harbour Deep."

Danny sat upright. "Mr. Pittman, my job is to protect game and from the reports I'm getting, the caribou in behind here need protection. I had a report from Englee and it wasn't very nice. I was told that the Ranger at Englee won't do anything about the reports he's been getting. It appears that he's not getting along with the people up there. I was told by the mailman that he spends most of his time playing cards and visiting the English nurse in Roddickton. He told me he even refused to issue dole orders to people who were almost starving. The mailman said that if it wasn't for a J.P. by the name of Stanley Hancock, he would have watched them starve. Hancock threatened to write the Lieutenant Governor."

Mr. Pittman replied quickly. "Yes. I heard that, and if Nat Johnston told you, then it's guaranteed to be true."

Danny then replied. "I guess I made a big mistake." He looked out the window, then at Mr. Pittman. "I told the mailman that if it was true, all those bad reports, I was going to write the Commanding Officer in Whitbourne and request that he be reprimanded."

Mr. Pittman pulled down his eyebrows. "There's one thing for sure. If you told Nat Johnston anything, he is sure to spread it around, and I'd say that the Ranger in Englee has that bit of information, but sometimes a threat makes a better man."

"Yes," said Danny. "But sometimes it makes them worse. A lot of people get stubborn and refuse to move."

"I guess so," said Mr. Pittman. "Maybe this feller is just the type. I don't know." He paused.

"He had a good reputation in training school. He was quite a bushman. I remember him."

"Ned," Mrs. Pittman called. "We have to go to Sam Cassell's for a couple of hours. Ask the Ranger if he will stay here 'til we get back."

The old man looked at the ceiling, then at Danny.

"Yes," he called. "He'll stay. I'm getting up there, you know," he said.

"Oh to be young." He looked at his hands. "You know, Danny, a man was made wrong, you know. He should be born an old man and get younger instead of older." They laughed.

"There's a saying, Uncle Edward," Danny stopped for a moment. "It says once a man, twice a child."

Barbara stood in the doorway. Mr. Pittman looked at her very keenly and said, "Will you sit down in the chair and rock me to sleep?"

Danny laughed as Mr. Pittman went out. Barbara put the broom back in the closet. "See you in a couple of hours!"

"Good enough!" was Mrs. Pittman's reply.

"You know, Danny, they're like a mother and father to me. This is my home away from home. I think I'm a lucky girl to be here in Harbour Deep with these people." She looked at Danny. He sat in the big arm chair. His red hair was combed neatly. He was always dressed very smartly whether in uniform or civilian clothes. She moved over and sat on the arm of the chair. He held her hand and looked at her beautiful face.

"I guess I'm a lucky man to be here in Harbour Deep, too. To be in the company of Barbara Gale."

"If you love me, Danny, then you'll call off that trip tomorrow to go on the open country or to Port Saunders, wherever it is."

He opened his mouth to say something.

"Please," she said.

Danny relaxed. He knew he loved this girl and he knew she loved him. "But, honey," he said. "I don't know why you're so upset, for this is just a normal trip, a part of my duty to protect wildlife. Imagine all those caribou being slaughtered, probably every last one of them. It is very important that I go on this trip. Duty requires it."

She looked at him with pain in her eyes. "I know you're a very capable man, but why don't you get someone to go with you. Suppose you fall in the water or break a leg. It happens to the best."

Danny sighed. "I'll be careful. Don't worry."

She put her arm on his shoulder. "I know your love for wildlife must be very deep."

"Barbara, I have seen men on the Avalon kill almost every living creature that they could get their guns pointed at, and I vowed that if I ever became a man, I wanted to protect the animals and the birds and especially the caribou."

She was silent.

"And besides, maybe the people here are saying the same things about me as they are saying about Peters up at Englee, and I would be the last to know. Therefore I am going to carry out my plans and go to Port Saunders, if you please, darling."

She sighed. "Well, I guess if you have to go, you have to go. So the only thing I can say is, be careful, and hurry back."

Chapter 10
March 12, 1936

The alarm clock brought Danny out of bed at a leap. He grabbed it and pushed down on the button. It stopped. Danny lit the lamp and looked at it. It read 5:45 A.M. Danny went to the porch. He opened the storm door and looked outside. It was beginning to dawn. The sky was a bit red but it had the appearance of a good day. It was not a cold morning. It gave him a good feeling when he thought of his trip across the peninsula and especially since he was going on a wildlife patrol. He wondered what the mailman would say today when the post mistress told him that he was gone on a wildlife patrol alone to venture into the wilds to chase caribou poachers. Would he spread the word around the Englee area? According to Edward Pittman, he would, and if he did, he hoped Ranger Peters would do the same.

He shut the door. Then he heard some dogs barking. He opened it again and peered out. He saw a team of dogs going past. "Must be somebody going to haul their seal nets," he said out loud. He shut the door and came back into the kitchen. He lit the fire, put the kettle on, and checked over his pack sack. Everything he needed for the trip was packed neatly inside. He double checked his list. Yes, he had not missed a thing. It's too bad Ches had to have his Easter test this week. He would have enjoyed the company on the trip and he was sure Ches would have liked it, too.

However, he thought, two's a crowd. Well, he thought, if all goes well, he should make twenty miles today. It's such a nice day. He wondered what the snowshoeing was like. According to Mr. Pittman, 14 inches of snow fell Saturday night and that should be a bit tough this morning. He then knelt down and said his prayers asking for special guidance and protection.

When he finished, he cooked rolled oats, and as he ate his breakfast he started to grin to himself. He remembered the morning Jave Pollard of Williamsport was here and cooked munge. What a man! He thought, if only he was going with him this morning. What a wonderful bunch of people lived on this coast, and some of the toughest men he had ever seen. He considered himself lucky to be here in Harbour Deep.

He washed his breakfast dishes and made his bed. He disconnected the radio battery and wrapped it up in a blanket. He checked his pocket watch. It was 6:30 A.M. He took his rifle out of the closet. It was a 303 owned by the Newfoundland Ranger Force. It had Nfld. Rangers stamped in the woodwork with a branding iron. He got his snowshoes and put them on in the kitchen. He carried extra slings. He put on his heavy sweater and Ranger parka with Danny Corcoran, Nfld. Ranger, written on the outside. His parka was black with black lettering on a yellow background. He had a glazed peak cap made of duck material with ears to fold down low around his neck. After he had strapped on the pack sack, he put on his black double wool mitts. He blew out the light and noticed the flickering of the fire, so he moved to push the fender in and in doing so almost fell down. The snowshoes were slippery on the floor. He steadied himself and crept outside. He shut the storm door. Mr. Pittman told him he would take care of everything while he was gone.

Noah Pittman made an early start today. He would swamp in a road across the arm to cut his summer firewood. After he had his breakfast, he went out to his woodhouse, filed his bucksaw, and put a junk of wood on his woodhorse to try his saw. While he was trying his saw, he heard a voice. "Good morning Uncle Noah!"

Noah stopped and turned around. It was Danny. He had just shut the storm door.

"Good morning, Danny. Are you heading out on your patrol?"

"Yes," was Danny's reply.

"'Tis pretty mild. I'd say we're gonna have rain. 'Tis almost like a morning in May."

"Yes, it is," said Danny. "Should be good walking."

Noah didn't reply to that. "Want me to harness up me dogs and give you a lift up to the bottom?"

"Not at all. If I can't walk up there, I don't guess I'll be able to walk to Port Saunders."

"Good enough," said Noah. "Have a good trip, and watch out for the brooks. There's not much ice on them." Noah looked at him as he passed a few feet away.

"I'll be careful. See you on the 17th." He broke into a run.

"Good enough!" said Noah after he had passed. Noah watched him as he continued to run. He noticed the snow was flying on each side of him about three to four feet. As he watched he said to himself, "you'll have a different tune when you get off the ice, sonny. Especially when you go in to Elige Newman's main road, because that place was made for snow." As he watched, he thought, "you'll be back here by 4 o'clock. But, then he thought, "maybe not. That young man's got pride. It's about a mile from here to the bottom. I wonder if he will run all the way." He was over half way now.

Uncle Noah put down his saw. "I don't know. Maybe them fellers from St. John's got everything figured out differently from us. We take it easy on the first of it." Uncle Noah watched as Danny neared the shore and then disappeared in the trail. "I guess he showed me he needed no dogs to give him a lift," he said out loud. "But to me, it looks mighty strange." He picked up a load of firewood and went into the house.

Danny stepped in off the ice near the mouth of Soufflett's River where it ran into the salt water and shut himself in from the town. He stopped and checked himself. He felt good after running a mile. He was not out of breath. The pack sack on his back felt light although it weighed approximately 38 pounds. He stepped into the cut line that used to be used as a portage line for the logging camps that had been shut down for four years, and he knew that this line ran in for nine miles. According to his map, it ran all the way to Hancock's camp. As he walked, he noticed he was sinking very deeply into the snow. The wind had caused high drifts in and across the trail. As he walked, he noticed he was sinking in places almost to his waist. At one point, he had to remove his snowshoes in order to get himself out of an area where he had stepped near a small tree. He sank down near it and went right to the bottom.

In about half an hour he had only gone about 200 yards from the shoreline. He sat down for a while and noticed that he was sweating. He turned up the ears of his cap and removed the sweater he was wearing inside his parka and put it in his pack sack. He stood up and felt more comfortable since his sweater had been removed. He started to move along the trail again. The snow was light and sandy. He estimated an average depth of snow about twenty-four inches and he was sinking to the bottom. He even had to trample down the snow in order to make a step. After four hours, he didn't think he had gone more than one mile from shoreline. He began to feel hungry. He checked his watch and it was 11:00 A.M.

"Well," he thought, "I'll punch on for another hour before I stop to boil up."

He got into a small cutover and noticed that the snow was not as deep. "This is great!" he said. "Maybe on the open country, the snow all drifted off." Yes, he thought, that is what has happened. The wind has blown the bulk of snow off the open hills and it has lodged in the valleys. This seemed to boost his courage. He got into the trail again and ran into the deep snow. He looked at his watch. It was 12:05 noon. He then decided to boil the kettle.

He took off his pack sack and got his axe. He beat his way to a birch that was off the trail and got some birch rind. He came back and chopped down a few small pieces of dry wood. "Well," he said, "I guess I'll have to melt snow because all the brooks are snowed over."

He then filled up his kettle with snow. After he had lit the fire, he put the kettle on and sat down and started to think. Should he continue on or should he return and wait a day or so for the snow to settle. He considered the options. Then he said out loud, "What would people say? Maybe they would say he was scared to go on the hills or maybe they would say that only men can go in there. One thing for sure, the comments would not be very good."

He grinned to himself. "I will not go back until forced to do so. This is great exercise."

The kettle was boiled. He threw in some loose tea and waited a couple of minutes. Then he took the kettle off before it boiled over. He opened his lunch bag and in it he had a piece of roast pork that Barbara had put in last night. It was wrapped in brown paper.

Danny looked at the note again. He knew he was very much in love with this girl and knew his mother would love her. She was the type that would like his mother. Maybe he should propose to her. But, he thought, she is a Protestant and I am a Catholic. I guess this was why they had never talked about marriage. But, he thought, this would not be a factor in preventing him from marrying Barbara. He was sure something could be worked out. "My tea is getting cold. What in the world was I thinking about, getting married. I'm only twenty-one."

His thoughts went back to his trip. Those poor caribou. He had to get in the open country. He ate his lunch without any further thoughts of Barbara. He packed his things back into his pack sack, strapped it on, and started to move again. He looked at his watch and it read 1:15 P.M. He estimated that he had gone about one and a half miles. As he moved again, he began to feel damp around the knees. He noticed the snow was beginning to melt around the top of his boots. He brushed it off as he fought to get through the snow. He started to feel hungry again. He looked at his watch and it was 4:00 P.M. Well, he thought, I'm not even to Elige Newman's camp yet. Is it possible that I haven't even gone three miles? He checked his map. Yes, it was true. But he was almost there according to the map. His feet were wet from the melting snow and sweating. His knees were wet and his elbows were wet right through his big parka. He had wrung out his woollen mitts twice today. It's good it's not cold, he thought as he struggled in the snow.

He could see the camp. What a welcome sight! As he neared the camp, he noticed that the door was shut. He walked up to it, untied the string which was near the top of the door and pushed it open. The snow was two thirds up the door. He took off his snowshoes and used it as a shovel to clear away the snow. He stepped inside. The walls were made of round logs not peeled. A window was high up in one end of the cabin, (the only window). There was an oil barrel for the stove with stove pipes wired together with haywire. Some firewood was behind the stove. A table of three boards was nailed to the wall and a big junk of wood served as a chair. A bunk was in the corner made out of a few boards with some boughs on it. Someone had stayed here not too long ago because the boughs were still green.

Well, thought Danny, not too bad a camp. He checked his watch. It was 5:15 P.M. I guess this is where I'll spend the night. He looked outside. It was not heavily overcast. I hope it will rain. It would settle the snow anyway. He brought in his pack sack and rifle and went out with his axe. He came back half an hour later with an armful of birch rind. He had to be careful lighting the fire not to shake the pipes in fear that they would fall down. He quickly had a fire going. He hung up his clothes and boots. He had dry underwear and socks and sat down on the junk of wood near the fire. He went to the door and looked out. Yes, it was beginning to rain. Ah, he thought, this was what he needed. It was now almost dark.

I wonder how far the water is from here? Maybe it's better for me to melt snow. He went outside and filled his kettle with snow and put it on the stove. He dug into his pack sack, took out a candle, lit it and sat back. He felt tired after such a hard day. What he would do tomorrow depended on the going. If the going didn't improve, he would return to Harbour Deep. Surely the people would understand and he thought, if it was too bad for him to get in the country, maybe it was too bad for the poachers. He quickly noticed that the kettle was boiled. He made tea and sat down to supper. How lucky he was to have a roof over his head. As he ate, he noticed the floor was made of sticks put into the mud and covered with boughs. But everything had been trodden down to a fairly smooth surface. The seams between the logs were caulked with moss. This made the camp fairly comfortable. He ate his meal, put more wood in the stove, and lay down on the wooden bunk with his coat and sweater under his head. He had one blanket. He put that one over him and before he could count to three, he was asleep.

Meanwhile back in Harbour Deep, Noah Pittman harnessed his six dogs and went to the area where he was going to put in his wood road. He stopped the dogs on the ice, put on his snowshoes, then took his axe and started to walk in through the thick woods. He got about one hundred feet in. After half an hour he said to himself, "What a batch of snow. It's the biggest one for the year. It's good this wasn't rain. If it had been, everything would be flooded." He walked a little further, then came back to his dogs. He noticed one dog was running loose. He caught him and saw the dog had chewed his trace off. He got the hauling rope and gave him four or five cuts with the rope. The dog howled but would remember the next time. He heard dogs barking further down the Arm. He saw a dog team coming in around the point. It was Albert Hynes coming in from his seal nets. It looked like he had a load. The team stopped and Noah decided to go out where he was. "Albert, looks like you're stuck in the slob. How many seals did you get?"

"Five," said Albert. "Old man, I'm glad you came out. Look, she's right to the bars."

Noah looked the situation over. "I'll take one on mine. Two old dog harps, isn't it?"

"Yes," said Albert. "The other three are out to Red Point."

"What a batch of snow," said Noah.

"There's a solid jam of ice outside. I was lucky to get me nets. Took everything up. Question if there's not a lot of White Coats handy to here. We seen a lot of old seals on the ice." He paused. "I seen the Ranger's light on this mornin'. You know he never tried to go in on the country. If he did, he won't get far today."

Noah laughed. "I'm expecting him to be home when I get in."

"Now tomorrow," said Albert, "tis gonna be pretty good going because it's gonna turn to freezin' late tonight."

Noah looked at the sky. "I'd say it's going to turn to rain."

"Maybe so," said Albert. "But we'll have the wind West right afterwards."

"You could be right," said Noah. "I hope so. I've got to get my road in."

They started their teams and went in to the stages. It was noon. Almost all of the men came around. They cleaned the seals and cut them up. Each man took a meal. Noah went up to his house.

"How are you today, Nellie?"

He looked at his wife with interest hoping she would say she was feeling good today. She sat down to the table with a cup towel in her hand. "Noah," she said, "sit down."

He sat at the end of the table.

"I'm going to tell you something," she said it in a very sad tone.

Oh my, thought Noah, I wonder if she has gotten any worse or if anybody told her anything about her sickness. "What is it, my dear?"

She sighed. "When I tell you this, you might think I'm crazy. But I've got to tell you."

Noah looked anxious. "Nellie, what is it?"

"It's about a dream I had last night."

Noah sighed. What a relief. He didn't care what his wife dreamed as long as she kept up and around. "Go ahead, my dear. Tell me about it."

"I dreamt I was in a room lying down and it seemed that the room was full of leaks. I thought I smelled smoke and I saw something like steam coming out of the seams in the wall. I looked closer and it looked like foam. Some fell down on the small bed where I was lying. I reached out and touched it but it wasn't foam at all. It was flesh coming out through the seams. It was coming out and dropping off. Then the flesh started to turn dark. I wanted to scream. As I looked I saw two feet coming out of the wall. They came out and hung down. I saw great bladders on the toes and legs. As I watched, I saw two hands come out all full of bladders. I tell you, Noah, it looked awful."

Noah looked astonished. "Go on," he said.

"I then saw the bladders burst and the water ran down over the bed. Then the flesh started to fall off. As I looked closer, I saw a face on the wall. It was too cloudy around the face and I couldn't see who it was. But there was one feature that I did recognize and that was that the person had red hair."

Noah swallowed.

"As I watched, I saw a man come in dressed in white. He crept over to the wall and put a sword over his head and made a chop with the sword. I saw the two arms and legs fall from the body and the red hair fell with it and fell on top of me. That was when I woke you. Remember?"

"I remember," said Noah. "You almost frightened me to death." Noah sighed. "It's only a dream or a nightmare. There's nothing to it."

Nellie looked at the floor. "The man dressed in white with the sword. I was thinking about him all day. He looked familiar and it wasn't until just now I could place him." She paused.

"Who was it?" asked Noah intently.

"It was Dr. Curtis."

Noah felt goose pimples come out on his neck. "Don't worry about anything, Nellie. As long as you're okay, that's all that matters."

"I am worried, Noah. I have been feeling odd all day as if something is going to happen. I'm glad Ches didn't go on the country with Danny."

Noah stopped for a moment. He felt kind of weak. "I got to go take the harnesses off the dogs."

He got up and left. He had a feeling like he'd never had before.

THE MUKLUK FACTORY
AND OUTPORT CHARTERS
116 WEST ST., P.O. BOX 665
ST. ANTHONY, NFLD.
A0K 4S0
PH: 454-8887

Date Aug 21 19 87

M_____

SOLD BY	C.O.D.	CHARGE	ON ACC'T.	ACC'T. FWD.	
1	Reflections from				
2	a Snow house			59.95	
3					
4					
5					
6					
7					
8					
9					
10					
11					
12					
13					
14					
15					

22

PRICE DAXION

o

Chapter 11
March 13, 1936

Danny shook himself, then sat up. He was shivering. He grabbed his flashlight and then looked at his watch. It was 5:10 A.M. He could hardly believe it. The last time he lay down, it was 11:30 P.M. last night. He had put the last two junks of wood in the oil drum stove and lay down. He had a fair night's sleep. In fact, he could not remember waking even once during the night, but now it was freezing cold. He moved to the door and peeped out. "Wonderful!" he said out loud. "The stars are shining. I'll bet it's a lot better going today then yesterday."

He moved quickly to the oil barrel stove. He noticed all the wood behind the stove was burned. "I guess I'll have to cleave the junk I have been using for the seat. He lodged his flashlight on the table and took his axe to start cleaving the piece of wood. He made a hard chop and put his axe in the center of the junk. He then lifted it over his head and slammed it down on the frozen ground mixed with wood. The axe hit first but the junk of wood split in two and one half bounced on the frozen ground and struck the stove. Danny's heart made a jump. He saw the stove pipes fall. When they touched the hard floor, they went to pieces.

"Well, well," Danny said out loud. "I guess that ends comfort - no stove." He looked at the pieces. He knew there was no way of repairing them.

"Well," he said. "I guess I'll move on. At least when I get walking, I'll be warmer. But it's not even daylight yet." Maybe he could get a fire going on the floor and even make breakfast, maybe get warm, although now he didn't feel uncomfortable. "Yes," he said. "I think I will get a fire going right here on the camp floor. It's frozen mud anyway."

He got some birch rind and tore it up into small strips. He placed it on the floor and took the boughs that he was lying on and placed it on the birch rind. He filled his kettle with snow. There was still some water left in it from the night before. He lit the fire and the camp quickly filled with smoke. He put down the kettle and opened the door. He started coughing but stayed low on the floor. In a few minutes, most of the smoke had cleared out and as the fire burned up fairly good, the kettle started to boil.

Danny made tea and had breakfast. It consisted of squashberry jam and bread. When finished, he went outside. It was just dawning. He would have to wait another half hour. The fire was almost out. He walked out to a tree near the camp and broke off an armful of green boughs and carried them in to the camp. He then threw them on the fire. He created an awful smoke, so much that he could not stay in the cabin. He had to watch for his chance to get in to bring out his pack sack and all his things. After three trips in, he got everything. He noticed that it was light enough to travel. He packed all his things in his pack sack and then put on his parka and snowshoes. He saw that the sky to the east was very red. "Hm," he said. "I wonder what the oldtimers would say about that? Usually it was "Red sky in the morning, sailors take warning." But anyway, he wasn't a sailor, now was he? He walked around the area near the camp. He could hardly believe himself. He could walk on the crust with snowshoes. "Wonderful!" he shouted out loud. He looked at the sky and said, "Thank you." He then thought about Uncle Jobie Randell. He stepped into the trail and started walking in the country at a fast pace.

After walking for what Danny estimated to be three miles, he stopped at an area on the trail that a lot of rabbits were using. "Lots of rabbits here. I think I'll tell the boys about this when I get back." But, he thought, the season closes the fifteenth and I definitely won't be back 'til the seventeenth. He looked at his watch. It was 8:30 A.M. Not bad, a mile and a half per hour. He knew he wasn't travelling at a fast pace. Now he had to be careful. The crust wasn't as hard as he thought. He sank down a couple of times, and once he almost wrenched his knee. He walked on picking his way up the trail. It was mostly all uphill now. At the base of some cutovers, he came to a small bog. He noticed water on the bog, so he had to trim around the edge. On the other side he stepped out on a cutover. This is great, he thought. I think I'll step it up a bit. So he started to hurry. He was halfway across when he sank down. He fell forward in the snow. He felt a pain in his right leg near his shin. He felt kind of sick. "What have I done? Is it possible that I broke my leg?"

He sat up and grabbed his leg with both hands. He removed his snowshoes and his pack sack. "Well, sir," he said, "this must be an unlucky day." He moved his toes in his boot and then moved his foot upright. "Thank God," he said. "At least there are no bones broken." He then took off his boot and pulled up his pants. Then he saw blood on his underwear. He pulled off his socks and pulled up his underwear. It revealed a gash on the front of his leg about two inches long. A sharp knot on a tree had torn his leg. It had also scraped his shin almost to the bone. He looked at the cut. "I don't think stitches are required.."

He got out his first aid kit and bandaged his leg. The pain had stopped quite a bit. He put on his socks. "This evening I will bandage it more neatly." He put on his boot and snowshoes. He stood up and walked around a bit, then picked up his pack sack and rifle. He checked his watch. It was 11:30 A.M. "I should be near Hancock's camp by now."

He walked down over the hill and sure enough, there was the camp. It was built out of lumber. He walked to the door. It had a string latch. He pulled down on the string and opened the door. Without too much pushing, he cleared away the snow with his snowshoes. He felt a pain in his leg but banished it. He then stepped inside the camp and found the camp very interesting.

Uncle Noah told him this would be a great place to spend a night. The camp was built good. At one time thirty-five men worked there. He shut the door and looked at his watch. It was noon. "I am now nine miles in from salt water and to the end of the cut road." From now on he would have to travel in timber using a map and compass and the lie of the land. He decided to have a quick lunch and move on. He checked his map and looked through the door. Yes. There was the river. The camp was right on the bank. He looked at the brook. It was at the junction of Soufflett's and Ben Hynes Brook. "Well," he said, "I will have to travel in by the brook 'til I see a good place to get across."

He went back to the camp, lit the fire, made tea, and got ready to move. He noticed the sky was overcast. He put on his snowshoes and pack sack and moved on. He walked in along the brook for two miles. It was all heavy timber. He then came to a place where the brook widened out. This should be a good place for me to get across, he thought. He got his axe out of his pack sack and cut a pole about twelve feet long. He tried the ice with his axe. He moved the pole further out on the ice and tried it again. It was thin but could take his weight. He did the same thing twice more and then he noticed the ice was starting to bend. He had about twelve feet to go. He threw his things across and pushed the pole ahead of him. Down he went, right up to his neck. He grabbed for the pole to prevent being pulled in under the ice with the strong current. While reaching for the pole he lost his axe and it sank to the bottom. When he got hold of himself, he discovered that the water was not over his head but it was only up to his chest. He quickly climbed upon the pole and slid into shore. He stood on the shore and looked back at the hole into which he had fallen.

"Well," he said, "What am I going to do now that my axe is gone?" He thought about his matches. He quickly opened his pack sack and took out his shaving kit. He unzipped it and discovered that his matches weren't wet. He took out his shirts and socks and surprisingly enough, his clothes weren't too wet in the pack sack. Well, at least he could change.

He moved into the woods and took off his clothes. He put on the clothes he had in his pack sack and started again on his journey. "Well," he thought, "I guess I can make it without my axe. I can start fires with birch rind. Thank God my matches didn't get wet. I'm glad I took Gill's advice and brought Eddies matches. If I took Sea Dogs, I would certainly have to return." He looked at his watch. It was 2:30 P.M. In this heavy timber, the walking wasn't too bad. He looked at his compass. Then all of a sudden he realized he had his maps in the inside parka pocket. He took them out. They were all wet. He wiped them off but they were blurred.

He noticed that if he took this ridge, it would take him to the open country. This is what he would do. It would put him slightly off course but it would be the best thing. He started to walk fairly fast. If he could make it to the open, maybe he could make it across the first lot of open country before dark. As he walked, he noticed his parka was beginning to dry out. He came across an area where moose were yarded. He had never seen one but had heard quite a lot about them. "However," he said to himself, "I have a rifle and I'll protect myself."

It was 4:30 when he walked out on the open country and he noticed that light rain was beginning to fall. He took off a compass course. He knew he was eighteen miles in. If he had not fallen in the water, he would have had a great day. But his leg, he had forgotten all about that.

He started walking across the open. It was good walking there but he noticed it was beginning to get thick. He walked even faster. As he walked he could not see very far ahead of him. He walked in a northwesterly direction for about another half hour. He stopped then and checked himself over. He thought for a moment. Since coming on the open country, I have travelled for sure, four miles. That makes it twenty-two miles in. I could be going a bit too far West. Maybe the ridge led me further West than I thought. He changed his course to the North ten degrees and started off again. He noticed that it was beginning to get dark. If only I could get to the woods, he thought, I could build a side camp. It was raining now. He walked to the top of a hill and when he looked over the side, he could see a black line of trees in the valley. It was a welcome sight to him. He quickly walked over the hill and into the woods.

"This is one time I feel like hugging the trees," he thought. He walked further into the trees until he came to a level spot. He took off his pack sack and took out his flashlight. He shone it around and noticed that the timber was long, scrubby trees overaged. He looked around more closely and found an old birch tree. He tore off some birch rind and brought it back to his pack sack. He went around and gathered some twigs. He sat down. After an hour he had a fire going. But in doing so he burned a full box of matches. He took out his blanket, which was wet and made a lean-to over the fire. This gave him some shelter from the rain. "Why didn't I take my rain clothes?" he asked himself out loud.

He sat quietly and looked at the small fire. He took off his mitts, wrung them out, and placed them by the fire. He opened his pack sack and checked his food. He had four slices of bread and some jam left. He had four cakes of hard bread. I might as well eat my bread, he thought. I will be at Port Saunders tomorrow evening. He thought about boiling the kettle but decided against it because of the rain. After he had eaten his bread, he got a few more twigs to put on the fire. He noticed they were not burning very well. He walked further away from the fire in search of something better to put on it but could find very little. Everything was wet. He found a few dry twigs and brought them back. He then noticed his leg was paining where he had cut it earlier that day. This was when he decided to survey the situation. He realized his feet were wet. He also felt his back was wet. Water was beginning to drip from his blanket all over him from his lean-to. He was also wet through the knees. He checked his watch. It was 8:30 P.M. He realized he was going to have a long night. He looked into the fire, then at the trees nearby. There was nothing he could do. He had no axe. If only he had not lost his axe. He would have sooner lost his rifle. Instead he sat quietly in the dripping rain and stared into the small fire. What was he to do? Nothing but sit and wait.

"I guess I made a mistake by not taking Uncle Noah Pittman's advice. He had said, "Son, don't go in on the hills. We are going to have bad weather. You could have a rough time and especially alone. The caribou are not worth the risk. We have been in there for as much as ten days unable to move. If the brooks burst out, there's no way you can even get out unless you really know where to go."

But now he sat in the very place where he was warned not to be and under the conditions that were supposed to be the worst. For a moment he felt discouraged, but got a hold of himself and said. "I am over halfway across. It's only about ten miles and I will be able to look down on Port Saunders." He thought about Barbara. He knew he loved her and he knew she loved him, but at this very moment they were in two different worlds. She was probably in that big arm chair in Uncle Edward's living room thinking about him and maybe thinking he was in Port Saunders. And here he was sitting in the driving rain thinking about her. But, he thought, we both are thinking about each other and that's all that matters. He felt the pain in his leg. "My, oh my," he thought. "If I was near Aunt   Martha now, how she would do up this leg for me. He remembered what she had told him about how she was the seventh ddaughter of the seventh son and that automatically made her a nurse, and after hearing the stories of the people in the town, it made her one of the highest order. Then he thought of Granny Randell. But maybe she was only good for delivering babies. He didn't know anything ath this moment. He would even let Uncle Noah Pittman dress his leg.

It was 7:10 P.M., March 13, 1936, when Nat Johnson stopped by Noah Gillard's house. He tapped on the window. A voice from inside shouted "Who's dat?"

"Tis me, Nat Johnson!" was the quick reply.

"Das you is it, Nat?" the voice from inside the house asked.

"Yes. 'Tis me. Where's Pleman? Where's he at? Tell him to come over I wants him."

The bag on his back was heavy. His snowshoes were squabbly from soaking in the water that he had been walking in most of the evening.

A man appeared at the door and said, "Nat, come in out of the rain. You must be nearly drowned. You must have had a hard tramp."

Nat replied quickly. "No. Got to go to the Post Office with the mail. Tell Plemen to come over at once. I got something to tell him."

"Good enough," replied Noah who shut the door as Nat moved on in the driving rain.

In a few minutes he was at the Post Office and put the mail in the holding room. He quickly went straight to his house. His wife met him at the door and helped get the oil skins off him. His shoulders ached and the skins in his snowshoes were soaked so much they could hardly stay on his feet.

"My dear," said his mother Dinah, "you must have had a bad day. This is a bad night. Not fit for a dog. I got your supper ready."

"Good," he said. "I'm some hungry." He sniffed his nose. "Smells good."

He moved to the table and started eating. He had fried seal and fried potatoes for supper. It tasted wonderful. He was almost finished when the door opened and Pleman Gillard stepped into the kitchen. He shut the door and sat down at the table. "Nat, me boy." He quickly looked directly at Nat. "What kind of a day did ye have?" He paused. "When did the rain come on? How much water is on the country? Did ye have a big load?"

Nat bolted the food quickly to get his reply in. "Yes, Pleman, yes."

Ple pulled down his eyebrows and spoke in a high-pitched voice. "What's you saying yes to? The weather, the food, or the water? Explain yourself."

A reply was quickly given. "Pleman, he's gone in on the country looking for the crowd killing game. I knew he was going to go, Pleman. I knew he was going to go. He's that type of person. Nobody could hold him back."

He stopped. Ple looked at him for a moment. "What are you talking about? Who's gone in the country? Come on, man, slow down." Ple said in rapid speed.

Nat bolted a half slice of bread and looked at Ple wide-eyed. The perspiration was on his forehead. "The Ranger, the Ranger, the one up in Harbour Deep. You know. The one I was telling you about with the red hair. They all begged him not to go because it looked like bad weather, but he still went. Said he was gonna stop the crowd from killing the caribou."

"Well, well," said Ple. "Did you say he was gone alone?"

"Yes," said Nat.

"Now, das very good. Too bad. If he had gone two weeks ago when he wanted Peters to go, das when the crowd from the other side and Belvy would have got caught. But I'd say he could catch fellers yet. I heard Whit Pilgrim and his buddies are going in tomorrow. Das if the rain hold up. But don't speak about dat. I hope Whit gets caught. Now listen, Nat, we will spread a good story just so as Peters can hear it. He should feel like a snake sitting here in Englee while Corcoran is walking all alone on the country looking for poachers. I wish him success. Hope he catches a whole lot just to make Peters feel small. Certainly I don't think there's any way making him look any smaller. All he is any good for is playing cards, keeping company with the English nurses, and sticking his nose in somebody elses business. Too bad he didn't go to Hooping Harbour the other day to meet Corcoran. We might have had an opportunity to take him."

Ple stopped. "I'd like to get the privilege to get him in the country. I would see if there was any bit of a man about him." Ple moved his chair back from the table. "Aunt Die, " he said, "have you got all your caribou gone yet?"

"No," she replied very quickly. She was a white-haired woman with a clean cut appearance who kept a very tidy home. When she was not knitting or house cleaning, she was visiting someone, especially the sick or shut-in.

Ple looked at her wide-eyed. "What's the weather going to be like in the next few days? Is it going to clear up?"

She looked at him and nodded. "Before twelve tonight, it will be as clear as a whistle."

She filled Nat's cup with tea. "It's going to turn off freezing, but we're going to have a lot of rain, all through the rest of the month."

"I'd say that will be snow in the country," said Ple quickly.

She looked at the two men and then asked. "Why does the Ranger here in Englee have a dislikin' for most everybody? He has done some weird stuff. You take what he did up to Uncle Sam Compton's. Sure, that was a mortal sin. Just because he owed John Reeves money on that stove, there's no reason for him to go up and take it from him." Aunt Die sighed. "Well, my son, what odds. Maybe some day he'll pay for things like that."

Ple grinned. "Yes, right, Aunt Die. Maybe you're right." Ple stood up. "I think I will go over and tell Joe Luther the news. He'll make sure Peters knows all about Corcoran gone in the Country."

It was 8:00 P.M. when Barbara Gale put down her pen. She sat up straight at her desk in her bedroom. She was trying to correct the test papers that were before her but she was too worried.

"Why would Danny worry me so much by going on such a trip? Why?" she said out loud. She looked at the ceiling. The lamp on the desk looked blurred. She felt a tear running down her face. "I wouldn't feel so bad if Aunt Martha had not told me Nellie's dream about Danny. My oh my, is it possible something could happen to him? But Uncle Noah says that he will be alright. I hope he's right. But the rain! I bet there's a flood. And what would he do if he came to a flooded river? I hope he will turn back and come home. This is the second night. I wonder where you are now Danny?" she said out loud. With this she fell down on the bed and started to weep. "That dream, oh that dream!" she repeated. She was crying out loud.

"Barbara! Barbara!" A voice called to her from the bedroom door. "Barbara, what's the matter? Are you alright?"

Barbara stopped for a moment, then sat up and faced Aunt Martha Pittman. Martha was a very dominant woman. She was the granddaughter of a Welsh miner who came to Newfoundland and was ordered not to return to the British Isles again. He refused to bow to the Grand Duke of London during a parade in Liverpool and his children and all his offspring have lived independent lives. Aunt Martha, it is said, was the seventh daughter of the seventh son. She had been known to have stopped bleeding with the touch of her hand. She could put away warts. She made medicine out of balsam buds, juniper roots, and bog-bean.

She now looked at Barbara very sternly. "Barbara, my dear," she said without any emotion. "I have spent many years here in Harbour Deep. In fact, most all my life. And if sorrow could have done it, I would have spent half my life crying over things that I thought were going to happen. You've seen Danny go in the country, and this is the second night he's been gone and you're crying because he may not return. You had better get a hold of yourself. It's not the end of the world."

Barbara looked at her with a tear stained face. "Aunt Martha, I've got a feeling like I never had before. I think the hand writing is on the wall. Something awful is going to happen to Danny Corcoran. I don't think I will ever see him alive again. I've got the feeling that Danny is a stranger. In fact, for some unknown reason, I can't even remember his features. I know he has red hair, but I don't remember what he even looks like. Aunt Martha, do you have a picture of him?"

"No," was her reply.

"Aunt Martha, what does all this mean?" She sputtered. "I mean, have you ever been in such a spot as this where Uncle Edward has gone away and you had the feeling that something had happened to him?"

Martha looked at the ceiling. She paused for a moment. "This part of the Northern Peninsula is full of stories of men who have suffered much hardship. I remember one time in particular when Ned and two other men from Harbour Deep went in on the hills. They had ten dogs. They went in on the East side of the Soufflett's. After they had gone it started to rain and every bit of ice and snow melted. After they were gone six days, four of the dogs came home. We got a search party going and after three days, the men came back. They picked up a jacket by the side of the river. It belonged to one of the two men with him. The whole area was alerted. There was no wireless here then. I took to the hills myself. We searched for five days. We could not even cross the river. We came back when Roy Ropson broke his leg. We had to carry him for eight miles. We were almost out when we met Ned coming in the trail. He was looking for us. They came out at Williamsport and came home by boat. When I saw him coming I was overjoyed."

"Do you know what I did when I saw him? I grabbed him by the ears and kissed him in front of the people that were there. Although most of the men were mad, everyone laughed. One man said it was a sight for sore eyes. Another said Ned would be plagued from then on with bad ears."

Barbara smiled.

"Don't worry, Barbara. Whatever is going to happen, will happen. Your tears won't change a thing."

Barbara dried her tears. "You're an expert in cheering people up." She paused and as Aunt Martha left the room, she called, "Thanks, Aunt Martha."

"Have a good night," said the grey haired lady who then shut the door.

Barbara sighed as she looked at the flickering light on the desk. "If I could only remember his features." She blew out the light and got into bed. It was 11:10 P.M.

Danny found a big dry limb that had partly fallen down from a tree. He brought it over and lodged it on the small fire. He looked at his watch. It was 11:00 P.M. The rain was beginning to turn to snow. He noticed it was turning colder. He felt a severe pain in his injured leg. He put his hand on the sore spot. It was very tender. It would have to stay as it was for the night. He was too miserable to have anything to do with dressing the wound. The pain kind of made him sick. He noticed it was beginning to blow. He felt the wind on his cheek. He was pleased with the thought of not having to sit 'til daylight in the driving rain. Then he wondered what would happen if it turned severely cold. "My oh my," he thought. "What a spot to be in. Yes," he asked himself, "what would happen if it did turn really cold? Well, anyway, I won't be wet."

The snow was beginning to hold up. He sat under the wet blanket. It had stopped leaking on him. He felt the water between his toes. He knew it was no use to change his socks, because the ones in his pack sack were almost as wet as the ones he had on his feet. As he sat near the small fire, he thought he saw something. He looked closer. He then stood up and looked through the tree. "Yes," he said. "It's a star! Thank God it's clearing up." He felt the temperature change and recognized the wind was North-West. It seemed to fan the small fire a bit. The fire was only giving one thing and that was a little light. There was no heat from it whatsoever, but with this little fire, he didn't feel so all alone.

He felt the tops of his fingers getting a little cold and noticed frost was forming on his pack sack. Yes, he thought, it's turning cold. As he sat and looked into the little fire, he started to size up the situation. He realized he was in on the open country about 18 to 20 miles from Harbour Deep. He wasn't sure if he could pinpoint his location on the map, though. That didn't matter because his maps were all soaked anyway. He had no food except four cakes of hard bread. He was wet to the skin from head to toe and had no dry clothes. The weather was turning cold, and from what Uncle Ned had told him, it could be raining one minute up here and severely cold the next. His plight at that moment didn't seem very encouraging.

As he thought, he noticed his pants legs were beginning to stiffen with the cold. He reached up and touched the blanket and it was almost stiff from the frost. He decided to put his mitts on, but they were almost frozen. After a struggle they were on his cramped hands. He stood up. It was then he realized his clothes were freezing on his body. As he stood he could feel the keenness in the air. He tapped the blanket and he found out that it was frozen hard. It could stand up straight like a door. Well, he thought, I'll stick it up on the North-West side of the fire. This will give me shelter from the wind. When he tried to move it, he found it was impossible because his mitts were frozen too hard to hold onto anything. As he looked around he realized he was in for a hard time.

The wind now began to pick up. He could hear it in the trees and he felt his feet beginning to get cold. I have to start moving around, he thought. He started beating his feet, one against the other, up and down, up and down. He would not be able to see his watch now either. He realized he was freezing.

"I can't stay here," he said. "I think I will move further down the valley. It seems I am on a hill." He picked up his pack sack. It was frozen into a funny shape. He was unable to put it on his shoulders. As he looked at it, he wondered if he had everything put back inside. He said, "Yes," to himself and then pushed the barrel of his rifle through a part of one strap and made a few steps.

He figured it was no more than an hour from the time it cleared up and already he could walk on frozen snow. He walked further down the valley, and as he walked, icicles started forming on his eyelids. He was now in complete darkness and the trees around him looked black. He stepped near a small tree. This gave him unsure footing. He sank to his knee, and in doing so, he scraped his injured leg. The pain stabbed him to the heart. He fell to the snow. His clothes were too stiff with the frost to even reach down and rub his leg. He felt as though he was in a suit of plaster of Paris. He groaned and rolled in the snow. He then stopped and lay still. He noticed he was crying. Waves of pain darted up and down his leg. The North-West wind seemed to bite at him from head to toe. He felt as if his blood was going to stand still. He then felt the numbness in his feet and said out loud, "Oh my God, my feet are going to freeze. Am I finished?"

He felt a sickening feeling like he never had before. "Do I deserve this? Is this my own fault? If I had only listened to even the smallest kid not to go on this trip, I would be at this moment in my bed back home in Harbour Deep. But now here I am and it doesn't look good."

It was then he remembered his training. He gathered all his strength and stood up. The only areas that bent were the knees, shoulders, elbows, and a little at the waist. He felt severe pain in his leg, and the numbness in his feet. He quickly got his rifle and pack sack on his shoulder and hobbled further down the hill.

As he walked further down into the timber, he noticed several birch trees and some dry wood. He noticed he had much more shelter. Now this seemed to raise his courage a little. "Well," he said to himself. "It's live or die. I've got to get a fire going." He tried to pick off some birch rind but was unable to do so with his finger mitts. "Well," he said, "My mitt has to come off in order to light matches." He started to take off his mitt but found it impossible. One was too frozen to catch hold of the other one and the handwrist was too small to let the hand come up. He started beating his mitts on a tree to try and soften them up. After a while he felt the mitt becoming a little slack. He put his hand under his knee, and bearing all his weight on his frozen mitt, he gave a pull with all his might. His hand came out of his mitt. He then tried to get his hand in his inside pocket to get his pocket knife, and after prying for about half an hour, he succeeded in getting his knife. He cut the handwrist off his other mitt and tore his hand loose from it. He quickly reached into his shirt pocket and took out his box of matches. "Thanks to Ches," he said. "I have matches." I'll tell him, he thought, when I get back how he saved my life. He picked off a bit of birch rind and lit it. He added more to it, and then he broke off dry twigs and put them on the burning birch rind. He held his hands close to the fire, almost right on the flame, and found a little heat.

"My feet, my feet!" he cried. "They're going to be frozen. Oh dear Lord."

He started to pray. He went and gathered more twigs and put them on the fire. He placed his boot bottoms about an inch from the fire but could find no life in them. He got up and gathered more burning material. He found a dry stump that had been broken down maybe ten years ago. He pulled it near the fire and sat on it. He put his finger mitts near the flames and watched them bend over as they started to heat up. He watched the steam rise out of his pants near the knees as he huddled close to the fire and felt its warmth. His blood started to heat up a bit. He took out his pocket watch. It was 1:15 A.M. It would be dawning at 5:30 A.M. The thought gave him hope.

He still couldn't find any heat or any feeling at all in his feet. If he could only get his boots off. He got up and went to collect more firewood. This would be the only means of survival. He was limping. As he walked, he started to feel something in his feet. It was a stinging sensation. He brought back two loads of dead brush and some rather old stumps. "If only I had my axe" he said out loud." I wouldn't be in this mess." He knew his axe would be the key to his survival. He looked at the kindling he had collected. He figured he had enough to last three hours. It would last 'til 5:00 A.M.

He sat on the old piece of tree near the fire. He almost put his feet right in the fire. It was severely cold. He sat with his back to the wind. He put his pack sack near the fire to thaw it. Then he remembered his flashlight. It was in his pack sack, but his feet, his toes, were still dead. There was no life in them at all. His boots had to come off. The strings of his boots started to thaw. He pulled at them. After an hour he managed to get one boot off. He looked at his foot inside the sock. He tried to move his toes but didn't see them move. He was afraid to look at them. He put them near the fire and he noticed his socks were beginning to scorch with the heat. Finally he could remove his sock. He could hardly believe his eyes. His five toes on one foot were like icicles, frozen solid. He reached down and caught hold of them and started to rub them. After half an hour he could scale the ice from his toes.

As the frost started to come out, the pain started to set in. What agony he felt! The saliva in his mouth ran down over his chin. He had never felt pain like it before. What would he do? What could he do? Here he was in the middle of the country, his toes on one foot frozen and maybe on the other also. He took his warm mitt and put it over his toes to protect them from the cold air and the hot flames. He started to take the other boot off. My, oh my, he thought, what have I gotten myself into? Oh dear God, what am I going to do?

He struggled with his boot strings and finally they were loose enough to let his foot out of his boot. There wasn't any life in his toes and very little in his foot. He slowly removed his sock and examined his toes. His five toes were frozen. It was then he realized this was his right foot and his right leg was the one he had cut. He didn't have the heart to look at his leg. He started rubbing his frozen toes. After half an hour he could feel life in them. He didn't know which foot to hold or rub. He started crying. The pain was piercing him to the heart. "Oh dear God!" he cried. "What have I done to deserve such agony?" His heart sank low. He tried to get a grip on himself but was unable to do so. He tore at his feet, severely slapping them with his hands. He fell on his back and looked at the twinkling stars through the trees. As he watched them, he remembered the words of his inspector in Whitborne: "Never give up. When you feel like quitting, push on."

He sat up. He could feel the fire on the bottoms of his feet. He looked at his toes. They looked a fiery red. What could he do? He knew about frost burns. He knew what was going to happen tomorrow. He knew what he was going to have to do when he put his boots back on. Now he would have to keep them on 'til he got to Port Saunders. He knew he would not be able to remove them for fear of not getting them back on again. He reached into his pack sack and found his socks. They were stiff with frost. He put them near the fire. Very soon he saw steam coming from them. Then he looked at his watch. It was 3:50 A.M. In about an hour he would be getting ready to leave. What would he do? How would he be able to walk? As he sat there and looked at the dying fire, he knew he would need much luck to get to Port Saunders before his leg and feet began to give him more trouble.

As he reached for his socks, he could see the fire was going out. He would have to get more wood. He pulled on the damp socks with much difficulty. With tears in his eyes, he examined the cut on his leg. Again he noticed it was red and swollen and was much deeper than it looked. It was a torn hole and his shin was scraped to the bone. When he did it, he thought it was the worst thing that could happen to him. But now his cut leg was nothing compared to his frozen feet. What would he do? He put his boots on and was unable to tie them firmly because it hurt so bad. He stood up. He felt a little weak. His 170 pound frame was almost too much for his tender feet to keep up. He made two steps and fell to his knees wincing in pain. He knew he would have to get a hold of himself. He felt hungry then and reaching into his pack sack, he got a cake of hard bread. He broke off a small piece and put it in his mouth and stood up again. This time he managed to stay upright. He walked around a bit, making circles around the fire. If I had a cup of tea, he thought. But it was no use. His tea had gotten wet when he fell into the river. There was only one thing that gave him any consolation. Although his feet were frozen and thawed, there was still life in them. But how tender would it be to walk over the hard snow and open country? By the way, his thoughts brought him another question: "Which way was Port Saunders?" Well, anyway, after daylight he would be able to pick himself up. He looked at his watch. It was 5:30 A.M. He could see the dawning in the Eastern sky.

Chapter 12
March 14, 1936

Earl Patey woke early. He looked through the window. The little town of River of Ponds looked as though it had been lodged on a silky cloud. There were icicles everywhere. The sudden change in weather last night from a downpour of rain to severe frost made ice candles reaching almost to the ground from some roofs. Earl lit the fire and put the kettle on. He was very quiet trying not to make any noise to wake his mother. He had his grub bag packed and his clothes bag was filled with two blankets and personal gear. It looked to him that the weather would be fair for the next two days. He went outside and took a better look. Ah yes, he thought, we might as well go today.

Earl and his two brothers had been rabbit snaring in around East Bluey Pond in February and were unable to get back to look at their snares since, due to bad weather. But the season closed tomorrow, so he thought it wise to go in today and take up his snares.

He walked over to his brother's house, which was about one hundred yards away, to see if he was up. "Well," he said, "what a morning this is." He went into his brother's house and found his brother up. "Good morning, Jack," he said.

"Good morning, Earl."

"Are you ready? I'm ready to go. Is Fred up?"

"Yes," said Jack. "I heard him calling his dogs just now." Jack looked out the window. "You'd better take your shot gun. We might see some partridge today."

"Okay," said Earl.

They looked at each other.

"How many dogs are you taking?"

"I'm going to take eight. You might as well get on with me. Fred is going to take the dogs' grub and a bit of lumber. We're going to make a couple of bunks. I'm not sleeping on the ground any more. He's also going to take his twelve knee slide. He's talking about hauling home a few dry sticks on the way back."

Earl heard the dogs outside. Then Fred called, "hey, Jack, I'm going on.

Let Earl get on with you."

"Okay. No problem. We'll catch you somewhere between here and the camp."

Jack winked and grinned at Earl. "I'll say we'll pass him on the big pond."

Earl laughed. Those two brothers of his, really got along together, especially in the fishing boat. They were good trapmen. Jack picked up his pack sack and walked outside, followed by Earl.

"Make sure you latch the door, Earl. The last time we went away I left the door open and when Meg got up, the dogs were after being in and had the pantry ramsacked. They even ate, or chewed up, the bread can, and you talk about a state they made."

Earl laughed. "I guess that fixed you. No more killing caribou for you."

"I guess not," said Jack. "Meg, since then has become my biggest enemy. I think she'd even tell the minister." They both laughed. "This is going to be hard on the dogs' paws. They'll chop themselves up this marnin'."

Earl said, "We'll have to keep a close eye on them."

They hooked the dogs to the komatik and away they went at full speed in the bright, cool, early morning bound for East Bluey Pond.

Meanwhile, Danny was making slow progress, but after walking only two hundred feet, he came to a pond. It was now daylight. The wind was still piercing cold and already his clothes were frozen stiff, but the morning looked like it was going to be a clear day. He could not get near the pond because it was flooded around the side. He noticed a high hill on the North side. He started walking along the side going West. He came to a bog and saw three moose at one end. As he limped out on the bog, he was quickly spotted by the large animals and they immediately disappeared in the woods. He crossed the bog and went into the woods at the West end and saw where someone had killed two moose. It looked about two weeks old and all that was left were the heads and legs.

After walking for a quarter of a mile he came to a large pond. His feet were so sore, he could hardly let his toes touch the hard snow. He had to be very careful not to let them touch against a tree. The pain was severe, but he had to push on. After trying to cross the pond he gave up because it was flooded so he started to walk around it. The sun was now shining brightly and the wind was beginning to die down. He felt hungry and tired but knew it was no use in even thinking about that. The only thing he had was a little hard bread. He looked ahead, and in the distance he could see open country. Well, he thought, just behind this area is Port Saunders. I think I'll step it up a bit. He started to move a little further. As he walked around the pond he came to a small brook. The water looked deep. He walked in along the brook a bit and saw a place where he could possibly get across. He knew if he was to get across, he would have to jump. He backed up a bit and ran five steps, then jumped. He landed on the other side, but sank through the hard snow. A blur of hot pain went through his whole body. He collapsed to his knees. He staggered, then fell to the hard snow on his face and lay motionless with his face on the snow. The rifle that was pushed through his snowshoes to make them easy for carrying fell on top of him.

There he lay, the young Ranger whom everyone loved dearly. He lay motionless, without any movement as if dead. The very morning air seemed to groan out the agony of this very moment.

Danny grew up with and knew hard work. He gave his widowed mother everything he ever worked for in goods and money to help her provide. This was the depression era in Newfoundland and St. John's was caught right in the middle. The job with the Rangers gave Danny the opportunity to help his dear mother get a few things that she had always longed for. Things such as a new dress and hat for Sunday church or a new pair of shoes. He was pleased that he could do this. He had spent this winter in Harbour Deep but had stayed in touch with his mother, his sister, and two brothers. He loved his family and they dearly loved him. He had just taken enough money from his pay to keep him and had sent his mother the remainder and did it with love for them. Whenever he put a money order in an envelope, his love for his family from deep down in his heart went with it.

But now this red haired young man with the heart of gold lay motionless, having endured enough pain to render him unconscious. If he had come in here on a pleasure trip and things of this sort had happened, things might not seem so bad. But he was here for a reason. He was here to prevent men who have no regard for the wild animal and especially the caribou, this magnificent animal that was about to be wiped out for greed. He was trying to prevent this from happening but had no help from his fellow officers. He decided to try this alone and here he lay wounded, doubting in his mind if he was going to make it.

The coldness of the snow on his face woke him up. He moaned and tried to roll over. He pushed the rifle and snowshoes off himself, then rolled over on his back. He could feel the awful pain in his leg and was sure he had his leg completely torn in pieces. He wept out loud. "Oh Blessed Saint of God," he cried. "Help me on this moment. I can't stand this pain and I'm all alone and without help. I just can't go on."

Danny was not a man who swore or used profane language. His people were not the type. They were men who sat and listened and made up their minds accordingly and if rough times came, they were ready to bear the burden.

Danny managed to sit up and look at his leg. He could see blood on his pants. He could feel blood in his boot. He moved his toes but could feel nothing because the pain was too great. He surveyed what had happened and saw that he had landed at a place where the water had honeycombed away the snow underneath near this brook. It was a wonder he hadn't broken his leg, and this thought gave him courage. If he had broken his leg, he thought, what would he have done? "What pain! I feel sick." He tried to throw up but realized there was nothing in his stomach to throw up. Anyway, he felt hungry but at least he didn't feel cold. The sun was shining.

"I've got to move on," he said out loud. He got his rifle, and with it he helped himself to his knees. He finally got to his feet, put his rifle and snowshoes on his back, and limping, started moving West hoping he was headed in the direction of Port Saunders.

Ranger Peters sat at the breakfast table and Joe Luther sat on the other end facing him.

"What a morning," said Joe to anyone who wanted to answer. Joe Luther was a pretty rugged man who took no foolishness from anyone and Peters was aware of this, and naturally, this gave Peters the notion to answer.

"It sure is a great day to go to Roddickton." He looked at Joe, but only for a second. He noticed Joe wasn't very pleased for some reason. He could tell.

"Hey Vie, bring the teapot in. The beans are getting cold," Joe shouted.

She brought in the teapot and set it on the table. Joe poured his cup of tea and carried the teapot out, then came back and sat down. She came back with the teapot and poured Peters' tea.

"Thanks, Vie," Joe grunted.

Peters didn't have to ask what was wrong. He knew, because last night Joe had said nasty things to him about Danny Corcoran. He knew of the wireless Danny had sent him asking him to come to Hooping Harbour for a meeting with him to arrange a patrol in the country. But now Corcoran was gone alone. Maybe he should get someone and go in. He quickly banished the thought, saying to himself, I'm not going to take any punishment for caribou. The quicker they're all gone, the quicker we'll be rid of a lot of trouble, he thought, and if Corcoran had nothing else to do but to go chasing people killing caribou, then he was welcome to do so. And if he got lost, he wouldn't be going in there either, to look for him. He got up from the table and left the house.

After he had gone, Joe called to his wife. "Vie," he said.

She answered, "What is it?"

"You know, now I know what the problem is. Yes. Now I know where the problem is. He should have been the nurse at Roddickton and she should have been the Ranger here in Englee."

Vie laughed. "Joe, my son, it's not all that bad. What odds. Let her slide. Let Peters do what he wants." She sighed.

Joe shook his head. "Maybe you're right. Maybe you're right."

He saw Peters go in the house where the young United Church Minister lived. He struck the table with his fist. "I make no wonder there's a depression in Newfoundland."

He got up from the table in anger.

Danny looked at his watch. It was twelve noon. It was a beautiful day. The sun was drying his clothes. Danny saw something about two hundred yards away. He looked closer and finally realized what he was looking at. It was caribou, three of them. They were snow white. They stood and looked at him as if wondering when he would shoot, because these animals were used to being stalked and chased to a point where there were not many places to go. They came nearer as if sensing something but then got wind of him and quickly moved away. Danny looked at his sore feet, then at the running caribou. He looked at the beautiful country. I guess it's worth it. Somebody has to sacrifice if the animals are to survive, so it might as well be me, he thought. He then turned his attention to his surroundings. He had made surprisingly good time in travelling. He had estimated his distance of ten miles since he had hurt his leg, and now he was on the hill where he was supposed to see Port Saunders. He looked, but his view was blocked by a wooded ridge in front of him. He would have to start going down to the low lands. In the distance, he could see the ocean. It looked a bright blue. The low lands were a pale green studded by the white patches which were the ponds and lakes. To the West he could see the splendor of Bluey Mountain with its shining white cap. It rose up high into the clear noon day air like a giant mushroom with its base surrounded by the thick green virgin forest.

And as he looked he could see haze rising from its white silky cap. Here I am, he thought, standing as if it was on top of the world with the ocean and the forest at his feet, but I am only a weakling. "What am I?" he asked himself. "Yes, it's true. I am only dust. I am only as the dew of the morning."

He looked at his feet. They ached. He had enough knowledge to know that frost burns were no small matter, and he knew his toes on both feet were frozen and maybe part of one foot. His leg didn't bother him too much as long as he didn't touch it against anything. He felt pains coming right up both legs. It seemed whenever he thought about it, it started to hurt more.

He had to move on. He started to move down off the open country, picking his steps as he went. He looked at his watch. It showed 12:45. He had gone quite a distance in 45 minutes, but now he was descending down in the valley. After walking a quarter of a mile, Danny discovered something that almost made his heart break. He sat down in the soft snow with his head in his hands.

On the open country, everything was cool and crisp. The cold air had kept everything frozen. There was no fear of sinking. No need of having to wear snowshoes on his tender, frozen, blistered feet. But now he had discovered the horrible situation. The snow had gone soft in the hot sun and now he would have to wear his snowshoes. He walked a few steps and sank to his knees. He stopped abruptly and lodged down his snowshoes and rifle. He sat down and put one foot into the sling and howled with pain. He lashed the snowshoe on. He was afraid to take a step. He bent over again and tried twice to get his other foot into the snowshoe sling, but he was unable to get it in. He surveyed the situation. "What am I going to do?" he thought. I've got no choice, but to put this snowshoe on. He knew his toes were all blisters. He looked at the backs of his hands and saw that they were beads of sweat. He loosened the slings as far as they could go, then slowly put his foot into the sling with tears in his eyes. Then he tightened up the sling around his boot. "My God, My God," he cried. "What am I to do?"

He put his rifle on his back and made a few steps. He howled in pain, made a few more steps, then stopped and cried. He looked around, then limped down over the hill through the timber. As he moved, he could feel the flesh tearing from his toes on both feet. Then he said to himself, "I've got to move on. I've got to move on." With almost every step he repeated, "Move on. Move on."

The sun was shining but the agony was too great to feel nature's pull. The pain drove away the colour of the trees and the sound of the squeaking Whiskey-Jack.

Danny paused for a moment. He had to concentrate on his direction. He had to be careful. Maybe Port Saunders wasn't very far away from here. Then he thought. "I never saw any town as I looked. There's no sign of either man or beast." That made the town at least a few miles away.

He was walking down a valley when he heard something. As he looked, he saw moose running through the timber. "My," he said, "if only I could ride one of them."

He walked on until he came to a round lake where he saw tracks. They looked like sled tracks. He started walking along the side of the pond, and at the end of the pond he found a dog team trail. Now he felt good. He walked in the trail for about three miles. As he was walking along a side hill, he was going due West when he saw in front of him a large opening. It looked big enough to be the ocean. He was almost running. His courage soared. As he stepped through the woods, he noticed he was on a large pond. But to the West, he could see what looked like a long bay. Maybe this is where the road to Port Saunders is. Then he remembered from looking at his maps that this was East Bluey Pond. "Yes," he said out loud. "There's Bluey Mountain." Well, at least he was off the hills. It was difficult for him to see westward because the sun was shining in his eyes. It was just above the horizon in the Western sky.

Where were the tracks he was following? They had disappeared on the lake. The heavy rain had taken them away. Now what was he going to do? He walked out on the lake. It was hard, so he removed his snowshoes with great pain. Then he started walking down the lake. After he had walked for about a mile, he decided to go ashore. He looked around. He was directly off the mouth of a river. As he looked he thought about what Mr. Edward Pittman had told him. "Stay away from the mouth of the brooks if you go on the ponds." As he walked he thought he heard the ice crack under his feet. He became very nervous. He knew he was past the mouth of the brook. "I'd better get in to the shoreline," he said to himself. He started sliding his feet across the ice. If only I had my skates, he thought, I would go the length of this lake very fast, but he thought about his feet. As he walked he wondered if the brook had a name. He thought he would call it Pittman's Brook after Uncle Ned Pittman.

He noticed the sun had gone down. It was now very chilly. Well, he thought, I had better stick close to the shore. There might be a camp near here. He reached the shore and started to walk along the edge. He noticed a raw nagging in his stomach and knew it was mainly from hunger. He knew he had to get to a hospital, that he could only go so long with such a condition. Because his toes were frozen and he had a bad leg, it made him feel uneasy.

As he walked along the edge of the pond, he realized he was going to have to spend another night out in the open. It was beginning to get dark. The stars were twinkling in the evening sky. He stopped near a bunch of large trees that were by the edge of the lake in a little cove. Danny decided this would be the place to spend the night. There were lots of birch trees and plenty of dry wood. At least he wasn't wet like yesterday.

Yesterday. It seemed like a year ago. He could hardly remember last night. Then he remembered the pain and the sight of his frozen feet. It made him shudder. He took off his pack sack and started gathering birch rind and dry branches. He put them near a large moor that had been turned up maybe years earlier when the wind had pushed over a large spruce.

He reached into his pocket to get his matches, but to his surprise, they weren't there. He checked his other pocket but they were not there. He checked every pocket in his clothes, but still no matches. He could hardly believe it. Where were they? He looked in his pack sack but couldn't find them. His heart sank. Then he went back over his trail in his mind. What could he have done with them? Then he thought, maybe they fell out of his pocket when he had hurt his leg earlier this morning. He knew he had passed out for ten or fifteen minutes and in such pain he might have even thrown them away. He could feel the keenness of the evening air on his nose. He knew this was not going to be a severely cold night, but if he had a fire, he might get some sleep. He had not slept now for almost thirty hours and his eyes felt as though they had sticks in them.

"There's not much use in staying here," he said out loud. "I might as well move along the lake." He put on his pack sack, picked up his rifle and snowshoes and began to walk westward along the lake. He walked for about three hours, then came to the mouth of a river running out of the lake. It was a big river, the main waterway of the River of Ponds River which was classed as one of the largest rivers in Newfoundland. Danny knew from studying the maps where he was, but he didn't know for sure in which direction Port Saunders was. He thought it was here.

He had heard talk of River of Ponds River. It was in the tourist guide as a sportsman's paradise for the Atlantic Salmon. But now here he was caught near its headwater with no hope in sight and not knowing which way to go to reach a town – any town. He needed help. He needed someone to give him medical attention and food, some place where he could get sleep. He knew he was far from giving in. He still felt his strength although his mind felt weak.

The rivers always run to the sea, he thought, and I might as well take advantage of this. As he started walking along the river bank, he stepped and struck his leg on a stick. A blur of pain went through him. He knew at once he would have to stop, so he decided to look for a place with a little shelter. This was the third night since he left Harbour Deep and already he suffered more than he had in all his lifetime.

There was a big difference in the spot where he was going to spend this night than what he was used to. He had slept all winter in woollen blankets, but now, he didn't even have a bed. It made him more appreciative of things back in his apartment in Harbour Deep. If only he had the floor near the stove. What a nap he would have! He broke off some branches and put them near a clump of trees and lay down. He looked at his watch and in the light of the evening and the brightness of the snow, it said 10:10 P.M. It would be a long night.

Earl Patey and his two brothers spent most of the afternoon taking up their rabbit snares west of their camp and spent the rest of the day doing repairs to their cabin.

Fred did all the cooking when they were out in their cabin, he being the oldest, and this evening they had cooked potatoes, turnip, some salt beef, and homemade dumplings. That day one of them shot some partridge, so for supper Fred had fried three. He made some gravy and when he served, the three brothers sat down in harmony.

At about 8:00 P.M., they were finished eating and had their dishes washed. Their dogs were fed. As they sat with their elbows on the table, Earl was holding a dog harness for Jack to repair. This was a beautiful night.

"What a night, Jack. I think we should harness up the dogs and go in on Bluey Pond for a ride."

Jack looked out the window, "Maybe we should," he said. "The only thing is, Earl, we just fed the dogs. If we harness them up now, they will run the supper right out of them."

"You're right," said Fred who was drawing some shavings to light the fire tomorrow morning. "I am not going to harness mine up. I got me harnesses and traces all ready for morning."

Jack went back to repairing the dog's harness. "I think, Earl, we had better wait 'til morning. We will get up early and take off."

"Which way are you going in the mornin', Jack?" asked Fred.

"I think I'm going over around Cobbles Ridge. I've got half a dozen traps over there on the brook."

"Well, Earl, you might as well go in around Bluey, and you'd better take the gun. That's a good place for partridge. The rabbit season closes tomorrow. Make sure you get every slip. That's what's wrong with the rabbits. Fellers don't take up their slips. I wonder what the forecast is for tomorrow and the day after?"

"I don't know," said Jack. "Never heard, but I'd say 'tis gonna be good for a day or two."

"How long are we gonna be in here now, Jack?" asked Earl.

Jack laughed and looked at Fred and winked. "Well, this is Wednesday. So, Earl, I think we'll go out on Saturday."

Earl laughed. "I don't mind, you know. I'm not married yet, so I can stay as long as I like, you know."

"Admit it, Earl," said Jack. "You have only been gone one night and you miss her already."

Earl said nothing.

"Lay off!" said Fred. "The boy is still wet behind the ears."

Jack laughed. "I don't mind, Fred. My turn will come. Wait 'til just before dawn tomorrow morning. That's my turn."

They all laughed.

Danny found himself in a very frightful situation. Here he was all alone under the stars with the trees around him. Their arms were not comforting. They stood motionless as through they were ready to fall. He began shivering. He thought of what Uncle Noah Pittman had said one time this winter about someone who was cold. He said they were so cold they were shivering like a dog in a bucket. And here he was shivering like a dog in a bucket. But what could he do? He knew of hypothermia. That was a part of his Arctic training. If hypothermia sets in, start moving around and here he was with the greatest symptoms.

Danny could not control himself, and he realized he was in a very serious state of shock. He also knew that he was going to have to get a very serious grip on himself. He knew he was on the verge of panic. He said to himself out loud, "Danny Corcoran, you had better stick to your training. What about the things you have been taught in training?" he could hear a voice saying down deep inside him. He began to fight for strict control. His teeth made a rattling noise, one against the other. His ears ached. There was a pain under his cheek bones. He felt the cords of his neck and it seemed they would not let his head turn, and his whole body ached from the pain that ascended up from his sore leg and feet. "This is not the end, Danny. You have to get up and move. Danny, you get up." the voice said again.

He rolled over on the bed of boughs and found himself on the icy hard snow. He tried to sit up but his strength was gone. He rolled over agian, then put his hand to his head and lifted it. "Is it possible that my head is as heavy as this?" he asked himself. He put his hand to his mouth and realized his mitts were frozen. He rolled over on his side and put himself into a sitting position. Lying on his side on the snow, he straightened himself out again and did this three or four times. As he put all of his strength behind his effort, he rose himself to one elbow. He was shivering badly and fell back again. He immediately got up on his elbow again and proceeded to push his upper body to arms' length. He held himself in this position. He then straightened out his legs and rolled over into a sitting position. He could feel himself going into shock.

As he sat there he found himself beating his frozen mitts together. "Oh, dear Lord," he cried, "help me." It was then he noticed the trees around him. They stood there like tall posts he had seen sticking up out of the mud from an abandoned wharf near the dock in St. John's. As he sat there it was only then he realized the stars were shining. He forced his face upwards and looked at the stars in the heavens. Yes, he thought, this was for real. It was true. This was really happening to him. He felt his body being pierced with the cold. What does this all mean? Then he remembered he had made one mistake. He had lain down in the cold with no heat or blankets and hypothermia had set in. Now he had to get his feet. As he struggled and fought, he found himself on his hands and knees. He knew what he had to do. He had to get his blood circulating. He rolled over to a sitting position again, then did this several times. He beat his hands and felt the rush of blood through his viens. He got to his knees and tried to get to his feet but fell. He tried several more times but could not make it.

He saw his rifle and dragged himself to it. He stuck it up, then used it as a crutch to help him to his feet. As he stood there he could feel the pain in his two feet, and his leg felt as if it had been stepped on by an elephant. He tried to make a step but stood as still as a frozen statue. He made up his mind. I must move around, he thought. "I just have to put one foot out slowly. What am I? A baby?" With this thought he made a step, then two, three. He almost fell. He slowly moved around in a circle staggering like a drunken man. Each step he made felt as if his two feet were in burning fire. He was sure that all the skin on every toe had fallen off in his boots. His leg felt heavy. The shivering which had made him so fearful had quieted down. Only his jaws seemed tight. The muscles in his face were tight because he'd had to clamp his teeth together to prevent them from rattling or even breaking to pieces. He feared that at one point.

He then walked out to the edge of the lake. He felt a little wind blowing. It was piercing cold, but the agony and pain from his feet took away the chill from his body. He only felt it on his face. He sized up the situation. It was fairly bright. The stars were twinkling brightly. He looked to the north and saw the northern lights. They hung low over the horizon and danced slightly up and down. His thoughts went back to his nights in Harbour Deep. "Oh my, oh my," he cried. "Barbara, I'm glad you don't know my present situation. If you could see me now. Imagine, Barbara, you think I'm in Port Saunders and here I am standing at the edge of a frozen lake gazing at the Northern Lights with no heat and no food for days. My toes are all frozen up, my right leg sliced to the bone, and there are tears in my eyes. And I'm lost." He cried out loud. "Barbara, I'm lost. I need help."

Barbara Gale sat up in bed with a sudden jolt. She was screaming. "Barbara, Barbara."

A voice called from the bedroom door. "What's the matter, Barbara? What's the matter?"

The aged woman of medium build walked over to the bed. She caught the wide-eyed screaming school teacher by the arm. "Barbara, for God's sake my dear, come to your senses. Please wake up." She shook the young girl.

There was silence. She looked up at the woman. This was her boarding mistress, but she was like a mother. Barbara Gale looked her in the face. The woman wore a flannelette night dress with a blue border around the neck. There was a wash towel on the end table, she picked it up and wiped the tears from her face. She sat down near her on the bed. "I think you were having a nightmare. You woke up screaming," she said.

The lamplight flickered on her face. It showed a glowing beauty. Her dark hair hung over her shoulders. Her tear stained face was dry, but her eyes glistened from the tears that still floated in them. The woman looked at this beautiful girl and admired her beauty. It was then she realized why Danny had told her how much he loved her. It was only one day last week he walked into Mrs. Pittman's looking for Skipper Edward. He wanted to ask him about the new bucksaws that he was getting when he found out Uncle Edward was not home. He turned to leave. "Danny, join me for a cup of tea," Aunt Martha recalled.

"That will be a pleasure, Aunt Martha," he replied.

She gave him a chair at the table. The tablecloth and the dishes were quickly put in place. She poured the tea for both of them and sat down. "Where did you get the cheese, Aunt Martha? I didn't think there was any in Harbour Deep."

She smiled and said, "That's some I keep for special people. Not that it's for Newfoundland Rangers only, but it's for people who live clean lives. It's for people who like to help people, people who don't mind work, who don't mind risking their lives to help others, and people who like the wild animals, and it's for a person who is in love with a daughter of mine." Then she looked at Danny.

"Thank you, Aunt Martha. You've flattered me. I just don't know what to say."

"Danny, I have been watching you ever since you came here in October and I have seen no change in you. I saw you the first morning you were here, even when you first saw Barbara out there on the road. That morning I saw the admiration in your eyes, not of lust as many men look at women, but you saw her as a beautiful girl and as a school teacher here in Harbour Deep doing a job. Do you know that, in fact, the two of you are one of a kind. You're away from your families and friends and you're here willing to sacrifice, willing to go at a moments notice." She paused, then said, "Danny, Barbara is a sweet girl. I see the other side of her. She is the kind that would make you a very happy man, and she has a good family."

Danny blushed and said, "Aunt Martha, I'm glad for this moment to sit and talk with you, and if my mother was here now in place of you, this is what I would tell her. 'Mom, I have met a girl that I am in love with. This is just not an ordinary girl. This is the girl I want to marry. She is in love with me. I don't love her, just because she is beautiful or just because she is a school teacher. I want to marry her because she cares about me. I saw the picture of you when you were young, and I know if Dad saw her he would want me to marry her, because she looks just like you when you were twenty. This girl is a help here in this little village and she loves children very much, and most of all she is a good cook. You've always said I was like my Dad. Well, Mom, for me to marry this girl would prove that what you told me about my father was true. He was a man of good taste'."

Aunt Martha looked at Danny with a tear in her eye and said, "Danny, what you told me I will keep a secret unless something happens."

And now Aunt Martha sat near this beautiful girl who was sobbing her heart out. She knew how she felt. "But why are you crying my dear? I'm sure Danny is in Port Saunders by now," she said.

"I had this terrible dream. I saw Danny lying in the water. In fact, it seemed his body was washed up on the shore. And as I watched, I saw an animal come out of the woods and tear the front of his right leg. Then I heard him groan. I tried to reach him but couldn't. Then I started to scream and that's when you came in." She then covered her face in her hands and wept. "Ever since Danny left I have had a strange feeling. Something tells me that our love affair has come to an end," she said and wiped her face.

"Barbara, Danny told Gill Ellsworth that tomorrow he was going to send him a wire, so let's wait until tomorrow, and don't you have any more nightmares."

"Aunt Martha, Danny left here Monday morning. If he had gotten to Port Saunders or anywhere he would have telegraphed me even Monday evening," she said.

Aunt Martha knew she was grieving, so she said, "Okay. If we don't hear from him by tomorrow noon, I will have a wireless sent to Port Saunders inquiring about him."

Barbara felt better. "Thanks, Aunt Martha. You are very kind," she said.

"You go back to sleep, my dear, and don't worry about anything. Okay?" Aunt Martha said, and pulled the quilts up to Barbara's chin.

Chapter 13
March 15, 1936

Danny looked at his watch. It was six-thirty and now daylight. He had walked what he thought could be three miles. He had walked through a narrow between Bluey Pond West to another pond. He walked along its shoreline. He had come to many brooks that ran into the pond. Twice he slipped and fell. His feet were numb and sore and he was weak with hunger. He was sure infection was beginning to set in his bad leg. It was tender. He had difficulty holding onto his rifle because his mitts were frozen. The sun was just coming over the tops of the trees. He looked back at the Eastern sky and noticed a redness. He was reminded of a couple of mornings ago when he got up after spending his first night on this trip in Elige Newman's camp. Suddenly he realized that was his last night he had his head under shelter. It seemed like months ago. Why didn't he turn around and go home? Then he knew from the radius of the sun and sky that it was the sign of rain or weather, and now the sky looked almost the same. It worried him as he looked down the lake. As he shuffled over the slippery ice, he felt cold.

The frosty morning air seemed to bite at his frame. His feet were too sore for him to move fast enough to warm his body up. He knew if he followed this river it would take him to the ocean, and he was sure that there was a trail going from town to town. Then maybe he would get picked up. He walked along the ice near the shore following all the coves. The ice was unsafe near the small brooks. He estimated it took about one hour to go approximately one mile under the slippery ice conditions and with his sore feet. "Where was the main river running out?" he asked himself. He noticed the sky was beginning to cloud over and the keenness in the air was gone. It was beginning to warm up. He noticed the ice was becoming a little better. As he walked along the shore, he saw old tracks in the snow along the tree line. "What was this?" he asked himself. He saw where someone had blazed a tree. He went ashore and examined the marking and the tracks. The rain had melted the snow around the tracks, and the snowshoe imprint was three inches higher than the rest of the snow. Then he noticed someone had put out a line of rabbit snares, and he noticed one set in front of him. At least, he thought, there was a sign of people and it seemed to raise his hopes.

He moved on further along the shoreline, slowly, looking for signs. Maybe there's a cabin here, he thought. He came to the mouth of the main river. This is what the people called the Running out of Big Bluey Pond (lake). He thought he smelled something. It smelled like burned wood. Not smoke, but like wood that had been burned. He walked for 100 yards along the river, then came to a steady in the brook. This was covered with ice. He would not cross for fear of falling in. He walked past the steady and started walking again. He could still smell burned logs. "There must be a camp or camp ground around here," he told himself. As he looked around he saw a flat rock about four feet square. He was fainting with hunger. This rock was near the river. He decided to take a rest so he sat down, stuck up his rifle and snowshoes, then lay down on his side on the rock. "I've got to be careful," he told himself, "not to go to sleep." Then he well remembered the ordeal of only a few hours ago when he awoke shivering and he was near death. The thought almost made him sick, but it seemed like a week ago. "What day is this?" he asked himself. He stopped and thought for a moment. It was the 15th of March. The rabbit season closed today. "I've got to get to Port Saunders. My poor feet and legs." He sat up and got his watch out. The time was 10:20 A.M. "I think I'll have a ten minute rest and move on again." He then curled up on the flat rock and shut his eyes.

Earl Patey woke early the next morning and crept to the door like a cat and looked out. He slept with his shirt, pants and socks on. He opened the door. It was dawning. He noticed the sky. It was red and glowing. The trees had an orange tint colour from the rays of the sky. It was a cold morning. The dogs that were tied on near the door were covered with frost. It had been a cold night, he thought. Good to have a roof over your head. He took another look at the sky, then pulled in his head and shut the door.

"I know one thing, Jack. Fred has been right with the weather. You should see the sky glowing red. We're going to have a wet week catching rabbits."

Jack jumped out of bed and went to the door. He looked outside. Earl heard the dogs barking. They must be up shaking themselves from their night's sleep. Jack came in. He shut the door, then opened it again and roared at some dogs who were fighting. "Tis goin' to rain before dark. I think Earl we'll take everything up, all our rabbit slips and fox traps. We might never get back here anymore this winter."

"You're right," said Fred from the bunk.

"Come on, Fred, the kettle is boiled," said Earl. "Put on some of that fish."

"I got some on," was Fred's reply. "No, 'tis not fish, 'tis rounders."
"Take a bit of fish out of that boiler over there. It looks like pretty good fish. I think those rounders are smatchy."

Earl looked at him for more instructions, then replied, "Good enough," when he didn't answer.

"We might as well take everything up today, Earl. We're going to have a lot of rain it seems. But I don't think we will be able to get out today. I've got a full days work to get mine up. The season closes today anyway." Fred said.

Earl laughed. "So you're getting honest. Imagine, Jack. Fred is getting honest. He is worried because the season is closing today."

Fred sat up. "It's not that bad, Earl. It gives us an excuse to take our traps and snares up. That's all, my son. We might never get back here before this spring."

Jack replied, "You're right. We will take everything up today according as we come to our gear, but I won't be able to take all mine up today, but I can finish it tomorrow on the way out. Earl, you take up the snares in around Bluey, but don't take the dogs. They'll cut themselves to pieces."

Earl looked up from the plate. "I'm going over to big Nord-East first."

"Good," said Jack. "Take the shotgun. You might see a few partridge around Bluey."

"The season is closed and Fred might get mad," said Earl with a grin.

Fred laughed. "That's alright, Earl. You can take it. I'll let you go." He paused. "How's the fish?"

"Tis ready," said Jack. "Get up."

Fred jumped out of bed, pulled on his boots, and went outside. They had boiled fish with fried pork, cut up in small pieces with homemade bread and steeped tea. After they finished breakfast they all left, each going in a different direction. Earl went in a south-westerly direction. After he got outside and on the trail he looked at his watch. It was 7:15 A.M. and it was a beautiful morning. Although the sky was pink, it was a cool crisp morning. He carried his pack sack with his shotgun pushed through his snowshoes across his back. He was walking over to big North-East Pond. It was approximately 6 miles. He had 200 snares to take up in this area, if he could find them all, and there were twenty traps.

When he got to the island in Big North-East Pond, he had a fox in his trap. It was dead. The jays had been at its hind quarter but had not spoiled the skin. He was very happy. He looked at his watch. It was 9:30. There was no wind. "Well," he said out loud. "This has been a great morning. This fox will sell for $5.50. That will be enough to pay for the wedding. He planned to get married next month. He hung the fox on his gun and started back. He figured he could go back in one hour to the camp. He began to feel a bit hungry. He noticed the sky was beginning to cloud over. "A mackerel sky," he said out loud. "Tis going to rain. I hope it don't rain before I get them snares up in around Bluey Pond." He started to walk fast. Soon he was at the camp. There was no one there but the dogs. They started to bark before he got to the camp. He could hear them in the clear morning air. He got to the camp, hung up his fox and rabbits inside the camp. This was to protect them from the dogs. He quickly lit the fire and made lunch.

After eating, he wasted no time. It was a 30 minute walk to the mouth of Bluey Pond. Some call it Bluey Steady. It was 10:30 when he had finished his lunch. He really made good time back from Big Northeast Pond with his load. Now he said, "I'm off again. I wonder if I will be as lucky this time."

He noticed the frost was gone out of the air and the sun was not shining. It was clouded over. "We're guaranteed to have rain, he thought." But it didn't matter since he had his oil clothes with him.

He moved at a very quick pace. He stopped to take up a snare. A rabbit had been in it but jays had eaten it. He took the snare up. He was walking along the trail thinking about his wedding day and the girl he was madly in love with. He was very concerned about making a living. He comforted himself by saying, "I've got my health and strength anyway, no matter what happens." And tomorrow night he would be back in River of Ponds. This made him sing. He was singing, "The Girl With The Blue Velvet Band."

He checked another snare, then walked out to the bank of the river. He saw a camp about 100 feet away which belonged to the Belburns Crowd. They had a real good camp. He wished he and his brothers had a camp as good as this. He took another snare with a rabbit in it. He walked along the side of the river for about 200 yards in a very happy mood. He noticed something on the other side of the brook. His keen eyes focused on the object "Well," he thought, "it's a bear. I hear they come out this time of the year."

He was stopped now staring at the object across the other side of the river. It was lying down on top of a flat rock about 80 feet away from him. He looked closer. It looked a funny shape. "What in the world is it?" He said out loud. "It can't be a bear."

He then called out, taking his gun off his back just in case. "Hey, hello." He saw the object move. He noticed the bottom of two boots facing him. He walked closer. "Yes," he said. "It's a man."

He then called, "Hey, over there."

That's a dead man, he thought. Then he saw a head lift and look around. The man was back on to him on his side on the rock with his feet drawn up behind him. He called again. The man sat up, then turned to face him.

The man answered, "hello"

It was then that Earl noticed a badge in his cap. It looked like a ranger. "Where can I get across the river?" the man called.

"Stay there. I will come over," Earl called.

Earl went about 300 yards up the brook and crossed the river, or the steady which was frozen over. He quickly walked down to where the ranger was sitting. He felt nervous and excited. Where did this man come from or where was he going? Imagine a Newfoundland Ranger in here. His thoughts raced and he had a shot gun and the season was closed. Maybe he should have listened to Fred this morning. But whoever thought this? Not in his wildest dreams. What would he say to him about the shot gun? But anyway, it was too late now. He could see him sitting on the rock. He noticed he was very pale. Well, he thought, this ranger looked very sick. He could see the badge in his cap. There was no mistake this was a Newfoundland Ranger. He had seen him before. This was the ranger from Port Saunders.

He stopped near him. This man looked pitiful. He looked like he needed help. "Hello, Ranger."

"Hello," said Danny in a shaky voice.

"You're a long way from Port Saunders, aren't you, old man?"

Danny looked at him with pain in his eyes and said, "I'm not from Port Saunders. I'm going to Port Saunders. I'm the Ranger stationed in Harbour Deep."

Earl looked at him with pity in his eyes. "You're going away from Port Saunders. You're walking about west. You got to go north."

Earl got close to him. He noticed the ranger shivering. "You haven't told me your name."

Earl was quick to answer thinking about the gun he had on his back. "What do you want my name for?"

"Cause you're carrying a shotgun and the season is closed."

Earl was quick. "You're carrying a rifle and the season is closed, and I think that makes you and I equal."

The Ranger laughed. "I won't hurt you. Don't worry about it. I'm Danny Corcoran."

"I'm Earl Patey."

The two men shook hands.

"Have you got any grub on you?" Danny asked. It seemed he was going to fall down. He was staggering like a dog in a tub.

"I got four slices of loaf here," he said. Then he motioned to the Ranger that 200 yards ahead there was a camp belonging to the Belburns crowd. "Come on. Let's go to the camp." he said.

They got to it and Earl opened the door and looked in. It was tidy. It had no floor but lumber benches. They had a 45 gallon oil barrel for a stove. "Have you got any matches?" asked Danny. "I lost mine yesterday morning and last night was a pretty cold night. I thought I was going to die at one point." He then told Earl about his ordeal. Earl lit the fire while he was talking.

The pain in his legs and feet was more than he could bear. He then decided to look at his leg. "I hurt my leg on the second day I was on my way over. I will show it to you."

"When did you leave Harbour Deep?" asked Earl.

"I left Monday morning, on the 12th. It has been four days. My bad luck started when I fell in the water. A little bit more and I would have drowned. I should have gone back then."

He told Earl of his story and what he had gone through in the four days. He pulled up his pants leg. His underwear was stuck in the wound. He pulled his underwear from the sore place and looked at the infected area.

Earl could hardly believe his eyes. He said, "Old man, you had better get to a doctor or nurse as soon as possible. If that gets any worse, you could lose your leg."

They looked at the cut again. It was swollen and infected. There was dried blood around the edge of the cut. The flesh had been scraped from his shin and it appeared as if the bone was protruding. He touched it and winced in pain.

"That looks like blood poisoning," he said. "There is a red streak up your knee."

Danny felt nervous. "I'll be alright." He paused and pulled down his underwear over the cut again. "I'll tell you what. How about doing me another favour?"

"I certainly will. What is it?"

"How about filling the kettle for me?"

"Right away," said Earl. He grabbed the kettle, ran to the river, filled it, and came back. Earl then opened his pack sack and took out the bread. He had some roast caplin and gave them to him. He also gave him some tea and sugar. "Why did you come over here, Ranger?"

"The Ranger I trained with is in Port Saunders, Roy Hiscock. I went on a wildlife patrol and tied it in with this trip. There would have been no problems if I had not run into bad weather."

Earl spoke up. "It's time someone stopped the slaughter or there won't be anything left."

Danny spoke up. "They say it's almost all gone now. Do you hunt caribou?"

"No," said Earl. "We don't get the time for that. All we do is catch a few rabbits and kill a few partridge."

Danny thought about his toes. They pained so bad. He didn't know what to do. "When did you come in here?" he asked Earl.

"We came in yesterday morning. Me and my two brothers are staying in a camp about three miles out from here."

"Did you walk in?"

"No. We came in on two dog teams."

A hope was raised in Danny that Earl saw. Then Earl said, "Now, here is what we'll do." He looked at the stove, "you eat your lunch and tip back here. Take your time. I'll go around Bluey Pond and take up all my slips. I should be back in about two or three hours. Then you can come out with me to our camp and you can get a ride home with us."

"Well, that will be great," said Danny. He paused. "By the way, which direction would you go from here if you were going to Port Saunders?"

Earl thought for a moment. "On the other side of the river, just across there, there's a bog. Now, if you stood on that bog you would have to steer on a northerly course. Then you would strike the line going to Hawkes Bay. Someone there would put you on the right road. But don't go. Wait for me to come back."

"Even if I wanted to go, I couldn't get across the river."

"You just walk in about 300 yards and you can cross on a steady. But stay here." He looked at the door. There was a nice heat on in the camp. "I'm going now before it starts to rain. So I should be back here by 3 o'clock." Earl immediately went out the door.

Danny sat at the table with the lunch in front of him. He ate two slices of bread the same way as you would eat cake. He poured up a cup of tea and tasted it as the liquid went down his throat. He closed his eyes at the wonderful sensation as the food moved down his empty stomach. It must be awful to starve, he thought, but thank God he had gotten into the land of the living again. He drank his tea and ate caplin and bread. Then he checked his watch. It was 1:20 P.M. "Earl should be back by 3:30 or 4 o'clock" he said out loud. "I think I'll lie down and get a rest." The young ranger lay down on the wooden bunk with his boots on. He put his hands under his head about 10 feet away from a hot stove. His thoughts were of Barbara. He had his hopes back again that he would see her.

Earl Patey saw where Danny had spent the night and couldn't believe it. He knew that Danny had suffered severely. It was open to the lake and although there was no wind, the draft from the lake would freeze you. He saw the bed of boughs he had broken off. "What kind of night must he have had? I make no wonder he said at one point he almost died." Earl shook his head. Earl looked at his last rabbit snare, then took it up. He put it in his pack sack and took out his oil clothes. He put them on, then tightened up his snowshoes. They had to be worn now. It was soft and whenever you stepped off the ice you would sink. He looked at his watch. It read 3:30 P.M. "Should be back to the camp where Danny is in half an hour." He quickened his pace. It won't take most of this to make it hard going. He came to the steady where the camp was that Danny was in. "I wonder why he wouldn't take off his boots? He could have dried himself. If he fell in the water, for sure his feet were wet. He must be a tough man."

Earl came to the door, opened it, and looked in. He was just going to call out when he saw the young ranger sleeping soundly on the bunk. He looked ghostly white but looked peaceful. He looked at rest. This was the first sleep he had in days. He was breathing fast as if someone with a fever. Although the fire had gone out, it was still warm in the camp. This camp was well insulated. Every seam was cinched full of moss. He thought for a moment. The best thing is for me to go out and get Jack to come in with his dog team and have him brought out, because he's in too bad shape to walk. That leg is serious and he looks too peaceful to wake. Earl very quickly shut the door and turned. He walked onto the steady and then crossed. He looked at his watch. It was raining hard. I doubt if he's got any oil clothes, thought Earl. That pack sack looked pretty empty. I guess I did the right thing. I think he'd have a struggle to make it out here on snowshoes. Anyway he'd get his brothers to come in on dogs. Earl stepped up his pace again. He looked at his watch. It was 4:15. "Not bad. I should be at the camp before 5 o'clock," he said. It was really raining. The water was beginning to drip from his cap. The mitt around the gun barrel was wet. He could smell the smoke from the camp and he could hear the dogs barking. They heard him coming. Jack came to the door when he heard the dogs barking.

"Hey," he called. "Fred, Earl is back."

Earl was near the camp. "What rain." He took off his snowshoes, then stepped inside. "Looks like we're going to get more rain. What do you think?"

Jack spoke up. "I think we're going to get a lot of rain. You got a fox. Looks like it's in good shape. Fred got you beat. He's got an otter. You know that trap we checked on the way in? He had an otter in it, a big one too. So I guess he got you beat." Jack paused.

"No. He hasn't got me beat. I got something bigger than an otter and more valuable."

The two men looked at him. Earl was not a fellow to kid around about things.

"Have a guess," he said.

"A silver fox," said Fred.

"You shot a moose," said Jack.

"No. It's not an animal."

The two men looked at him. Then they asked. "What was it, Earl?"

Well Earl didn't know how to begin. "Don't think I'm crazy, but I found a Newfoundland Ranger, a fellow by the name of Danny Corcoran. He's from Harbour Deep."

The two men looked at Earl with surprise. "Where's he to?" asked Jack.

"I took him to the Belburns camp and that's where he's at now. I was supposed to bring him out with me, but he got his leg torn up. You should see it. And he's got a red streak going up it. I was going in by the river and I saw this black thing on a rock. I said imagine a bear out this early. Then I saw something strange, a pair of boot bottoms facing me. I knew then it wasn't an animal. I roared out, "Hey, Hey!. He was on the other side of the brook. I roared out again, Hey! Then a head came up. I saw the badge. I knew it was a Ranger, so I went over to where he was, and sure enough it was a Newfoundland Ranger."

"Well," said Fred. "Let's go in for him."

Jack spoke up. "It's pouring out of the heavens now. Do you know what I'd do? I'd leave him alone for the night. If we go in after him now we got to stay all night, and it will be dark almost before we get ready. I don't like crossing that steady after dark. He's in a camp and you gave him a bit of food, and if he survived last night outdoors without any fire, surely goodness he will have home comfort there tonight.   "But his leg, Jack," Earl said. "I never saw anything like it. He's got to get to a nurse."

"We've got to wait until daylight before leaving here," said Fred.

"Yes, but if we had him out here we could clean his leg and bandage it up."

The older brothers didn't want to go into Bluey with their dog teams tonight in the driving rain and dense darkness.

"He can't leave, anyway," said Jack. "So we'll get up early and take off at daylight."

"Good enough," said Earl, and started taking off his clothes. "He must be a tough man, boys. I saw where he slept last night in by Big East Bluey Pond. Dogs would freeze there. He told me he had a rough time."

"How old is he?" asked Fred.

"I don't know, maybe 25, but then maybe 18. It's a job to tell. He looked terrible. The only thing I knew about his features was that he had red hair."

"Well," said Jack, "must be an Irishman."

"Yes, could be," said Fred. "Corcoran sounds like he must be from St. John's."

"He didn't say," said Earl. "But he told me he was having a boat built in Harbour Deep and he's going to come all the way around to Port Saunders from Harbour Deep."

"He must be older than 18 then, to be able to do that," said Jack.

"He got a rifle with him. He told me that he lost his axe when he fell in the water."

"It's something fierce. It's something fierce," said Fred who sounded so concerned.

Barbara Gale awoke. She looked at the clock. It was 7:15 A.M. and the sun was shining through her window. She looked again. No, it wasn't the sun. It was the bright rays from the sky. They were in a valley among high hills. But the sun would be over the hills soon. She thought about Danny.

This was the 15th of March. Danny had been gone four days. It seemed like months. She jumped out of bed. She had a busy day ahead of her. She was in the midst of Easter exams. She was having problems concentrating on her work in school due to being so worried about Danny. The older kids like Ches could notice it. He had comforted her on two or three occasions, but she thought, I just have to get if off my mind. It's no use giving up. My whole world has been turned upside down. She banished the thought of anything being wrong with Danny and tried to make herself believe everything was alright.

She quickly dressed, took the wash basin, and went into the kitchen to get some warm water to wash. Mr. Edward Pittman was sitting at the table. He was a broad featured man with a mustache. He had a glorious personality. He had snow white hair and it was always neatly combed. There was one outstanding feature about this man. It was a joy to be around him in the morning. As Barbara walked into the kitchen he looked up from his breakfast and smiled. "Good morning, Barbara, and how are you?"

She smiled at him. "Good morning." She paused. "I am fine." She made the "I" stand out.

He understood immediately. "I am going to get your breakfast, if you will allow me."

"Uncle Edward," she said, "I would love for you to do that."

His face lit up. She poured hot water from the kettle and added cold to get it to the right temperature. She then disappeared into the room. In ten minutes she came back into the kitchen where Uncle Edward was. He had an egg fried and toast made.

"Where's Aunt Martha?"

"She went down to Noah's. Nellie is not too good. Noah was here a few minutes ago. He told us she was up almost all night, so Martha went down to see her. I don't think she's too serious."

She sat at the table.

"Well, my dear," he said, "it will soon be Easter. You'll soon have a week off."

She paused. "Yes."

He looked at her then and laughed to himself. Mr. Pittman knew beauty. He looked at this beautiful girl. She was simply beautiful. She was wearing a light blue dress which seemed to blend with her long black hair which hung over her shoulders. She was full busted. Her long eyelashes and blue eyes seemed to match the firmness of her features. The old man sat for a moment and looked at her. He had been married twice. Martha, who was not Noah's mother, was a very beautiful girl when he met her. But the years, like everything, takes it toll. Mr. Pittman had been a businessman all his life. He had retired and let Joe Norecott run it for him on a fifty-fifty basis. He was one of a few on the Northern Peninsula who had money. He was not wealthy but was well to do. "Do you mind if I compliment you on your beauty this morning?"

She blushed. "Thank you, Uncle Edward."

He smiled and the two of them sat at the table.

"Welcome to the Newfoundland Hotel," he said. "What would you like to have?"

She grinned and flashed her eyelashes at him. "Nothing, sir, thank you."

She looked at him and thought, when this man was young, he must have had taste and class.

The latch of the door clicked and Aunt Martha walked into the kitchen. "Good morning, Barbara," she said.

"Good morning, Aunt Martha," she quickly answered.

"Martha, I was just about to tell Barbara how beautiful she was, seeing that we were dining together. You came and disturbed us." He was grinning from ear to ear.

"I'm sorry," she said. "But anyhow, your days for dining young girls are over. I will be the most beautiful girl you will ever have your arms around."

They all laughed.

"I am going to send Ches over to tell Gill Ellsworth to wire a telegram to see if Danny is over there for sure."

She paused. "If I don't do this, Barbara could be up all night."

"What time is Ches going over?" asked Uncle Edward.

"He is going now. I told him to get his dogs harnessed, he should be over there as soon as the telegraph office opens."

"Did you write the message?"

"Yes," she said.

"Good," said Uncle Edward. "It shouldn't take him very long."

Aunt Martha spoke up. "I told Ches to wait for a reply, even if he's there for two days."

Uncle Edward grinned. He knew Ches would wait if his Grandmother told him to. If she said, "jump", Ches would say, "How high?"

Uncle Edward had a feeling that a negative reply would be received. They'd had too much rain since Danny left. He was expecting him to walk out here any day. "I must go and see Ches," he thought. He took his cap and then left. He could hear Ches getting the dogs ready to go over to the small settlement. It was also called Harbour Deep although it was three miles away. Where they lived it was called Harbour Deep North East Bottom Brook. This was at the mouth of Soufflett's River, although no one used that name.

He went where Ches was. "Hey, Ches, Ches," he called, "come here."

Ches came over. "What is it, Grandfather?"

Uncle Edward motioned to the stage. "Come down in the stage. I want you for a moment."

The two men went to the stage. He shut the door, then turned to Ches. "Now this is what I want to tell you. I've got a dirty notion that Danny Corcoran is not over in Port Saunders. I've got a feeling that something is wrong. I haven't told anybody because it will only upset the women. Keep what I just told you to yourself, and if you get a reply back saying that Danny is not over there, tell Gill Ellsworth to notify the head fellow in Whitbourne immediately. Wait for a reply from him and whatever it is, come to me when you get back. Don't go to the women. Tell Gill not to tell anyone. We'll handle it."

"Okay, Grandfather."

The two of them walked out of the stage just as Barbara was walking along. She looked at them with worried eyes and motioned for Uncle Edward to come near her. They watched as Ches left with the dogs at a fast pace. Then the noise quieted down. "Uncle Edward, you look worried. In fact, you're more worried than I am, only you think you're not showing your emotions, but you can't fool me. I know honest men."

He got close to her and they turned to the school house. "Can I walk you to the school house, Miss Gale?"

"Yes, you may."

They started walking together, this 20 year old school teacher and a 71 year old businessman. All the neighbours stood back from their windows where they could not be seen and gazed. Something was not right for Mr. Edward Pittman to be walking Barbara Gale to school, and Mr. Pittman had nothing on his head. His white hair was like snow in the orange glow of the sky. When they reached the school he said, "As soon as Ches gets back, I'll let you know if he has any message."

"Okay. Thank you, Uncle Edward."

Then she ran into the school house. Uncle Edward turned and went back to his house.

"Look, Ed, you're going to catch a cold out with nothing on your head."

"Maybe you're right," he said, "but Martha, I'm worried something has gone wrong. We should have had word back by now. If he's fallen in any of the brooks, things could be bad."

Aunt Martha spoke up. "Keep that to yourself. If Barbara knew you're worried, she would lose more sleep."

Uncle Edward sat down. "I just told her I guess I could not control my emotions."

"What did she say?"

"She said she knew all along I was worried. Anyway, when Ches comes back he'll have all the news."

She sighed. "The sooner the better."

It was 9:30 when Ches walked into the wireless office in Harbour Deep. Gill Ellsworth was busy sending a message. Ches went to the wicket and peered in. Gill had a mirror in front of him. He could see behind him without looking around. He held up his hands indicating three minutes. Ches nodded. When he finished the dots and dashes, he took off the headphones and turned around. "How are you, Ches?"

"Not bad," said Ches. "You haven't been over since Danny left. The old man was talking about you yesterday wondering what you were going to be doing in Easter."

Gill put a junk of wood in the pot belly stove. "Not very much. We got Good Friday, Saturday, and Easter Monday off this year. I'd say we'll have a day trouting."

"Good," said Ches. He paused. "Grandfather sent me over here to get you to inquire about Danny. He said he's prepared to pay for the message."

"I just inquired. The operator told me that she hasn't seen him and knew nothing about him coming, but she sent someone to ask the Ranger if he is over there. I told her to get back to me immediately."

"That's fine," said Ches.

"How's Barbara," said Gill.

"Don't be talking," said Ches. "She'll soon be ready for the mental hospital. The old man said she's going to have to be put in a strait jacket pretty soon." Ches grinned.

"Look, Ches, Danny should have never gone in the country. I wouldn't go if they shot all the caribou in Newfoundland, not this time of the year. I tried to talk him into not going, but it didn't work. You won't catch that Ranger up in Englee going in the country."

Gill turned and moved quickly to the keyboard. He put on the headphones. This is the message he received.

FROM PORT SAUNDERS, NFLD. 10:20 A.M. 15TH OF MARCH, 1936. TO GILL ELLSWORTH, HARBOUR DEEP. HAVE CHECKED LOCALS. RANGER CORCORAN NOT SEEN THIS SIDE. HAVE PEOPLE CHECKING. WILL KEEP INFORMED. SGN. RANGER HISCOCK.

Gill replied with an "okay" of received. He put down the headphones and slowly turned to Ches with the message in his hand. "Ches," he said very soberly, "I've got something to read to you."

Ches waited. Gill read the message. Then he said, "This could be serious. What do you think, Ches?"

"It's a job to know what to think. We've had so much bad weather since he left."

"Ches, close the door. Let's make some plans." He paused looking out the window. "Come inside."

Ches stepped inside. It was the first time he had been inside a post office where the mail had been sorted. It looked funny inside looking out. They sat by the table. "Now what do we do? We know Danny is lost or overdue on a trip across the country. There are many facts to be considered. Number one, the conditions were bad when he left, 18 to 20 inches of snow."

"Yes," said Ches, "and the worst kind of snow for walking in with snowshoes, right sandy."

"Number two, then we had hard frost turning to snow and then a downpour of rain for about 10 hours." Gill looked up from the pad where he was writing this down.

"And in the 24 hours of his first day out, that was not all," said Ches, "about two in the morning it turned off to freeze. The old man said it was about 10 below."

"Number three, the brooks here, especially Soufflett's, are flooded. It busted out."

They looked outside.

"If he got to the brooks and couldn't get across, he would have come back on his tracks, which meant he got across the river before the rain came. Maybe he couldn't get off the country on the other side due to the same thing. The rivers might be flooded."

"Yes, this was his problem," said Bill. "He's up in the middle of the country and can't get out, caught between two brooks."

Ches spoke up. "No, that's not right. Everything has frozen up since then. That's since we had the rain three nights ago."

"Yes. You're right, I don't know," said Gill with a sigh. "If we make an outcry and there's nothing to it, who's going to take the responsibility?"

Ches looked up. "What if we don't and something happens? Suppose they find him frozen or drowned and we know he is missing, who will take the responsibility then?"

They stopped with their heads down.

"I know," said Ches. Although Ches was only 15, he was very mature. "Grandfather is a J.P. He asked me to notify the head fellow in Whitbourne if there was any trouble."

Gill clicked his fingers. "Why had we not thought of that before? Ches, you're right. The J.P. got the authority."

He got up and ran to the keyboard, put on the headphones, then started with his message. After the keyboard stopped he came back. "Listen to this."

Ches's eyes were bulging. "HAVE CHECKED ALONG THE COAST. NO ONE HAS SEEN RANGER CORCORAN. WILL KEEP YOU INFORMED. SIGNED RANGER HISCOCK, PORT SAUNDERS."

The two men stared at each other. "Well, let's put together a telegram to the Captain of the Rangers at Whitbourne from Mr. Edward Pittman, J.P. Harbour Deep." "RANGER CORCORAN LEFT HARBOUR DEEP MARCH 12TH, 1936, TO DO A TWO DAY TRIP TO PORT SAUNDERS. HAS NOT ARRIVED. SUSPECT HIM TO BE LOST. REQUEST YOU HAVE SEARCH PARTIES INVESTIGATE. I'M AT YOUR SERVICE. SGN. EDWARD PITTMAN, J.P. HARBOUR DEEP, NFLD.

He jumped to the keyboard and sent the message. In ten minutes he gave Ches the carbon paper. He signed for it. "Don't go back to the Bottom yet, Ches. Stay around for a couple of hours. I might have a reply from the head Ranger."

"Good enough," said Ches. "I'm going down to skipper Jim Pollard's. He's got a big block made for the old man, so I might as well pick it up and for sure I'll have to have a cup of tea with him."

"Okay," said Gill. "If I get a reply I'll let you know."

Ches shut the door. "What a heat in there," he said out loud. "I know Gill Ellsworth is going to dry up and blow away." He laughed out loud.

He straightened out his dogs and went down to Jim Pollard's. Gill Ellsworth was sorting out some old telegrams. It was 11:30 A.M. when the dots and dashes began calling him. He jumped to the keys and was at them before he sat down. He picked up the headphones in the other hand and put them on his head. He started writing. "TO MR. EDWARD PITTMAN, J.P. HARBOUR DEEP. TIME 11:30 A.M. WHITBOURNE, NFLD. MARCH 15, 1936. RECEIVED WIRELESS RE RANGER CORCORAN MISSING. I AM CONCERNED. WOULD LIKE YOU TO HAVE SEARCH PARTY GO ON COUNTRY SEARCH. WILL CONTACT OTHERS TO SEARCH. COMMANDING OFFICER, STAND BY."

The wireless started again. The same message was sent to Williamsport to Herb Randell, J.P. He relayed another message to Ranger Hiscock in Port Saunders. He also included the report in the news of the day to be posted in all the telegraph offices that Danny Corcoran, Ranger stationed at Harbour Deep, was missing on a patrol between Harbour Deep and Port Saunders and for everyone to be on the lookout. "He is wearing a black Ranger trench coat, black peak hat with ears, and dark Ranger whipcord briggs."

With this done he quickly sent for Ches, and in a few minutes Ches came on his dogteam. He hitched them on a fence outside and came in. Carl Ricketts was in the Post Office at the time.

"I got a telegram for Uncle Edward Pittman, Ches."

"Good," said Ches.

"Would you mind giving it to him when you go back home?"

"Sure," Ches said.

"By the way, I got a notice to go up in the office. It's the news of the day."

He then posted the lookout report for Danny, the same as the one to be posted in every telegraph office. Ches and Carl Ricketts read it. Then Ches walked out without a word. He guessed Barbara had a reason to be uneasy. He unhooked the dogs and went over the hills to North East Brook. It didn't take him very long. Uncle Edward was watching for him, but Aunt Martha was the first to see him. "Ned, hey, Ches is coming."

They went to the window. Ches came straight to the house. He stopped the dogs, took the harnesses off them, and turned the komatik over. He walked into the house. Uncle Edward and Aunt Martha said nothing. Before Ches could say anything, Noah walked in. "Ches, did you hear from Danny?"

"Yes," said Ches and pulled out three wireless messages.

"Read them, Ches," said Aunt Martha.

Ches looked at his grandfather before attempting to open the envelopes. His grandfather nodded. There was a silence. The first one was from Ranger Hiscock to Gill Ellsworth. It was a copy of Gill's message telling of Danny not being seen. Then there was a copy of the one his grandfather sent to the commander. Then there was the one from the commanding office to Edward Pittman, J.P. telling him to have a search party arranged to search for Danny Corcoran.

They looked at each other in silence. Noah went to the table and sat down. "You have to be a madman, anyway, to attempt to go across in this weather. We begged him not to go."

Uncle Edward spoke up. "There's not much use talking like that, now that he's lost in the country somewhere. So now our job is to find him."

"Well, there is one thing that is for sure," said Noah. "He got in past Hancock's camp, because if he didn't he would have been back. Maybe he fell in the water."

Aunt Martha looked at Ches. "None of that out of your lips. Look at the bright side first. What am I going to tell Barbara?"

Uncle Edward spoke up. "We'll just have to tell her the truth." There was a brief silence.

"She had the feeling all the time. I guess to tell her wouldn't make her any worse than what she is now," said Aunt Martha. "She should be home in a few minutes."

Noah spoke up. "It's going to rain the once, don't worry. So there's not much use in us leaving and getting nowhere. So we might as well get arranged for tomorrow morning. I'll start getting a crowd together."

"Good for you," said Uncle Edward. "You're right. It is going to rain, and I think it is going to rain hard." He looked at the sky through the window. "I figure it will clear up after midnight, but I don't think we'll get any hard frost."

"Father," said Noah, "I can't stay in the country for more than one night. Nellie is not feeling so good. I think she got the flu. She coughed all night. If we go in we'll be staying in Hancock's camp and working out of there. I had a mind to take the dogs, but I suppose you won't be able to do anything with them."

Uncle Edward spoke up. "There's not much use in taking them. Half of them will be foundered before you get in because there's so much soft snow, and if you get frost, it will cut the paws right off them. So there's not much use in taking them. A good pair of snowshoes will be the best."

Ches hushed the crowd. "Barbara is coming."

"I'll handle everything," said Aunt Martha.

"Good enough," said Uncle Edward.

They were all watching the door when Barbara walked in. She stared at them with eyes wide open. She was the first to break the silence. "Uncle Edward, give it to me straight," she said. "What is the news about Danny, and from the gathering, it appears the news is not good."

Uncle Edward cleared his throat. "It's not all that bad either, Barbara." He paused, then moved his body into a leaning position on the table and shifted from elbow to elbow. He then said, "Barbara, we sent a wireless to Port Saunders and asked for Danny. So the operator in Port Saunders checked and a wireless came back from the Ranger over there. They haven't seen him. He then checked along the coast, but no one has seen him."

"I knew it," she said. "I had a feeling this is how it would be."

Uncle Edward motioned with his head. "I have sent a wireless to the commanding officer in Whitbourne notifying him that Danny was overdue on a trip from Harbour Deep to Port Saunders. He came back with a reply to organize search parties to look for him on both sides. We are going to get everything ready this afternoon. We were going to leave now but it's almost raining, so we'll leave tomorrow morning at dawn."

Barbara looked at Noah. "Uncle Noah, can't you leave this afternoon?"

"There's not much use, my dear," he said. "I doubt if we would get in the camps before dark and besides, we would get very wet, but if we leave tomorrow morning, then we got the whole day ahead of us and we can go a long way in one of those days. But I'm expecting him to come home this afternoon anyway."

Barbara put her head down. "And I've got a feeling you're in for a big surprise. This situation seems to be very strange, but maybe you're right and I hope I am wrong." She took off her coat and walked into the room.

"Your lunch is ready, my dear," said Aunt Martha.

"I'll be out in a minute." She closed the room door.

"Come on, Ches," said Noah. "I think I must round up a crowd." The two went out. It was beginning to rain outside. "Someone is in for a hard time before this is all over and I have a dirty suspicion that Danny is in for a rough time."

"I got the same feeling," said Ches. "Can I go with you?"

"You have to stay." said Noah. "Your mother is not feeling well. I'm not going for any more than one night."

"Good enough," said Ches, as the two of them walked down the small snowy road.

It was 3:30 in the afternoon and Pleman Gillard was walking along by the wireless office in Englee. It was raining hard. The operator waved for him to come in. Ple tapped himself on the chest and made a "me" sign with his lips. The operator nodded, "Yes."

Ple was not a fellow to hang around public places and he was not called into places like this for a chat or to hear gossip. He quickly opened the door and called, "What do you want me for?"

The operator said, "Close the door."

He closed it and then walked over to the wicket. "What is it?" he asked.

"I got a bulletin in, got it about an hour ago. I'll read it to you. Just a minute." She walked back to the counter, then came back. "This is from the commanding officer of the Newfoundland Rangers, Whitbourne, Newfoundland. It reads: "TO ALL ON THE NORTHERN PENINSULA. BE AWARE A RANGER IS MISSING ON A TRIP FROM HARBOUR DEEP TO PORT SAUNDERS. HE IS DANNY CORCORAN, AGE 21, RED HAIR, BLUE EYES, WEARING DARK RANGER WINTER CLOTHING AND USING RANGER EQUIPMENT. ANYONE SEARCHING, LISTEN FOR RIFLE SHOTS BECAUSE HE IS CARRYING A RIFLE. HE IS TWO DAYS OVERDUE. ANY INFORMATION, PLEASE CONTACT ANY TELEGRAPH OFFICE."

Ple got her to read it over again, then cleared his throat. "I want to send a message."

The operator said, "just a moment." She went to the table and returned in a minute with a pen and piece of paper. "Go ahead."

TO THE COMMANDING OFFICER OF THE NEWFOUNDLAND RANGERS. WILL PUT TOGETHER A SEARCH PARTY TO LOOK FOR DANNY CORCORAN. WILL LEAVE AT LIGHT TOMORROW MORNING. SIGNED,, PLEMAN GILLARD."

Ple said nothing more and walked out the door. "So," he said out loud as he walked along the road, "Danny Corcoran is lost in the country, and I am going to find him if I can get one man to go with me." His thoughts raced.

It was pouring rain. "This won't last," he said. "It came on too sudden."

"Hey, Wilf, come here, I want you," Ple called to a young twelve-year old boy.

"Yes. What is it, Ple?"

Ple side stepped over to him. "I'll tell you what I want you to do, Wilf. I want you to go down to Art Compton's and tell Art to come up to the old man's and on your way up tell Gus Compton to come up too. The reason is that the Ranger up in Harbour Deep is lost, and I am organizing a search party to go look for him. I am going to get Jack Brown, so tell Art and Gus to come up as soon as possible."

"Okay," he said and took off.

Ple went over to Jack Brown's. He went to the door, opened it, and put his head inside and roared, "Jack, Jack!"

Mrs. Brown heard him calling. She came to the porch. "you is it, Ple? I thought I recognized you. Come in."

"No, I haven't got time, Aunt Mary. Is Jack in?"

"Yes," she said, "he just went upstairs. He should be down in a minute."

"I'm going over home. Tell Jack to come over, I want him. It's important."

She looked at Ple with a suspicious look, but said, "Yes, I'll tell him."

Ple went on home. He stepped into the kitchen. His father looked at him as he came in. "Looks like it's going to break up, Ple."

Ple looked at his father, then answered, "Naw. Nothing to this. This will be cleared up again after twelve."

His father was bald. He was a very religious man, kind of meek and humble. "Ple, you got a wild look on your face. Don't say you're going in the country again. My son, the Ranger is going to catch you guys yet, and I'd say the sooner the better."

There was a silence.

"Peters will never catch me, father. You know the difference of that. He wouldn't search your house because he's too much in with Rodrick and Rodrick is too much in with you."

His father looked at him and grinned. "Maybe you're right, but maybe you could push your luck too far. Maybe the Ranger up in Harbour Deep might catch you."

Ple answered slowly. "Father, that's where I'm goin now or tomorrow morning, on a search party to look for the Ranger from Harbour Deep. His name is Danny Corcoran. He is lost in the country and has been gone for days. So I doubt if he'll catch me now."

The old man felt sorry. Then somebody came in the porch. It was Art Compton.

"Come in," said Ple.

Art kicked the door facings on the way in to knock the wet snow off his boots. Noah Gillard looked at him standing, then at the pile of wet snow in the doorway.

"It's only water, Uncle Noah," he said with a jaw puffed out with tobacco.

"Now, Art. If you want to spit, spit in the stove. The last time you were here you spit in the water bucket, and I almost had to light a fire in it to get the stink out."

"Uncle Noah," said Art, "I'm glad you were my Sunday School teacher when I was a youngster. If you hadn't of been, there's a question as to if I wouldn't have gone astray."

Art and Ple laughed.

"There's a day coming when you might be found because the two of you are lost, not only Danny Corcoran."

Art spit on the floor behind him. "Old man, did you say the Ranger up in Harbour Deep is lost?"

Ple interrupted. "Yes, but I'll give you the details when Jack and Gus come."

"They're coming," said his father.

Jack Brown and Gus Compton came to the door.

"Come in, boys," said Noah. "I'm glad to see you boys."

Art winked at Ple. When Noah turned away from him, Art spit on the floor behind him. There was a big brown streak of tobacco juice. Ple started to laugh. He knew that if his father saw it he would drive Art out. He had to start a conversation right away. "Come over to the table, boys," he said.

They all moved around the table and Ple took a notepad and pencil, he knew their plans had to be made right here and put on paper.

"Just a minute, Ple," said Art. He went out in the porch, opened the porch door, took his tobacco chew out of his mouth, and threw it in the water barrel in the corner of the porch. He pretended that he threw it outdoors. He shut the door and said to himself, "This serves you right, Uncle Noah. You don't like me and I don't like you." He came back in and sat at the table.

"Now, boys. I had a telegram this evening. To put it this way, I read the one that came to the Post Office." He knew there was no telling Jack and Gus lies. "It was about Danny Corcoran, the Ranger in Harbour Deep. Remember we were talking about him the other night. He went on a wildlife patrol. Well, he hasn't come back and he's not on the other side. A message came in from the head fellow of the Rangers to have a search party go look for him, so I sent him a wireless telling him I was leaving the the morning with a search party. So this is what I want you for."

Ple let the words sink in. "Are you planning on going?"

No one spoke. Each man was leaning on his elbows. Art spoke up. "It's raining pretty hard, isn't it?"

Ple turned to Art. "Rain won't stop you, Compton, if you want to go."

Jack Brown was next to speak. "Are you sure he hasn't showed up on the other side? I've been over there on the edge of the hills looking down on the fields of timber inside of Hawkes Bay. If he got out in that he could be lost for weeks."

Ple spoke up. "Do you know where I think he's at? I'd say he's in around Red Sea Pond or somewhere in behind Williamsport."

Gus spoke up. He was the oldest of the bunch and had spent much time in around there after caribou. "Well, boys," he said slowly,, "according to what we talked about the other night, and the kind of weather we have had since, I'd say he hasn't come east of Harbour Deep River. For sure the river has busted out or flooded. That's the reason he's not on this side of the river. It's that simple. He can't get across."

Ple spoke up, "Maybe he crossed inside the Wolfe Barren. If he did, he could come out on this side of the river. He could cross the Rocky Stent and then Camping Pond under Lucky Strike, then come in over to the Red Sea Pond."

Gus looked at Ple. "No," he said. "If he got over on that high country out behind the Wolfe Barren, he would be able to see the woods behind Hawkes Bay. I have been out there. We were out there once and just made it back. Jack, you went with us."

Jack nodded.

"He is either between Little Harbour Deep or Big Harbour Deep Brook or over on the Lowlands in behind Hawkes Bay as Jack had stated."

Ple said throughfully, "Well, boys, that's one thing we don't know. Fellows do some queer things sometimes. But there's one thing for sure. If he's out in the open all this time,, he must be having a pretty rough time. And if I was in his place, I would want someone to look for me.

Jack spoke up. "I'll go Ple. But I guarantee you I won't be taking any chances."

Gus butt in. "I can't go."

"Why?" asked Ple half standing up. "What's the matter?"

"Boys, Clair is pretty sick. I'm getting ready now, myself and Arch, to take her to Roddickton on dog team. We may have to take her to St. Anthony."

"Well," Ple said. "Then the three of us will go. No. We need four men, two dogteams, two men to a team. We have to get someone else. Who can we get?"

"I know who we can get," said Gus.

"Who's that?" asked Ple.

"Get Ranger Peters."

"Then you go ask him," said Jack grinning.

"Well, no, old man," said Art. "If he goes, I don't go."

"I know who we'll get," said Ple. "We'll get Nat Johnson."

"Is he finished carrying the mail?" asked Jack.

"Yes," said Gus. "I think he is. In fact, I think this is his last day. This is the 15th, isn't it?"

"Yes," said Jack.

"Well, there's our man," said Ple. "I'll ask him."

Gus spoke up. His advise was from experience. "I'll tell you what to do." He started motioning with his fingers on the table.

"You can leave here now and go straight to Devils Cove Lookout, but instead of going in on Rock Brook, go in over Flyoil Hill. Rocky Brook is busted out. We were over there yesterday. Stay in the open all you can. You may have a bit of trouble around the big hill due to the brooks. So when you get on Rocky Pond,, go across and take Hynes Barrens. There's no brooks that way. Then go up Johnson Flats, but keep a bit to your left and go on the outside of Dung Hill. You'll see my marks, one rock on top of the other. We got caught in Charlie's Skirt one time for six days, and it was the best kind of going. Just outside of Dung Hill the brooks fill right up with water and you can't get across one of them. Now listen, when you get to the Hay Pooks, make a straight dart for the Blue Skirt. If you get there the first night, you've got it made. You can search all the Williamsport - Harbour Deep area even on bare ground. When you get to Harbour Deep Brook, take the west fork, because if you cross outside of that,, you're going to run into a bit of t rouble. And do you know what I'd say? If you're goiing to see any sign of Danny Corcoran, 'tis going to be around there." He paused.

"Ple, you remember the time we were up there and Sam Randell shot the two moose on Copper Brook? See, old man, you got the Wolfe Barren there on the north side of the pond. And if I were you, I would stop my dogs and I'd walkk up on the Wolfe Barren and have a look. You know a man. If he's got either grain of sense at all he's going to go up on all the lookouts."

They thought for a moment.

"What tents are you going to take, Jack?" asked Gus.

"I'd say we'll have to take yours. It's the best one in Englee."

"You can have it," said Gus. "And take the canvas flap too. I'd say you'll need that to keep your shirt from getting wet before you get back. I was talking to Zack Canning just now, and he told me we were going to have a week's rain."

Jack Brown spoke up. "If Uncle Zack said it's goin' rain, then it certainly will."

"What about the grub, old man?" asked Art.

"Everybody will have to take their own."

"Don't take any meat, just salt. I'm taking my rifle. We'll kill a caribou as soon as we get in. We'll take my stove."

A knock came on the door. "See who that is old man," said Ple to his father. "Maybe someone wants the loan of something."

The old man walked slowly to the porch. They were all talking when he rushed back. "Hey, boys," he said in a kind of a whisper. "It's Ranger

Peters. Ple, he wants you."

They all looked at one another. Art turned and indicated he was going to spit, but decided not to. Uncle Noah was looking straight at him. Gus spoke up quickly. "Tell the Ranger to come in."

Ple was going to say no, but Gus caught hold of his arm. They heard boots clinking on the porch floor, then the Ranger appeared in the doorway.

Peters was 24 years old, medium built, and had a round face. He was one that liked to give orders. He came to Englee in October and didn't like it there, he was just waiting to move out.

He stood in the kitchen doorway with his hat and gloves on. "Good evening, gentlemen," he said and looked at Art who showed a gold tooth with kind of a fox grin.

"Good afternoon," said Jack and Gus.

"Ple," he said kind of bold. "Could I speak to you?"

"You sure can, Peters." He paused for a moment. "Go right ahead."

"Well," he started to say. "I am looking for some people to go with me in the open country to search for Danny Corcoran, the Ranger from Harbour Deep. He's lost."

Ple looked at him. "Where have you tried?"

"I've tried a few places, but I can't find anybody that will go."

Peters took off one glove. He needed help, and here he found the country experts gathered all in one place. He looked around the table. Here were four tough men, and he needed them.

"There's no need of you searching for Danny Corcoran. We're going to find him. We got our trip planned and we're leaving in the morning," said Ple.

Gus spoke up. "Ranger Peters, would you please join us?"

He thanked Gus. Than Uncle Noah got him a chair. He sat down near the table, then took off his cap. He had thick dark hair. He was what you'd call soft. He taught school for two years before joining the Rangers.

"You know," said Gus, "that this is a pretty serious matter. A man is lost on the open country in the winter, maybe with no food or shelter, and maybe injured. We don't know. Perhaps the worst has happened." He paused. "But there is one thing we know for sure. That is if he's out there in the open in this kind of weather, he needs help."

Peters nodded.

"And at this time we're the ones who are responsible for finding him because we have the country experience. It is no good to send kids up there this time of the year, because there are going to be many problems, for instance, the weather. We know the weather, and we can battle that due to experience. Then there's the country itself. We know the directions, clear or foggy, night or day. The equipment, we have good dogs, country dogs. We have a good camping outfit, and we're healthy."

Peters nodded.

"But what about the supplies? I mean the grub?" He looked at Peters. No one spoke.

Then Peters cleared his throat, "I will get the food supplies for everyone if I go."

Ple got up from the table and walked around the kitchen. He came over again and sat down. "Now boys, it's like this with me. I am going to look for a man who's lost in the country. When I leave I'm staying in until I find him or until the snow goes away."

"Yes, me too," said Art. "I'm prepared to swim out Harbour Deep Brook."

Peters nodded in agreement, but he knew what he was getting himself into. He had no choice. If he was to advance, he would have to take chances, even if he had to travel with a bunch of radicals. "Who will be in charge?" Peters asked.

The men looked at Ple. They knew he was the senior man when it came to the country. But Peters looked at Gus. "How about you, Gus? Being in charge?" he said.

"I'm not going, Peters. If I was, I would be in charge, but Ple is next in line."

Peters heart sank. He hated Ple and Ple knew it.

"But," said Gus, "all important decisions must be voted on."

Gus noticed a sigh of relief on Peters face. He knew he had to go. He had strict orders from the commanding officers to mount a search, and as far as he was concerned, he had to put his life in the hands of the worst men he had ever known. As far as he was concerned, Art Compton and Ple Gillard should be in jail. And as far as they were concerned, he should have stayed a school teacher.

Ple said, "Okay, gang. Let's start getting ready. We should be over Flyoil Hill by daylight. We will get up at 4 O'clock, be ready to move at 4:30 A.M. Jack, you take Peters with you. I'll go with Art."

"Good enough," said Jack Brown.

"How many dogs are you taking?"

Art Compton had savage dogs. He had 14. He used them mainly to bring patients back and forth to St. Anthony. "I'm taking eight."

Jack then spoke up. "I'm taking 10 of the old man's."

Ple spoke up, "We'll take my riding sled and komatik box. We'll let four of my dogs chase us just in case any of ours get cut up or foundered. That will give us 22 to work with."

"Good," said Gus. "But, boys, there's one thing you make sure not to do, that is not to split up. And if it gets too bad, go out to Williamsport or Harbour Deep. Then send me a wireless and I'll come up after you in boat."

Jack spoke up. "Boys, if we find him, how are we going to know?"

"Well, I'll tell you what," said Gus, "Ple, you know where that cross is up on Harbour Deep Brook just out from Brengies Flats. If they find him I'll have Pittman put a ...". He stopped. "No, forget it. We'll get word to you somehow. Don't worry about anything. There's an old washing tub down by the house. You know, the one we had the last time. Take that again. It's the real one for feeding the dogs in."

"Okay," said Ple. "Jack, you and your buddy get the grub. We'll take some salt fish."

"Don't worry about that," said Jack. "Everybody will have to take their own bread."

"Good enough," said Gus. "Now, boys, take lots of rope and at least three axes."

"Yes, we'll make sure."

Gus got up and left.

Peters left. He had a headache. He hoped the rain would hold up, but anyway, rain or shine, they had to go on. He made for home at a fast pace. He knew he was an intruder. He had forced himself on these men, and he knew he would be having little to say. Anyway, it didn't matter. It would only be a couple of nights, maybe three. If they got to Harbour Deep, he would not be walking back or coming on dogteam because he would make sure he told Rodrick before he left to have a boat come to Harbour Deep and get him. Yes, that's what he would do. He would get a boat to come to Harbour Deep, Williamsport or Canada Harbour, whichever town he came out to. That's where he would get picked up. He felt better.

Ranger Roy Hiscock sat at the table with his arms folded. He was lost in thought when Mrs. Taylor asked him if he wanted a cup of tea. Mrs. Taylor was his boarding mistress. She was a good humoured person with blond hair. She was beautifully built and knew it.

"If you don't mind, Mrs. Taylor."

She did not want anybody to call her Mrs. She had told Jack so many times before that there was no use in telling him any more. She put down the two cups, then poured the tea. She made sure sugar and milk was on the table before she sat down.

"Jack, you look worried, but I don't think there's much to it." She stopped.

"I got a feeling there's a lot to it," said Roy. "I've checked from Eddies Cove to Belburns, and no one has seen him."

"There have been a lot of people in the country since Monday."

Roy reached for the sugar. "But what puzzles me is why he didn't let me know the day he was leaving to come over. I could have gotten Guy Gould to go with me on the hills to meet him. It would have been fun. You know, for a man to leave by himself, and according to Gill Ellsworth he hardly took any grub, and come across over here to me, Danny must be gone out of his head."

Mrs. Taylor moved around on her chair. She seemed to be uninterested. Her concern was her kitchen, her boarders, and anywhere else she could pick up a few dollar bills. Roy knew there was not much use in carrying on a conversation with her regarding Danny Corcoran. The fact that he was lost in the country made no difference.

"I am going in the woods this evening, Mrs. Taylor. I won't be home tonight unless we find Danny. If we find him, he will be staying with me in the spare bed."

Her face lit up. "Good." She could see another dollar.

"If there's a message for me, I will be in around Middle Pond or Pikes Feeder. Pass it on to Martin Lowe. He will have someone send it in to me."

"Good enough," she said.

He thanked her, then walked out. He walked down to the little office that the Government had rented, a 16 x 12 foot room as part of the Post Office-Telegraph Office. It was heated with a wood stove. He opened up a map of the area between Harbour Deep and Port Saunders. He studied it for a moment, took out his compass, put it on the map, and began to turn it. The door opened and Guy Gould came in.

"Guy, is everything ready?"

"Yes," he said. He had peering eyes and long sideburns. He was built strong and very thin. He was known around that part of the Straits for poaching. He had spent the most part of his winters on the country. It was said that one winter he and two other fellows killed 45 caribou and 30 moose.

But Roy Hiscock was not afraid of them. He was a rough, tough fellow who would not be pushed around. They would be doing whatever he said or else they would be returning home. He grew up rough and under a lot of discipline. His father was a tough man who cared nor feared for anything. Roy could wear his father's boots but he put his ability to law enforcement and was well respected by the Headquarters personnel in Whitbourne. There was no doubt that if Roy Hiscock stayed in the Ranger Force, he would go places.

"Take a look at this, Guy."

He invited Guy to the table with a wave of his hand. Guy moved over. "What's that?" He looked at the map.

"How much do you know about the Harbour Deep area?"

Guy pulled down one eye. "I've been over there. We used to have a tent over in Big Gulch. We usually hunt over around the big ponds just in from Williamsport." He pointed to the ponds on the maps. "We were over there this winter and met a man in there. Now, this is what they call Red Sea Pond. The man's name was Mr. Sam Brenton. He's from Williamsport. But you got no worries about Danny Corcoran in there. He's where we said he is. He's probably in around Pikes Feeder or Bluey."

Roy looked at the map. "Maybe you're right. Listen, did you get the lantern?"

"Yes, and I got a gallon of kerosene and an extra chimney."

"Good," said Roy, "I sent word to Fred Hoddinott at Hawkes Bay to be ready to join us."

He stopped and looked at the map. "What would you say if I sent Fred and his group to search around Raft Pond?"

"It might be alright," said Guy. "But tell him not to go any further west. Tell him to go up around the Moose Flat. It's a good place to go."

"I don't want anyone to go in on the hills. We both discussed that."

Guy remembered he wanted to go in on the hills, but Roy and the boys changed his mind.

"Good enough."

"I'm going to send a wireless. Just a minute."

He went out and locked the door. He went to the telegraph office door which was about 10 feet away.

"You're going to search for Danny Corcoran now?"

"Yes," he said. "I just had a wireless go through to Whitbourne. There's a bunch leaving from Englee. A Ranger Peters said he was putting together a party and leaving in the morning."

Roy kind of sneered his face at the sound of Peters. Sue Lavers didn't ask what the problem was.

"I want to send a wireless to the commanding officer. You know the orders. I'll tell him what I want him to know, then you send it in the fewest words possible. Three parties have been sent out in the Eddies Cove – Port Saunders areas. I am joining a party to help search for Corcoran. Would appreciate any information you receive. Will keep you informed. By the way, mention weather conditions here. Heavy rain. Sign my name to the wireless."

"Good enough," she said.

"That will be collect, please."

He thanked her and left dressed in his oil skins.

She admired this man. He was six feet tall, good looking, built strong, and was feared and respected by almost everyone. He was a man who mixed with everyone. But she often wondered why he hadn't mixed with her. She wanted a date with him, but he was taking out Wavey Tavers.

Anyway, work came first. She heard the dogteams leave. She put her mind back to the wireless. She began. "MARCH 15, 1936 PORT SAUNDERS, NEWFOUNDLAND.

Danny Corcoran awoke cold and tried to move but was unable to. He opened his eyes and stared at the wall. It was built of logs. It seemed like every part of him was frozen solid except his eyes. He closed them and tried to think. He sucked in a few gulps of air. It burned his lungs. He knew he was in a building. He opened his eyes again. He looked towards the ceiling. He was in a camp. "Yes," he moaned. "It was the Patey fellows. It was almost dark."

He turned his head. He was supposed to come back for him. Certainly he should have known better. I guess he was afraid because of the gun he had. But he gave him his word. I guess he didn't trust him. He had showed him his leg and he was sure he saw pity in this eyes. But why? Why would he leave him? Is it possible that man would stoop so low as to forsake his fellowman? He felt the pain in his leg and his two feet. It hurt him right to his heart. His head was aching and waves of pain seemed to roll over his brain. He put his hand to his mouth. Then he rolled over on his back. He was almost flat on his back when he felt himself go. Before he knew it he had landed on the floor. There was a big junk of wood on the floor near the bunk that he had used for a seat to sit on while having supper. This is where his bad leg hit.

Danny felt the lights go out. He fought for consciousness. His body went into kind of convulsions. "What am I to do?" he cried. "What am I to do?"

He felt pain in his heart. It was piercing. He was sure he had his leg broken. He got sick and started to throw up the supper he had eaten. The supper had done him no good now. It was all gone. He started to come to his senses. He knew he had passed out, but for how long he wasn't sure. He had difficulty pinpointing an area in his body where the pain hurt most. But his feet. He tried to move them but was afraid for fear of more pain. He felt a throbbing in his leg. Finally he opened his eyes. He noticed it was dark, but he could see the oil barrel. Then he remembered where he was again. Now he knew he would have to get this body going.

He put his hand on the bunk and pulled, but the only thing that moved was his head. He rolled onto his side, then pushed himself up on his elbow. He then caught hold of the bunk and put himself into a sitting position. He felt nauseous. His head started to roll. He felt like one time when he had gotten sea sick, only this time it was much worse. He held onto the bunk and put one hand on the piece of wood. He gradually lifted himself, after three attempts, to the bunk, and sat up. The light from the snow outside glowed a bit in the camp. It wasn't pitch dark. He sat there for five minutes, then reached down and felt his leg. It was so sore that he could not bear his hand on it. Even the slightest touch on his leg made his feet ache. After a few more minutes he started to think. The words of Earl Patey started to ring in his ears. "It looks like it's getting blood poisoned.

There's a streak going up your leg. You be careful. You could lose your leg."

These words sounded over and over in his ears. Danny noticed the tears running down his face. He could not keep them back. Waves of pain were in his legs. He knew he had to get to a nurse or a doctor. But what could he do? He was so weak he could hardly sit up. Then a voice said to him, "Danny, you must never give up. You must fight all odds. Never give up. Never give up." It went on and on. It was so clear he sat up straight.

"Well," he said out loud, "I've got to get the body going."

He tried to take his own weight on his legs, but screamed. Then he tried again. This time he kept his thoughts on his feet. He got to the table helping himself along the bunks. He found the matches that Earl had given him. He knew there was birch rind on the floor. He bent over holding onto the table. He picked it up and tore the strips in small pieces. He then lit it and put it in the stove. It glowed. He noticed it was not very cold. It was still raining outside. He also noticed that his blood was moving a little in his veins. The pain in his leg seemed to be eased a little.

He got some wood and put it on the fire. He put more birch rind on the flames. He now had a good fire going. At least it was not like last night. He put more wood in the stove, then sat back on the bunk. He thought for a moment. It seemed like every time he lay down and slept, his blood seemed to stand still giving him much pain when he moved again. Was it possible that the poison from his leg is what was giving him this problem? He knew that infection could spread throughout his body. If this was the case, he wouldn't be able to move again until he received medical help. "What will I do? What can I do?" he asked himself silently. He had only two matches left in the box, and he didn't have much wood left. He knew Earl would not be back again. Maybe he was right about the direction over on the bog.

"I must be able to make a move at first light in the morning. Yes, that's what I will do." He had to get on the move and the sooner, the better. He dare not lay down again and go to sleep. "But how long did I sleep?"

He looked at his watch. It was 7:30 P.M. He knew it had gotten daylight around 6:00 A.M. He would have a long night. He didn't have enough wood to last all night, but there was the lumber in the bunks. Then he remembered he had tea. "I think I will make tea. And I still have three cakes of hard bread. I will boil the kettle and have a lunch."

He sat up very pleased that the pain had eased in his feet. Well, he was going to have a look at his leg very soon. He still had tea left in the kettle from earlier that day. He put the kettle on the stove where it could boil. He moved over near the stove and started to loosen his boot. "Yes," he said out loud, "I got to take my boot off." He slacked it, then started pulling slowly, a little at a time. His underwear was stuck in the cut. He noticed fresh blood around his pants leg. It seemed like his toes were stuck in his boots. He pulled harder and it seemed like the flesh was pulling away from his toes. He almost fainted with pain. Then he thought, if I get my boot off, what can I do? I don't even have a first aid dressing, not even a bandaid. "Oh, dear God," he cried, "I guess I am finished. Why did Earl Patey run away from me when he knew I had a sore leg? I showed it to him?" He then put his foot back in its place.

He noticed the kettle was boiling. He filled his enamel mug up with the strong tea and added some sugar. The hot tea seemed to revive him. He took out his three cakes of hard bread and started to eat one. It reminded him of the story he had heard or read of the Newfoundlander who had been in prison. Being punished for crimes, he had to eat hard bread and drink cold water. There was no humour in the thought. It seemed like he was being punished. But why? He had not done anything wrong. Thank God he had nothing on his conscience.

He put more wood on the fire. He started to move around a bit. His feet didn't seem as bad although he had a bad limp in both. He wasn't sure if he would be able to walk in the morning. But he just had to walk if he was ever able to survive. He limped to the door and peered out. It was still raining outside. "Thank God for a roof over my head," he said. "That's one thing I can at least thank Earl for, showing me this cabin."

Then the thought came to him. Tomorrow the going would be soft. He would have to wear snowshoes. "My, oh my," he said out loud, "how can I do it? But I have to. How will I be able to strap the slings around my poor feet?" He stopped and tried to move his toes. "But it has to be done. It has to be done." How he dreaded tomorrow. But it would come and he would go. He went to the bunk and sat down and with his feet in his boots, he waited for daylight.

Chapter 14
March 16, 1936

Earl Patey awoke and jumped out. He had slept round. It was dawning. He went to the door and peered out. The rain had stopped, but it was mild. Last night there was no frost at all. He stepped outside for a moment. It was soft. He could see his breath in the air. "It is a good morning for travelling with the dogs, good on their paws."

He stepped back into the cabin. "Hey, you guys, let's go. I bet the Ranger is up now wondering what happened to us. Or maybe he will soon be out."

"I hope he is," said Fred. "Don't you think 'tis not goin' to be a hard drag gettin' in there this mornin'."

"Don't matter," said Earl. "Come on. Get up. Let's get in there." He paused. "I know he must have had a rough night, my son. You should have seen his leg. What a sight! I'd say by now it's blood poisoned."

"Naw. He'll be alright, Earl. Certainly the two of us is enough to go in. Fred, you can stay and get everything packed up. Then when we get back we can leave right away."

"Good enough," said Earl.

Earl looked at Jack. "I think we should go on now. We can have breakfast when we get back."

"No, not me," said Jack.

"Why not?" said Earl in a very eager voice.

"Listen, Earl," said Jack in kind of a crooked voice. "Some of them brooks might be full this morning after all that rain. Eat your breakfast and don't be so crazy. Another half an hour or so won't hurt."

There was a silence.

"Anyway," Jack said, "I'm having my breakfast. It's up to you if you want yours or not."

"Okay," said Earl. "But let's hurry."

Fred started to laugh. "Jack, I think you should go on right now without any breakfast."

"Why?" asked Jack.

"You see, Earl, he's not worried about that Ranger. He wants to get home to that little girl out there. Maybe we should forget about the Ranger and let him make his own way out."

They laughed.

"Okay, okay, boys. Let's have breakfast first."

They ate in silence. Earl knew he had put his foot in his mouth. He would make sure it wouldn't happen again. When finished, they quickly harnessed the dogs and took off. It was 7:05 A.M., Thursday morning.

It was just after daylight when Noah Pittman and four other men stepped into Danny's tracks on the trail near Soufflett's River. They noticed he had made a trench through the snow. And although it was five days later, it was still visible. They were having quite a job crossing the small brooks that were crossing the trail going in by the river. It was the same trail Danny had walked in. They had a problem to getting around the bogs. At 1:30 P.M. they reached Elige Newman's camp.

"He was in this camp," said Noah. "Let's have a look, boys."

He opened the door and looked in. He looked all around, then stepped inside. "Hey, Nat, come here and take a look at this."

Nat Cassell stepped inside and looked around. "Look's like he had a fire lit on the floor."

Noah looked at the fire. "What do you think of that? He was burning green boughs."

"Why didn't he light the stove?"

"Look, there's stove pipes in under the bunk."

They paused and looked at where Danny had boiled the kettle on the hearth floor after the stove pipes had fallen apart.

"Now, he don't know very much about the woods. Imagine, he lit the fire on the floor with green boughs."

"How did he ever live with all that smoke?" said Noah. "Why he didn't put the stove pipes back on the stove? For sure he had to have seen them."

"Well, there is one thing I have to say," said Noah, "I don't think he knows very much about lighting a fire or the kind of wood that burns. There's plenty of dry wood around."

They were not even considering that Danny had stayed all night in this cabin and he had broken the old stove pipes into pieces. In the morning it was plainly evident, but they were satisfied to say that Danny knew nothing about lighting a fire using dry wood, only trying to get green boughs to burn. When they went outside, Noah said to the men, "Hey, boys, we found out something. Danny doesn't even know how to get a fire to burn. He was even trying to burn green boughs. So you can imagine what kind of a time he's having in the country, if he got in."

Bill Randell asked. "Did he stay here overnight?"

"Yes," said Noah. "He must have had a rough night. He left here

Tuesday morning. You can tell by the tracks. We won't be able to track him very much. It froze that night. Let's go into Hancock's camp."

"Good enough," they said, then moved on.

By the time they reached Hancock's camp, they were feeling hungry. They could also track Danny more plainly now. He was beginning to sink in the snow. Although it was five days later, his tracks were still visible. They noticed his tracks went to the door and moved on again. They cleared the snow away from the door. It was mainly ice. They went inside. This was a good camp. This was the place where Hancocks had a contract for I.P.N.P. to cut pit-props. They took their lunch bags off. Nat Cassell got the fire going.

"He didn't stay here," said Noah.

"I know why he didn't stay, because he couldn't get a fire lit on the floor," said Nat.

All except Noah laughed.

It was 5:00 P.M. when they had finished their lunch. "We got an hour and a half, boys, before dark. Let's pick his tracks up and see where he crossed."

They put their snowshoes on, took their axes, and followed Danny's tracks. They walked in along the river to the little steady. The water had gone down on the steady because the brook had busrt through near the mouth of it. They saw where Danny had cut a small tree. Then they saw the tree out on the ice. The ice was lodged on the bottom because the water was gone. They walked out on the ice and noticed a hole near the cut tree. They examined the hole, then Noah shouted, "Hey, look Nat."

Nat looked under the edge of the ice. He saw it, the red handle of the axe.

"That's the old man's axe," said Noah. "Do you know what happened here? Danny fell in the water. Yes, that's just what he's after doing."

"Well, well," said Nat. "You just imagine that, Noah. He fell in the water." He went on. "I'd say there was about six or seven feet of water here when he fell in. Look at the ice there. That was the high water mark."

There was a pause. Another man reached down and got the axe. "For sure he never made it. I'd say you wouldn't have to go very far before you would pick him up frozen to death."

Noah nodded. "Why did that man come in here? Why did he come in?"

There was a silence. "Well, boys. It's after 5 o'clock. I'm going over to check the trail to see if he went through to the open country. Nat, you might as well come with me. Gill, you and Sam might as well go back to the camp and get everything ready for the night. Get a nice bit of wood. It looks like it's going to be a cold night."

"Okay," said Gill, "try and get back before too late."

"Don't worry. We won't be late," said Noah.

They turned and followed Danny's trail. He didn't take the old country road. He went into the woods and was following the timber. They walked in his trail for a while, then turned back to Hancock's camp. The camp was right on the edge of the river. When the water was high it almost touched the camp, and it was near Soufflett's. The roar of the river at night would almost keep you awake.

After they ate supper, Noah said, "Now, boys, I'm only spending one night in here because Nellie is sick. I shouldn't be in here now by rights, but for Danny I came."

They all nodded.

"Tomorrow morning we'll take up his track over on the other side and follow it. I got a feeling we won't have to go far before we'll pick him up frozen to death. Remember last Tuesday evening it snowed, then it turned to rain, and it poured out of the Heavens. Then it started to freeze, and it froze all day Wednesday. Remember?"

There was a silence. "We will stay together. But if he went on in the country, then I doubt if we'll be able to track him."

Not much more was said. "We'll get up around 4:30. That will be time to get everything ready. I hope it freezes."

They all turned in for the night.

It was 7 A.M. when Roy Hiscock put on his snowshoes and stepped outside. He noticed it had stiffened a little last night, but it was still soft going. Guy Gould, Bill Hyre, and Roy Hiscock were searching the area between Pikes Feeder and Lady Worster. He hoped to find some trace of Danny in this area. He had not gotten much sleep last night thinking about Danny. He knew that something was wrong. How could he sleep? Danny had been a good friend of his from the very beginning. From the first time they shook hands until now, they had kept in contact with each other.

The two men were different in many ways. Danny was brought up by his mother after his father had died. She brought him up to be a real gentleman, to be fine cut, to use good English, to wear his clothes neatly, and always to be on time, to respect the King, the Governor and the Mayor. He was taught above all to help your fellow man.

But Roy Hiscock grew up differently. His father was quite respectful, but he ruled with an iron hand. His father was the toughest in town. They lived raw and ready. Roy got his education early and had taken to the woods in Howley. Roy Hiscock could have made almost anything. He had the ability. He didn't drink, but he did like a girl in every port, but refused to practise this for fear of any disrespect for the Rangers.

Danny Corcoran was a fellow who stuck to the one girl, but the two of them had one thing in common – will power. If they made up their minds to do something they could stick to their decision no matter what. Facts would have to prove otherwise.

So now Roy found himself searching the Lowlands for Danny Corcoran. He had been on four search parties and this made the fifth. Some of the men wanted to go up on the high hills inside the treeline to search for Danny, to use the hills for lookouts, but it was decided against until they were sure Danny was not in the treeline. What they hoped to do was search between Pikes Feeder and Lady Worster Brook. Then tomorrow they would search further to the West. The next day they would search the South East of Pikes Feeder in the Upper Torrent River area, then to the west near Raft Pond. Fred Hoddinott and his crew of four were searching between the Moose Ridge area and East Bluey Pond. Another bunch from Hawkes Bay were searching an area near the Cobeaus Ridge. The other parties were moving in almost any area between River of Ponds and Pikes Feeder as directed.

They were a roving band. The parties found their biggest problem to be so many people in the woods poaching moose. They couldn't establish a pattern of searching. Almost everywhere they went there were men, dogs, and moose running all over the place. Shots were fired different times of the day, but when the searchers located the area where the shots were fired, they found dead moose and the men running away. On two occasions two groups of searchers were sent on wild goose chases. And after going in a certain direction, they found out there was nothing to this search because the poachers only wanted them to leave so they could carry on their killing. The first day they didn't find out anything about Danny. There were no signs, no tracks in the snow or anything. Tomorrow they would search as planned.

Danny looked at the last glimmer of fire in the stove. All the wood was gone. He tore cardboard from the wall and threw it in the stove. It made a flame. He had his snowshoes all ready to put on his feet. What would he do? He must try. He started with his left foot. This one was frozen, but only his toes. It was a nightmare for any man to try and tackle putting on a snowshoe, especially the kind of slings Danny had on his. They were the kind that had a two-inch strap across the toe of the boot. He grinded his teeth and tried to get the toe of his boot in the sling. He was unable to. Saliva ran down over his chin. Tears came to his eyes. He tried again, but this time he held his breath.

He cried, "What am I going to do? What am I going to do? I can't stay here and die."

The sweat poured from his forehead. He noticed that he was unsteady. His hands were trembling. He knew what the problem was. His toes were blistered so much that they were too big to go in the slings. Every time he put pressure on them, it seemed like the flesh was being pulled from the bone. "Oh, what will I do?" he cried. "Oh, what will I do?"

He had to move on or else perish, or perish, or perish. The words seemed to echo in his ears. "You've got to put on your snowshoes. You might as well put them on now. It has to be done," a voice inside was saying. He then stooped down, put the toe of his boot in the sling, and gave it a push. His toe slid into the sling and it seemed as if he had torn himself to the heart. He had to hold onto the bunk.

The flames flickered and there was a silence, and only the sobbing and the sucking in of air broke the early morning stillness. No birds were singing at that moment near the lofty Bluey Mountain. No stars were shining in the sky over Hawkes Bay. There was no one to pity this mother's child or this orphan son. It seemed like God had forsaken this young honest Ranger. And it seemed to Danny that fate had sealed his doom and it was only a matter of time until he would fade slowly out into the endless ages of eternity where forever he would drift with frozen feet and a rotten leg. But when it would come only God knew. But 'til then he would push on.

The pain was so great he hardly knew anything before he had the other snowshoe on and was standing up in the middle of the cabin with his parka, cap, and mitts on, his rifle on his back, and tears streaming down his face. It was dawning. He must move on.

Earl and Jack Patey stopped the dogs near the Belburns cabin. It was 8:00 A.M. Earl ran for the cabin. He opened the door and stepped inside very quickly. "Hey, Danny! Hey, Ranger!" he called. He stopped in his tracks. "The Ranger is gone. He's left."

His thoughts raced. He could hardly believe it. He turned to leave. "Maybe he is outside somewhere. Maybe we can catch him."

Jack stepped into the cabin. He looked at Earl. "Where is he, Earl? Where is he gone?"

Earl swallowed. "Yes, he's gone. Let's see if we can find him."

"Just a moment," said Jack. "Let's have a look around."

They felt the stove. It was a little warm. They looked on the table. His mug and spoon were left. Then Earl said, "Jack, look there on the stool. There's two cakes of hard bread. He only had three cakes yesterday when I met him, and there's only two here. He must have eaten one for his breakfast."

They picked up the hard bread. It had been soaked around the edges. This happened when he fell in the water.

"I know what he's been after doing," said Jack. "He's gone out in your tracks on the other side of the river."

Earl's heart lifted. "Maybe you're right Jack. Let's find out."

They went out of the cabin and closed the door. They could easily track him. The dogs were barking loudly. "You walk on ahead, Earl, in his tracks. I'll come up behind with the dogs."

"Okay," he said.

They quickly went to the steady. When Earl had crossed, they followed him to the bog that Earl told him about. Then feared at what he thought Danny had done.

"Yes. It is true. He walked straight to the middle of the bog and had taken the wrong course. Jack, you got your compass?"

"Yes," said Jack.

"Then take off a course and see which way he's gone."

Jack took out a little round compass and held it in his hand. He turned it and studied it for a moment. "He's gone North, Earl, my son."

He checked his compass again. "Yes, North it is."

"Now, why did he go that way? Why?" asked Earl.

"Why?" repeated Jack. "That puts him right into the heavy Cobeau's Ridge."

Earl stopped looking North for a moment, then said, "Jack, let's track him. I don't think he's gotten far. His feet and leg are too bad."

"Maybe we should," he said.

They let go of their dogs and walked in Danny's tracks. They saw where Danny stopped and lay down in the snow on two occasions. They moved on. He was travelling in a northerly direction. The going was soft. He was sinking badly in the snow. After a mile Jack said, "Earl, he might have left here before daylight. We will never catch him. If he keeps on in the same direction, he will strike Raft Pond. Fred Hoddinott has a camp in there, and for sure he's in moose hunting. So I don't think there's much use in following him any further."

Earl felt better. "Good enough," he said. "But I'm still worried." Then he paused. "Yes, we might as well turn back." They called the dogs, turned around, and went back.

Noah Pittman was moving along the river as dawn broke. He was walking at a good pace by the side of Ben Hynes Brook. They knew where to pick up Danny's tracks. Without tracking him, they would pick up his tracks near the river where he fell in the water. They crossed the river and picked up his tracks. They noticed his tracks were much clearer now. This was due to the fact that he had sunk further in the snow because he was wet. They followed for 200 yards. Then Danny went into the heavy timber and kept following the Ridge.

"Noah, why do you think he's following the timber?" asked Nat.

They stopped. "Well, Nat, there's only one thing I can say and that is it must have been blowing and it was too cold to go up on the open country and he decided to stick to the woods."

Nat looked at the other two men. "You just imagine, boys, I don't like the look of this."

"No more do I," said Noah. "Anyway, let's go on."

The four men moved in Danny's tracks. They followed him through the timber. Then they started to turn and go higher up the Ridge. He had turned at a 45 degree angle and was walking up the Ridge. They followed him looking at every detail expecting to see him at every turn, frozen. But, no. He had gone on. They then followed him out on the open country where they lost his tracks.

It was now 9:30 A.M. when the four men sat down on a barren hill and looked over the country. "What do you think of everything, Noah?" asked Nat. "I mean, where do you think Danny went from here? What direction did he go in?"

Noah looked worried. During this past winter he had been very close to Danny. He had talked to him about his family, about his upbringing. He knew everything about him and about his family. If anything ever happened to Danny, his mother would go crazy. And Barbara, it would almost kill her. "I don't know what to think of this, Nat. I think we're looking for a dead man. We know he fell in the water, therefore he's wet. He has no axe, maybe no matches." He paused. "Boys, this is winter, and on this side of Ben Hynes Brook, there's no cabins, not for me to know about. So as far as I'm concerned, we got a job on our hands. We can't give up this search. But which direction do we search in?"

"I wonder if he turned to his right and crossed the main river and went over around Red Sea Pond."

"No," said Noah. "I guarentee he didn't go that way. I told him to steer about Norwest, when he went from the trail. So if he went in that direction, when he got to the open country here, that put him too far West of the Inner Gulch."

"According to that," said Nat, "he could be over in that valley there." He was pointing to the area to his left.

"Let's boil up," said Noah. He looked at his watch. "I wonder," he said out loud. "I wonder."

"What's that?" asked Nat.

"I only intended to stay in here one night because Nellie is sick, but I got to stay in here. I wouldn't be able to leave Danny Corcoran in here. And for sure he needs help. So we'll stay another night. Someone will stay with Nellie."

He looked over the country. It was almost bare of snow. He knew there was no use in looking for tracks on the open country. They would have to search along the edge of the treeline. If they had some more men they could search both sides of the open country. He looked again straining his eyes.

After they had their lunch they would search the edge of the country to the Sou-West. Maybe he fell to his left. "Hey boys, we'll search over along there first," pointing to the area.

It was a fair day, just a light breeze. The sun was not shining but it was warm. It was still cold enough to keep your ears inside your cap and to have gloves on. They all stood up and moved along the open country to the woods at its edge. As they moved along, Noah thought about his wife and family. What would he do if Nellie died or if he had to take her to the hospital? Who would he get to look after the children? There was Herb and Max. Max was only a year old. Ches and Maude could look after themselves. "My, oh my," he thought. He knew Nellie could not last much longer. To think of losing Nellie almost killed him, the girl he had married and lived with for years in peace and harmony, the girl whom he loved. What would he do? Oh what would he do? What was he doing in here? He should be spending every day with her because each day was precious.

But Danny, he thought. Imagine Danny Corcoran. But can it be true? Maybe he's dead. The thought struck him heavily. Could this be true? Could this be true? Is he thinking right? Yes, it was true. Danny was lost and here on this country, and maybe the worst has happened.

"Hey, Noah. Hey, Noah," said Nat pointing.

Noah snapped out of his thoughts. Right in front of him were two moose. They were out on the edge of the open country lying down. The men walked down on them. Noah jumped. The moose turned quickly and ran in the woods, a cow and a calf.

"We should have brought our rifles, Noah. We could have gotten the two of them," Nat was excited. He looked at Noah.

"Not so likely, Nat. We're lucky if we get ourselves back out of this, because it's going to rain tonight."

They went into the heavy timber and made a fire. This is where they would have lunch. It was 10:30 A.M.

Danny took off his course standing on the bog where Earl Patey had pointed out to him saying that he should go in a northerly direction. And if he stuck to this course, he would strike Hawkes Bay. He tried walking fast along the shoreline near the river but could not due to the pain in his feet. He had his snowshoes strapped to his feet and it seemed like the blood had stopped in them. But he knew they were as loose as could be. They were almost falling off his feet now. He looked at the brush in front of him. He knew he would have difficulty getting through. Trying not to strike his feet, however, he thought, it had to be done. He had to go if he was to keep his feet. He had to reach medical attention today. If not, he knew he would have serious problems. This thought made him very determined. He picked up his rifle and started moving north. He got into the bush. It was just daylight, that is clear. He walked for two hours. He was sinking deep in the snow. As he moved along he felt weak and hungry. But he pushed on. He could not stop to rest. He had to move on. He came to a small brook that was flooded which went to the North East. He tried to cross but was unable to. He then started to follow it. He knew this would alter his course, but he hoped it would swing north soon. He noticed trees marked which were not very old. Maybe it was from this winter where someone had snares out. He walked along the small brook for about a mile until it turned east. "This is not good, he thought. I have to cross this brook."

He started looking for a narrow place. He took out his compass and checked his bearing. Yes. He was going East. He walked a little further and saw a place where he could cross. He sized it up. "Yes," he said out loud. "I can cross here."

On the other side was a high bank. If he had an axe, all he would have to do was cut a tree and cross on it. But the snow on this narrow brook looked hard enough to walk on. He put one foot ahead of the other. First he estimated he would have to make five steps. He walked out two steps, then made a dash as best he could for the other side. His third step proved fatal. He sank to his waist in the cold thick slob. He leaned forward throwing his rifle. He tried to steady himself but found he was falling forward on his face. The snowshoes on his feet would not allow his feet to come back. He reached out ahead of himself with his hands at arms length but could catch hold of nothing.

He steadied himself a bit, then made another effort to lift his feet, but couldn't. The heavy wet snow was on top of his snowshoes. He started to take his weight on his hands. He looked around but knew he could not get back. He felt water running around his waist. He made another plunge forward, and this time he freed a foot. It came up. He made one giant step and plunged towards the other side dragging his other foot behind him leaving a trench full of water. He lay for a moment on the snow half in the the woods. He pulled his legs up behind him, then sat up and looked at his two feet.

He could hardly belive his eyes. "My snowshoe," he cried, then looked back at the hole in the brook where he had fallen in. "I am finished," he cried. "My snowshoe is at the bottom of the brook."

It came to him to get back into the water and try to fish it out but he realized he might have the sling broken beyond repair and d ecided against it.

"Where is my rifle?" He looked around. He saw it sticking out of the slob. He reached out and got it. His compass. Where was it? Panic struck him. He knew where it was. "Could it be possible," he thought. "I am finished without it," he said out loud. "Why did I decide to cross here? I should have gone back and followed Earl Patey's tracks on out to River of Ponds. "My compass," he said, "without it in this area, there's not much I can do, especially in this jungle of a forest."

He was wet to his waist. He was lucky it wasn't frosty, but it was chilly. He sat for a moment and looked at his feet. The pain was gone. The cool water had made his feet numb. But what if it turned to freezing? He would have to take his socks off and wring them out. He had no choice, and he would have to do it now. He looked at his feet. "Maybe if I started walking the water might serve as an insulation." He stood up and looked around. Which way would he go? He knew he was walking North East and that this was the direction this river lay. He picked up his rifle and started moving through the woods. He was sinking to his knee with one foot and was only sinking to his ankle with the other. He was lucky the snowshoe was on the right foot. This was the one where he had the sore leg. He steadied himself, catching hold to every branch within reach. He walked for about one hour. He was beginning to feel the going very difficult. He was working hard. He thought about Nat Johnson, how he saw him walking with the mail on his back. He knew that if this man could see him, he would be looking for him. Then he thought, 'I have been out now for five days. I wonder if there's anyone out there looking for me.' He stopped. "Maybe there are," he said. "I had better size up the situation and make a decision of what I am going to do."

He noticed an open place ahead of him. He walked to it in a hurry and found himself at the edge of a lake. He walked out on the lake and noticed a large mountain across the lake. He looked at it for a moment, then said, "I have walked in a circle. I have walked back to Bluey Pond again. He noticed the valley where he had come out through. He paused. That was two days ago. It was across on the other side of the lake where he had spent the night, and the thought of that made him shudder. It was the closest time he had ever come to death. But now what was he to do? He took his wet mitts off and checked his watch. It was 12:30 P.M. He looked westward down the lake. He knew about six miles from here was the cabin he had stayed in last night. He knew that there he could pick up yesterday's tracks of Earl Patey. Maybe he could find the camp where they were staying. But maybe Earl was lying. Perhaps they were staying in a canvas tent, and yesterday when he had met him he went back and packed everything and left. He stopped for a moment and thought about his personal welfare. "If anyone is looking for me, it will be Noah Pittman for sure, and he will be looking between Hancock's camp and the edge of those hills.

He looked at those hills to the East on the other side of the lake. He estimated the distance across the lake to be three miles and another three miles to the open country. That was six miles to the area where possibly someone was looking for him.

"Well," he said out loud. "There's no use travelling through this dense forest with no compass. There's no use looking for Earl Patey's tracks. He might never be from River of Ponds. So that leaves one thing for me to do, return to Harbour Deep."

He thought about his feet. His boots were full of water. His feet were not paining too bad because the water had soaked his frozen toes. They were very tender. He had to be careful stepping not to touch them. His leg was aching and a steady throb was going up and down his leg, but no great pain like he had experienced earlier. He had no food, just two cakes of hard bread. He had no matches, no light, and no shelter. But he figured he could make the edge of the open country within two hours. That would give him 2:30 P.M. Then he had about four and a half hours to cross the open country to Hancock's camp. He estimated this distance to be ten miles, or this is what they had measured on the map before he had left Harbour Deep. He looked again at the west end of the lake then at the forest behind him, then at the hills. "Yes. My best bet is to go back to Harbour Deep."

He then stepped out on the ice with one snowshoe on and both logans full of water. He gave a sigh of relief because he was going towards Barbara.

Earl Patey stepped off the komatik and took his two packsacks off. He took his axe out of the komatik box. "Okay, Jack, I'll be over in a minute to give you a hand at sawing the wood."

"Good enough," said Jack, as he whistled to his dogs to move and with that signal they quickly moved into hauling position and at Jack's command the komatik made a sudden jolt forward.

Earl carried his rabbits and fox into the house. His mother, who was a tall slender woman, greeted him pleasantly. "Well Earl. I'm glad you're home. What kind of a trip did you have?"

"Not bad," said Earl. "I got over 40 rabbits for my share, and best of all I got a fox."

He told his mother this with pleasure. She saw the smile on his face and knew what it meant. "Earl, that's wonderful," she paused to smile. "What color is it?"

"It's red with an almost white tail. I'd say it's worth $5.50."

She looked pleased and was anxious to see it. She went into the pantry and brought out the butter and sugar and placed it on the table. She put the teapot further on the hot portion of the stove. She quickly had dishes put on the table. "I got some pea soup leftover from dinner. I was expecting you out around this time. Do you want some?"

Earl was hungry. He hadn't eaten since his breakfast, "well. Yes, I want some. I am starving. I haven't had anything to eat since seven this morning."

She looked at him. "How come you never had your dinner, my son?" She looked at him with surprise.

"We left the camp early this morning and went in around Bluey to see where that Ranger went."

She put the teapot down, wiped her hands in her apron, and walked towards him with her eyes wide open. "Earl, what are you saying?" She paused. "Did you say there was one of them Rangers in there? Did he catch you with a gun? What will happen to you now? Oh my. Oh my." She turned red. "Earl, will you have to go to jail?" She started to wring her hands.

"Now, Mother, the Ranger never caught me at anything, neither Jack or Fred."

She sighed, then sat down. "What was he doing in there? Was he in rabbit catching?"

Earl thought for a moment, then replied, "No." He looked at his mother. "No Mother. He was lost. I saw him yesterday. He was asleep on a flat rock. You should have seen him. What a pitiful sight. He is from Harbour Deep. I took him to the Belburn's camp where he stayed all night. He showed me his leg. He had an awful gash in the front. I never saw anything like it."

His mother looked at him wide-eyed. "Where is he now?" She asked kind of looking outside. Her hands hung by her side.

"I told him to stay in the cabin until we came in after him. When we got in there this morning, he was gone. He's on his way to Hawkes Bay. We tracked him a bit but he was gone on, so we came straight home. We were afraid it was going to rain. You know what Jack is like."

She smiled. "Yes, I know he hasn't got the patience to wait for anybody."

"You're right," said Earl.

"Have your dinner. It's almost 2:00."

He sat at the table. "Earl, I'm going to run down to Mrs. Sampson's for a few minutes."

Earl nodded. He knew his mother liked to go and chat with almost everyone in the community.. He was glad she had spent a lifetime raising kids. And now that he was the youngest, she deserved to do as she pleased.

Mrs. Patey quickly went to Mrs. Sampson's house. This was the home of Lucy, the girl that Earl was supposed to marry. She walked into the house with her hands in her apron pockets and sat down. "How are you today, Agnes?"

"I'm fine. I'm fine," she replied.

"Did the boys get home? I thought I heard their dogs barking just now."

"Yes, they got home a short while ago." she said wiping her hands.

"Oh," said Mrs. Sampson. "How did they get on with the game?"

"Not bad," said Agnes. "They got a lot of rabbits. Earl got home with 40 for himself."

"Wonderful," said Mrs. Sampson. "That should do you all spring."

"He got more than that. He got a fox worth $5.50."

"Well, that is good news."

With the sound of this, Lucy came out of the pantry. "Yes," thought Lucy, "this was wonderful," but she said nothing.

"But," said Agnes, "thats not all he found. He found a Newfoundland Ranger."

Lucy and her mother looked at each other. "Why, Agnes," said Mrs. Sampson, "do you mean he found a Ranger? I mean a policeman in the country?"

"Oh, yes." she said. "His name is Danny. He is from Harbour Deep. He was on his way to Port Saunders and got lost. But Earl and them sent him out to Hawkes Bay."

"Why that's wonderful, Agnes," she said.

Agnes looked up. "Earl said he had a bad leg from a cut in the woods. Earl said he is afraid he might lose his leg."

Lucy looked worried. She felt sorry for people like that. "Well," she said. "I hope he'll be alright."

"I hope so, too."

Agnes changed the subject. "When will the minister be here?"

"This afternoon," said Mrs. Sampson. "He always stops by here, never passes. I am expecting him here at 3:00 P.M."

"Oh. I had better go," she said as she left.

The clock on the shelf said 2:30 P.M. She dashed out of the house leaving Lucy and her mother there.

"Well, Mother," said Lucy, "what do you think of that? Finding a Ranger in the country? I mean, a lost Ranger in the country. Did you ever hear talk of that?"

Mrs. Sampson looked at her daughter very keenly and said, "Maybe we should find out more about this before we have anything more to say. You go over and talk to Earl, because the minister will soon be here and he might know something about this."

"Good," said Lucy with excitement. She was dying to see Earl.

"Now, don't stop a moment. We don't know who the minister got with him. They will want a lunch for sure. So hurry right back."

"Okay, Mother," she said and dashed out smiling to her mother as she left. She ran all the way to Earl's house, opened the door, and went in. Earl was sitting at the table not expecting Lucy. His mother was in the bedroom. She quickly ran to him after noticing Mrs. Patey's absence the kitchen. She put her hands over Earl's eyes. He put down his spoon and said, "It's Almeta."

"Hurry up and guess," she said. "I want to kiss you."

Earl jumped. "Lucy," he said. "I missed you this week." He looked into her eyes. She was a beautiful girl, tall and slender. He kissed her.

"Earl, I want to know more, or Mother wants to know more, about the Ranger you found in on the country. The minister will soon be here."

He tried to kiss her again but she stopped him. "First, about the Ranger."

"Okay," he said.

"Hey, Earl, you talking to me?" asked Mrs. Patey.

"No," he said.

"Well, who's there?"

He looked at the ceiling with a quick glance as if to say, what's the use. "It's Lucy, Mother."

His mother came quickly from the bedroom. "Well, Lucy, do you want anything?"

She looked at Earl.

"Mother wants to know more about the lost Ranger, because the minister is coming."

'Well," said Mrs. Patey. "There's not much to it. Earl saw a lost Ranger and put him on the right trail. That's all there was to it. Isn't that right, Earl?"

They heard dogs barking. Earl ran to the window. "Hey, it's the minister. They're stopping at your house."

"I'd better go."

"No, I'll go with you. Those dogs might be bad."

Earl left with her. He walked part of the ways. It was a short distance. Lucy ran to her house and went inside. Earl went back to his house. "Did you find anything out?" said her mother.

"No," she said. "Never had a chance. They came too quick."

"Okay," said her mother.

The door opened and Rev. Griffin stepped inside. He was a tall man and well respected along the coast. He was well known for his ability to travel on dog team. He looked at Mrs. Sampson and said, "Good day Mrs. Sampson. How are you today?"

"I am fine," she said. "And how are you?"

He looked at her and smiled. "I am fine, only it's a bit chilly on that komatik box."

"The weather has been bad, almost everything falling."

"You're right," he said.

"Where did you come from now?"

"Port Saunders, we had to go right in around the bay. We had to cross Big East and Torrent River in a boat. It delayed our trip."

"Will you give me your coat, Reverend," said Lucy, trying to be of assistance."

"Why, of course," he said smiling at her. "And how are you, Lucy, my dear?"

"I am fine," she said, "thank you."

"Well," said Rev. Griffin, "the last time I was here you were going to get engaged. Are you still planning?"

"Yes, Rev. Sir."

He looked at her mother. "You said it was a young man by the name of Earl Patey if my memory serves me correctly. Is this right?"

"Yes," said Lucy.

"Well now, that's wonderful.. What has be been doing this winter?"

Lucy looked excited. She was glad to be able to talk to the minister.

"He has been trapping mostly. He just came out of the country."

"Did he get anything?" This man was very concerned about the welfare of the people.

"Yes," said Lucy. "He got a big fox and about 40 rabbits.

"Well, that's wonderful," he said looking pleased.

"He's got something else, or he found something else," she said with excitement.

"Hey! Hey!" he said. "Don't tell me he's been poaching."

"No," said Lucy blushing.

"Well, my dear. You tell me what he saw or found. I want to know."

She wasn't sure if she should tell him. She felt nervous. Suppose Mrs. Patey misunderstood Earl. But now she had no other choice but to repeat what she said. "Mrs. Patey told us..." she said. "She told us that Earl found a Ranger in the country. She said he was from Harbour Deep."

The minister spoke up. All smiles left his face. He held up his hand. "My dear," he said very sternly, "I just came through Port Saunders and the Ranger is out on a search. The Ranger from Harbour Deep has been lost for quite a spell. The whole Northern Peninsula is looking for him."

They looked at him wide-eyed.

"Lucy," he said, "would you go and have Earl Patey come to this house immediately?" A command was in his voice. "Don't tell him what he's needed for. Just tell him he's needed immediately."

"Yes, Sir," she said as she went through the door.

In less than five minutes Lucy came back with Earl almost on the run. They came through the door and Earl found himself standing face to face with the most popoular and feared man on the coast. He sat at the table with a pencil and paper in front of him.

"Sit down," he said to Earl motioning towards a chair that was near the table.

"Thank you, sir," he said then sat down.

"Now, young man, what's this I hear about you finding a Ranger?"

Earl spoke up. His voice was unsteady with excitement. "Yes, sir, I did find a Ranger. His name was Danny Corcoran."

"That's his name alright. Now, you tell me the story. I want the time you saw him first, where you told him to go, and the time you saw him last."

Earl told him the full story. When he finished telling him all the details, he said. "Okay, Earl, I want you to go to Belburn's right away on dog team and send a wireless for me. You go get your brother to harness his dogs, then come back here. I'll have the wireless ready. Now hurry. You got to be there before six. It's 3:15 now."

"Yes," said Earl as he hurried to the door. He was glad to be out of the presence of this man. It made him nervous to even have to look at him. He ran to Jack's place and told Jack what had happened.

Jack grinned. "Wait till he marries you. There's one thing about the people he marries. They stay together if nothing else, just for the fear of him."

"Why would he have to make a wise crack like that?" thought Earl.

"Start harnessing the dogs, Earl. I'll get the traces ready. We should go up there pretty quick."

The dogs were put in harness.

"Hey, Earl, you better go up to Mr. Sampson's and get that letter. I'm afraid to go over with me team, because if they get where those from Rocky Harbour are, there could be a big tangle."

"Okay," said Earl.

In spite of fear of the minister, he left and ran to the house. He was thinking about Danny. If they had only known they were searching for him, he would have never let him out of his sight. But now it was too late to think about that. He had to do whatever was required of him to do. It was very mild out. He was glad of that. Maybe Danny was almost to Hawkes Bay by now. This made him feel good. He quickly reached the house and saw the minister sitting by the table. He had a wireless message. It was a rush message. It read:

TO MAJ. F.A. ANDERTON, COMMANDING OFFICER, NEWFOUND-LAND RANGERS, COLONIAL BUILDING, MILITARY ROAD, ST. JOHN'S NEWFOUNDLAND. DANNY CORCORAN, NFLD. RANGER, SEEN MARCH 15, 1936. NEAR RIVER OF PONDS. ST. BARBE SOUTH. SHOULD BE IN VICINITY OF HAWKES BAY TODAY. WILL KEEP YOU INFORMED.

SGN. REV. GRIFFIN B.D. CHURCH OF ENGLAND PARISH, ROCKY HARBOUR,, NFLD.

Gill Ellsworth heard the wireless tapping a message to relay. He quickly jumped to the keyboard and put the headphones on. He tapped out "Ready". The goose bumps came out on his arms as the message came over the wireless. "Thank God," he said out loud. "He's found at last. I knew you could do it, Danny."

It was 5:05 P.M. He quickly put the message through to Gander. It had top priority. He put the headphones down and stood up. Two men were at the wicket. Gill clapped his hands. "They found Danny," he said.

The two men look relieved. "Where?" said one of the men.

"Over near River of Ponds. He is gone out to Hawkes Bay. What a relief."

Gill went to the pot belly stove and put in some wood. He noticed it was dull. He reached up and lit the kerosene oil lamp. He sat down and finished filling part of the days work. Barbara was going to be a happy girl, he thought. "All that foolishness about dreams and nightmares. Women can drive you out of your mind if you'd only listen to them. Boy, oh boy," he said. "They almost had me convinced I would never see him again." He shook his head.

He was just going to sharpen a pencil when the keys started squeaking. It was for him. He quickly jumped to the keyboard. He touched the keys. A message came.

"MARCH 16, 1936. TO ALL STATIONS FROM HARBOUR DEEP TO RODDICKTON. HAVE ALL SEARCH PARTIES RETURN TO STATIONS. RANGER CORCORAN SEEN NEAR RIVER OF PONDS. PARTICIPATION IN SEARCH GREATLY APPRECIATED. SGN. MAJ. F.A. ANDERTON, COMMANDING OFFICER, NFLD. RANGERS."

Gill looked at the clock on the window bench. It read twenty to six. It was a dull evening. A blanket of fog was beginning to roll in, but he didn't care now that Danny was found. That was all that matteered. He would have to send word to North-East Bottom right away to have someone locate Uncle Noah and the crowd who were searching for Danny. He sat down and wrote a message.

"TO MR. EDWARD PITTMAN, J.P. MARCH 16, 1936. DANNY CORCORAN SEEN NEAR RIVER OF PONDS, POSSIBLY AT HAWKES BAY BY NOW. WOULD LIKE FOR YOU TO CALL OFF SEARCH. HAVE PARTY RETURN TO STATION. WILL KEEP YOU INFORMED. SGN. MAJ. F.A. ANDERTON, C.O. NFLD. RANGERS."

Barbara sat at the table. She said very little in the way of conversa- only commenting on her school work. Danny was on her mind day and night, every minute. There were times when she thought she would go crazy. She was carrying a heavy load and all the people in the little town knew it. She ate supper in silence with Mr. and Mrs. Pittman. When they finished they sat and talked about Nellie. She was very sick. With Noah gone looking for Danny, it meant Ches was taking full responsibility. They were expecting Noah home this evening. He only went for one night. Maybe he was on his way in.

It was 6:30, time to wash the dishes and clean the house. They heard a dog team.

"A team is coming," said Uncle Edward. "I wonder who it is."

The door opened and Jim Pollard stepped into the kitchen. Uncle Edward grinned. "Hello, Jim."

"I got a message for you, Uncle Ned."

"Oh, a message. Okay."

Barbara and Martha stopped in their tracks and everyone looked at Jim. He reached into his pocket, took out the message and handed it to Mr. Pittman. He took it and turned to the table. He sat down, opened his pocket knife, and cut the envelope open very keenly. Barbara held her breath. He unfolded the sheet of paper and very slowly read the message. His words sounded like the beating of a drum. When he was finished he said, "Thank God. Thank God."

He looked at Barbara. She had tears in her eyes. Aunt Martha went over to her and put her arms around her and said. "Don't cry, my dear. I knew everything would be alright. I am just as glad as you."

She went to her bedroom and shut the door. She was so relieved. She wanted to be alone.

"Well, well," said Mr. Pittman. "All this fuss for nothing. Now we got another job on our hands, finding Noah and the boys. In Hancock's camp, that's where they're at." He stopped for a moment. "Now we got to get a word to Noah. Nellie's pretty sick. I'm expecting we're going to have to get the nurse up here from Roddickton for her. But we got to get Noah out of the country first. He said he was only going to be gone for one night. He knew she was sick. That's funny." He looked at Jim.

Jim was an able man, very strong and quick. He was also very intelligent. He was an extra good fisherman. He had a crew of men when he was young. He was also a very obliging man. He looked at Mr. Pittman and said, "Uncle Ned, what do you want me to do?"

Mr. Pittman looked at him and said, "Do you think it's possible to get someone to go with you into Hancock's camp and get Noah? You've been in there before, haven't you?"

"Yes sir," he said. "I worked in that camp. In fact, I helped to cut the line from the salt water into the camp. I know every inch."

Mr. Pittman looked at Jim then said, "Jim, will you go?"

Without hesitation he said, "I certainly will go."

"Okay," said Mr. Pittman. "I'll get someone to go with you.. When can you leave?"

"Right now, and the sooner the better."

"Very good. I will tell you the reason for going tonight. If we wait until the morning, Noah and them will be gone out searching again, and they won't be back to the camp until tomorrow evening, but if you leave now, you should be no more than two hours going in." He paused.

"Well, it's a pretty dark night. I figure it will take three hours at least, but that don't matter."

"Okay," said Mr. Pittman. "I'll send someone down to tell Susie where you're going."

"Okay," he said.

Then the two men left the house to go check on someone to get to go.

It took Danny a full hour to cross the Northeast side of East Bluey Pond. It was two miles. The ice was glassy smooth. When he reached the shore, he was tired. He walked along the shore until he came to the narrow path where he had come down three days before. He examined the tracks. They were very faint, but they were his. He looked at his watch. It read 1:30 P.M. He looked down the lake, then up the trail. This was it. He had to move. He stepped into the trail. The foot with no snowshoe on it was sinking very deeply. He started walking as best he could. Every step he made seemed like it hurt his foot more and more, but it seemed the pain was slackened. This was due to the water in his boots. He walked on up over the first hill, then along the side of the river. He thought he heard rifle shots, but after listening for five minutes he decided against it. He was exactly one hour from Bluey Lake to the Round Pond in the valley. He knew this was not what he had planned. From where he stood he could see the open country to the Southeast. There were three high hills. The one to the South looked closer, but he knew it was further away. He thought the matter over. "I had better stick to the trail I came over here on," he said. "If Uncle Noah is looking for me, they will be on my trail for sure because I came over on the planned route." He felt a bit secure. He also felt very hungry. All he had since yesterday noon was one cake of hard bread. But he decided he would not eat his other two cakes, so he thought, 'til he got to Hancock's camp. Maybe he would find his axe when he got over there.

With this thought he started walking along the edge of the pond. He noticed he had a terrible limp. The rifle that he had once moved so swiftly doing drill in Whitbourne seemed so heavy now. As he walked he thought of the cobblestone streets near Water Street in St. John's, how he used to run along them early in the morning while getting in shape for the Regatta Sports Day. If he could only run now he would be over at Hancock's camp in an hour. But it was no use in thinking about that here. He came to the tracks where he had come out of the woods three days ago. It seemed like three months. He stepped into his tracks. It was easy to follow because he had been sinking very deeply when he came down. This made it a bit better because the snow was more compact and could support him. This gave him more courage and he moved on.

Noah Pittman searched around Harbour Deep River for most of the day up until 2:00 P.M. Then they decided to cross the open country to the West branch of Soufflett's River and look there. Then they would work their way back to camp. They decided to stay another night and search until noon tomorrow. If they saw nothing then, they were going to go back home. It was a sultry day, no sun shining, but visibility was good and very warm for a March day. They reached the edge of the woods just up from Camping Pond and started walking along the edge. After walking for a mile, they saw tracks of something going in the woods. Nat called to Noah. "Hey, Noah. Come here. Come and take a look at this."

Noah came over where the tracks had been made. "It's tracks from something. That's for sure."

He looked closer, then lifted his nose into the air and sniffed a few times. "I thought I could smell something. Could you?"

Nat did the same. "Smells like smoke," said Noah. "Let's follow those tracks."

They stepped into the woods. The tracks were hard to follow. They went for about 50 feet, then Nat said, "Look at this. It's a snowshoe track for sure."

They looked at it. You could see the shape of the front cross bar. It was where Danny had sunk deep in the snow near a small tree.

Nat spoke up. "I just smelled something. Look there."

All four men stared at the grey blanket. They saw the place where Danny had the fire in. The blanket had thawed and folded over it looked like someone was underneath it. Noah went over to it, stared at it, and touched it with his toe. "Could it be possible that you're under there?" he said. He moved it again with his toe.   He then stooped down and hooked the corner of his axe in the blanket and gave it a pull. He gave a sigh when he saw there was nothing underneath it.

They looked at the area and saw where Danny had broken off bits of firewood. He noticed a lot of burned matches. He knew that Danny had problems getting a fire going. It made him feel better. It was not what they had expected. They were expecting to see a frozen body. How could anyone survive falling in the water in these temperatures?

While they were talking, one of the men said, "Let's walk down to the pond. For sure that's where he went."

"Okay," said Noah. "But just for a look. We got to get off this open country before dark."

They had not walked far when they could smell a campfire. "I smell something," said Noah.

"Me, too," said Nat.

Then they saw Danny's other campfire.

"Well, what do you think of this?"

They picked up his kettle.

"This fire was a big one," said Nat.

"Yes, it certainly was," said Noah. "Maybe he dried himself and his clothes. But why would he leave his blanket back there?"

"I don't know," said Nat, "unles it was frozen too hard for him to carry."

"Maybe you're right," said Noah. "Anyway, boys, this is a ray of hope. I'd say that by tomorrow morning we will find something else. It's only a two hour walk from here to the edge of the hills. I've been out here before."

They looked at the old campfire. "It's too bad we didn't bring the dogs. We could put them on his tracks. For sure they would find him. They could track him. We can't see a track. He could walk on the hard crust and the dogs would track him."

"Yes," said Noah. "But we should see where he crossed the river tomorrow morning. We'll cross the open country further west and take the brook further up about a couple of miles. I saw the map before he left. He had his trail marked out. He was supposed to cross at the upper end of Camping Pond."

They all agreed, went back up to the open country, and headed back to Hancock's Camp.

It was 4:10 P.M. Danny started up the valley. He noticed a large lake below him and he saw open country near the end of the pond. There was Woody Hill Pond. He had to cross a brook three days ago, but now it might be better for him to leave his tracks out of Bluey. With this in mind he turned Northeastward. He travelled on.

His feet were beginning to get cold. His leg pained terribly. Now he was making slow progress. He finally came to the edge of the pond. He felt like he was going to faint. This is due to hunger, he thought. Then he thought of his leg. "You be careful you don't lose your leg," a voice said. It made him move on. He started walking along the edge of the pond. It was slow going.

It took him about one hour to walk the length of the pond. The distance was approximately one and a half miles. He stood on a bog at the end of the pond and looked back. The open country was about one mile away. He started out. His feet were numb with the cold. The air was chilly, and he was unable to walk fast to keep himself warm because of the tenderness of his feet. He tramped on and as the open country got nearer, he looked at his watch. It was 5:00 P.M. He got to the edge of the open country. There was a skirt of trees near the base. He walked through the trees and started up. It was a very bad experience. He was sinking badly, even the foot with the snowshoe on. The other foot was sinking to his knee. With every step it seemed his toes were going to come off. He got halfway up the hill, sat down and took a short rest. He started moving again, finally reaching the top. He looked eastward. All he could see was open country. There was a small pond to the east of the hill he was on and a large ridge to the Southeast. Maybe on this ridge he could see the South West Branch valley of Soufflett's. With this he started down the hill to the pond.

He made a few steps and found himself on the edge of an overhang. He tried to stop his downward walk but he was unable to do so. He quickly fell down on his side. With this movement he started to slide. He let go of his rifle and tried to get his balance. He found this impossible and continued to slide. He then started to roll. He felt himself drop over the edge. He was in the air. He closed his eyes, then found himself falling. He hit the bottom with a jolt. He felt numb. His body was limp and for a moment he just lay there. He opened his eyes and noticed he was on his back. He felt pain. There were waves shooting up and down his leg. The first thing that came to him was that he had broken his leg. He lifted his arms. There was no snow on top of him. He lifted his head and looked around. He felt a terrible pain. He put his hand to his head. The right side felt a little tender.

He noticed it was still light. He sat up, then moved his legs. They were paining severely. He must have struck his head. He didn't know how long he had been lying there. He still had his pack sack on his back. His rifle was nearby. His snowshoe was missing. He looked around, then saw it. The sling was broken.

"Well," he said out loud, "I guess it's not much good. I don't think I'll even pick it up. I'm on the open country anyway."

With this he staggered to his feet, whimpering as he took his weight on them. He picked up his rifle and started towards the pond. He was sinking to his knees. After floundering in the snow he finally made it to the pond.

He looked at his watch, it read 6:15 P.M. He walked straight across the pond to the narrows, then on to the East side. There was a chilly wind blowing from the Southeast. He started up the steep ridge with great difficulty. After an hour he was near the top. To the south he saw what looked like a bank of fog rolling in over the hills. It was beginning to get dark. He knew it was no use to go for Hancock's cabin, because between him and the cabin was a bank of fog. He knew it was only a matter of hours and it would be dark. He looked east and north. All he could see in the twilight was open country. To the southwest about two miles away was what looked like a small bunch of trees. This is where he would head for. This is where he would have to spend the night. The thought of this made him sick. Another night out. What would it be? What kind of a night was it going to be? He looked again at the blanket of fog rolling in. If only he had walked out by the side of the river. He took a quick glance at the small skirt of trees to the southwest, then at the open country in the direction where he had to go tomorrow morning. He thought if it's foggy he would come here and go straight. This would take him to the river valley. He looked helplessly at the open country. If only he had his compass and maps.

As he stood there, just a young boy of 21 years, for the first time his hopes started to fade. And as he thought of his possible destiny, tears came to his eyes. It's a very scary feeling to be alone on the open country with the sun gone down, no food or shelter. But Danny's case was worse. His two feet were partly frozen. His injured leg was to the point of serious infection. He had no axe to cut firewood, and the fog was rolling in.

As he stood there with tears running down his face, he heard a fox howl. It is the call for everything to prepare for the long night, he thought. Then he wondered if Uncle Noah Pittman was out on the country now looking for him. With this he put his partly bent frozen mitts to each side of his mouth and called Uncle Noah. He heard an echo. "Uncle Noah, Uncle Noah." He cocked his ear to listen, then called again. "Uncle Noah. I'm here." His echo seemed to bounce back.

He looked at his mitt, then at his feet. He felt the string of pain shooting up his legs. He wiped the tears from his face with the back of the frozen mitt, then with great difficulty picked up his rifle and limping badly, he started for the bunch of trees two miles away.

Art Compton was in the nose of the komatik and in his hand he had a 16 foot leather whip coiled up. His jaw was bulged out with tobacco and juice ran down his chin. He was sweating. He told Ple he had four extra dogs which brought the team to 16. He said he had stolen them. Ple was delighted. If anyone said anything they would blame it on Peters. This gave him a good feeling, but when Jack Brown told him that the dogs belonged to Uncle Al Hancock, this almost made Ple sick, because Uncle Al Hancock was not a man you could play around with. If ever there was a man you should be scared of, it was him. Ple knew that either Art or himself was in for a hard time when they got back. But they were on a mission of mercy and this could make a difference. Ple was not a man who worried. He just said, "I'll wait until that comes."

It was 10:30 A.M. The sun was shining and after a rainy night the going was soft. Every step was to your knees. They were just upon the height of the country or at least up over the worst hill. They had come up Flyoil Hill and were now on Rocky Pond. Peters wanted to have lunch but Ple said, "No. We'll go on to Big Pond. There's a camp there."

The two dogteams moved on again. Each had a big load. At 12:00 noon they reached Big Pond. The sky was overcast and it was almost like a spring day, but it was only the 16th of March. There was slob on the ponds and Jack Brown didn't like it. "Boys," he said, "if it gets any milder and this water starts running, we could be in for trouble."

Art turned over the chew in his jaw. "Tis going to freeze like guns tomorrow turning off after twelve tonight."

"Yes, I bet," said Peters. "I think we should go back while we're ahead."

No one spoke.

"Or at least we should stay here in this camp 'til it freezes."

Ple turned red. He blinked his eyes and with a high pitched voice said, "I'll tell you what to do, Peters. Now you shouldn't have any trouble finding your way back. You only got to go up on that hill we just came over and you can almost see Englee. It will be great going, all downhill with snowshoes on. You shouldn't have any trouble and another thing, you could be needed back home."

Peters looked at Jack Brown. "What do you think? Jack, what are you going to do?"

"I'm going on," said Jack.

There was a pause.

"Old man, Ranger, you never asked me what I was going to do," said Art, showing his gold tooth through the juice.

Peters knew it was an insult but said, "Yes, Art, what are you going to do?"

Art cleared his throat, then dumped out his chew. "Do you see them dogs?"

Peters looked at them. "Yes," he replied.

"Well," said Art, "before I go home without Ranger Corcoran, I'm prepared to eat every one of them and then turn on the bakeapples because I'll be here until August." He stopped. "And you'll be in here with us, because if you leave here now and go home, you'll go down in our books as a deserter and we'll let your commanding officer know about that."

Peters sat on the komatik box like a little boy with elbow on his knee wondering what would happen to him. "For sure I've fallen amongst thieves," he thought.

"Okay," he said. "I'll go on."

Ple laughed out loud. Jack Brown shook his head. "How far do you think we'll get tonight, Ple?"

Ple looked at his watch. "If we get to the Blue Skirt, I figure we'll do good."

"Yes, I guess we will," said Jack.

"Let's boil up and get going," said Ple. He felt disappointed that Peters didn't go back, but he would have to live with his presence. This he was prepared to do.

Noah Pittman and his party ate a late supper and lay down for the night. Their plans were made. They would go in at daylight to where they saw the old campfires in the snow. Noah lay awake and watched the flickering firelight which on one side of the oil barrel stove, was orange from the fire. He felt warm under his blankets. He thought about Nellie. He knew she was sick. But Danny, is it possible that he is somewhere out there, maybe huddled under a tree, cold and hungry, maybe waiting for someone to find him. He knew that if Danny was out there he was sure that Noah Pittman would be looking for him. Then he thought he heard something, a dog barking. He sat up. "Hey, boys!"

There was a pause.

"Hey, Nat!"

"What?" said Nat quickly.

"Boys, I think I heard dogs."

With this Noah jumped on the floor. He already had his clothes on. He went to the door and stuck his head outside. It was foggy. Then he heard a voice call to the dogs in the distance.

"Yes, boys, there's a dogteam coming. Get up."

The other three men quickly jumped up. They put their boots on.

"Something isn't normal for a fellow to be coming in here this time of night. What time is it?"

Noah looked at this watch. "Quarter after ten."

The fire in the stove lit up the camp.

"Light the lamp."

The kerosene oil lamp was quickly lit and placed on the table. The four men went outside and in a few minutes the dogteam pulled up to the door. There was a commotion. Dogs barking and two men trying to control them brought the cabin area alive.

"It's Jim Pollard," said Noah.

The four men just stood there and said nothing. After they had settled their dogs down and tied the komatik on, Jim came over to them. He was smiling. "A fellow needs three eyes in this fog," he said.

"You're right. 'Tis pretty thick. What's up, Jim?" said Noah.

"Your father sent us in to tell you that Danny Corcoran was found over on the other side, and he sent me in after you."

Noah felt a burden lift from him. "Did he say how he was?"

There was a pause.

"I mean is he alright?"

Jim looked at them. "No. Why?"

"Well," said Noah. "To tell you the truth, I was never expecting to see him alive again. We saw where he fell in the water. We even picked up some of his stuff. We didn't think there was ever any way for anybody to survive from what we saw."

"There's no need to worry about that," said Jim. "He's over on the other side. Your father had a wireless from the head man in St. John's."

"Good," said Noah. "How's Nellie? I was supposed to be home tonight."

"She's okay. We want a cup of tea before we leave. Is the kettle on?"

"That's no problem. Come on inside."

The six men went inside feeling relieved. They would take their time. Danny was tucked away in some comfortable bed in Port Saunders as far as they were concerned.

But little did they know that only a few miles away huddled under a tree freezing and chilled to the bone was Danny Corcoran. The cold fog and Southeast wind added to his disappointment when he found out he had left his only food _ two cakes of hard bread _ on a stump seat in the Belburn's cabin. And now his mind pondered the agony of his desperate situation. His eyes seemed to twitch in their sockets from the pain that came from almost every part of his body. He knew he would not take a chance on going to sleep or even staying still for more than five minutes for fear of hypothermia setting in. He knew this was going to be a long night. He had four matches and had lit a little fire from twigs which he had gathered in the dark from the scrub spruce. There was no heat from it, just a little light. And as he sat there he thought of his mother and how she had taught him to pray.

Chapter 15
March 17, 1936

It was getting light. Danny saw the outline of rocks around him through the fog. He felt weak. His head rolled. This must be caused by hunger, he thought. "Well, thank God, I'll be able to get on the move in about half an hour," he said out loud. He stood up straight from his cramped postition. "If only I had my compass."

His feet pained. His teeth rattled in his head from the chill of the morning. It was winter and he was lucky it was a mild night. It could get to 40 below zero in this neck of the woods and Danny was quite aware of this. The thought put fear in his heart. If only he could get to Hancock's camp. He would make it there without any problems, he thought. "What day is this?" he asked himself. "When did I leave Harbour Deep?"

He thought for a moment, then figured it all out. This was the sixth day. In fact, this was St. Patrick's Day, March 17th. He was supposed to have a party tonight with Barbara's high school pupils. He could think about it no more. He put the thought out of his mind.

He noticed it was getting light. He decided to walk around a bit. As he did, he stumbled and almost fell. He got his balance and walked around a bit more. He had a bad limp. He didn't know which foot to put ahead of which. He was a little relieved after he walked around a bit and got his blood moving. It was light enough to move. He started out in the direction that he came last night. He could see no tracks because on the barrens it was mostly bare ground and ice. He started to walk near the top of this barren. He followed it for a mile. It was now light but quite a bit of fog. He walked for another 15 minutes but could not find the area where he had left yesterday evening. Well, he thought. I might as well follow the lie of the land and he saw a large rock and put two more small ones on top of it. He would mark this place because he might have to come back to it again. He started off at a fairly fast pace, limping badly. To see him go would make any man's heart ache. One foot was completely turned in, and he was walking on the side of his foot. He was also walking on the heel of his other foot, but he made quick steps. He was in such good physical condition, with lots of exercise during the winter. This gave him an advantage over any ordinary man. He didn't know it, but he was walking in a southwesterly direction away from Soufflett's River in the dense fog, but his hopes were high. He thought he was going towards Hancock's camp.

Ple Gillard and his crew were camped at the Blue Skirt. They had arrived there late last night. It was raining hard and fog had set in. Jack Brown advised the men to set their tent up on fairly high ground because it looked like they would have a lot of rain. They took his suggestion and were glad they did. At midnight it began to rain hard. Art Compton was up before daylight. He called Ranger Peters telling him it was a beautiful morning. Jack and Ple knew the difference. Peters got up and went outside. After a few minutes he came back again. He looked at Art without any smiles. Art's face showed a grin and you could see the shine from his gold tooth through the tobacco juice. He was cooking rolled oats.

"How do you want your rolled oats, Peters?"

Peters sat down on the komatik box which was used for a table in the tent. With his elbows on his knees and his hand to his head, he looked a sad sight in the candle light.

"You can have it well done, I mean the bottom part nice and brown. It tastes really good that way, espcially when it's stirred a lot."

Peters said nothing. He knew the taste of burnt rolled oats. Ple, who was half sitting up, said, "Art, what are you going on with?"

There was a pause. Art knew Ple was up to something. "You know the Ranger don't like burnt rolled oats," Ple said with a kind of sneer. "What you should do, Art, is mix up some rolled oats in cold water and give it to him to drink."

There was a pause. Art laughed. Peters said nothing. He took his boots off again and got under his blankets. Ple got up and stretched himself like a dog. He had his clothes on. He slept in them all night. Art and Ple were countrymen. They were not used to sleeping under blankets while on the country, especially when Gus Compton was with them.

Ple went outside and had a look around, then came back in. He knew he had Peters mad, and how. He was happy. "It is not a good morning. Looks like a flood of rain. I'd say we're here for a week." He winked at Art.

"You know something, Ple," said Art. "I'd say we'll have to go out on the grass or the blackberry bushes."

"Yes," said Ple. "We're going to be stuck here for a long time."

They heard Peters sigh under the blankets. "Do you know what we're going to have to do, Art?"

"I don't know, old man. I don't know."

"I'd say we're going to have to shoot our dogs before we get home, because we don't have much grub, and this is only the second day. You can notice the grub gone already, and I'm kind of worried."

Art almost laughed out loud. "Yes," he said, "them dogs of Uncle Al Hancock's should taste real good."

"No, Art," said Ple quickly. "I didn't mean that. I mean we got to start right away eating the dog's grub."

Art showed his gold tooth. He shook all over with laughter but didn't make a sound. Tears ran down over his face. "Yes, old man," he said. "I wonder which ones taste the best? The white ones or the black ones?"

Ple kept a straight face although he wanted to laugh. Jack Brown sat up. He knew what the two men were up to. He would have to distract their attention from the present conversation. "Boys," he said. "Who brought a rifle?"

Both were silient.

"It's too bad. Someone should have brought a rifle."

He knew Ple had one because he saw it. "If you had brought one, I'm sure the Ranger would give us permission to shoot a caribou."

He paused. "Because now would be the time to get a bit of meat before we run out. It would be a great save on our grub."

Ple knew right away what Jack was trying to do. He was trying to shut them up, but before he could answer Art spoke up. "I got a rifle, old man. I got a rifle."

Peters didn't move. His voice sounded hollow under the blankets. "Yes. Go get one."

His answer was flat. The two men winked at each other. They knew Peters won this round but wouldn't win the next one. They quickly put their clothes on and moved outside.

Danny had spent the day going around in circles in the fog. He had fallen down a couple of times and had a job to get up. His two feet were wet. His mitts were also dripping with water. This dense fog was like walking in steam. He was on the open country. He could not find any trees, and it seemed like the more he walked the more barren it became. He noticed the small ponds on the open country were beginning to get water on them. He had to walk around them to avoid falling down in the water. He looked at his watch. It read 4:45 P.M. He sat down and put his elbows on his knees. He was, wet, cold and hungry. His two feet pained and he felt weak. Then the thought struck him and he said out loud, "Is it possible I have to spend another night out on the open country?"

He looked around. He could see nothing but rocks and snow. "Dear God," he cried, "don't let this happen to me."

He was sitting on a clump of wet caribou moss. He looked at the ground with tears in his eyes. He knew this was going to be a long, cold night. As he looked at the ground with pity in his eyes, he saw some partridge berries. There were three or four that had thawed out of the snow. He reached out, picked them and put them in his mouth. For a moment he forgot the horror of the coming night. The berries tasted sweet. He looked for more to put into his gnawing stomach but was unable to find any. He slowly got to his feet with the help of his rifle and for a moment he was unable to stand. He could hardly put his feet to the ground, but slowly they took his weight. "Maybe I can still find woods before dark. At least I would have something around me."

His voice was unsteady. He could taste the sharpness of the berries in his mouth. He looked at his watch again. It as 5:30 P.M. He noticed it was beginning to rain. He walked on and on but saw no trees. He saw a couple of boulders in a small valley. This is where he would spend the night. It was raining hard. Now he was wet through the knees, elbows and shoulders. His back was dry thanks to his pack sack. He got to the boulders and sat down by the side of one. This rock was about 12 feet high and was leaning enough to give him shelter from the rain. He sat down at its base and pulled the hood of his coat down over his face. He prayed out loud.

When he was finished he looked at his boots and wondered what his feet and leg looked like. He knew they were in terrible shape, but the cold water in his boots kept the pain down. The only thing he hoped for was that it might not get cold because if it did, he knew his feet would freeze solid. He wrung his mitts out, put them on, and put them inside his coat. It was pitch dark now and raining hard. As he sat there he thought of his youth, of his days in school, of his struggle to get his education, of the sacrifices his mother made, how she had to go around scrubbing stores on Gower Street in order to put him through school. It would have been better if he was never born. His job helping to unload dry fish from the schooners was better than being here. Then he thought about these poor caribou, how they were almost all gone. It made him feel sorry for the thoughts of not being a Ranger. Then his thoughts went to Barbara. He knew she must be worried, but was helpless. His main concern now was staying alive. He knew he couldn't afford to make any mistakes. In order for him to stay alive he would have to be careful. He would not cross any more ponds or brooks that looked dangerous and be extra careful not to fall down. He would look for berries as he travelled. Maybe he would come up on a lot. This fog and rain might thaw the snow off them. The thoughts of survival made him slumber as he huddled with his head in his arms. He asked himself, "Is there a reason for this?" Then his mind went silent.

It was a foggy morning. Not much of the surrounding hills could be seen, just the dark outline letting one know something was there.

Barbara Gale walked from the steps onto the hard surface of the snow road that led to the school house. Although she was told last night that Danny was at Port Saunders, she somehow didn't believe it for the single reason that he had not wired her. When she demanded to see the wireless, she knew he was not found. It read: "DANNY CORCORAN HAS BEEN SEEN NEAR RIVER OF PONDS." But when Uncle Edward pointed out that every pond over there had a cabin near it, this had eased her mind. He said that if he was held up in a cabin somewhere, it could be a week or more before someone got to him because the weather had been so bad. But she thought, it had been seven days since he left. It seemed like a year. Her mind was not on the road or the school. She had passed the school, and her attention was brought back when she found herself up to her knees in snow from stepping outside the hard snowy road. She looked around. People were watching her. She felt embarrassed but quickly got back on the road and almost ran to the school.

It was late in the evening when Guy Gould returned to the camp on Middle Pond. He had been searching now for three days in the rain and fog. He took his snowshoes off and struck them together to clean off the wet snow. He stepped inside the cabin, and the look on his face was not pleasant. Guy was a young man who knew the country like a book. He had been in this area almost from the time he could walk. He was not a big man, but every ounce of flesh on his bones was compacted with power, and everyone around the West Coast respected him.

He was eighteen but was one of the most dependable men in the Port Saunders area. He shut the door, took his coat off, and threw it on the floor near the stove. He looked into the pot, it was full of half cooked dog meal. Eight other men sat near the table but none spoke. There was a strong smell in the camp. This was caused by the dogs' harnesses and traces that were hung up over the half oil barrel stove. The lamp was just lit and glowed yellow. He wrung out his mitts and hung them on a nail on the post. The skin boots on his feet were all soaked and squabby. He then looked around the camp. "Where's Roy?"

There was a pause. Then Joe Patey spoke up. "Roy's gone out."

Guy put his hands on his hips. His eyes blazed. Then he spoke. "Joe, what has he done? Run away? Or is it too wet for him?"

No one spoke.

"Listen boys, I got something to tell you."

Everbody strained their ears.

"Today I was up around Kill Devil on that bit of country. You know, that bog just below."

Joe nodded.

"I heard 27 rifle shots. It ranged from East Bluey Pond to Lady Western. I checked on a couple of people yelling, but not the Ranger. What I am saying is this, if we want to find him we got to go in over the open country."

There was a pause. Guy picked up a plate and took up some salt beef and potatoes, then sat at the table.

"Now boys, I am mad. We are seaching in vain on the lowlands. Look, there's only nine miles from Middle Pond to East Bluey Pond. You got the coast outside and the open hills on the inside. There's camps all over the place, and there's men all through the area shooting rifles. Therefore, there's only two things. He's either dead or he's gone back in the country."

The men looked at each other. "We got a note here for you. Jack left it here before he went." They handed it to him.

Guy opened it up. It read: "Guy, I am going out to contact Earl Patey and have him come to Port Saunders to hear first hand what went on between him and Corcoran at Bluey Pond. I am going to find out if there are any reports from the other search parties. I will be back as soon as possible. Tomorrow, you, with the rest of the men, search the Pikes Feeder Pond area, Sgt. Roy Hiscock."

Guy struck the table and the lamp almost went out from the impact. "It is ridiculous. Tomorrow will be another day in vain. If I had a rifle, I would go moose hunting."

He pushed back his plate, rolled up the note paper, walked over, and threw it in the stove. "Boys, it amazes me. Here's that man in there on the open country dying, and we're not allowed to even go in and look for him."

The men nodded in agreement.

"Well then, let's go in tomorrow morning over Lady Western and go over to the inner Gulch. The fog shouldn't bother us too much."

The men looked at each other, then Joe Patey spoke up. "I'll tell you what we'll do. Guy, let's search in the Lowlands two more days. If we haven't found him by then, we'll go in over the hills with you."

Guy became furious and walked outside slamming the door. He couldn't wait another day.

Chapter 16
March 17, 1936

Danny spent most of last night moving slowly around under the shelter of the rock. The hours dragged on like years. He was shivering to a point where his teeth made a rattling noise, one against the other. He was damp all over. The rain had stopped around midnight, but it was a dungeon. It was so dark he couldn't see the snow just five feet away. There was no feeling in his feet. They were numb with the cold water, but his legs pained from the chill. He had been sitting down for a while and had dozed a couple of times but awoke with a start just in time to catch himself from falling over. He was beginning to feel weak from hunger. There were times when he felt dizzy, and he felt a pain in his left arm. He knew that his body would break down sooner or later. He had to get something in his stomach. If only he could find a few more berries. He tried to move his toes but was unable to. He was glad it wasn't frosty. It was beginning to become light. He could see the outline of the boulders near him. He was glad. But where could he go in this fog? He got his thoughts together. This was the seventh day since he left Harbour Deep and three days since he had anything to eat. But today, what would it bring forth? He knew he would have to travel. If only he could find trees. At least he would have shelter. He started to move. It was getting light. The fog was even more dense than it was yesterday. He walked upon the barren. He used his rifle for a cane. There was no wind. His feet were numb. He could hear the water sucking in his boots. At each step he took, he noticed his legs were weak.

He had to be careful steppping over rocks. He walked for an hour from one barren to another. He wondered if anyone was looking for him. He stopped and gave a loud holler, then waited. It seemed like his voice travelled nowhere. He yelled again but felt the same. All was in vain. He started walking again. He didn't know which direction he was walking in, but he had to keep going. It was the only comfort he had. "To move, to move," he heard himself say. "Move or die. Move or die." A voice inside him started to say, "Danny you're finished. You're finished. You're finished."

He stopped for a moment, then got his bearings. "It must be lack of food," he thought. He had to fight this dreadful feeling inside of him. Is it possible that things like this could happen? Especially to him. He never thought anything like this could happen. The feeling left him. Then he thought, what was this thing he had just experienced? He felt as if there was someone present. It must be the poison from his leg. He started walking again. He was looking for berries mostly, just following the barrens. He looked at the caribou moss and wondered what the caribou saw in the stuff but knew it was no good as food to him.

Every hole in the country was flooded. There was at least four inches of water over the ice. He had to walk around all the ponds. He spent most of the morning walking around the barrens looking for something to put in his mouth. If only he could see a partridge or a moose. He had his rifle. He could shoot it. But he saw nothing.

It was 12:30 P.M. It started to blow. He started walking with the wind. It was not a cold wind but a little chilly. The pain in his feet was still being numbed by the cold water in his boots. But as he started walking fast with the wind helping him, his feet began to come alive and the pain started to come back.

"Well," he said out loud, "at least I have a sense of feeling." As he went on, he started to notice Juniper trees every once in a while. "I must be getting near some woods," he said. He walked across an open barren and came to a large pond. He tried to get out on it but was afraid of falling on the glassy ice. He walked around. It took him an hour. At the other end there was a bunch of trees. He sat down in the shelter of them and tried to collect his thoughts.

If only he had his compass. He wasn't sinking in the snow very much, just to his ankles. This was an advantage. It was more or less a cushion for his feet. He sat there for an hour, then moved off again. He walked out of the trees and out on the open country. He was on a wide barren. All the snow was gone on it, but there was ice under the moss, and each step made him wince in pain. He still had a bad limp. It was blowing really hard and he could hardly stand up. "I wonder where I am?" he asked himself out loud.

This was the second day he had been travelling in the fog. Maybe the wind is Northeast. If it was he would keep the wind on his left shoulder and move on. This would put him in the direction of Harbour Deep. But then he thought maybe it was Southwest. If it was, then he had to travel with the wind at his back and walk to his right on an angle. It was then he felt more discouraged than ever. He sat down on a rock. As he sat there he noticed something a couple of hundred feet away. It was an outline of something in the fog. He stood up with difficulty and walked towards it. As he walked toward it, he noticed it was a pile of rocks. They were put there by man. He picked up a few empty rifle cartridges. He examined them. They were 44 calibre. He estimated them to be between one and three years old.

It was really blowing. The fog was travelling fast on the ground. "The wind must be Southwest," he paused. "Maybe I'll walk along this barren for an hour."

As he was trying to figure out what to do he noticed he could see a little further than he could all day. Maybe the fog was going to lift. He checked his watch. It was 3:30 P.M. He then sat down. "Maybe I should wait," he thought. "It might clear."

He put down his rifle and lay back on the moss. If only he had something to eat. He shut his eyes and thought of the big sausage his mother used to make. Then all of a sudden he felt cold. He opened his eyes and saw blue sky. With a start he sat up and it hurt. What was this? His head rolled. He looked around. "Yes," he said, "it had cleared up. I must have gone to sleep."

His two legs seemed as if they were paralyzed. He felt the coldness in his feet. He bent one knee, brought it up, and placed the bottom of his boot on the ground. The pain in his foot was not that great. He moved again, and with one hand on the rock near him and the rifle in the other hand, he slowly got to his feet. He just stood there. He tried to move, but couldn't. He leaned forward and dragged one foot forward. "I've got to move," he said, then moved the other foot. He cried in pain. He found himself moving his feet around. How long have I been lying here, he thought.

He looked at his watch. It was 5:00 P.M., almost two hours. He had difficulty in getting his mitts on. They were beginning to freeze. Then he realized it was turning cold. He knew he would have to get to the woods. Where he was he could look down in a valley. This was where hunters waited for the caribou. He then started to walk east. He walked for an hour. The wind picked up from the northwest and his clothes started to freeze. In the distance he saw the outline of a skirt of trees. He walked faster. The pain in his feet was not as bad, he knew what was happening. They were getting numb with the cold water. He didn't know what time he reached the bunch of trees. It was really cold now. His clothes were frozen stiff. He was going to check his watch but could not get his mitts off. He could only bend his arms at the elbows. His pants were frozen except around the knees and hips. This was due to his moving as it froze.

The sun had gone down and the stars were bright. He knew this was going to be a hard night for him. The thought scared him. He looked around for the best shelter. He saw a tree that had partly blown down and stood in under it. His hands pained with the cold in the frozen mitts. He kept striking them together. They made a clinking noise. He moved his weight from one foot to the other trying to keep his blood moving. He stopped for a moment and almost fell over. There was a terrible pain in his legs. The snow under his feet was now ice. He stamped his feet hard on the snow but felt no pain, no feeling at all. It worried him. His fear was freezing his feet. He knew he had frozen his toes and that they were in bad condition, but they might not be beyond repair. But what would he do if he froze his feet? "Oh, dear God," he cried. "What am I going to do? What am I going to do?" He bowed his head. "Don't let my feet freeze." There were tears in his eyes.

There was no way he could even check. His mitts were frozen on his hands and were as hard as plaster. There was not one thing he could do, only wait, hope and pray. His fingers pained, but there wasn't anything he could do. All he could do was try and beat his frozen mitts together. He tried bending his feet at the ankles, but from the top of his logans down it was nothing only one junk of ice. This frightened him. He continued to lift his feet up and down slowly and beat his hands. He estimated the time to be around midnight. He knew his feet were almost impossible to bear. A couple of times he found himself fainting but had to fight to stay upright. His fingers were dead. He knew they were frozen. "If I can only hold on for another five hours. I will get moving again."

He knew the direction now he had to go in. He looked at the twinkling stars. Then the wind dropped out, and he noticed it was beginning to cloud over. It was not as cold. This gave him hope. He stepped outside the area where he had been standing to get a better look at the sky when all of a sudden he found himself falling. He had stepped on frozen ice and fell flat on his face. He landed on his hip. The pain from the blow went through his whole body. He lay motionless unable to even put his hands to his hip. He also felt a pain in his left wrist. He took part of the blow on his
and wrist. He finally passed out.

When he came to he was face down. He slowly raised his head and saw snow coming down. He rolled over and wondered how long he had been there. He didn't know. The pain in his hip was still severe. He pushed himself up on his knees, after a long struggle. He lay down again and rolled over a few times to the side of the tree. He got near it and got to his knees again. He put his right arm around the tree and slowly got to his feet. He then held on with both arms around the tree. As he stood there he looked around. It was snowing very heavily. "What in the world is going to happen to me?" he asked himself. The frost was gone now and it was snowing really hard. His mind went back to Uncle Edward Pittman's saying that evenings clearing was no good. It would be bad the next day. He saw during the winter that this saying was true, and again he was right. He would now have to wait until daylight before he began to travel.

This was his eighth day. He didn't think he could take much more. He would have to make it to Hancock's camp today. If only he could get to the Soufflett's River Valley. Maybe today he could. He closed his eyes. His morale lifted a little. He now longed for daylight.

Art Compton awoke with an urge to move on. He lit a match and checked his watch. It read 5:00 A.M. He quickly jumped out from under his blankets. He opened the tent flap and got quite a surprise. It had cleared up around five last evening and turned really cold with a northwest wind. But now he stepped out into a snowy morning with a northeast wind. He stepped back into the tent and called Ple. "Hey, Ple. Get up. Time to move."

Ple didn't speak or move.

"Come on, boys. Get up. There's not a cloud in the sky."

Jack Brown got up. He walked to the tent door and looked out. He saw the snow that was falling, then said, "Ple, we got to move on this morning. It froze last night pretty hard and with snow, I figure this should be a good time to go up along by Tom's Knob. Maybe we could get as far as Red Sea Pond."

Ple coughed under the blankets. He then threw the blankets back, very slowly. He got up on one elbow. "What do you think of it, Art?"

Art was lighting the fire. He already had a chew of tobacco in. He lit the birch rind and shut the stove door. "Get up, Peters. We're moving." He looked at Ple. "It's sure a good morning for travelling. We might get a caribou today. Come on. Get up."

Ple sat up. "Well," he said, "two nights in the ashes." There was a pause. He looked at Peters who had not moved. "You know something, Art?"

"What's that, old man? What's that?" Art looked excited.

He saw Ple looking at Peters who had his head covered. He then winked at Art. "I had a bad dream last night."

"Go on, old man. Go on." Art grinned.

"Yes. I dreamed we were travelling in a storm and someone on the rear komatik shot off a rifle and shot Peters. 'Twas awful."

Jack Brown warned them. "Boys, take it easy. This is too serious for horseplay."

The two men laughed and shut up. "Get up, Peters," said Jack Brown.

The men ate their breakfast in silence and broke tent. It was just getting light. They started towards Harbour Deep River.

Chapter 17
March 19, 1936

It was getting light and Danny decided to move. He was standing under the tree again where he had spent most of the night. His rifle was stuck up by a tree. He walked over to it. His mitts were frozen solid. It would be impossible for him to pick it up. He had a strap on his rifle. If only he could get the strap over his shoulder he might manage. He put his hand through the strap and tried to lift it but was unable to. His coat was still frozen. A lot of snow was falling. He then reached down and caught the strap in his teeth, put his arm through the strap and used the tree to push the rifle over his shoulder. Then he let the strap go with his teeth. With this done he moved out. The minute he stepped out of the woods he met a strong northeast wind and blowing snow. There was also a lot of snow falling. Visibility was not more than two hundred feet. Danny had planned to go in a southeasterly direction, but now he fell with the wind. He noticed his clothes was beginning to thaw. His mitts were starting to get a little softer.

He was walking slowly, just dragging his feet. He was almost afraid to look down. He knew his feet were frozen. His hands were numb as if he had none at all. There was pain in both arms and legs. As he went, evrything was blurred in front of him, but he continued. He thought he heard something but realized it was his imagination. He walked for about three hours. The pain in his hands was so great he could not stand it anymore. He stopped. He could move his fingers on his right hand. His mitt was almost thawed. His left hand was paining so severely it almost drove him out of his mind.

He sat down and caught hold of his right mitt with his teeth and started to take it off. After a while it came off. His hand came into view. "Oh my God," he cried as he looked at his hand. He could hardly believe his eyes. His four fingers were frozen. He quickly put them down in the snow. He kept them there for a couple of minutes then reached up and put them under his cap which was still on his head. He kept them there for a while then put them in the snow again. When he lifted them out of the snow, he saw ice coming out of them. The pain was so severe he fainted, but the

The Barrens where Danny travelled while lost.

The Devil's Lookout.

Near Devil's Lookout where Danny may have spent nights.

In the area where Danny was lost.

The cabin at Blue Skirt. This is where the Englee search party camped.

Norman Pilgrim standing on the top of Gravel Head near
where Danny Corcoran was lost. (Note the height of The
American Man.)

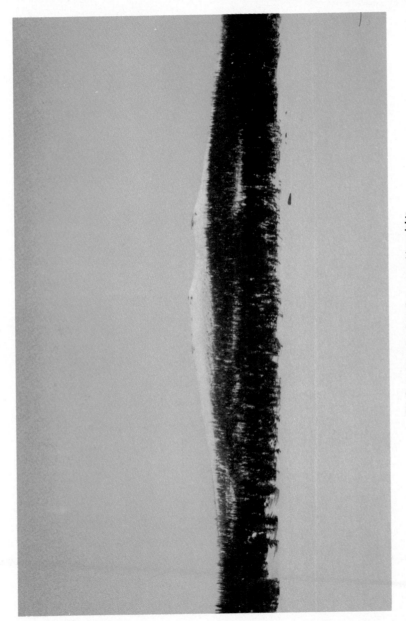

The Copper Barren where Danny spent two nights.

Looking down Souffletts River from the Wolfe Barren. X is where the search party first saw Danny's tracks.

Launching the Pioneer in March, 1936 to go to Harbour Deep to get Ranger Corcoran.

The shoreline of the Great Northern Peninsula during winter.

Iceburg in the White Bay.

Caribou in the summer.

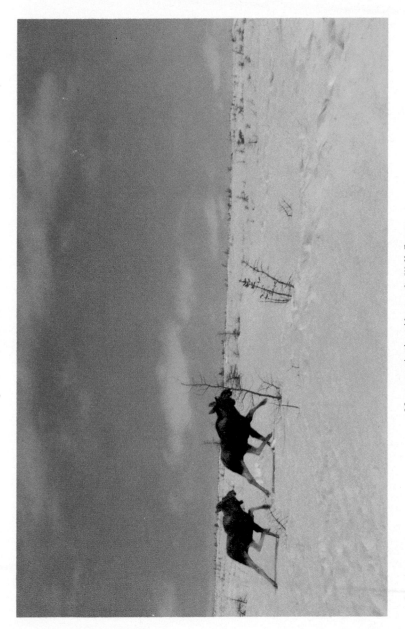

Moose running in stride near the Wolfe Barren.

Shrubs on the Great Northern Peninsula.

Typical dog-team scene in winter.

Art Compton and Uncle Noe (Noah) Gillard in later years.
The young man with the dog is Bobby (Robert) Gillard.

Noah Pittman family. Nellie Pittman is second in from left (back row).
The buildings in the background are where Danny Corcoran stayed during the winter 1935 - 36.

cool snow falling on his face quickly revived him.

He put his hand back under his cap again. He started to move his fingers. He knew he was going to have a very bad hand.

"My! Oh my!" he said out loud. His coat was not thawed so he put his hands inside of his coat. He bent over and started to weep.

He looked at the surrounding boulders and the blowing snow. It seemed like he was out on the open country and couldn't get off. He would just have to stand the pain. He took the mitt that was already off and put it inside of his coat next to his shirt. He could now use his right hand. He put his rifle strap across his chest. "Well," he said, "the next time I take off my rifle it will be in Harbour Deep."

He got to his feet and started walking again. "I wonder what time it is?" he asked himself, as he reached painfully inside his pocket and took out his watch. It had stopped at 5:30. He guessed the time to be about 12 noon. He couldn't set his watch or even wind it up, so he put it back in his pocket. "I guess it doesn't matter, anyway." He reached inside of his coat and got his mitt and put it on. He said to himself in a very shaky voice "I've got to move on. I have to get to Hancock's camp. Where is the valley? Where am I?"

His red hair hung down over his face, the same face that only a few days before had been full and clean. Now it was hollow with hunger and dark from smoke and frost burns. As he staggered on limping with his hand inside his coat, the other dangling helplessly at his side, he knew now that if he were to survive it would be a miracle.

Ple Gillard and his companions including Ranger Peters pushed their way westward along Toms Knob, it was noon. They were one mile east of the distinguished Landmark.

They had only travelled six miles in seven hours. It was not 1:00 p.m. They stopped near a small pond. It was raining hard. The dogs were all in. These were bad conditions for using sled dogs because there was fear of them foundering. (A problem with sled dogs in the spring from pulling too hard. When the going is tough, their hind legs become useless).

They then checked their dogs and Peters wanted to make camp. He was in bad condition. He complained of being chafed from walking. The water and slush was up to the komatik bars. Every brook was flooded. They had to go around all the ponds.

"We shouldn't have left Englee," Peters said to Jack Brown. "Look at the mess we are into now." He pointed to the tent and stove which had been dragging from the sled into the water and slush. "What are we doing still going further in the country?" He paused, "Oh my, Jack, don't these fellows know when to quit?"

Jack Brown was not soft. He knew when he left Englee with Ple Gillard and Art Compton that the word was 'go'. He knew there would be no turning back until all hope was gone of finding Danny Corcoran. "Peters," he said, "what's wrong?".

Peters did not answer.

"It seems to me it's more than the bad travelling conditions that's putting you in a sour mood. I'm beginning to think like the boys now, about going on."

There was a pause. "You know something. Out there," he pointed his finger to the open country that they could not see for the mist and fog, "there's a Ranger out there and maybe he's on the verge of dying and by pushing hard we might be able to save his life. I'm not here for pleasure or to get my fortune. I'm here because a human being is lost and I'm going to keep pushing until we find him."

Peters looked up from where he was sitting on the komatik box and said "Corcoran had no business going in there on a wildlife patrol. He wanted me to go with him, but I wouldn't go. Look now at the confusion he has put everybody into, everybody is looking for him."

Jack turned to him with stern eyes. "Is it possible you refused to do a patrol with one of your fellow rangers and left him to go alone? I am amazed at you. I didn't know this at the start of our trip or I would have never let you come. If anything happens to Danny Corcoran, you know what will happen to you? You'll be hung." Peters hung his head.

"I want to tell you something," Jack said quietly. "Don't let Ple and Art know what you have just told me. They could run away and leave you here and I wouldn't blame them."

The conversation halted when the two men came back. Ple and Art were both wearing oil skin clothes. "Jack," Ple said, "about a mile further up this skirt of woods the Hooping Harbour fellows got a tilt built there. We'll go up there now. I know where it is so I guess we'll move on. Are there any problems?" he asked. He looked at Peters who was still sitting on the komatik box. Then he looked at Jack and said, "Yes, I guess you got problems," and walked away. They each caught hold of their hauling ropes and along with the dogs moved on.

Danny was standing in the driving rain and the pain in his hands was too much for him to bear. He had not looked at his left hand. His feet were so sore he could hardly put them on the snow. He was walking with great difficulty. He knew his two feet were frozen and maybe part of his legs. The thought of this made him sick, but his left hand hurt the most. He raised his hand and saw blood on his mitt. "I must have cut my hand." He looked around for a place to sit down. He saw a rock that was barely out of the snow. He walked to it and sat down. He took off his right mitt. His eyes could not believe what they saw.

From the tips of his fingers to his hand and the back of his hand was blistered. The water in the blister on the back of his hand was about half an inch deep. A part of the palm of his hand was also blistered. The pain was unbearable. He looked at it and wept.

"Oh my," he said, "I'm finished. What am I to do and I am so far from home. Is there any hope?"

He put his right hand inside his coat and wept. "Whatever have I got myself into?" He paused and had to move as quickly as he could to keep himself from falling over. He felt weak. He tried to stare at the barrens near by, but his vision was blurred.

His right hand was in a terrible condition and it looked like it was beyond repairs, but the most pain was still in his left hand. He knew it must also be in terrible condition. He could not even move his fingers and the weight of his mitt was beginning to hurt. He thought if it was any worse than his right hand, it would be better to let it stay in his mitt and rot. He didn't have the nerve to look at his hand, but he must. He had to take his mitt off to dry it inside of his coat because if it turned cold, his hand would freeze again. With this in mind he decided to take off his left mitt.

He brought up his hand close to his face and closely looked it over. Blood was coming from both the front and back of his mitt now. There was so much pain that sweat was rolling down his face. He was never in this situation before. "What can I do?" he cried. "Oh, what can I do?"

He took hold of the mitt and gently tugged it. Pain darted up his arm. He could hardly believe it. "My hand must be crushed," he said out loud. He caught hold of his mitt and clamped his teeth together, then gave a little pull. The mitt moved slowly, just a little. A bolt of pain stabbed right into his heart and it registered on his face. His vision was blotted out by tears and he said out loud, "Dear mother, help me. I think I'm going to die." He bowed his head and sobbed.

After a few moments he finally got hold of himself and started to take his mitt off again. He pulled slowly. It felt as if the flesh was tearing from the bone. Blood started to come. He stopped with his mitt half off. The rain was still falling hard, but he didn't notice it, and during this time he did not think about his feet at all, although his two legs were burning as if he was standing on hot coals. He looked at the part of his hand that was now showing. It was blistered badly. Bags of water were visible. He took hold of his mitt again and gave another gentle pull. He felt himself fainting and had to fight to stay conscious. He gathered all his nerve together, then closed his eyes and pulled his mitt off with a quick jerk. He kept his eyes closed for a few seconds, then opened them. What he saw made him sick to his stomach. Before he could control himself, he fell over on his side and fainted.

There he lay, Danny Corcoran #14 of the Newfoundland Rangers, a man whom his instructors knew would be an asset to whatever part of Newfoundland island he went, a young fellow who just a few days ago thrilled a young lady with just the sound of his voice. A young man who just a short while ago thrilled two old midwives and made them wish they were young again by looking at the life in his eyes. Now he lay motionless and at the point of death in the driving rain on the open barrens, with not as much as a tree or even a rock for shelter.

The rain beating on his face revived him after awhile. He rolled over on his stomach and with his nose flat on the moss, he felt as if a great weight was on top of him. He felt pain in every part of his body. He lifted his head to look around. It was still light, but he knew it was late in the evening. "What am I doing to do?" he thought out loud. Then he remembered the agony in his hands. He sat up slowly and brought his left hand in view.

"Oh my God, what have I done to my hand?". He looking at it more closely. It was swollen to an almost unbelieveable size. Then he remembered it was the fall when his fingers were frozen. He had slipped and fell and broken off his fingers like icicles and without even a bandage. He looked at his hand closer. He noticed that each finger was broken between his hand and the first joint, each finger was cut half off on the palm side. He was losing some blood but not a great amount.

His fingers were swollen four times the normal size, with huge blisters on both sides. About the only thing that wasn't blistered was his finger nails. He knew he was going to have to let the water out of these blisters to ease the pain or he would not be able to bear it much longer.

His pocket knife was in his left pocket and it was impossible for him to get it with his hands as now they were swollen so big that he would not get them in his pocket. He looked around for something else and remembered he had 10 rifle bullets in his right parka pocket. He managed to get his thumb into his pocket and with the bottom end of his coat on his knee, he managed to roll out a bullet. It was of a 303 caliber.

He took it in his hand and looked it over. It was hunting ammunition which had a lead tip. He knew it was not sharp enough to open the blisters. He noticed the roughness of the rock surface he was sitting on, so he took the bullet and scrubbed the tip several times over the rock. This made the bullet sharp and pointed on one side. He then began to push the sharp lead tip into his left thumb. The pain was severe, but he didn't care. He pushed it farther and the water began to run out and he watched as it went flat.

He did the same thing with the fingers on his left hand. It semed to ease the pain a little. He put the bullet between his left thumb and the base of his index finger. With great difficulty and pain, he let the water out of the blisters on his right hand. With this done he felt a little better.

"If I only had a bandage," he thought, but then remembered, "I have a handkerchief in my pocket." With a struggle he got the handkerchief from his seat pocket. Danny Corcoran had quite a task trying to bandage his frozen, broken and blistered left hand.

Twice he stopped and cried in pain. It was still raining and water dripped from the hood of his parka. What would he do if it would start to freeze, he thought. He finally finished bandaging his hand and looked at the weather. It was late evening. The sky was heavy and dark. He didn't know from what direction the wind was blowing. The only thing he knew about his whereabouts was that he was on the open country between Harbour Deep and Port Saunders.

He stood up after some difficulty and found he was very weak. His legs could hardly keep his body up. He staggered and had to keep himself up by the rock. He finally moved on slowly. His coat was soaked with rain and felt as if it weighed a ton. He knew he would have to spend another night on the open country without shelter.

"Should I pray for a clear night, or fine weather? No," he thought. "With that kind of weather would come frost and wind. I would be better off standing in the rain all night, than to go through what I went through last night." With this he started to limp across the barrens. He didn't look like a human being, but resembled a mobile scarecrow that someone had forsaken and decided to get up and walk away.

Guy Gould and Joe Patey sat at the table. They were beat out after a hectic day searching around Pikes Feeder Pond and around Lady Western Brook without seeing anything, only tracks of men moose hunting. They had fired several rifle shots and had yelled and called Danny's name on many occasions, but all was in vain. They now sat and looked at Roy Hiscock after telling him of their day's events.

"Roy," said Guy, "did you intend to continue to look any further on the low lands?"

"Yes," was the Ranger's reply. "Corcoran is somewhere between the mountains and the salt water."

Everyone was silent. They looked at each other. "Night before last we decided that if we didn't find him today, we would go in on the open country," said Guy. Roy Hiscock tapped the table with his fingers and looked at the ceiling. "Is that so?" he said in a voice of stone. "So you've decided to take over," and stared right into the face of the young man, this mere boy. His stare was cold and challenging. But what Roy Hiscock did not expect to see was that he was looking right into the eyes of what looked like an untamed wild animal. He saw eyes of flaming fire ready to strike at him like the deadly fangs of a snake.

He noticed the hands of the young man on the table without even changing his stare and his finger nails almost clung to the wooden surface of the table like claws on a mountain cat. His knuckles showed white through the skin. The other three men moved away. They knew that Guy Gould was a tiger that was untamed, but they also knew the reputation of Roy Hiscock. He was afraid of nothing. He was highly trained and experienced and much older and bigger than Guy.

Roy Hiscock spoke in a voice that everybody understood. "Gentlemen," he said, "I am here on a mission, and that mission is to find the Ranger that is lost somewhere in this area and I don't know where to put my finger on this man. In fact, I am not sure we will even find him, but there is one thing I am sure of, and that is as long as I'm in charge here, I am going to be in control and I mean in complete control. If you're not willing to sit down and be men enough to talk in a sensible manner, then we will have to see who's boss some other way."

Roy was a master at words. He had the technique of handling most any situation. Although Roy was uneasy about this man, there was a lot of talk in the surrounding towns, the only things he saw about him were good. But at this very moment words couldn't change the present situation, and if blood had to be spilled, then it would.

Joe Patey walked back to the table. He turned the kerosene oil lamp down low. He looked at the two men who were about to spring at each other. "Gentlemen," he said, and his voice seemed weak and frail, I've got an idea. What we should do, if you will hear me out..."

There wasn't a sound to be heard. "And you think I want to take over, hey, Roy?" Guy said, in a quick sharper voice. "And you don't want that to happen."

"You are perfectly right," was Roy's reply.

Guy seemed to settle down a little. Guy shifted on his stool. "I know why you don't want me to take over, Ranger."

Roy motioned to Joe who turned up the lamp again. "Put it this way, Guy. When I can't do my job I'll call on you to take over."

"Now you listen here Hiscock. We have been searching the Lowlands for a week now and haven't seen eye nor hair of Corcoran. Hundreds of men have been searching, but no one has seen anything. I think it's high time someone stepped in and had a say in this operation. The reason you won't let anybody else have anything to say, is that you are afraid we might find Danny Corcoran."

Roy Hiscock could take an insult, but what Guy was saying was a little much. "Ah, what's the use," he said and motioned a keep quiet gesture with his hand. He turned to Joe before Guy could comment. "Joe, you said you had an idea. Let's hear about it."

There was a silence and the men all looked at Joe. "Well," said Joe, "I'm going to make a recommendation to you Ranger, and that is to put Guy in charge for one day."

No one spoke. A dog outside made a howl and it seemed that the flame on the lamp jumped like a keyboard. Then Guy spoke up. "I'll tell you what Hiscock. Put Joe in charge. They say a change is as good as a rest."

Roy took a pencil out of his pocket and reached up on the shelf and took down his notebook. He opened it and started writing. When he finished writing, he looked up and cleared his throat. "Gentlemen, let me read this to you please." He tipped the noteback toward the lamp and read.

"Friday, March 19, 1936. Due to disagreement with one of our searchers, and he seems to be influencing others, and to avoid bloodshed, I am prepared to hand over the reins of command for one day March 20, 1936, to Joe Patey."

He read the last sentence very clearly. "I hope that Joe does a better job than I have in finding Danny Corcoran. If they find him on the open country I'll crawl."

He looked at Joe who got up from the table and put some wood in the camp stove. Joe walked back to the table and turned the lamp down a bit, then picked up the empty dishpan, walked to the door, opened it and emptied it outside.

"Joe," said Guy, "you're emptying an empty pan."

Joe came back to the table. "O.K. boys," he said, "tomorrow we'll go in over Lady Western and search the open country around Red Rod Feeder Pond and the Devil's Lookout, and, Hiscock, I'm sending you to check on the rest of the parties around West Lake and Raft Pond."

They all agreed. Peace was restored.

This was the eighth night that Danny Corcoran was about to spend away from his comfortable apartment in Harbour Deep. He had spent two nights in cabins in great misery and had spent five nights under the trees, and out on the barrens, suffering the misery that only men from insane institutions, or men that went through great tribulations in wars, had ever suffered. But today he had an experience that only dead men had ever witnessed before giving up the ghost and had never been able to tell their experience, before the agony and the pain had snuffed out their lives, perishing by the wayside or collapsed trying to hang on.

What must it be like this very moment, to be lying on the frozen barrens with a southwest wind blowing and a stone for a pillow? His legs bent at the knees, he was on his side, his left hand was inside his coat, his right hand was underneath the hood of his parka, which was partly pulled down over his face. The night was fairly light and a few stars were beginning to peek through the clouds. The wind made a groaning noise and moved the little shrubs that were nearby. Although the sky at times was broken, it was still foggy, but warm.

Danny had cried himself to sleep. His mind was a jungle of foolishness. There were dried tear stains on his face, making streaks on the face that had partly turned dark from the smoke of campfires from previous nights. His red hair was no longer neat and tidy. It was matted and streaks were hanging around his bony forehead and partly hiding his eyes. His eyes were two sunken holes. He had lost a lot of weight from almost a week of not eating, and using up all his strength trying to fight off infection. To look at the young man now, at midnight, lying wet to the skin and as if he were barred from the very existence of civilization, all alone with no place to go, to watch him would make the most stalwart man bow his head and weep.

As he lay there motionless, and in the mind that was brought to a standstill, he thought he saw something. He strained his eyes and looked. "My," he said, "what a gorgeous sight. All these flowers." Danny was dreaming. He dreamed he was standing inside the gate of a beautiful garden. And oh, the sights he saw, as he looked up through the garden. He could see the valleys of green and the mountains of blue with clean crystal water. As he looked at it in bewilderment, it seemed so peaceful here. Then he heard someone call, "Danny, Danny."

He quickly looked around and saw someone coming through the gate. It was the most beautiful girl he had ever seen. She was dressed in a light blue dress with red slippers on her feet. She had a basket on her arm. "Danny, I work here," she said. He nodded. "I have come here to pick flowers for my master. Will you join me?" she said.

She held out her hand, he caught hold of it. The touch of her hand made his heart leap. She reached up on her toes and kissed him. Danny looked her in the eyes. There was something in her eyes that looked familiar. He then joined her as they started to walk through the beautiful garden.

"I am not going to pick the white ones this morning," she said. "My master only wants the most beautiful flowers."

Then Danny directed her attention to a flower far out in the middle of the field. It was a different colour and it was very noticeable. They stepped along through the ranks of tulips. He noticed the ground under their feet was like a carpet of wool.

She started to sing a most beautiful tune and it seemed the air was full of music and it was in tune with her voice. She stopped singing then asked, "Do you like the garden?"

He looked her in the face and said, "I really haven't looked around enough yet."

"How much would you like to see?" she asked.

"Maybe I would like to see beyond the mountains," he said, "or maybe I would like to see away up those valleys."

She looked at him and he noticed a large tear fall from her eye and run down over her face, leaving a wet streak on her cheek and a dark spot on her light blue dress.

"Why are you sad, my dear?" he said in a voice that he himself recognized as weak.

"Danny Corcoran, I am sad because this is my master's harvest field and all those flowers have to be harvested. I must get at least one today, but where?"

She looked at him. Then he said, "Look over there."

She tried not to see it and pretended not to look that way, but he insisted she would look in that direction of the beautiful flower. He then put his arm around her shoulder and pointed in its direction.

"I see it," she said. She then turned toward him and he stood there with his arms around her. He reached down and kissed her. She did not respond to him with her lips but her arms went around his neck and with love she hugged him. He felt the wetness of her tears on his face. She then stepped back, picked up her basket and walked over to the beautiful red rose. He noticed some of the petals were dropped and turned dark at the tips. This seemed to make it more beautiful and give one the urge to pick it more.

She had her back to him now. She bent over. He noticed she was having difficulty bending. He stood motionless, watching her and something seemed to grip his very soul deep down. She reached down with a pair of scissors and started with difficulty to cut its stem.

He saw a red liquid run from the stem and unto the scissors, then unto her hand. He looked. "My God," he thought, "it's blood." He noticed the slippers had turned to black cobble shoes and with weak legs she struggled to her feet. She held the red rose in her hand, but before she turned, she started to sing. The music was in tune, but the voice was changed, yet full of melody. The words hit home like bolts of lightning on a steel wall.

> Though like the wanderer
> The sun gone down
> Darkness be over me
> My rest a stone
> Yet in my dreams I'll be
> Nearer my God to thee
> Nearer my God to thee
> Nearer to thee.

Then a strong wind came in and blew the flowers and the wool from under his feet. The crystal lake became frozen.

The girl turned around with the red rose in her hand, when she turned he saw she was no longer the young and beautiful girl, dressed in a pale blue dress. She was an old lady, bent at the shoulders, wearing a long black shawl with a white apron. Her hair was white and a wrinkled face, but the same eyes. Then he remembered. "My God," he cried. "It's you, Granny Newman."

She bowed her head, then looked up at him and seemed as though she stood on the verge of eternity. Her lips trembling with pity said "My son, be careful. God always picks the most beautiful flowers." With this, she was carried away with the wind and the sound of music.

Suddenly he realized it was a dream, that he was alone at night on the barrens, and his condition was so severe he could not think. But then he thought, those were the words of Granny Newman. This was only a dream, but it was true. It was unfolding. This was for real. He rolled over on his back and wept.

Chapter 18
March 20, 1936

Danny came to and realized it was the dawning of another day. He thought for a moment and wondered what this day would bring forth. His mind went to the dream he had last night, how real it was. "What does this mean," he thought. Is it possible this could be the end, that he would perish soon and that his bones would be scattered throughout the country, distributed by the birds and animals?

He sat up straight. His legs felt like two dead logs. Then he thought, "my hand, my hands." For a moment he was afraid to even think about them. His left hand was inside his coat. His right hand was on the wet moss by his side.

It was not getting light. The fog hugged him like a wet cloak and it seemed to talk to him and say, "Today will be your last."

"Oh, no," said Danny out loud. "I'll keep moving." Then for a moment he felt as if he was going to faint. "I'm hungry," he thought. "My nerves are being torn apart. If I could have something to eat, just a morsel of bread, even the food I have been feeding my dog during this winter." He then thought of Uncle Jave Pollard and his cooked munge. The thought of this made his stomach rumble. Right now it would taste like honey.

He could see his right hand now. He lifted it up and looked closely. 'What an ugly mess,' he thought. He didn't think that human flesh could get in such a horrible condition. He thought he could even smell the rotten odor coming from his hands. Is it true? Yes, it was true. He looked closer. Great bags of water hung from both sides of his hands and parts of his fingers looked to be infected. "I've got to let the water out again." He felt pain. He would have to get the bullet out again and open these blisters. He noticed between his fingers were terribly infected, but how would he get his hand in his pocket to get the bullet?

"It must be done," he said out loud, "whatever the cost." Then he thought about his left hand and slowly took it out from inside his coat, where he had kept it all night. It seemed whenever he moved it, a pain tore a hole in his heart.

It was daylight now and the melting snow around him gave him a chilly feeling. His hand was still wrapped in the handkerchief he had used for a bandage. It was full of blood and it looked like a blood pudding he had seen in the mess hall in Whitbourne.

His hand was swollen out of proportion. His fingers were at a very funny angle. They throbbed with pain. High blisters were on them now and on the back of his hand. He touched the bandage and found it had a spongy surface. Around the edges it looked dark yellow. He knew from the look of things that the bandage was stuck in the blisters.

To hold on to some sharp object with his fingers seemed to be impossible but it had to be done. He thought for a moment he was going to faint and he had to rest on his right elbow to steady himself. For a moment he closed his eyes until the dizziness passed. Then he sat up again with difficulty and tried to get his hand in his pocket. It was a very painful experience. He got his fingers partly in, but a big blister on the back of his finger prevented him from getting his hand in.

He pushed again, turning his hand. A sharp pain seemed to make sparks fly from his eyes. His hand went down in his pocket, felt the bullet and pulled it out. He quickly noticed what he had done. The skin on the back of his fingers was pushed back to his hand. Water and yellow like substance was running down his fingers. It was bleeding.

"I'm finished," he thought. He looked at his surroundings, then bowed his head and with tears in his eyes he prayed. "Please, dear God, give me courage. I'm about to fall by the wayside and I'm in trouble. It seems like the whole world is against me. Please help me. Amen."

He wiped his eyes with the sleeve of his coat, then punctured the blisters around the edge of the bandage. He watched as the water and blood ran out of his hand. The bandage became loose. He put the bullet on his left knee and put his left wrist on it holding it firmly, then let the substance out of his right thumb.

He pulled up his pants legs and looked at his legs above his boots. His socks were not visible, but above the logan tops his legs were horrible to look at. His feet and legs were frozen almost up to his knees. They were completely blistered and swollen. He took the bullet and slit the blisters open. What a mess!

When he saw it, it gave him a funny feeling. He thought for a minute he heard something, "You be careful. You could lose that leg."

He put his hands to his face and smelled the stench of rotten flesh. He quickly pulled down his pants legs and lay back in the caribou moss.

The rain had stopped and the fog was lifting. He shut his eyes and in a hail of pain he collapsed and lay motionless.

The rocks covered with barnacles were perched around the barren like headstones that some of the English writers had written much about, when describing some one-legged pirate captain, coming out of the grave with a patch over his eye, about to avenge his death of some jealous mutineer. The moss around the rocks was a light brown shade and it looked ready to roll up Danny Corcoran and seal him for time and eternity, but no.

Guy Gould, Joe Patey and two other men reached the top of Lady Western Hill. They sat down. "What do you think, Joe?" asked Guy.

Joe stood for a moment, then sat down. All the snow was gone on the top of the hills and they sat down on the side of a two foot wide caribou trail. It showed no signs of wildlife and had not been used for years. It was now one of the main arteries for poachers. "It's pretty foggy, but I think it's lifting," he said.

Guy looked at him. "Don't sit down, Joe. Let's move on."

"Now take it easy, Guy. 'Tis pretty rough going for me. I think I'm going to wait here till it clears."

Guy pulled down his eyes. "Let's walk into the inside part of the hill. We'll do a lot of hollering in there and maybe he might hear us if he's in there."

"Okay," said Joe. He stood up then picked up his lunch bag. "When we get in to the edge, I think we'll lunch."

"Sounds good," said Guy.

It was a half hour walk across Lady Western and from where they stood, they could see a lot of the open country under the fog. There were three piles of rocks built up on the edge of the hill. They were called "Amercian Men". They were there as a marker for poachers coming out of the country when it was foggy and in snowstorms. It is said that even the dogs from Port aux Choix knew these three marks.

"I think, Joe, we'll go over on the Devil's Lookout after we have lunch," Guy said. "If 'tis any place a lost man would be, 'tis around there because it's a remarkable looking place."

"Maybe so," said Joe, "but I wouldn't go there. The name is enough for me. I've heard it said that the old people wouldn't go handy to the place. I think we should go in around there and look around."

Guy started to laugh. "Imagine Joe Patey afraid. You've heard too many granny's wrinkles."

"Okay, okay," said Joe, a bit impatient for some kettle tea. "Let's get a fire going, boys," he said. He looked at his watch. It was 9 a.m.

"Danny Corcoran. Danny Corcoran. Hello. Hello." Guy's voice sounded flat and hollow in the fog. This was big country up here. It was barren as far as the eye could see.

"You're wasting your time roaring out up here, Guy. Save your energy until we get further in the country. If he was anywhere here, he would be up on top of the hill."

Guy stopped and took his hands down from his mouth. He could tell, by the flatness of his sound, that Joe was right.

They quickly had their lunch and were moving again at a fast pace. The fog had lifted a bit and you could see down the country. It was warm and snow stuck to their wooden snowshoes. They had to walk around all the ponds due to the flooding. The sides of every barren were covered with snow and overhung like great waves, caused by winter drifting.

Around 10:30 a.m. they walked across the top of the Devil's Lookout. This barren, windswept cliff looked like the skull of a great giant that had turned black in the blazing sun, and it gave Joe Patey the spooks at even the thought of coming up here. He wouldn't be here, only Guy had insisted, telling him he didn't care even if the devil himself was up there. The light brown moss up there was like a carpet of sponge. It was warm and the fog was just over their heads, giving him a feeling that the sky was about to fall on him. It seemed to him that they were on top of the world.

Guy was ahead. He climbed upon a large boulder, about twelve feet high and looked around. They put down their packsacks and took off their snowshoes and had a good look around in all directions. They saw nothing. "This is a queer place," said Joe. "I'm not going to spend very long up here."

Guy laughed, "To me this is no different than the old man's kitchen,". he paused. "If anything is going to grab me and carry me off, I figure it will be something with brass buttons on it, and instead of going to hell, I'll be going to St John's."

Joe had to laugh. He was glad there was only one Guy Gould. "Now you can do your yelling," he said to Guy.

Guy put his hands up to his mouth and looking southwest, sucked in a chest full of mountain air and gave a loud roar . . .

Danny was trying to pick his way around a small pond. He was walking in slob water to his knees. He was finding a bit of relief. The cold water was helping to kill the pain in his feet. Although his feet were numb, each time they touched the surface the pain would be so severe he would groan.

When he got to the end of this small pond, he felt very weak. He walked to the side of the pond near a huge snow drift and sat down for a while. He sat with his elbows on his knees unable to think straight. Then he lay back, still unable to think straight. 'What can I do next?' he asked himself. He was motionless.

"Hello, Danny Corcoran," a voice said very clearly. Danny sat up with a jerk. "It's my name. Somebody is calling my name," he said with excitement. "Hello," he called. Then staggering to his feet he called again, "Hello." His voice was roach and squeaky. He called again, "Noah, Noah."

Then he heard, "Danny, Danny, hello."

Danny shook himself. I am not dreaming, then kicked the snow, that hurt his foot. "It's somebody," he said and called again.

There were two high cliff rocks on the Devil's Lookout. Guy stood high on one and looked down in the valley a couple of times. They heard a voice call, "Hello."

Guy turned to Joe, "Did you hear that?" he said. "That's a man."

Everybody's attention was focused to the southwest. Guy called again, then another reply. "That's him," said Guy all excited.

"I have a funny feeling," said Joe. "They say everything happens here on this spot."

Guy looked at Joe and his stare was not pleasant. He called again and another reply.

"Do you know what you're doing, Guy? You're waking up all the crows in the country."

Guy put his hands on his hips and looked at him. He couldn't believe Joe Patey could be so stupid. Image calling that sound a crow. "Joe, that is a man calling."

They listened and heard more sounds coming from the southwest. "Hear that?" said Joe. "That's Noah."

They listened again, not even their breathing was heard. A deathly silence capped the top of the Devil's Lookout. Then, "Noah," again.

"Hark," said Joe. "I told you that's the sound a crow makes. I've heard it before. Sometimes they'll answer you back, too."

"Boys, I have something to tell you," Guy said, then paused. "Let's walk over there and check it out." Guy himself felt a little bit spooked. It was weird.

"Not me," said Joe. "You can, if you want to, but for me, I'm going straight back to Lady Western. 'Tis half past eleven now."

"Maybe you're right, Joe," said Guy, "but if I was here alone, I'd be heading out for the gulch over there right now." He pointed with his hand where the sounds came from. Then all four men turned and headed back to Lady Western.

Danny didn't know what to do. He had called until all of his strength had gone, but after the first ten minutes, there was no reply. He sat down again and began to cry. There was so much pain in his hands and feet that it made his head throb. Just then the sun came out. He wiped his eyes with the sleeve of his coat. He noticed the fog still hung low, but was being pushed away by the sun's rays. Danny shaded his eyes with his right hand and looked around. He was down in a hollow. He knew he would have to move to higher ground and to move now was a great burden to him.

The sun told him it was about noon from its position in the sky and if he walked towards it, he knew he would be walking south. He was sure this would be in the direction of Harbour Deep. Maybe he was near the Souffletts River.

It was late evening. The sun was about an hour and a half high. The snow was soft. It seemed like the snow on the side of every hill was going to slide down into the valleys. Danny came to a small pond on the back side of the Wolfe Barren. His plan was to walk to the top and have a good look out the valley. He walked around the small pond with great pain, groaning as he went. Everytime he put down his feet he winced in agony. His two hands were terribly infected by now. He started up the hill, falling after every dozen or so steps. The snow was soft and he was sinking in the brush, sometimes very deep. His determination drove him on and finally he reached the top.

His eyes pained severely from snowblindness and he could not look without shading his eyes with his arms. Water streamed down his face. As he reached the top he felt himself fainting and lay down motionless. Then he thought he smelled something and for a moment everything around him blazed with bright lights. He sat up shading his eyes. "What is this? What is this?" he said aloud.

He looked along the horizon with bloodshot eyes. He could hardly believe himself. He saw someone walking. He tried to move, but he couldn't. He blinked his eyes, but couldn't clear his vision. Everything was blurred. He called, "Help". He then saw a whole lot of people. They were going into a building. He focused his stare on the building. Then he said half screaming, "It's a hotel, the Newfoundland Hotel. I'm home! I'm home!"

He got to his feet and without feeling any pain ran to the door with both hands out in front of him, reaching as he plunged forward. The street. How good it was to be on a street again, he thought as he ran toward the hotel. Then all of a sudden the first part of his body that hit the rock was the tips of his fingers. The roughness of the square large rock tore the flesh that was infected and blistered off his hands.

The handkerchief which was on the left hand, wrapped around his broken fingers came off and took with it two of his fingers, leaving the other two dangling. The flesh on the backs of his fingers on his right hand was torn to the bone. He struck the solid rock with his chest. The jolt knocked him senseless and there he fell in a heap, in a pool of water, and it's only a miracle he didn't drown. Maybe it would have been the best thing. This dying ranger now was lying unconscious here alone on the top of this hill, with no one to pity or even lift a helping hand or give him a morsel of bread.

Where he lay was in the trail of caribou, that had been worn deep over the years, but now had been covered with moss. No tracks now were visible because man had almost wiped out this beautiful animal due to senseless slaughters.

As he lay there on his side, partly in the water, the evening sun shining on him, casting a shadow, his breathing was slow and his mind was a blank. The only one watching was the great God, who was permitting this to happen.

Six hundred miles away in a humble home, sat a silver haired woman with her hands holding her head and groaning in agony. Tears ran down between her fingers. She wept and shook as if her heart would completely leave her body. "Danny, my Danny," she cried. "Will anyone search for Danny?" She started to cry again. The commanding officer sent her a note this afternoon telling her not to worry. Danny would be alright and that he could be holding up in some cabin in the dense forest of Hawkes Bay and it could be another few days yet, maybe before he could be found. "Everything was okay," he said, but the newspaper said, "Danny Corcoran has not been found and the weather in that area hasn't been good and the forecast is bad for the next three to four days. Fear is expressed for his safety."

She thought about this. She had a bad feeling that something was dreadfully wrong. Her two hands were numb to her elbows. They had never been like that before. Her oldest son, Bill, told her it was worry that was causing it, but she had the feeling it was something more. Her feet and her legs up to her knees were like flaming fires. She had not slept now for three nights. The pain was too great. She looked out the window at the south side hills of St. John's and her mind went back to the days when Danny was a boy.

You would hear him coming, whistling a tune. He would holler out "Hey mother, I'm hungry." The neighbours would all come to the doors and want him to come in. Some of the elderly women would call his name and wave. His Irish Setter would run to him barking. The whole street would seem to come alive when Danny stepped on the scene. But now sat this elderly woman, bent in sorrow. She knew something was wrong and as darkness cast its shadow over the land, she dropped her head and wept again.

Danny sat huddled, shivering, trying to control his teeth that were rattling against each other. He had lost a lot of blood. The last thing he could remember was running towards the hotel asking people to let him in, when he saw a huge flash of light and fell down on the doorstep. But now he realized he was still lost, hungry, and in a worse condition than ever, here alone. But how real was that hotel! He could hardly think of it. He had read of men that had been lost on deserts who had seen springs of water and had run and thrown themselves into them, only to find themselves face down in burning sand.

Danny knew what it was all about. He had seen a mirage, but usually in the stories he had read, these men were near the end, but not him. He was not going to die here on these snowy barrens of the Long Range Mountains. No sir. He would get to Harbour Deep if he had to crawl. He looked at his hands. The right had the skin off the back of his fingers. He noticed the infection was gone and it didn't pain as much. His left hand was in bad shape. The two smaller fingers were gone. His hand was swollen. The bleeding had stopped. "I can live with this," he said out loud as he clamped his jaw tight. The muscles in his face pained, but his feet, this was his real problem. He could hardly put them to the ground now. It seemed that even when he looked at his logans, it increased the pain.

But regardless of pain and hunger he knew he had to move on. He looked up on the trees around him. "It's dawning. It looks like it is going to be a clear day." It had not frozen at all last night. As he looked up he could see the top of the Wolfe Barren. Then he realized where he was. He was near the pond under the Wolfe Barren . He was now in the Soufletts River Valley. His courage seemed to give him strength. His rifle was still on his back. How he had gotten from the top of that barren to this position, he didn't know. He looked through the trees and saw the pond. He would have to cross it and pick up his tracks on the other side. It would only be a short distance to Hancock's camp.

He looked with pain at his feet that were lying flat out in front of him. For a moment he was afraid to even attempt to move them. But he had to move them. He had to get going. With this in mind, he started to move his legs. He rolled over on his face and pushed himself up with his right hand. With great difficulty he finally got to his knees. Oh what pain! He thought for a moment he was going to faint again. He had to hold on to a tree that was near him. He reached up with his right hand and caught hold of a branch and gradually pulled himself up. He howled in pain as his feet gradually took the weight of his body.

"I just have to get moving," he said, as he clenched his teeth. For a moment he stood there and reeled like a man in a daze. Any normal man would have collapsed and fallen in a heap, but the will to live and the will to move on towards Harbour Deep, combined with the tremendous athletic condition this young ranger was in, made him stay on his feet and move out.

He noticed the pond was covered with snow about a foot deep as he stepped out on its edge. He was sinking past his knees in places. Water was between the snow and the ice, but the water didn't matter. He was wet now anyway. He slowly trudged out on the pond. He got halfway across and started staggering. He fought to keep himself steady. He noticed the island in the middle of the pond. This was near where he had frozen his feet after falling in the water. He went across to the other side. When he got to the shore, he sat down and looked back in his tracks. On the pond they looked like black marks on a white board. He looked at the Wolfe Barren. The sun was coming up. This was going to be a warm day and he knew travelling was going to be difficult, due to the melting snow.

He had lost his mitts somewhere but it didn't matter. It was warm and he hoped to be in Hancock's camp by this evening. With this thought in mind, he struggled to his feet again and moved in through the woods.

Chapter 19
March 21, 1936

Art Compton awoke. It was still dark. He lit a match and looked at the clock. It was 4:30 a.m. He got up and lit the fire.

"What kind of a morning is it, Art?" asked Jack Brown.

"Haven't looked out yet," said Art, with a kind of a sarcastic attitude. He had been mad now for two days. Stuck in one place for three days was not Art Compton's way of life. He stuffed his mouth full of dark beaver tobacco and went outside.

Jack Brown laughed to himself. "When you get all of that dirt gone that you are chewing, I will be a proud man." He rolled over and pulled the blanket back over his head. "Not much use getting up yet," he said. "Won't be daylight for another hour." He heard the dogs barking then Art came back in.

"We're moving, boys. Let's try and get up to Red Sea Pond I think it's stiffened up a bit overnight." He paused. "Come on, Peters, get that fat frame of yours up off the broad of your back. You must have bed sores by now."

Peters groaned and rolled over on his side and mumbled under his breath.

Ple motioned for Art to be quiet. Then he waved his hand and whispered to Art, "Get the dogs in the tent."

Art lit up and grinned and nodded. Jack Brown jumped out of bed, "Oh, no, you don't," he said. "The first one comes through that door, I'm shooting him."

Ple laughed. "Well, Jack, put Peters out with the dogs," he said.

Jack said nothing. He knew Peters would have a nervous breakdown. "We'll move today," said Jack, "even if it's only a hundred yards."

"You're right," said Art.

"You know something?" said Ple. "This is the first day of spring, March 21."

Art took the cover off the woodstove and unloaded a mouthful of tobacco juice in it. "I got spring in me bones, old man. I got spring in me bones. Let's get going. We don't need breakfast. We got to find Corcoran."

The light from the lantern cast a large shadow on the tent roof. "The only place I'm going is towards Englee". The voice sounded flat and had a quiver to it, and although the words came from a man of authority, it lacked all the substance of a command.

The three men looked at the form covered with blankets, then looked at one another without saying anything.

"Do you hear me? We're going back home."

"Jack, put the kettle on," said Ple. "Art, you start getting the dogs harnessed and traces ready." He paused. "Now here's what we're going to do."

He spoke kind of loud. "Harness them three dogs of Uncle Al's and two of ours. Get them ready and hook them up to my komatik and put Jack's riding box on it."

Art looked pleased. "Good enough," he said.

"Listen here," Peters said. "I want to go back home. We're soon going to run out of food."

Jack Brown knew what was coming, but kept his mouth shut.

"You're going home Peters as soon as Art can get a dog team put together for you, because I got a feeling that if you wasn't here on the country, the weather would be alright. You got us jinxed."

Peters at up. He looked wide eyed at Ple. "Who me?"

"Yes, you," said Ple.

"What have I done?"

Ple looked at him furiously. "What have you done, Peters? Ever since we left the battycater (frozen edge of ice along shoreline) in Englee there has been nothing but trouble with you. I've had enough. I can't take any more. You don't like the grub. You don't like the weather, nor the country. You don't like dogs. You don't like Danny Corcoran and I don't expect you to like us. What amazes us is why you don't want to look for someone who is lost. What do you think the government is paying you for? I don't know how you got a job as ranger."

Peters lay back.

"But you can go back if you want. There's only two people you like Peters, and that's Rodrick and yourself, and between us, when I get back, I'm going to tell this story to the right people."

Peters laughed. "If there's any stories to be told, I'll tell them," he said.

"But," said Ple, "the story is about yourself. How we had to send you home, bag and baggage to stop your crying, and home you're going. This is final."

Before Peters could complain, or even answer, Art Compton started laughing. He sat down on the box and really laughed. "We can't do it, Ple. We can't do it."

"Oh, yes, we can," said Ple. "Can you imagine him going in Englee with Uncle Al Hancock's dogs."

Jack Brown began to laugh also and said "Maybe, Peters, that's what you need, a sudden bring up. I got no other choice, only agree with Ple and Art. You should be sent home, but if we did you would never be seen again, and we would be put down for murder. So I guess we got no other choice, but to drag you along. You see Peters, you are a drag and you'll get no more sympathy from me. Imagine. Since you came on this trip, you have never gotten any wood or water for the camp. We have cooked all the dogs' grub. You have never yet offered to cook a bite. We almost have to challenge you every morning to get you out of bed and you complain almost every moment. On top of all of this, you don't want to look for your fellow ranger. What kind of man are you?"

With this, Peters hung his head. For a moment he sat speechless, then he said, "Please give me another chance."

With these words, Art and Ple went outdoors. It was getting dawn. "Take down the tent," Ple said to Art. "We're moving."

Jack Brown looked at Peters and his look carried the full weight of disgust. He didn't speak but Peters knew what it meant. "Why do they hate me, Jack? I haven't done anything."

Jack Brown didn't reply to this question.

"Do you think I could make it home alone on dogs?"

"No," was Jack's flat reply.

"Will you come back with me? Oh, come on. Let's you and me get back out of here. Let them two crazy men search all they want for Corcoran." He paused, then added, "I can prove that they're crazy. For instance they were out in the driving rain looking for Corcoran and the other night 12 o'clock the two of them walked up on Toms Know roaring at the top of their lungs like mad men. The dogs even went wild and when I complained, Art threatened to set the dogs after me."

Jack poured a cup of tea. He was mad.

Peters spoke again. "Corcoran is in Port Saudners by now. I don't even know why we're in here. Jack, I've had enough. Why don't you and I go back?"

Jack Brown looked over at him and said, "I volunteered to come here. You came because you were ordered to do so, but listen, we are going on up the country to look for Corcoran. That is what we set out to do."

"Even if you die on the way?"

"I don't know what you're so upset about. What do you want to go back for? We have plenty of food and we're not lost. No one is sick and your salary is still going on. Is it possible you don't want Danny to be found?"

Peters said nothing. The light from the lantern made his face look round and white.

"Every day," said Jack Brown, "I am beginning to dislike you more and more. I don't know much about your background, but judging you by the way you've performed on this trip, from the time you left Englee, up until now, I'd say your people had a lot of trouble raising you."

Jack felt bad having to say this to him. He awaited his reply, but the barking dogs indicated Ple and Art were about to enter the tent. He kept quiet.

"Okay, Peters, we're getting the dogs and komatik ready. We're going to give you three of my dogs and my leader. He'll take you home. Get out of the bunk old man, you got my stomach turned," said Art, as he hawked out his chew and threw it in the stove.

Peters turned even whiter than ever. He stood up. "If I was near a jail, I'd lock you up." He clenched his fist.

Art Compton feared for neither man nor beast. Peters did not know his background. The Comptons of Englee were tigers and Art was known as the tiger of the bunch.

"So you would have me locked up in jail for gettin you out of the bunk, eh, Peters? Well I got some news for ya." He paused, tension mounted. Jack Brown felt nervous. If Peters had the guts to fight, to stop Art, he knew would be impossible.

But Ple stepped in. "Boys," he said with a grin and a squeaky voice. He had a very satisfying look on his face. "'Tis just dawning and I wouldn't want this day to start out on any better note than to see Peters get his front teeth knocked out, but 'tis hardly light enough yet and if you fought now, me and Jack would miss some of the fun. Why can't we wait until we get back to Englee. I'd like for Bob to see this." (Bob was Ple's younger brother.)

Peters sat down. He put his hand to his head. "Rodrick said I was crazy to even attempt to come with you fellows. He told me there would be trouble, that you didn't know when to quit. I asked you for another chance," he said. Then he looked up. "How about it?"

"Okay," said Ple, "but you have to agree on one thing."

Peters looked at him wide eyed, wondering what great thing he would have to do now. He knew his back was against the wall. "Okay, I agree. What is is?"

Ple pointed his finger at him. "Keep your mouth shut and speak only when you are asked a question."

He looked relieved, "Good enough," he said.

"Let's move," said Art.

Jack Brown blew a sigh of relief. "Yes," he said. "Let's get out of here." Then the barking of the dogs and the red glare of the sun's rays brought everything alive.

"Barbara, get up my dear. It's 7:30," said the soft voice of Aunt Martha Pittman. "Breakfast will soon be ready."

"I'm up, Aunt Martha," said Barbara. Her voice sounded weak.

Aunt Martha walked back into the kitchen. She stood for a moment in the sunshine that was streaming through the window. "Good morning, Aunt Martha," said Barbara.

"Good morning, my dear," said Aunt Martha. She looked at the young school teacher. She could see by the redness of her eyes that she had a terrible night. This girl was living in pure agony, both night and day. "Your breakfast is ready. You can sit in whenever you want to."

"Thank you," she said, then sat down at the table. She was a girl that loved to sit down and have breakfast with Uncle Edward and Aunt Martha. But the hurt in her eyes was so great that Edward Pittman couldn't even look her in the face any more, especially in the mornings, without feeling guilty.

Aunt Martha sat down with her. "Do you know something, Barbara? This is the first day of spring and what a glorious morning it is. You can almost hear birds singing. I guess a month from now they will be here. We will be glad of that."

Barbara bowed her head and asked the blessing. She kept her head bowed a moment longer and moved her lips silently. Aunt Martha knew what she was saying, although she did not speak any words out loud. When she lifted her head a tear fell from her eye on the table. She picked up the spoon and put sugar in her tea. She swallowed hard to keep back the lump that was rising in her throat. "Aunt Martha, I am more worried this morning than I have been before. I feel like a bird in a cage, just being fed, but unable to do anything else. It has been ten days since Danny left and for a whole week now all I've heard is 'don't worry'."

Aunt Martha said, "Barbara, Danny is over around Hawkes Bay somewhere, held up in a cabin, and the brooks are too high for him to cross or for anyone else to get to him."

Barbara said, "I have a feeling Danny is somewhere in the woods around here." Aunt Martha glanced towards the window. "You know, Barbara, I got a feeling maybe you could be right."

Barbara, for the first time had her thinking her way. "What puzzles me, Aunt Martha, is why are these men all standing around gossiping night and day, talking about Danny, each one having his own version of where he might be, but no one doing anything about it. I wonder what's wrong."

Aunt Martha struck the table with her fist. "I will tell you what's wrong, my dear. For the first thing if we started from the top right to the King of England and come down the line to Ned, you'll find that the world is controlled by men, and if you'll notice, the whole thing is a complete failure. I'm of the opinion that if this island was being run by women, we would not be in such a mess as we're in now. Can you imagine what I'd do if I was in charge here today, and with Danny Corcoran lost on the country. There would be no man left in either town. I would have them all out, but you can't get a word in edgeways where they're to." Aunt Martha cooled down a little. "When Ned comes home I'm going to have my say."

"Your're right, Aunt Martha," Barbara said. "Imagine Danny lost on the country and men contented to go out sealing, moving around day after day without a worry. Do they really care?"

"My dear," said Aunt Martha, "I'm led to believe that nobody cares." She paused. "You know, Barbara, it dangerous not to care."

Barbara said, "Maybe we're wrong, Aunt Martha. Maybe we're wrong. I hope we are. Maybe we don't really understand, but something makes me sick inside and I can't help it. I guess it's because I'm a woman."

She looked out of the window. It was a beautiful morning. If anything happened to Danny she would never set foot in Harbour Deep again. "I'm going to tell you something, Aunt Martha. If anything does happen to Danny, this place will disappear. Do you believe that?"

Aunt Martha didn't answer. Uncle Edward was coming to the door. She got up from the table and went to open the door for him. He had his arms full of wood. "You're carrying too much, Ned," she said.

He looked at her puzzled. "Oh," he said almost out loud. "I'd better get out of here. I think Martha is going to take a strip off me hide." He dumped the wood in the woodbox and bolted out through the door, saying as he left, "be back soon," and quickly shut the door.

Danny had been walking for about three hours, treading softly through the soft snow. Everytime he put down his feet, he felt a terrible pain that made him sick. He could only walk about a hundred yards without having to take a rest. At one point he passed out. He completely collapsed and fell on his face, losing all control. When he came to himself, he was so hungry that it seemed like his stomach was going to digest itself. He noticed his hands were still bleeding, but he was too weak to do anything about it. He slowly walked on.

He was walking along by a brook, Copper Brook. He walked out on a bog and ahead of him he could see a barren hill. He had been pointed out this spot on the map before leaving Harbour Deep. This was the Copper Barren. He looked back to the pond where he had just come from. He had not travelled far since leaving the pond, but he had to move on. He crossed the bog and started walking by the brook again.

He came to a windfall and sat down on it. The rifle on his back weighed like a ton. He had not taken down his parka hood for days now. It was bright to the eyes and the glare from the sun made his shadow on the snow. He stood up and started walking again toward the open country along the brook. He was sinking deep in the snow now. He estimated the time to be about 10 a.m.

"Maybe I can find a few berries on the barrens," he said, and slowly walked through the low brush. As he slowly staggered along he came to a place on the bank of the brook where the snow was gone and the moss was soft and dry. Danny sat down and leaned his back against a tree. His mind went quickly back to Barbara and for the first time in days, he could see her face in front of him.

"Barbara. Oh, Barbara," he said. "What does this all mean? Will I ever see you again? Why did I leave? Why didn't I listen?" His voice slowly faded as he fell into a deep sleep.

This was the first day of spring, March 21st. The forecast in St. John's on this day set an all time record, 68 degrees F in the shade and 79 degrees F in the open. (Mar. 21, 1936 Evening Telegram) but the forecast for the St. Anthony – Horse Islands areas said 'warm with fog' (Mar. 21, 1936 Evening Telegram.) But on the high country of the Long Range Mountains this day was clear and warm. This caused Danny to sleep for about five hours. He awoke around 5 p.m. He had been lying on the rifle that was strapped on his back. He sat up and looked at his hands. Just ahead he could see the Copper Barren about a quarter of a mile away. He got to his feet slowly and stood for a moment as if paralysed, holding on to a tree with his right hand.

He screamed with pain. The sweat on his forehead felt cool. He let go of the tree and stood for a moment ready to catch himself. He began to walk out into the open. He was sinking to his knees in wet snow and each step he took, it seemed as if the bone was piercing into the ground. In agony he moved on. The land seemed to roll in front of him and his vision was blurred.

"If I only had something to eat," he said. He looked at his left hand. Part of two fingers were gone. He could hardly believe it, but he slowly tramped on, staggering as he went. Then he sat down in the snow. He couldn't stand on his feet any longer. He was only about four hundred yards from the Copper Barren.

The snow was gone on the side of the hill. It was then he decided to crawl on his knees and using his right hand he slowly dragged himself through the wet melting snow. The rifle and packsack on his back made him look a very odd shape, almost like a camel. He was limping like a dog that had one front leg missing, but no, this was Danny Corcoran.

The young ranger, who just a few days ago was proud, full of life and very nimble while walking around Harbour Deep, at this very moment was unable to stand up. It seemed he was on the last leg of his journey, using up the last bit of energy as he crawled along trying to get off the open country. As he moved along he said over and over again, "I've got to make it. I've got to make it."

He crawled to the top of the Copper Barren, his two hands were bleeding. He looked over to the Wolfe Barren, then at the valley below him that led out to Harbour Deep. He moved around the top of the hill found a few berries. He picked them and put them in his mouth. They tasted bitter. He had difficulty swallowing them. His throat was dry and swollen. He saw some partridges a few yards away from him and watched as they flew away making a squeaking noise.

He moved around slowly on his knees looking for more berries. He moved around the side of the hill but found only a handful of berries. He noticed the sun was low and estimated the time was about 6 p.m. It was really warm and water was running in the brooks.

The pain in his feet was too much to bear. His hands were bleeding. He had torn off some skin from crawling. He sat down on the edge of the barren with the sun to his back. He looked down the valley. He gave a sigh of relief when he realized he was at last off the open country. He would be in the woods anyway. It was a matter of getting enough energy to move on.

If he could only get to Hancock's camp, he was sure Noah would be there. He knew he would have to move on. He lay back on the caribou moss and looked out the valley. The snow was too soft to move on now. Anyway it was warm here. Maybe he would stay here for the night, but changed his mind. He had spent the last five nights on the barrens and had nightmares. He decided to move down the valley and into the timber. At least he would have some shelter. With this he moved slowly down the hill and into the heavy woods.

It was dark when he got to an area where the thick woods were. He looked around for a place to camp. He saw a windfall and crawled under its branches. He lay down and looked up at the stars through the trees. He wondered how far he had come from the Copper Barren. He felt disheartened when he realized he was only 200 yards from the barren. With this he fell asleep. This was the 11th night out after leaving Harbour Deep.

Noah Pittman and three other men from Harbour Deep walked into Ben Hyne's camp. They noticed that no tracks were around the camp or near the entrance. Inside they found the same thing, as it was over a week ago. Danny had not returned to this area or to this camp.

They had left home at 6 a.m. this morning. The going was so soft it had taken them ten hours to come in. They couldn't even attempt to use dogs due to the soft going. What a hussle they had on snowshoes. Almost every step was to their knees, they were almost exhausted when they arrived. The fire was quickly lit and the kettle put on. The four men sat down at the table. "Well boys," said Noah, "he's not here."

No one spoke.

"'Tis a question if every peck of snow don't go. 'Tis only fer it to turn to rain now and you'll be able to go on the drive."

One man spoke up and said, "I'm heading home in the morning. If we gets caught in here, they'll have another fuss on their hands."

Noah looked at the man, but didn't say anything.

"Only for Martha Pittman we wouldn't be in here anyway." This was Noah's mother he was talking about. It hurt him but he kept his mouth shut.

"Can you imagine," he added, "she drivin men on the country and what she'd do if she was a man. I wuddn't be in yer iffen fer me wife."

Noah looked at him then added, "No, Henry, I guess you wouldn't and I expect there's a lot of things you wouldn't do only for your wife, and one of them things is"... he paused. "Look," he added, "Only for the old woman you..."

The man got up quickly and went outside.

Noah looked at the other three fellows. "Maybe Henry's right. We could be in here on a fool's errand, but that's something we don't mind. But the going is so bad you can't step anywhere without going to yer waist and the snow is like slob. Be alright if it freezes."

The water was now boiled and the kettle was brought over to the table. Noah called for Henry to come back in and have lunch. He had nothing against him. In fact he had to agree with him.

Henry came in and apologized. "I tell you what we'll do, boys. We'll stay all night and when we leave in the morning, we'll leave so much grub here in the camp just in case Danny would happen to come along. You never knows and we'll leave just at daylight." They all agreed.

It was dark when Art Compton rolled out the tent in Red Sea Pond woods, it was in the Western Cove. They had been hauling their komatiks through slush and water all day. It took them fourteen hours to travel seven miles. The dogs were almost 'all in'. Everything was soaked. The ponds were covered with water and Art Compton, who was an experienced traveller in all seasons, never saw the like for this time of the year. He said it was a hot July day in March.

Jack Brown was cutting up herring for the dogs' supper. They were so tired they hardly ate. "Art," he called, "what do you think of it?"

"What's that?" was Art's reply.

"I mean, 'tis pretty hard on the dogs."

"Oh," said Art. "Looks like one of mine is on the verge of foundering. I hope that doesn't happen. I know one thing for sure, Jack, no matter how much it freezes tonight, I'm not moving tomorrow. I got to rest me dogs."

"Good thinking," said Jack Brown.

"We're in a good spot," said Art. "It's good travelling from here to Harbour Deep Brook. When it freezes it won't take us long to go up to the Rocky Stint."

"I know," said Jack. "This is where they had the big slaughter of caribou four or five years ago. They said the whole pond turned red with blood."

"Maybe that's the reason they called it the Red Sea Pond," said Jack.

"Maybe so," said Art.

Everything was soon prepared for the night and Ple had the pot on, the men were all set to settle down for the night. Ple checked the food supply. They had very little. All the bread was gone. They ate their last slice that morning. The sugar was scarce and very little tea was left. From now on Jack Brown would have to make 'Damper Dogs' (Dough cooked on the outside of the stove without being put in a pan, just stuck on, usually on the side of the stove. When the dough falls off, it's supposed to be cooked.).

They had salt pork, but up until now they had been unable to kill a caribou. In fact they had not even seen one. But now they were in a prime place for caribou. This was the center of the Williamsport herd. (This herd was almost completely wiped out due to poaching. Only 25 animals could be found. Earl Pilgrim, a Wildlife Officer, brought the herd back to a healthy state with the help of the local people.)

However, with supplies or not, Ple knew they could not turn back now even if they wanted to. They had to go on to Harbour Deep. It was the only way now for them to get out of the country, but he wasn't going to tell Peters. Maybe tomorrow they would get a caribou, but caribou or not, they would go on.

Chapter 20
March 22, 1936

Danny awoke just before dawn. The sky was red and glowing. It was mild and looked like a warm spring day. He lay there and tried to move but found it impossible. He was wet from where he was lying on the snow and the wet ground. He knew the brooks would be rising from all this melting snow. His hands were swollen but most of the pain was gone. For a moment as he lay motionless in the early dawn, he wondered what the day would bring forth. He knew his chances of survival were growing dimmer day by day. A man could last only so long without food. He tried to move but couldn't. It seemed as if he was numb all over. He would have to get moving. "Maybe I'm finished," he thought. "This could be the end." With this he closed his eyes and went to sleep.

When Danny awoke the sun was shining through the trees. He felt the warm rays. He looked at the sun. It hurt his eyes and he put up his hand to shade them. He thought, "well I can lift my hand." Then he lifted the other one. He attempted to sit up and did so with a lot of difficulty. He tried to move his feet but couldn't. He could hear Souffletts River just behind him. He then, with all his might, started to move his legs. This was when the pain started to drive him crazy.

After about an hour he got to his feet with the help of a nearby tree. He looked at the sun and guessed it was now past noon.

After hobbling around in a circle he started moving down towards the river. With each step he screamed with pain. He knew it would be impossible to travel along the river so he started back towards the Copper Barren. Every few steps he would fall and then would crawl some. Finally he reached the side of the barren. It was late afternoon. He felt so weak. He noticed he was shivering. He knew he wasn't cold. It must be from the lack of food. He could move no more under these conditions.

It was then he felt himself passing out. He fought against it but collapsed. A short time later he came to again and noticed the sun was going down over the nearby hill. "Oh God," he prayed out loud. "Don't let this be the end." With these words he passed out again.

Chapter 21
March 23, 1936

It had turned cold during the night and the snow stiffened a bit. The snow surface had a crust on it but not hard enough to stand a man's weight walking. After an hour suffering severe pain, he finally got to his knees, then to his feet. He tried twice to walk but fell. When he did step on the frozen snow, it tore the flesh that had been hanging off from his legs. Due to the frozen and thawed condition he knew that both his feet were badly infected.

It was now daylight. He then decided to crawl on his hands and knees. With this thought he started out. This was much better. His weight was more evenly spread out. The only part which broke through was his knees.

He came to a hill and a thought came to him. 'I should be able to slide down on my back. The canvas packsack on my back would serve as a sled. It should slide real good.

With this thought in mind he rolled over on his back, but the rifle was across his back. He sat up and reached for the strap across his chest. It was then he saw his hands. He could hardly believe his eyes. The sight of his hands made him sick. He felt weak and almost fainted. A wave of pain blurred his vision. Both hands were bleeding and flesh just hung off. This was caused by crawling on the hard crust snow. He didn't feel it because of the pain in his legs and feet.

He had to get the rifle off his back. He reached up with his right hand. His left hand was useless now. He got his thumb under the strap and lifted it from his coat far enough to get his left elbow under the strap, slipping his arm out under the rifle strap and rolled over on his back. Using his packsack as a sled, he went sliding down the hill about forty feet, coming to a halt at the bottom just barely missing a tree. He then rolled over on his hands and knees and started crawling again.

By late evening he had crawled and slid about six miles since early morning. He got to the side of the Big Steady and sat down under a tree. He passed out for a few minutes feeling pain everywhere. "If I only had something to eat," he thought. As a result of the sliding on his packsack and the many times it almost came off, the strap hung down over his shoulder. For the first time he decided to look in the packsack. "Maybe," he said, "there's something in there to eat." He sat up straight. After a struggle he got his pack off. He opened it. He saw his enamel mug. He took it out and dug deeper. He took out his tea bag. It was half full of loose tea. He then saw his flashlight. He took it out. After trying to push the switch without success, due to the bad condition of his hands, he lay it down. Then he saw his pipe. He had not smoked it since he left Harbour Deep. He smoked it only occassionally. It was full of tobacco but he had no desire to light it. Even if he did, he couldn't, because he had no matches.

He had nothing there to eat. He knew the only possible place he could get anything to eat maybe, was at Hancock's camp. From the way he had studied before leaving Harbour Deep, he was only about two miles from the camp. This gave him courage and for the first time in many days, he felt like travelling on. But he knew it was impossible. It was getting dark. "Well," he said, "it's not much use putting these things back in my packsack." With this he hung them up on some short limbs over his head then sat down. He put his hand under his chin and with his hands on his knees bowed his head and groaned. "I am only about eleven miles from home." His thoughts wandered. The pain was severe. He knew he could not go on much longer. He had to fight to keep from passing out. Souffletts River was roaring with the large amount of water caused by the melting snow. As he thought he fell back against the tree unconscious.

From Red Sea Pond to Camping Pond it is eight miles, all open country, mostly barrens and ponds. The two dog teams slowly picked their way around the brooks and large rocks. Several times the four men had to wade to their knees in water. The going was slow. The dogs paws were cut from the sharp ice made from the coldness of the night, but melted very quickly in the morning. Little was said that day because the task of hauling the komatiks loaded with gear made every man work very hard.

They had their breakfast early then broke camp. Some of the dogs were still limping from the cuts on their paws. Ple and Art made stalls for some of the dogs that were cut badly. Jack Brown put liniment on some which took the tenderness out. However at 4 p.m. when they reach Camping Pond under Lucky Strike they couldn't go any further.

Art put up the tent and Jack put the pot on the stove and started preparing supper. Ple and Art then got wood for the night. Peters sat in the camp. He was partly snow blinded. Water ran down his face from his eyes. "What do you think of it, Jack?" Peters asked.

"What do I think of what?" Jack answered.

"Where we're at?" was his reply.

Jack Brown handed him a knife and some potatoes. "Here, peel those,"
he said.

Peters picked up the knife.

"It's too late for that now," Jack said, putting salt beef in the pot.

"Too late for what?" Peters asked.

"Too late to go asking foolish questions like that. Why don't you ask Ple
what time we're going to get to Harbour Deep?"

Peters said nothing.

Art came in with a load of wood. He looked at Peters. "Old man," he said
through a mouthful of tobacco juice, "what are you crying for?" He knew
what the problem was with Peters, snow blindness, but he couldn't stand
to see him sitting in the tent and he had to bug him.

Peters didn't answer.

"Hey, Ple," said Art, "come in the tent I wants yeh."

"What do you want, Art?" Ple put his head in the tent.

"I think we'll leave here and go back home and call off the search."

Ple looked surprised, but caught a hint of something. "Why, Art, why?"
he said quickly.

Art rolled over the wad of Black Beaver in his mouth. "Corcoran must be
dead. Peters is crying."

Peters was about to do something serious. He threw down the potato he
had in his hand. Then Jack Brown asked Art to get out of the tent, which
Art did very quickly.

"I can't take much more," Peters said. "If I can only get my feet in
Harbour Deep, I'll never touch the open country again. This place is
strictly for fools and mad men."

Jack said nothing. In one way he pitied Peters. He really didn't know
how much of a sissy he was, but what amazed him most was that he was a
Ranger and Rangers weren't supposed to be like this.

"The man's a fool," said Peters.

"Maybe you're right," said Jack, "but fool or not, you got to depend on
him to get you to Harbour Deep, so the less you say the better for you."

Peters knew this was right and he held his peace.

The sun shone brightly and its rays made a reflection from the harbour
ice that looked like a mirror. There was an inch of water over the surface of
the eighteen inches of ice covered by melting snow. Barbara Gale walked
into the house. It was noon. She had heard that Noah and the other men
had returned from the country. She heard from Ches and the others that
they saw no sign of Danny, but she wanted to hear more details.

Uncle Edward sat on the couch. Aunt Martha was busy with lunch.
"My dear," said Uncle Edward, "Noah just left. He was telling us about

the rough time they had searching for Danny. They almost all got snow blinded." He paused.

Barbara sat down and stared at him, then asked. "How far in the country did they go?"

Uncle Edward said, "They went in to Hancock's camp. They stayed all night in Ben Hyne's camp." He shifted his weight on the couch nervously. "They listened almost all night, but never heard a sound."

Barbara sat with her head bowed and slowly unbuttoned her sweater. "Uncle Edward," she said softly, "is there any hope?"

He spoke up with words that to himself had confidence, but to Barbara it was only a flat sentence just something to break the silence. "Don't you worry, Barbara," he said. "Noah left food and things at the cabin and if Danny came out, when he got to the cabin he would have it made."

Barbara said, "This is Tuesday, the 22nd. At least the nights are not cold."

"No," said Uncle Edwards.

"What happens if it turns cold?" she said.

"If it turns cold, my dear," said Uncle Edward, "it will be good travelling." He stopped. "Has Gill Ellsworth heard anything yet?"

"I don't guess he has," she said. "If he had, he would have let us know."

Aunt Martha said, "Maybe we should send somebody over to ask him to try and find out if they are still searching over on the Port Saunders side."

"Yes, I think I'll send someone over after dinner."

He was glad he had something else to do to get away from the conversations.

"Your dinner (lunch) is ready, my dear," Aunt Martha said. "You'd better eat it while it's hot."

With these words Barbara moved slowly to the table.

As Danny regained consciousness he could not get to his feet. He crawled and slid out to the steady. The rifle he was dragging was now a great burden to him. He knew he could not take it with him any further. He would have to leave it. This was going to be a hard thing to do. He could hardly think now. He had to fight to keep his senses and stay awake. He fell on his face on the snow. Its coolness revived him and as he gazed across the snow, it seemed the trees along the bank of the brook were trying to jump off the ground.

Everything seemed to be in waves. He sat up and crawled to a tree and stuck his rifle against it, feeling too discouraged to look back. "After I get to Harbour Deep, I can send Noah back after it because it is owned by the Rangers." But there was nothing else he could do now. He felt lucky if he could get himself back to Harbour Deep.

He then started to crawl along the ice near the shore at the end of the steady. He went into the woods. It was mostly downhill. The sun was up now. It had not frozen very hard last night.

The pain in his hands and legs was too great to feel the chill of the night air and now as he crawled and slid on his back, he knew that Hancocks camp was only a short distance away. He just had to move. This was one thing he had to do. If he was to survive he had to keep going.

The roar of the river made him shudder when he thought of the cold water. That was the beginning of his troubles when he fell into the water just up from here, Ben Hynes Brook. If he had only turned back then, he would not be in the mess that he was in now. All day he had been moving on all fours like an animal. His hands were dead and skin was hanging from the bone. His feet and legs throbbed with pain. He was also wet to his waist. This helped to keep back some pain.

At around 4:30 p.m. he knew he was getting near the spot where Ben Hyne's Brook empties into the Souffletts River. He crawled on then. All of a sudden he found himself on a wooded point of land with a major river on his left and a fast moving brook on his right. He crawled out near the edge of the snow. Then with the help of a tree he got to his feet. He could not believe himself. The thought struck him, "I am finished. The rivers are so high, it is impossible for me to get across. This will be the end".

He sank to the soft snow. He sat and put his head down and wept. "Dear God," he cried aloud, "this is the end of the line for me. I will never see my home again." He then looked up at the blue sky. "What have I done?" he asked in a clear voice. "I haven't done anything, only tried to help someone and wildlife. I have been a good son and have loved my mother. I've worked hard."

He held up his two hands in front of him. His left hand was almost unrecognizable. It was partly bangaged in a dirty pocket handkerchief. His right hand was swollen and dark with blood stains all the way up to his coat sleeve. The tears from his eyes ran down into his red beard like streaks of sunbeams. Then he cried, "Barbara, Barbara, please send someone to help me cross the river. I am about to die."

The water made a rumbling sound on both sides of him. He knew there was no use walking in along the side of Ben Hyne's Brook. The amount of water running out by him and the swiftness of it told him that it was running free for many miles back. He cooled himself again and stood up holding on to a tree. He then walked a little nearer to the edge of the river and looked across it. He couldn't believe what he saw. Just across the river, near the edge, was Hancock's Camp.

"I am dreaming," he thought. "This can't be possible." He rubbed his eyes with the arm of his coat. The strap from his packsack hung almost to his right elbow. He looked again. Then he saw the stove pipe sticking up from the roof. The cabin was less than a hundred feed away. He fell flat on his face and the sun sank, casting a long shadow from the trees around him. Danny Corcoran would have to spend another night in the cold with a stove less than one hundred feet away, ready to be lit. Although Danny didn't know it a box of food lay on the table, left by Noah Pittman, and as he lay there he suddenly realized his wounds and fate were against him.

Chapter 22
March 24, 1936

It was 5 p.m. The search party from Englee arrived at the southwest corner of Rocky Stint about one mile northeast of the Souffletts River. They had been travelling all day (three miles) when they arrived at the camping ground.

Art Compton was in no mood to even speak to Peters. He was mad and very concerned about Souffletts River. They could hear its water roaring. They knew the brooks were running high and if they couldn't get across the river, they knew they were in for a hard time. Jack Brown and Ple Gillard said very little, but Art knew what they were thinking. Most of the dogs were 'all in'. They had to leave four. They were too tired even to drag themselves, but he hoped they would catch up later after they had some rest.

After they had the tent up and some wood sawed off, Ple and Art walked down the large bog to the river. There was a small brook at the end of the bog. Even that would be hard to cross, but they would manage. They could fall a tree across it if nothing else, and cross on it.

"Art," said Ple, "the going is getting pretty tough. The thing I'm getting worried about is the dogs."

"Old man," said Art, "das not wat I'm worried about now. 'Tis crossing the river. If we can't cross now, 'twon't be much use going back home. Never get across the bay." Art paused.

"Don't worry about crossing Souffletts," Ple said. "The steady under the Wolfe Barren we're guaranteed there. That's the last pond up here. We could have problems crossing Ben Hyne's Brook though. He's a wild brook. There's no steady on it, but if we got too, we'll make a rear boat." (a raft made of logs nailed together, used while driving logs) He looked at Art, "Can you swim?"

Art grinned, showing his gold tooth through the tobacco juice, "No I can't, but Peters will." They both laughed aloud.

Danny had spent most of the evening leaning against a big white spruce tree, gazing across the brook at the cabin and looking at the water. He could not understand why someone wasn't at the camp. "Is it possible" he asked himself, "that no one is looking for me." He paused. "Where is Noah? Surely he could depend on him." He looked again at the camp. "Maybe there's someone further up the river at Ben Hyne's camp. If I call, somebody might hear me." With this he started yelling, but he found out he was too weak to continue for more than four or five yells. Everytime he called it seemed the top was going to come off his head.

"It was no use," he thought. "I will just sit and wait. Maybe someone will come by." But when he thought about the cabin and that he was only ten miles from Harbour Deep, it made him more restless.

He sat in the snow for a few minutes, then got up and looked at the cabin again. He would try and cup his mouth with his right hand and call again, but all was in vain. The sun had gone down. It was getting dark. He knew he could not last much longer. This was going to be a chilly night. The thought made him shudder. He looked at his hands and the sight made him scared. He knew what was happening. He looked in the direction of the cabin again, then at his boots. He then fell back on the snow and lay motionless.

Danny Corcoran's mother sat at the table. She stared at the oil cloth covering on the table. The red and white blocks that formed the pattern looked a blurred mixture. This was caused by the tears that ran down her face and fell in a pool on the table. She couldn't believe her son was lost on the mountains, and that no matter how hard she tried, she could not get any news of what was going on.

Many questions were on her mind, but there wasn't anyone she could ask or talk to about getting anwers. She had tried to get to see Mr. Anderton, the Commanding Officer, but she was told by his aide that he was out of town. The men of lower ranks said that everything possible was being down.

"Sirs, can you tell me exactly what is being done?"

They just shook their heads and looked at her in pity.

They knew very little was being done, but kept their peace. She bowed her head and with her hands limp on the table, wept out loud.

"I wonder where you are this very minute," she sobbed and it seemed as if her heart was going to leap out of her body. "I've got a feeling you're at the point of death. What can I do? Dear, God, what can I do?"

Pain was in her voice. She shook all over. The gold ring on her finger was wet and glistened from the tears that showered from her eyes. The palms of her hands were hard and rough from cleaning floors to help give her family bread, butter and education. The backs of her hands were wrinkled from the many trials and sorrows of 55 years.

As she sat there she looked up at the ceiling and asked herself a question. "Have I done all I could possibly do for my family?"

She quickly surveyed all her labouring and toiling. Nowhere could she find anywhere she had been neglectful or treated her family unfair. She looked out of the window at the Southside Hills of St. John's. They were painted a gold colour by the flickering rays of the setting sun. Then the thought came to her. "Have I not done enough for you, God, that in times of trouble I could receive protection? Have I not prayed enough? Have I not given enough time to the sick? Have I not helped the blind and the lame?"

She hung her head for a moment and her memory came back crystal clear. Maybe she had been too busy, but what else could she have done. These were hard times. If bread was to come your way, it was from the sweat of your brow, but in this case it was different. Danny was a Ranger and his job would be helping people. Then she thought , "maybe he should have become a priest, at least he would not be out lost on the mountains."

She slowly got up from the table and walked over to the stove to put the kettle on. Maybe tomorrow she would hear something. If she didn't she would have to go to the Governor. She knew he would get some answers.

Only the great God and the angels will ever know what really went on at the north junction of Ben Hyne's Brook and Souffletts River during the nights of March 24 and 25, 1936. Danny tried to relate some of his story to the Englee search party, Barbara Gale, and the doctors and nurses at the hospital. But each time he talked about it, his memory focused on the misery of the two days and nights, living in the snow and water and he would become so overwhelmed with emotions, that his body would shake from head to foot and he would have to be held down until the memories passed.

He arrived at this spot on the evening of the 23rd and had collapsed at about 8 p.m. under a large spruce tree. He lay resting his head on its moor. There was such a roaring in his head that his vision became blurred when he tried to look around him. He finally slipped into unconsciousness. He didn't know how long he lay there, but the next time he came to his senses, the sun was shining. He lifted his head and looked around for a moment. He was startled when he found out where he was. He had to fight to stay awake. Then he realized where he was, just inches from the bank of the river. It was only for him to roll over and he would tumble into the river.

He tried to move his legs but couldn't. He looked at his hands. They were still bleeding. He had to get back from the edge. He twisted his upper body trying to roll away from the river's edge. He tried again without success. Then with all his strength he made a side lurch and rolled away from the river.

He stopped for a while but couldn't think. Finally he knew he had to get further away from the river. He looked around and there about ten feet away he saw the tree where he had stayed last night or at least where he had lain down. For safety sake he would have to get back to that position. After many attempts he finally got back to the tree. "Now what must I do?" he thought. "I know what happened. I must have been up in my sleep." The thought of this made him sick. Maybe this is how the end would come. He knew if he fell into the water, it would be the last of him and with this he passed out again.

The search party from Englee spent the night at Rock Stint Pond. Very little was said. The men were so tired they all laid down after supper and fell asleep. They awoke around midnight and each got under his blanket and turned in for the night. The dogs were curled up near the tent all twenty-seven of them and not one made a sound all night. They were so tired they could not eat properly. The stragglers staggered into camp before dark. They ate some of the food that was cooked and fell a victim as if dead.

Chapter 23
March 25, 1936

The next morning, the three men got up early and ate breakfast. They then took a look at things outside. It had not stiffened up at all last night. The three men walked to the pond. "What do you think of it boys?" asked Jack Brown.

The question wasn't directed at anyone in particular, but both men knew that Jack was concerned about the situation and espeically the dogs.

"There's only one thing I'm worried about, old man," said Art. "And that's having to haul the komatik meself, because sure as you're here, the dogs are going to give out."

They all agreed.

"I'm not moving me dog team today at all, fraid they give out," said Art. "Some of them are in bad shape now."

"You're right," said Ple. "I tell you what you should do, boys. You should go off, the two of you and kill a meal of partridge."

Jack spoke up, "Yes, 'tis a good idea. What do you say, Art?"

"Get the gun and let's go," said Art.

"We'll pass the day anyway," said Jack.

After they left, Ple went to the tent. He opened the tent flaps and stepped inside. The flaps fell closed behind him. It was almost dark inside. He opened the flaps again and tied them back. He went inside again. The sun was just coming up. It cast its rays through the trees.

Peters rolled over in his bunk, then looked at Ple.

"Where's Art and Jack ?" he asked. His voice sounded roach.

Ple looked at him and squinted his eyes. "They're going off to see if they can kill a meal of partridge." His voice had a tinge of an insulting tone to it.

Peters sat up. He pointed his finger at Ple after sensing the tone of his voice. He looked at Ple with cool eyes, then said, "Now you listen to me for a minute." His voice began to quiver, not from fear or excitement, but from the opportunity he had now to say something to Ple in private. This would put an end to this misery he was going through.

"I have had enough of this from you and Art. Ever since we left, the two of you have been continually on my back. I want a halt to this immediately."

He paused and looked at Ple. "Do you understand, Ple?"

Ple looked him in the eyes and saw he meant business.

"This is the first time I have had the opportunity to talk with you in privacy since we left Englee."

Ple said nothing.

"Do you know something, Mr. Gillard?" he said to Ple with a snarl in his voice. "It's only for me to tell the boys about the deal I made with you and you're going to have trouble on your hands."

Ple kept quiet.

The night before the search party left Englee, after their meeting at Uncle Noah Gillard's house, Ple met Ranger Peters and told him that he had changed his mind about going to search for Danny Corcoran. Peters could get someone else in his place. "Why aren't you going?" said Peters. "What's the matter?"

Ple looked him in the eye and said, "I'm going in to Roddickton. I got a chance to go to work with Uncle Simon Canning. He wants me to come in and help lay boom sticks, so you'll have to get someone else."

Peters knew that Ple was up to something and right away he sensed it was money. "Ple," he said, "we're all ready to go. Now you're backing out. I'll tell you what I'll do. I'll pay you $70.00 if you will go on the trip.

Ple could see that Peters had to go in the country. He had his orders. There was no way he could get out of it. He had to go and search for Danny. "What do you say, Ple?"

Ple rubbed his head under his cap. "I'll tell you what, Peters. I'll make a deal with you."

Peters stopped for a minute, then said, "Okay, Ple, let's hear it."

Ple cleared his throat. He said, "We'll go on this search for Ranger Corcoran who is lost." He picked his words very carefully. "I've been thinking it over, Peters. I don't want to bite the Ranger Force." Peters almost laughed. "But here's the deal I'll make." He paused. "$70.00 to go, but I'm not going to accept it. Here's mine. If we go on this search and we're gone for two months and don't find Ranger Corcoran, then you don't owe me one cent." He looked at Peters, who had his mouth partly open and was wide eyed. "But if we find him, dead or alive, you have to pay me $100.00."

Peters couldn't believe why anyone would want to get paid such a large sum of money as this. He had never heard the like before. He knew the force would never go along with that. "Ple, I can't do it. I got no authority to make such a deal." He paused, then he looked at Ple. "Look, you must be trying to get me fired."

"Well," said Ple, "if I don't go as your guide, then you can't go. So you'll get fired anyway."

"Ple," Peters said, "I've got no other choice but to make the deal. Okay I'll pay you the $100.00 for the trip on these terms." For a moment he thought, "our chances of finding Corcoran are slim and on the other hand if the force disapproves, he can always work something out. It's his word against mine."

"Okay, Ple," he said again. "The deal is made $100.00."

"Okay," said Ple. "I want you to come over to Mr. Reeves (a business tycoon in Englee and the local Justice of the Peace) and sign a letter to this effect."

'Well," Peters thought, "this makes it hard." "Well, I guess I don't have much choice, if that's the way you want it, Ple."

"That's it," said Ple and away the two of them went over to John Reeves, J.P. and drew up the contract, word for word as they stated it.

When they finished signing the contract, John Reeves, a white haired gentleman, turned to them and said, "Gentlemen, this is the first time I ever had anything to do with putting a price tag on a human being, but it seems there's a first time for everything." He paused, then added, "Do you know what we should call the contract?" He looked at them and said, "One Hundred Dollars for Danny."

All three men were silent. Peters took the contract and folding it, put it in his pocket.......

And now as the rays of the early morning sun peered in the eyes of Ple Gillard, sitting near the tent door about a mile from Souffletts River, he knew Peters had the trump card. With this thought he walked quickly out of the tent. As he was leaving he heard Peters laugh out loud as he lay back on his bunk.

Danny lay under a tree all day. He couldn't move. He had tried many times, but it seemed as if his legs were paralysed. He could move his arms and the upper part of his body, but was unable to do anything else. He lifted his head to look around and saw that he was sunk down in the snow and that his feet were in water. As he tried to move his feet, he realized there was no way out for him unless someone found him.

He tried to think, but found it impossible. He could see part of the river from where he lay. It looked wild. As he lay there and thought about his end, he became very upset.

'Why didn't I listen to the men of Harbour Deep when they warned me about going in the country." But his mind kept saying "Those caribou. Those poor caribou."

He wept openly and tears ran down his face. He started calling to Uncle Noah Pittman. He called louder and louder. Each time he called his voice seemed flat and dull. He guessed this was caused by the way he was positioned, which was flat on his back. The sound travelled nowhere only around the base of the trees.

If there was anyone, only about a hundred yards away, they would not have heard him. The calling took most of his energy. He started to get weaker. "I know I'll never see Barbara again. I'll never see Mom again."

His body started to shake. He trembled all over and then passed out. He just lay there, wet almost to his waist and the hunger and infection were beginning to take there toll.

When he awoke he looked at his hands and thought about the days in St. John's as a high school student. He thought about how he could run and jump and play ball and clap his hands and take part in almost every sport. As the thoughts went again through him, he looked at his hands again and through his tears he said, "It's better if I die. I will never be any good anymore. My hands. My feet." He wept. "I am finished."

With the sun shining in his face, he lay still for a moment. His red beard was in streaks and looked like the side of a pier with the tide gone out. His eyes were pink from the strain of trying to endure pain. His hands slipped slowly down by his side and came to rest on the snow. He slipped into unconciousness as the sun steadily sank in the bright evening sky.

Gill Ellsworth pushed back his chair and stood up, taking off his headset and laying it on his desk. There were two red marks around his ears left by the head set. He was disgusted. He had wired Port Saunders asking if anyone had seen Danny. The answer was no. Not one trace. Some of the search parties had returned due to the rain and mild weather, but Ranger Hiscock was still looking.

He had sent a wireless to Englee, but no one had heard anything. The search party from Englee was still in the country. They were not expected to get very far due to the mild weather.

The people of Williamsport came back the same time as the search party from Harbour Deep.

"Where could Danny be?" he said. "I am worried something is wrong, very wrong,'' he heard himself saying, "but what can I do?"

He put his headphones on again and sat down. He put together a message to Major Anderton, Commanding Officer of the Newfoundland Ranger Force. It read as follows: DANNY CORCORAN HAS NOT BEEN FOUND-STOP-HIS CHANCES OF BEING FOUND ARE SLIM-STOP-SUG-GEST YOU COME TO HARBOUR DEEP OR SEND PERSONNEL TO CON-DUCT A MORE INTENSIVE SEARCH-STOP-AN EARLY REPLY NEEDED. SIGNED GILLARD ELLSWORTH, GREAT HARBOUR DEEP.

Gill put down the headset and stood up again. 'What does all of this mean', he thought. He checked the cash box, emptied it in his briefcase and walked out the door. This had been a rough day. Maybe tomorrow would bring good news. He hoped.

The search party from Englee sat around the small stove. The kerosene oil for their lamp was all used. They were now using candles for light. It was a clear night, but very mild. Art noticed that Ple was very quiet this evening. He had asked no questions. He thought it must be his concern for the travelling conditions, and the problem he suspected about crossing the river, which he knew was going to be difficult.

He put a piece of wood in the stove and took out a small piece of Dark Beaver Tobacco from his shirt pocket. He held it in his hand for a moment, then said, "Old man, this is the last of me baccy. I got a message for yous. Tomorrow morning I'm going' to harness me dogs and I'm not takin' the harness off un ' till I gets to Harbour Deep and if the dogs can't walk, I'm goin' on to Harbour Deep meself." He paused. "I don't mind gettin' out of grub, but not outta baccy." With this he bit off a small piece and put the rest back in his pocket.

Jack Brown spoke up, "Boys, everyone knows about the problems we're facing. We got about one more meal left for our dogs, which means the longest we got to use them is three days. As for our grub, the only things we have left are flour, hard bread and a bit of salt beef and a small bit of tea. I would say about two more days grub left and after that well your guess is as good as mine."

They were silent for a while, then Ple spoke up. "Well," he said, looking at the candle that was burning brightly. "We know the brooks are all flooded, which means we will have to take the long route around. First we have to go in to the steady (pond). It's about two miles in from here. It's right under the Wolfe Barren. We will cross there then we might go up across the Copper Barren. Then go straight from there to the steady on Ben Hyne's Brook. That's about three miles in on the brook."

He looked at Art. "Were you with us the time we were in there with the surveyors?"

"No," said Art, "never there."

"No I think 'twas Gus Compton. Anyway we will go out along the side of the brook, then to Hancock's camp. From then on we can take the cut line to Harbour Deep. 'Tis ten miles out from there."

Jack Brown looked at him. "It's all up to you, Ple. We don't know the way. What do you think the ice is like on the Wolfe Barren Steady?"

"You got no worries about that," said Ple.

"I never seen the like before. Mild every day," said Art. "'Tis the sou-west wind that's causing it"

Ple quickly spoke up. "Thats one reason why I want to move quickly," he said. "We're going to have a change. Put the kettle on Art. I'm going to have a cup of raw tea."

Art got up and put the kettle on and sat back down again. "What about Corcoran? Are we going to give him up?"

They looked at Peters who said nothing.

"I'm not," said Ple. They all looked at him.

Jack Brown shifted his weight. "What are you going to do, Ple?" asked Jack.

"Well we'll put it this way, Jack. We haven't even looked for him yet. All we've been doing is looking after our own skin ever since we left home and trying to get up here. Do you think I'm going to fold up now? Not on your nerve!"

No one spoke, but Ple said, reaching for his mug, "I bet tomorrow we'll see something. There's one thing for sure, if Corcoran had any intelligence about him at all, he wouldn't come on the northeast side of the Souffletts River. Which means if he's anywhere on the other side, he is between Souffletts and Harbour Deep River." Nobody spoke. "Now if he's over on the other side towards Port Saunders, then they got him found. If not then he's a gone goose."

Jack Brown spoke up, "Ple," he said sternly, "what do you intend to do tomorrow?"

Ple stood up. He looked at the other three men. He blinked his eyes and said, "I intend to keep my eyes open." With this he walked outside.

It's hard to sit in the snow in the weather, even with a buddy around a campfire, when one side of you is freezing and other side is roasting, at least there's light. But at night all alone, without a fire, weak with hunger, and your feet and hands having been frozen and thawed a couple of times, with stabs of pain piercing the heart at almost every twitch of the muscles, and when a man opens his eyes and looks at the twinkling stars from his position of lying on the flat of his back on the icy snow, one must have nerves of steel, a will to live and a controlled mind beyond all comprehension in order to stay alive.

It was long after midnight, Danny did not or could not relate or estimate what time it was, he lay motionless all evening. At about midnight the pain was so great that he went unconcsious again. At one point he had an encounter with a waitress in a restaurant.

He thought he was walking down Water Street in St. John's. He turned on the sidewalk and went into the restaurant. He sat at a table. He noticed on his feet he had a pair of snowshoes. He had his parka on with the hood up. People looked at him and with wide eyes quickly got up and ran for the door.

A little girl who sat at the next table looked at him and fainted and was quickly carried inside the kitchen. A waitress came out wide-eyed and screaming. She had a mop in her hands. She looked at him and in a screaming voice she said, "Get out, get out, you bum."

He looked at her and said, "I'm not a bum, I'm a Ranger."

"No, you're not," she said, "you're a bum dressed in Ranger clothes."

He tried to explain. "No. no," he said, "I'm Ranger Corcoran. Danny Corcoran."

She looked at him closer, coming nearer to him, "I know Danny Corcoran and you're not him. What do you want anyway? You look like a man from the North Pole."

Danny put his right hand to the hood of his parka to keep the hood out of his face. "I'm from Harbour Deep," he said. "I'm hungry, would you give me something to eat? It's late I don't have much time left."

She looked at him again, "Where are you going?"

He lowered his eyes and looked at his hands. "I think I'm going to die," he said.

"You're mad. Get out," she said.

He stood up and looked her in the eyes. "Would you give me a drink of water, please?"

"Get out," she said screaming, lifting the mop handle. With this he stood up and staggered out the door.

His hands hung at his sides as he stepped outside. He noticed the sidewalk had disappeared. The street was turned into a river. He looked back as the tide caught him. Then he heard the waitress say, "Yes, it's you Danny. Come back. Come back." She ran to the door. "Come back, Danny."

But it was too late. The tide was sweeping him away. With this he awoke and found himself holding on to the ice. He was screaming and crying. He opened his eyes and saw the stars, then closed his eyes, and before he knew anything he had passed out again.

It was just before dawn when Danny heard something. It was music. He turned his head. It got louder. He saw a light. It was from a window in a house. He walked closer. The music became clearer. It was a piano. Then he heard a woman singing. He caught his breath. "I think I'll go in," he said.

He walked to the door and stepped inside. He was in the kitchen. He looked all around. What cooking utensils he thought. Everything was shining. The walls were shining. He looked across the room and saw a lady sitting at a piano. She had a white crown on her head and several crowns were placed on the piano. She started to sing. Her voice melted Danny. He sat down near the counter. The aroma of fresh fruit filled his lungs. He looked at the lady with amazement. He felt relaxed. Her hands moved over the keys with ease.

She started to sing, "Amazing Grace, how sweet the sound, that saved a wretch like me." The hairs on his body stood on end. From the soles of his feet to the top of his head, he felt as though he was at the edge of eternity. He had a wonderful feeling like he had never experienced before. He felt so wonderful that tears of joy ran down his cheeks. He sat just drinking in this golden voice. As he sat there he heard a man praying. The words pierced his soul.

"Dear God, we come to you this morning and Lord we're in need. So many this very moment don't have the privilege as I've got. So many are drifting without any hope. Please help them."

Danny knelt down. "Lord," said the voice, "I'm on my knees this morning at the dawning of this new day to again pay my respect to you and I'm asking you to do something for me." He paused and when he started again it seemed that his very breath could be felt by Danny.

"You said, if I came to you with an honest prayer that whatever I ask, believe and you'll do it. I'm not asking you to do anything for me. You've done too much for me already, that I'll never be able to repay you. Lord, here's what I want." He paused for a moment. "You know where Danny Corcoran is right now. You know if he's lost or suffering." The music continued to play. "You know his situation. Whatever it is, if its bad please help him. If he's hungry please feed him. If he's lost please have somebody find him. If he's suffering please ease his pain. Lord, I'm going to follow you until I die. I ask everything in your name. Amen."

The lady at the piano started to sing, "When we've been there ten thousand years, bright shining as the sun," Danny looked at her again and remembered. It's Granny Randell. She smiled and nodded her head. Tears were running down his face. Then he remembered the voice. It was Uncle Jobie Randell. Danny felt good. He put his hand on the table and while the music played, it seemed like a huge orchestra came and played all around him. He felt himself falling into a deep sleep right on the table. Danny must have been in a kitchen of heaven.

Chapter 24
March 26, 1936

It was just before dawn when Ple Gillard put some wood in the stove. The kettle was boiled. He called the rest of the boys and stepped outside the tent. "It's a dungeon of fog," he said. He could hardly believe his eyes. The weather was so uncertain. He came back into the tent.

"Did I hear you say it's fog, Ple, old man?" Art had a chew in already.

"Yes," said Ple, "as thick as mud."

Jack Brown sat up, "what's the going like? Did it freeze at all?"

"No," said Ple, "in fact I think it's even softer going than it was last evening. We're going to have trouble travelling in this. The dogs will sink right to their ears."

Art spoke, "Old man, I'm moving. I don't care how bad it is. We've been here now for two days and nights and it's time we moved on. Or maybe we should go on over to Hawkes Bay."

Peters sat up rubbing his eyes, "Enough is enough," he said, "I'm going to issue some orders."

They all looked at him. "When it gets daylight we are going to break camp and move. Do you hear that? Move."

Art looked at Ple and then at Jack and then looked at Peters. "I've got to take back all the things I've said about you since we left home." He rolled the tobacco chew over in his mouth and juice ran out of the corners. He was grinning and his gold tooth was glistening in the candlelight. "I got some more orders for you, too, gentlemen." He was about to get up. "Come, on Peters," he said with glee in his eyes. At this very moment Peters was his man.

"The fact of the matter is," Peters said, "we're not going any further up Western. We're going back home and we're going back the way we came."

The wad of tobacco that was bulged in Art's jaw fell out on his lap. Art got such a jolt from this statement that he sat there with his mouth open and it looked for a moment that Art was going to hit him. "Now you listen here, old man," said Art, in a tone that had such hatred in it it almost made them jump. There was a snarl on his face. His ears moved. Art Compton was not a man to play around with. He then opened up at Peters. The argument was so firy that Jack Brown had to step in to avoid bloodshed. Peters ended with the words, "I'm not going any further, I'don't care if Corcoran is ever found. You can go on if you want to, but not me. You hear, Not Me!" He was screaming.

Ple and Art moved out of the tent. When they were outside Ple looked at Art and started laughing. "You sure got sucked in on that one, Art," he said.

Art said nothing.

"I knew what he was getting around to all the time. You could see the yellow streak showing."

Art looked around, "Tis getting daylight."

"You're right,"said Ple. "You know there's nothing' to this fog, Art. 'Tis only vapour from the brooks and 'tis hanging around the side of this hill. I'll tell you what we'll do, Art. Let's you and I put on our snowshoes and walk over to the Copper Barren. 'tis about two miles away. We'll walk in along the brook to the steady, then cross and walk up to the Copper Barren. By the time we get over, this stuff (fog) should be cleared up."

Art looked at Ple. "Ple, now you're talking my language. Anything to get away from that slob."

"Good," said Ple.

"Do you know something, Ple? This fog is going to haul the wind around nar-west as sure as you're here, old man."

"I dare say you're right," Ple said. Then both men went inside the tent.

They tried to explain to Peters what they were about to do, but to no avail. He wanted to leave immediately for home. They just ignored him and came back out of the tent. They put on their showshoes. It was light now but still foggy. They crossed the big bog at the end of the pond to the small brook at its base.

It took them about half an hour to get across. They had to cut a large tree and use it as a bridge. Finally they crossed and headed west on the bogs called Brendy's Flats. (This is where an old hunter, Leander Rowsell of Englee, had to destroy one of his sled dogs, so he named the bog after his dog, Brendy.)

Finally they came to Souffletts River. The water was high. They were too busy to notice the weather until the sun shone on them. "Tis gonna be a good day, Ple," said Art.

"It's only the vapour from the pond back where the tent is," said Ple.

"We'll never cross the river. Too much water," Art said.

"I didn't expect to cross it anyway. We'll walk into the steady."

They stepped back away from the edge of the river and started to pick their way through the black spruce and scrub.

It was close to half a mile up to the steady from where they were now, and the going was soft. The snow had no bottom to it. Finally, about an hour later, they reached the steady.

"Do you think it's safe to cross?" Art asked. "There's a couple bad holes up there." Art pointed with his hand.

Ple squinted his eyes. "I wonder where Corcoran is?" he asked. "For sure he's somewhere along the river. Keep your eyes peeled, Art."

Ple walked out on the ice and cut a hole. The ice was soft, but he thought he would move out further and cut another one. He cut another hole and so on, until they got across safely.

"Well," said Art, "where do we go from here?"

Ple motioned to an area by the side of the pond where a lead ran up the side of the Copper Barren. "That way," he said, "takes you up to a big bog with woods on your right. It's the old camping grounds."

The two men started up the opening. They had walked only a few steps after they got off the pond, when Ple stopped. He caught hold of Art's coat sleeve and motioned for him to stop.

"What's that?" said Art.

"Look at this," said Ple. He put down his axe. "Look at that, Art," he said. "I think that's what we're looking for."

Art was quick to observe. "Yes, I think you're right, Ple. It's a man's track alright."

Ple examined it more closer. "And he's walking out the river, too." They both examined it now. "I think you're right, Ple. Who do you think it is?"

Ple sat down. "Well it's got to be Corcoran. For the simple reason if it's a search party, there would be more than one track, and if one of the search party got lost, this place would be crawling with people because they would know near about were he got lost."

Art looked at the track again. "Yes," he said. "I think 'tis Corcoran."

"I think so, too," said Ple. "Let's go back and get everything together and get on this track."

"What time is it, Ple?"

Ple took his watch out of his pocket. He squinted his eyes and looked at it. 'Tis 7:30."

"Well," said Art, "we got the whole day in front of us."

"You're right. Come on."

With this, the two men hurried back with new courage.

As they got near the camp, the sun broke through the fog. It made everything glow a bright orange and vapour was rising from the snow. The dogs were barking loudly and stretching themselves. One could hardly hear himself speak. Ple roared to the dogs to be quiet, then met Peters at the tent door.

"Ple, are you ready?" he said in a voice that tried to have a tone of command.

Ple stood for a moment with his hands on his hips and stared at him. He noticed that Peters was shaking with emotion. Ple was about to open up on him but sensed something.

Jack Brown came out of the tent. He was furious. "The biggest mistake I ever made in my life, Ple, was when I came on this trip. Why did we take him with us? Why?" he asked aloud.

The dogs were all quiet now. They stood and stared at the three men. Art stood near the komatik. In his hand he held a dog whip, partly coiled up. Tobacco juice ran down his chin and a look of satisfaction covered his face. His fingers twitched. He could almost feel the end of the leather snake licking the ears of Peters.

Peters looked at him but turned away quickly. Peters and Jack Brown started a very heated argument, but Ple stepped in although it pleased him to hear them quarrel. "Hold everything, boys. I got something to tell you." He held up his hands. They looked at him.

"What is it, Ple?" Jack asked.

"We have found fresh tracks of Corcoran," Ple said.

Both men looked with wide eyes. Jack Brown spoke up, "Where?"

"Over on the side of the brook."

Peters spoke up, "Are you sure?"

Ple didn't answer him.

"It could be someone else. What are you getting us into now?"

Ple spoke up quickly with a very cutty tone of voice. "Someone made the tracks. It doesn't matter to me. Someone's lost, but I'd rather for it to be Corcoran."

Peters replied, "I bet you would."

The two men stared at each other, knowing what was meant by the remark, referring to the $100.00, but said nothing.

"Now," said Ple, "We're moving, boys, over where we saw the tracks. Art, harness the dogs. Jack, get your team ready. I'll take down the tent and stove."

"Good," said Jack.

They went to work breaking camp. This only took about ten minutes and they were ready to go. Ple kept on his snowshoes and walked ahead.

After they had crossed the brook at the base of the bog and got on Brendy's Flats, they moved fairly well. It took them one hour to go through a skirt of scrub, before they got to the barren under the Wolfe Barren. They crossed swiftly and stopped the dogteams on the other side. They tied on the kotamiks and Peters put on his snowshoes. He had problems walking in them. The four men walked to the tracks. For a moment Peters didn't believe it was a man's tracks. "It's caribou tracks," he said looking at Jack Brown.

"You know something, Peters," said Art. "You should have a straight jacket put on ya."

Peters didn't answer him.

"Come here," said Ple. "Look here. This is a boot print."

Peters still didn't believe it, but said nothing else about it.

"Where do we go from here to get to Harbour Deep?" Peters asked.

Ple spoke up. "We just crossed the Souffletts River. It empties out in Harbour Deep. So all we have to do is follow it and we'll come out in the logging roads. That's about 15 miles from here."

"So," said Peters, "we're about 25 miles from Harbour Deep."

"Yes," said Ple.

Jack Brown spoke. "What's the plan now, Ple?"

"Come here, Art." Ple motioned for all three to get around. "Now boys, we have reached our objective. We left Englee to look for a lost man, Ranger Corcoran, and after days of arguing and fighting and draggin our stuff through the water and slob, we have finally come upon a track of a man..." He paused. No one said anything. "We have to make a decision right now. Shall we continue and proceed with a 'knife at our throats,' or proceed at least on a workable condition."

Still no one spoke.

"If we do the right thing, we could find the person who made these tracks and maybe find him alive, but if we work contrary to each other we could miss him completely."

There was silence.

"From now on all eyes and ears are to be completely on alert if this job is to be completed, and listen. If we move fast and find Corcoran without too much difficulty, we can be in Harbour Deep tonight, or at least in one of the wood camps before dark, or even sometime tonight, anyway."

Still no one said anything.

"Now what do you say, boys?"

Each man nodded in agreement that they would work together.

"Good enough," said Ple. "That is what I think we should do."

They all looked at him knowing that he was capable of making plans and carrying them out.

"It looked obvious to me that Danny crossed this steady and went up to the Copper Barren. It would be a wise thing to do. From there he could look down the valley and the going would be better.for sure. He don't know about the bogs along the side of the river, but what I'm expecting once he gets on top of the barren and can see the bogs, he'll go down there on them and follow the river out."

They all listened carefully.

"Now what I'll do is follow his tracks and see where he went. If he crossed the open I'll cut back and meet you between 12 and 1 o'clock.

There's a place about four miles down from here where there's a big cross near the river. You can't miss it. Whit Pilgrim nailed it up there about three or four years ago. It's a big juniper slabbed down with an axe. Just outside of that is a bog. You wait there. If I'm there before you, I'll cut a top and stick it up. Then you come on and follow my tracks." They all agreed.

Peters seemed to perk up a little. He shifted his weight from one foot to the other.

"Good enough, boys," said Ple as he stepped into the tracks of Danny Corcoran. The other three men with the two dogteams started cutting a road through scrub out along the river.

Ple Gillard was a man who 'grew up on a pair of snowshoes', as the saying goes. He spent years on surveys both summer and winter travelling the wilderness. He had been poaching caribou, for food only, every winter since he was big enough to handle a dogteam (This man is now a friend of the wildlife.)

As he walked along in the tracks of this Ranger, although it was soft going he was walking with ease, he noticed the tracks he was walking in were made with difficulty. The tracks were without snowshoes and he noticed that the traveller was falling down and laying down every few hundred feet. He walked across a large bog about a quarter mile up from the steady.

Someplace on the bog the tracks disappeared because the snow was melting. Someplaces it was down to the ground. He came to the edge of the Copper Brook. As he walked along the brook's edge, he saw where the traveller sat down under a large spruce tree. He looked around for clues but saw nothing. He then picked up the tracks and followed them along very carefully. The man making the tracks was sinking deep in the snow. He noticed that the man was either crawling or dragging something. It was hard to tell under these conditions.

He looked closer and after seeing no tracks, he was sure the man was crawling. He must have been sinking too deeply. Finally, he got to the edge of the Copper Barren. The snow was gone along the side of the barren. The tracks disappeared. He walked up on the top of the barren and looked around. It was a clear day. He looked at his watch. It was 10:30. There was a slight breeze from the west. The weather was going to change, he knew. It was going to freeze tonight.

He could hear the dogs barking down by the river. "The boys are making pretty good time," he said to himself. "I wonder where you went from here Corcoran," he said out loud breaking the silence.

He walked along the edge of the barren towards the valley. Then he saw the same track leading from the open and going into the woods. "Great," he said, "just as I thought. You're going to stick to the river."

Ple quickly stepped into his tracks and followed him into the heavy timer. "Maybe you're in here," he said looking all around. As he walked he came to a windfall. He saw tracks leading under it. For a moment the blood rushed to his head. He stooped and had a better look at it. He felt relieved. No one was there. Then he saw tracks leading away from the area, but they were much plainer. He knew the traveller had spent a night there. Again he looked for clues to try and establish identity but found none.

He stepped into the tracks again and following very quickly, the tracks turned and went back to the barren again. He saw where more tracks had left the barren and started back into the woods again. This time the tracks were very plain. Now he knew the person had spent another night near here. He followed the tracks down towards the river, expecting any minute to see somebody. He came to a hill where he noticed someone had slid down an embankment. At the base of the hill he saw where quite a fuss had taken place. He suspected the person had a terrible time getting up. Then he saw something on the snow. It was bright and shining. He stooped down and picked it up. It was a belt buckle.

Ple knew now who's tracks he was on. It was Danny Corcoran. He saw Ranger Peters with the same kind of buckle on his belt. He put it in his pocket and started following his tracks. He noticed that he was walking very little, crawling and sliding whenever possible. His tracks led out to th bog where he told Art and the boys to meet him. He got there before they did. He listened for a moment. He could still hear the dogs barking.

He stood there and thought for a moment. When Corcoran passed by here they were so close to him that if they had been looking they could have almost seen him, because from where he now stood he could almost see the trees where they camped at the Rocky Stint. "He must be suffering severely," he said.

The bog where he was standing was almost bare of snow. He walked to the edge and picked up Danny's tracks again where he left the bog heading out the river. He looked in the direction of the dog teams and saw movement. He put his hands up to his mouth and gave a few "Hellos". They heard him and came at a fast pace to where he was. The dogs were making a loud noise, all twenty-seven of them, barking at one time and jumping savagely. Their traces were all tangled around the trees and snags on the bog.

Art was ahead with his team and Jack Brown was behind with his tied up out of the reach of each other. There were about half of the dogs running loose, just milling around. The three men came where Ple was. They tried to talk but the barking of the dogs was too much. Art got the dog whip out and silenced them. "What have you found, Ple? Did he come down here?"

Ple reached into his pants pocket and took out the buckle. "What do you think of this, Peters?" He handed it to him.

He took it and looked it over. "It's a belt buckle off a Ranger's belt,"

Peters said. "Where did you get it?"

Ple pointed to the heavy woods under the Copper Barren. "Boys, I think we'll find a dead man when we find Corcoran. He's not walking hardly at all. He is sliding and crawling on his hands and knees. He's not very far ahead of us either. I saw a couple of places where he fell down. That's what it looked like. There's some awful looking tracks in places coming through the woods. It looks like he was dragging himself a couple of places."

No one said anything. They only stared at the woods ahead wondering if Danny was there.

"The tracks look a day or so old. It's a job to tell. "It's been so mild. Between the steady and where I left you fellows, he spent two nights. You could almost see our tent from where he spent one night. If we had only known."

Art looked at Ple and asked "What do we do now, Ple? We can't lose no time now."

"You're right," said Ple. "Let's get going. I'll go ahead same as last time. If I see a hard place, I'll swamp a little, but I want to move as soon as possible. I'm not expecting to go much further before I find him."

"Okay, Ple, you go on," said Jack Brown.

With this Ple headed for the heavy timber and picked up Danny's tracks. He could see now what was happening. Danny was sliding on the down grades and crawling the up grades. He was walking on the level but his boot prints were very uneven, which indicated to him that his feet were bad.

He followed him for about four miles. He walked out of the sound of the dogs and the men. He came to the bank of the big steady. He walked along the bank of the steady for about a hundred feet. He saw where Danny had walked out on the ice. It seemed he rolled around on the ice then dragged himself ashore. He saw where his tracks disappeared in the trees. "Ah," he said, "this could be the place where you crashed in."

He walked over to the place where Danny walked into the woods. He saw where he crawled under a couple of trees then out again. He walked about twenty feet further and saw a place beat down under a big tree. Suddenly he saw a 303 rifle. He picked it up. There was one round in the chamber. He had a job to get it ejected. He pushed the bolt a couple of times, finally he got it out. The round had been fired. It was an empty cartridge.

He looked under the tree where he had spent the night. He saw a flashlight hanging on a tree, also a mug and some tea in a bag held together by a drawstring. He looked closer and found a pipe filled with tobacco. He looked at the tracks leading away from the tree. They looked real fresh.

"You're not far ahead now Danny," Ple said. "Now I'm not so worried. At least you haven't got your rifle."

Then Ple thought for a moment, "Suppose you're out of your mind. You could have shot me, but now I got your rifle, so that's that" thought Ple. He took all items including the rifle and carried them to the edge of the steady. Well, I have to go back now and meet the boys. He looked at his watch. It was 1:30 p.m. "We'll boil the kettle when we get there," he said out loud. With this he started to swamp back to meet the men and dogs.

Gill Ellsworth sat in the telegraph office and looked at the message that just came in from Commanding Officer Major Anderton, Newfoundland Rangers, St. John's:

TO GILL ELLSWORTH. SORRY UNABLE TO SEND ANY PERSONNEL TO NORTHERN PENINSULA-STOP-HAVE RANGERS OUT WITH SEARCH PARTIES FROM ENGLEE AND PORT SAUNDERS-STOP-WILL KEEP YOU INFORMED. SIGNED MAJOR ANDERTON NEWFOUNDLAND RANGERS.

Gill took off his headphones and got up from the desk. "What does all this mean?" he said. He walked over to the Dixie stove and put in a few birch junks. "I am helpless," he said, throwing his arms in the air. "There's nothing I can do." He put on his coat and went to his dinner (lunch). It was almost 2 p.m.

It was about 2 p.m. when Danny awoke. He had lost track of time. He lifted his head and looked around. He thought for a moment 'where am I?' Then said aloud, "I am stuck here on the river." He sat up, the pain in his legs gone. His hands looked horrible but there wasn't any pain in these either. This was a relief, but he felt weak and hungry. His stomach was rolling with hunger, but he felt good as far as pain was concerned. He staggered to his feet and had a look around He was so weak he could barely hold the weight of his body up on his legs. (This would be the last time Danny Corcoran would ever stand or even attempt to get up. It's enough to make one sick to think of such a thing, but it's good to know that a person in such a condition doesn't know what his future holds.) He looked across the river and then up at the sky. He was too weak to make a step. He held on for a moment then lay down again in the same position. The shape of his body was imprinted in the snow. He wanted to urinate but was unable to do so only in his pants, as his fingers were too sore to unbutton his clothes. He closed his eyes. Something was making him feel good. His mind then wandered off to a faraway place. Everything was warm and wonderful. Then he heard the sound of music and it seemed as if some great orchestra opened up playing in his mouth and Danny fell into a deep trance. The die had been cast sealing his destiny.

The search party from Englee reached the big steady. Ple called the men over to the area where he found the rifle and the rest of the things. Each man examined the items. "It's no mistake," said Peters, "it's Corcoran's tracks we're on. What do you think, Ple?" His tone was now filled with a little bit of excitement. "I mean, what should we do now?"

"We'll have a quick snack and move on," Ple said. 'It's 2 o'clock now. We got about four hours before dark. We will soon catch him. These tracks are pretty fresh. He's crawling most of the time. I'd say he got his feet frozen. He can't cross Ben Hynes Brook, that's for sure. So if he got as far as that, that's where we'll find him. We'll continue the same way unless Peters, you want to got on ahead or come with me."

Peters opened his eyes wide. "No," he said quickly. He looked as if he wanted no part of it. He was scared of what he was going to see.

"I'll go with you," said Art.

Ple looked at him, "Who's going to take your team?"

"Maybe Peters."

Ple grinned.

"No, thanks," said Peters.

"Art, you'd better stick with the dog team. I don't want anyone with me."

Jack Brown called, "The kettle is boiled boys. Come on."

They all got their mugs out and continued the conversation as they ate.

The tracks leading along the river that Ple Gillard was following looked like someone had been dragging a bunch of old clothes or something tied on a rope. If someone else had been out travelling and not looking for someone lost, they would have passed the track and thought it to be something foreign or some kind of an animal that was now extinct. At almost every step, Ple thought he could see something moving just ahead of him. It was 4:30 p.m. when he came to another wide embankment. He noticed that Danny had actually gone down this one and it looked like he had lain in one position for some time. The snow was trampled down by his weight. He had got to his feet and walked for about fifty to sixty feet and then began crawling again.

It was getting cold now. The snow was starting to freeze. The wind was northwest. "It's going to freeze," he said. He could hear the dogs barking. It seemed they were making good time now. He went on a little further. He saw where someone had chopped a tree about a year ago. This was the first sign he had seen along the river. "I must be getting close to Ben Hynes Brook," he said. He followed the tracks again. They kept out near the river. All of the sudden his progress was stopped by a slow moving brook. "Ben Hyne's Brook," he said. "You've got to be out on this point."

He saw where Danny moved around in circles on his feet. He looked around and saw the roof of the camp on the other side of the brook. "I suppose he wasn't fool enough to try and get across the brook to get to that shack," he said. He could still hear the dogs barking. The boys were coming fast.

"My God, there he is," Ple said aloud. His voice almost made him jump. He moved over near him and looked at him. "Hey, hey," he said in his direction. Danny never moved. He walked closer. The man was dressed in a dark brown, almost black parka of the Newfoundland Rangers. He saw what looked like a pack sack under his head.

Ple was excited. His heart pounded in his body and his face felt hot. For a moment he felt funny. He had not prepared himself for this. He could see his face. It was in the parka hood. Ple called, "Hello, Danny Corcoran," but he didn't make a stir. Ple was now about 10 feet away. "Now Ple get ahold of yourself," he heard himself say. "This job has to be done."

He walked closer and saw his hands. He couldn't believe his eyes. He got near him and knelt down beside him. He lifted the hood back from his face. What he saw will always be in his memory as if put there by a red hot branding iron. Ple tells the story.

"I walked over to him. He was laying on a pack sack. The pack was full of holes and all ragged from where he was sliding on it, when it was on his back. I couldn't see his face because the hood was covering it, but his hands I saw. Earl, it was a sight to behold. The blood was oozing out of them from his wrist down. They were raw. The bones were sticking out through the flesh. I felt sick. There was blood all over the snow. (Ple is now in his seventies with a clear mind but had difficulty telling the story) I very slowly reached down and lifted the hood from around his face. This was when I got the biggest surprise. I thought I had been following Danny Corcoran, the Newfoundland Ranger, but when I saw his face I said, "Tis not you at all." I had heard Nat Johnson describe him as young, tall, good looking and very physically fit, but the man I was looking at now was an old man with a beard. For a moment I forgot the uniform. His eyes were sunken in his head. His face was partly hidden by a dirty redish beard. His teeth were partly showing. "I wonder who it is," I asked myself. I felt his face. "You're dead who ever you is." Then he saw the badge on his cap and under the parka the Newfoundland Ranger uniform. Is it possible? I reached into the pocket of his tunic and took out his note book. In it was his identification card. It said, "Danny Corcoran, #14 Newfoundland Rangers."

"Dear Lord," I said, "at least you're out of your punishment. You're dead."

The dogteams were stopped about a hundred yards back. He heard Art calling, "Ple." The dogs were quiet now. "Ple, where are you?"

Ple put his hand to his face and roared back. "I'm here."

"Have you seen anything?" Art called.

"Yes," Ple called back. "I have him found."

There was a pause. "Did you say you had him?" said Art.

"Yes," said Ple.

"How is he?" said Art.

"He's dead. Danny's dead," said Ple.

There was a silence. Ple looked in the direction of the dogteams.

"I'm not dead, sir. I'm dying."

Ple Gillard says he has had many scares in his lifetime, but that day on the Soufletts River, he heard a voice that almost made his blood run cold.

I heard a dead man speak," said Ple to Earl (the author) in 1983 while relating the story. "I almost jumped out of my 'wits." When I landed, I was facing Danny. I stared at him. His eyes were wide open. He lifted a hand and smiled at me, but he sank back into an unconscious position."

"How are ya?" Ple asked him, but Danny didn't answer. He let out a puff of air and yelled back to the others, "He's alive, boys. He's alive."

Ple turned back to him again. He was still breathing. He noticed his body had thawed down in the snow and water was all around his feet. He could smell urine and human waste. He knew no one could take down their pants with their hands in such a condition as his. He had to do everything in his clothes. He took off his jacket and put it around him after he had hauled him up nearer to the tree, to get his feet out of the water.

The next man to arrive on the scene was Art Compton. He had one of his blankets with him. It was homemade and smelled of smoke from the use in the tent. He looked and shook his head. "Ple, is he alive?"

"Yes," said Ple. "He just spoke and opened his eyes."

"Old man," said Art, "if he's alive, he's not much of it."

Art put the blanket around Danny. Some of the dogs came around sniffing Danny. At one point it looked as if the dogs would jump him, if it had not been for Art cracking the whip.

Peters came up to where Danny was and looked at him. "I wouldn't know him," he said, "only for the red hair." He looked again. "It's him alright," hauling back his coat with no mercy in how he was handling him. This was noticeable to Ple and Art.

"Has he got his ID on him?" asked Peters.

Ple answered quickly, "Yes, I have it here." He took the notebook out of his pocket and handed it to Peters.

"Yes, it's him."

Jack Brown came up to them, "Boys, is he alive?"

"Yes," said Peters, who had now taken over. "Jack, get that bottle of brandy out of my bag for me, will you?"

"Yes," said Jack and went to the sled and got the bottle and brought it back to Peters.

"Hold his head, Ple. I'll pour some of this in his mouth. It might wake him up."

"Now, you listen here, Peters," said Art. "You want to kill him right off?" Peters got furious with Art.

"I can't believe it," said Ple. "My son, you're crazy. You mean you're going to pour brandy down his throat. Not on your life, Peters. Put that bottle away."

"Let's boil the kettle and get some hot tea or broth in him," said Art.

Before anyone could say anything else Ple spoke up. "No, this is what we got to do. We have to cross the brook. We're only ten miles from Harbour Deep and if we can cross we wouldn't be long. 'Tis freezing like a flint now. Once we get to the Portage Road we shouldn't be long."

They looked at Ben Hyne's Brook.

"Jack, you get your komatik down here and we'll put Danny on it and wrap him up in heavy blankets. I'm going to look at the brook. We got to work fast."

Jack went back to his sled. Art and Peters lifted Danny up out of the snow. Ple walked over to the edge of the river. There was too much water to wade across. To make a raft would take too long. "Ah, ah," he said, "I see a way."

He walked over the point between the two brooks where large pans of ice were gathered. "We could use these pans to cross on. Art, come here."

"Yes, what is it?"

"Do you see these pans of ice there about a foot thick? We could load everything on them and go across."

"Maybe," said Art, "but it's a tricky business. We should cut a couple of poles and cross two at a time. There's a lot of tide there."

Ple said, "Yes, we can do it. Let's you and me go across first. We'll put Danny on the komatik and go across. Let the dogs swim. If we can get across before dark, we'll go out to Harbour Deep tonight."

"I'm willing to give it a try, old man. Let's go," said Art.

They cut two long poles. The ice was about twenty feet square. It was just a slush pan. They put the komatik with Danny on it on the ice and pushed it off with the poles. They found themselves floating down the river with the tide. Their dogs were swimming along behind them. At one place they could not reach bottom with their poles, but the ice pan soon got into shallow water. They then pushed it into the shore and grabbed the trees near the edge and pulled the ice pan in close. They had done a good job. They had crossed the river.

They waved to Jack Brown and Peters to come on. They took Danny ashore on a small bog. He was strapped on the komatik with the tent and blankets under him. The ice was still around the edge of the steady. They watched Jack Brown and Peters coming down the steady on a pan of ice and the dogs swimming after them. Everything was in a loud commotion, dogs barking and the four men talking loudly.

It was now beginning to freeze hard and the wind was also blowing hard. The two other men had landed a bit further down the steady. Ple and Art met them and pulled the komatik ashore rapidly. Their dogs came ashore and shook themselves, sending water everywhere. After everything had quieted down, Ple called the group together near the komatik that Danny was on. "Boys, we done a good job getting across the river." He looked at Art. "I know it's dark, but we can still move on. Art, you used to work in here, didn't you?"

"Yes," Art said, "in to Stan's camp."

"So you know the road, Art?"

"Yes," Art said, "when we get to it. I went out here only once before and I never took much notice to it then."

Peters spoke up, "Unless you know what you're doing, we should stay here all night."

Ple said, "Look, it's about ten miles to Harbour Deep. Once we pick up the road, there will be no problems. We can go on out. 'Tis a good night. Danny has to get medical treatment as soon as possible. I don't think he can last much longer, maybe not before daylight. I'll tell you what. I'll go on up through the woods until I come to the road, then I'll come back. You get the dogsteams ready while I'm gone."

"Good," said Art.

"Now make sure you stay close to each other. I'll walk on out the road and if I come to a bad place, I'll stop."

"Okay," said Art.

"But keep a close eye on Danny. He don't look much of it," said Ple.

"I will," said Art, as Ple stepped into the woods.

Ple walked for about a hundred yards, then came to a wood road. In the twilight he could see snowshoe tracks that were leading out. They were about three to five days old from Ple's estimation. "This is great," said Ple. "I think I'll go back and tell the boys." He spoke out loud. "Harbour Deep tonight."

He quickly went back to where the men were getting the teams ready. "Art, the Portage Road is not very far away, just through there. I'll go on and you keep coming behind me. O.K.?"

"Okay, Ple."

Ple then left and went quickly through the woods and picked up the Portage Road and started towards Harbour Deep at a fast pace. He had walked for about an hour. He had crossed a couple of small brooks but nothing to stop a dog team. Once or twice he stopped and listened for the teams but heard nothing. This was funny because they should have caught up to him by now. He thought about this, sat down and waited for about ten minutes, but still heard nothing.

"Maybe something has happened to Danny. I wonder what is the matter. I'll have to go back and meet them."

Then he turned around and headed back to where he had first taken the snowshoe track, when he heard the dogs barking. Ple saw the light in the tent door. He called to Art. Then heard Art shouting at the dogs. "Is that you, Ple?" called Art above the dogs barking.

"Yes, 'tis me. Is Jack's dogs tied on?"

"Yes, come on."

Ple went to the tent and met Art. First he took off his snowshoes then said, "I thought I could trust you, Art."

Art clenched his fist. "'Tis not me, old man. I wanted to go on."

"Why did you stop?" He paused. "The going is the best since we left home. It might be raining tomorrow."

Art spoke up. "Peters issued another order. He said it was too hard on Danny to travel tonight. He could get shook up bad."

"Where is Peters?"

"In the tent," was Art's reply.

Ple went into the tent. He was mad. He shook his fist at Peters. "Why did you stop and put the tent up? I told you to keep going. What's wrong?" He looked furious at Peters.

Peters was lying back on his blankets, he sat up. "Now you listen here, Ple. I ordered the teams to stop. We got a very sick man on our hands, an unconscious man. It would be too rough on him to travel tonight. All these bumps would cause too much pain on him. He would not be able to take it."

Ple stood there. The three men stared at him as if he was going to take the place apart. "I should have known better. That's about how many brains you got Peters. Are you aware that Corcoran is unconscious. He would not feel any pain at all, even if you dragged him and by now we could have been almost to Harbour Deep. But when the heat here from the stove hits him, he's going to wake up and you're going to hear screams like you never heard before. No I don't expect you to understand that because you're too dumb for anything."

There was a pause. Peters lay back on the blankets again, then Ple said. "All I've done since I left Englee is row, row. It seems if you have to get anything done you have to get in a fight over it. I'll tell you something, Peters, if Gus Compton was here now in my place you would have to get a new face put on you because he would bat the face off you. But if anything happens to Corcoran and we don't get him out, I'll have you hung."

Peters answered without even looking up. "I've made the right decision, Ple."

"What's the use?" said Ple.

"The soup's ready," said Jack, as Ple turned his attention to Danny.

"Has he come too, yet Jack?"

"No, said Jack. "Not a stir."

Ple said, "Okay, boys I'll stay up with him."

"Leave my blankets around him. I'll stay up with you," Art said.

"Good," said Ple. "Jack, you might as well turn in now. We might need you later on tonight."

"Okay," said Jack.

They noticed that Peters was already under his blankets. They ate their soup using the komatik box for a table. This was the eighth night they spent in the canvas tent and not one night was there any peace. Their finding Ranger Corcoran was not luck. It was the results of guts, hard work and skill and now the three men sat there eating fried dough and soup. They smelled of sweat and grime.

If Peters had not been with them, there would have been times when they could have told jokes, but his presence kept a scrowl on everyone's face for most of the time.

The candle light flickered. Ple and Art sat motionless looking at the candle burning. They could hear Danny breathing. Jack Brown and Peters were sleeping.

"Hey, Art, wonder what his feet are like. They must be bad because he crawled all the way from the Wolfe Barren and what a set of hands he has on him. Never seen the like before. 'Tis awful, the bones are sticking through. I wonder what in the world did he get involved in. He froze his hands and lost his mitts. I'd say the same thing happened to his feet. They are frozen too."

"Do you know what we should do?" said Art. "Let's take off his boots and take a look."

"Yes, I think we will," said Ple.

"Okay," said Art.

They took the candle and put it down near his feet so they could see what they were doing. Ple took his knife and cut the logan string. He pulled his pants and underwear up. The smell was terrible.

"Phew," said Ple. "He smells like an outdoor toilet."

Ple lifted Danny's left leg. He could hardly believe his eyes. His leg was black almost to his knee. The skin was rolled down over his leg and dried blood was on his underwear.

"What a mess," said Ple. "Take off his boot."

Ple rolled the top of his boot down and lifted his leg more. Art pulled on the boot and it seemed stuck to something. He pulled it again while moving it side to side. The action was similar to a dentist pulling out a tooth. The boot came off. Ple felt something grip his stomach. His eyes bulged out at what they saw. Most of the foot, the heel and the bottom of his foot stayed in the boot. His sock was rotted and the ankle bone was clearly visible, sticking through the hole in his sock, and decayed flesh was clearly showing through.

Danny groaned and moved his head from side to side. "Put the boot back on Art. There's nothing we can do."

Art put the boot back on and hauled the top of the sock up. "Ple, do you know what I think?"

"I don't know, Art. What?"

"Gangrene is after setting in. Look how black it is and look at the two red streaks gone up his legs."

"You're right, Art. I think if he makes it through the night, he'll be lucky."

"The heat from the stove is going to get him," said Art.

"Hey, Art," said Ple. "I hear the old man, (his father) say, they had to put hot presses on Uncle Billy Canning's leg the time he had a blood poisoned toe. The gangrene did not kill him."

"Yes," said Art. "I heard some of the older women talking about that. Aunt Louie Ellsworth was telling Sue (Art's wife) about that gangrene stuff. She said that if you put hot rags above the gangrene, it would prevent it from spreading and maybe even kill the germ."

"See, Art, there's no cure for it. That's what they say."

Art looked at Ple, "Old man, lets put some hot presses on Danny. We can put them on him just above his knees. That might keep the gangrene from spreading any further."

Ple spoke up. "Yes, I think we will. It might save his life."

"We can tear up one of my blankets," Art said and reached for his blanket.

"Just a minute, Art."

Art looked at Ple.

"Maybe we should check with Peters first. For intance if something should happen to Danny, he would have us hung."

Art nodded his head. He knew it was true.

"I'll wake him up and ask him. I'm sure he won't mind, especially if it hurts him," said Ple.

"Yes, go ahead," said Art.

"Hey, Peters," said Ple, trying not to wake Jack. "Hey, Peters," he said almost in a whisper shaking Peters.

Peters woke and looked at Ple. "What is it Ple. What's wrong?"

"We just looked at Danny's legs and we think they're full of gangrene."

"So what? What can we do, Ple?" His voice was low and unconcerned.

"We think the remedy for that is to put on hot presses every hour above the gangrene. That's what the old people used to do and still do. Myself and Art, that's what we're going to do with Danny."

Peters sat up. "Now you two, you listen to me." He looked at them both. "I know first aid and there are no such things in the manual. Do any of you know first aid?"

No one spoke.

"It's obvious to me that you don't. Now, that makes me the only one qualified. Now both of you don't lay a finger on him."

Ple was furious. "Peters, you want him to die. The thing is to do something. It's better than doing nothing. Can't you see he could be dead before daylight."

"Listen Ple," said Peters. "Is he complaining? Has he asked you to do anything for him." Then Peters lay back and covered himself with his blankets.

Ple and Art sat staring at each other. Their thoughts were on the dying Ranger and their hands were tied as far as doing anything to try and help him. "Why would Peters want him to die." they thought.

"Art, you lie down and get a couple of hours sleep. You will need it in the morning. If I get too sleepy, I'll call you."

"Okay, Ple."

With this Art lay down and put his blanket over him. He was lying on a bed of boughs. Almost as soon as he lay down he went to sleep.

Art Compton was rough and tough. He had a bad heart. In his lifetime he had spent many a day and night hauling sick people to the hospital on dog teams in blizzards, without getting paid one dime. When he lay down, the world could fall around him as far as he cared. There was almost complete silence, except the deep breathing of Danny. Ple looked at him and wondered what must have happened to him and what he went through.

"I wonder if he will live to tell the tale." Ple put more wood in the stove, then lay down on the wood near the stove. He looked at his watch. It was 1 a.m. We could have been in Harbour Deep by now, he thought. Ple heard a groan. He quickly sat up. It was Danny. In the dim light of the candle he could see him rising his head. His eyes came open and he stared at Ple. It was a very serious moment. He lifted the hand that the flesh was hanging off and the bones sticking out through. Any other man would have screamed, but not Ple Gillard. He had nerves of steel. Danny opened his mouth and looked at Ple, his teeth showing. His face was boney and covered with his dirty red beard. "Who are you?" he asked in a deep voice, that made the hairs on Ple's head tingle.

Ple looked at him.

"Who are you?" Danny said, "I'm a Catholic. Who are you.?"

"I'm a Protestant."

Danny groaned, then said, "Please don't touch my feet. Don't touch my feet mister."

Danny lowered his head and moved it from side to side.

"Hey Peters. Peters," said Ple, shaking his leg.

Peters opened his eyes.

"I think Danny is coming to. He was just talking to me."

"What did he say?"

"He just asked me who I was and told me he was a Catholic."

"Is that so?" said Peters. Peters sat up and reached over and shook Danny. "Corcoran, Corcoran." He shook him again. "Corcoran you know me. I'm Peters. We trained together. How are you?"

Danny tried to speak but could not.

"Peters," said Ple. "You should know the difference than to get a dying man to go talking like that. It will take all his energy. Leave him alone."

"Well, what did you call me for?"

"Okay, Peters. The next time I'll call you is for breakfast or when he dies."

Peters lay back in his blankets again and went to sleep.

Chapter 25
March 27, 1936

Ple looked at his watch. It was 5:30 a.m. He had not gotten any sleep. His thoughts had been with Danny all night. He could not see any hope for him. He had examined his left hand closer. All the fingers were broken and a part of two were gone. "What must have happened" he thought. "He must have gotten them caught somewhere. It looks as though they had been in a bear trap." He then got up and went outside. It was dawning. The wind was northwest. Everything was frozen as hard as steel. He could hear the river roaring. "If you were out last night, my son," said Ple, then glanced up at the stars, "you would have been done now. Frozen."

He again looked up at the starry heavens, then thought, "If the old man knew you were in such a bad condition as you're in Danny, he would pray for you." Ple was not much of a Christian and he knew it. "What am I saying?" he said out loud, kind of blushing at the thought. "It's time for the boys to get up."

The dogs stirred and Ple went back into the tent. "Heave out, boys. It's getting daylight. The kettle is boiled. Come on. Get up."

The three men then got up. They rolled up their blankets and at a little breakfast of toutons (fried dough) and tea without sugar or milk. They then took down the stove and tent. They rolled all their blankets around Danny and spread the tent on Jack's Brown komatik and lashed Danny on tightly. "I'm going on ahead," said Ple. It was light by now. "You can take your time, boys."

By now Danny had come too and wanted to sit up. Then for the first time he recognized Peters.

Ple asked Danny if he had any pain. He said "no."

Danny asked then how far they were from Harbour Deep. They explained to him where they were. He smiled and said, "We should be out in a couple hours."

Then Ple Gillard hung his head. He knew this man was not just an ordinary man. Maybe, after all, it might be possible he could survive, if he could get to a hospital right away.

It was a clear morning. Peters had told them about the plane in Norris Arm. A Major Cotton was flying it and for sure he would come immediately if he sent for him via wireless.

The sound of the dogs brought Ple's attention to the wild surroundings. The sun was coming up. Art was beginning to hook up the dogs. "Art," said Ple, "Don't hook up too many to that komatik. They'll tear everything to pieces."

There were dogs milling around and fighting. They were all colours. Some were limping from the cuts to their paws and others just shook themselves and scuffed the hard snow. The two komatik boxes were on Art's komatik, full of gear. The part of an oil barrel they were using as a pot to cook dogs food was discarded and left where they camped.

"Art," said Jack Brown, "don't go too fast. We have to take it easy. You know how rough it is on this hard snow. Danny could get shook to pieces, so take it easy, alright."

"Alright, old man," said Art. "If I only had a chew of beaver now old man." He rolled his eyes.

Jack Brown said nothing. He just grinned. Ple looked at his watch. It was ten past seven. They should be in Harbour Deep in three hours, maybe less. The signal was given then to move and the two dogteams were unhooked. All the dogs that were loose made a dash to the front. Art suspected this and was ready with the eighteen foot coil of plaited seal skin. He threw it and it went forward like a leaping cobra. It caught one dog on the ear bringing blood. It yelped. Another crack of the whip brought three dogs to the snow. The rest quickly stopped and ran to the rear. "Good," said Ple. "That's it, Compton. Do your duty."

And with these words, Ple knew Art had everything under control. They moved on at a steady pace carrying Danny Corcoran, whom they had snatched from the jaws of death.

Noah Pittman got out of bed, long before daylight. He couldn't sleep. Nellie was not well. She tossed and turned all night. He rubbed her back trying to ease her pain and sometime around 2 a.m. Herb started to cry. He got out of bed and got him a drink of water. He looked out through the window and said quietly, "Ah, it's turning real cold. The wind is nar-west. 'Twill be just just like the flint in the marning. Danny, me son, if you're out tonight, you've had it."

He then went back to the bedroom. He came out into the kitchen and lit the fire in the waterloo stove and put the kettle on. The dogs harnesses that were hung behing the stove were in the way, so he carried them out into the porch. He came back then and set down to the table. His thoughts went back to this winter. He would be glad when it was over. It was the worst he had ever experienced. Nellie was sick most all winter. Everyone was on the dole. The ice was bad in the ponds and on top of it all, Danny was lost and it was possible he might never be seen again.

And now, here he was. What could he do? He shook his head. "I've got to put this out of my mind," he thought. He noticed the kettle was boiling, then said, "I think I'll put on some salt fish to boil." He then picked out a couple pieces of fish and put it on the stove in a dipper. He went back to the bedroom and said, "Nellie, my dear. Do you want a cup of tea? The kettle is boiled."

She looked at him and smiled, "Yes, alright, but don't have it too strong, please." Her voice was weak.

"Okay," he said. He got her the tea and sat down to the table. The oil lamp was smoking. He reached and turned it down, then ate his breakfast in silence.

He went to the door, just as the sun was coming up. "'Tis a beautiful day," he said. "I think I'll spend the day sawing and cleaving wood. Nellie is sick and I think I'll stay around home today,"

He heard dogs barking and knew it was someone going in to haul wood. He put on his canvas clothes and heavy cap and stepped out into the cool morning air. Almost all the snow was gone around the houses. He decided first to bring a barrel of water using buckets. This took him about an hour. Then he took the bucksaw and started sawing off wood. Every half hour he would go back into the house and put wood in the stove.

About 8 a.m. he called Blanche (his daughter). She got up and he went back sawing wood. Everyone in the small town of seventeen families was up and around. They were glad the sun was shining after all the foggy weather. At one point Noah started to whistle. It was about 10:30 a.m. when he straightened up from sawing and wiped the sweat from his forehead with his arm. He then saw something move up near the brook. He looked closer, then saw a team of dogs come out on the ice from the Portage Road. He shaded his face with his hand and looked closer with his keen eyes. Then he saw another team come out on the ice. "Well, now what's this," he said out loud. "I don't know who that could be. I wonder where they came from."

The dogs from the village started barking as the teams drew nearer. People started to notice and rushed to their windows. After hearing the dogs barking, the doors of the houses came open and the town started to come alive.

"Who's that coming down dar?" said a voice.

"I don't know," said Noah.

The teams got near and stopped just from where Noah was standing. He strained his eyes to see if he could recognize anyone but couldn't. Some of the dogs from the village ran out but the man on the lead team struck out with the whip and almost slivered the head off one dog. The man coiled up the whip and stopped his dogteam and walked up towards Noah. As he got closer he recognized him as Art Compton.

"Nore," said Art. "Give us a chew."

Noah went into his pocket and brought out a part plug of Beaver Tobacco and gave it to Art.

Art looked at Noah with a scowl. "Wase you're doin Nore?" asked Art.

People started to mill around and gaze in wonder. "It's not what I'm doing, Art. It's what in the world is you doing?" said Noah.

Art clenched his fist and said, "Nore why idden you out looking for Corcoran?"

Noah cleared his throat. "They got Corcoran found over near River of Ponds. That's over on the other side."

" Now, Nore," said Art, through a mouthful of tobacco juice. His words pierced the soul of every man, woman and child that was in hearing of his voice. "You're wrong, Nore. You're wrong. We got him der on the kotamik. He's half frozen and I think he's dying."

Noah's eyes filled up. He dropped the saw. "My God, Art, what are you saying?" He could hardly believe his ears.

"We got Corcoran. Where can we put him?"

"Up the old man's," said Noah.

The news quickly spread around the town. Everyone started to gather around. The dogs from the two teams started to come ashore. Art threw out the whip and it cut the clear morning air with a whistle. Everyone, especially the kids, jumped back as the whip cracked. The dogs quickly jumped back on the ice.

"Bring em up along here, Ple. We're going to put him in Uncle Ned Pittman's house."

Ple then motioned to Jack Brown to come near him. He pointed out Uncle Ned Pittman's house to him. Almost everyone in the town rushed to the scene. Jack Brown hooked up three more dogs to the kotamik to help them haul their human cargo up to the house.

Barbara Gale was going over some test papers. She was trying to concentrate on the work she was doing. She looked out the window a couple of times that morning. Her mind was constantly on Danny. She had lost weight and at one point a couple of days ago, she even looked closely at her hands. She thought she was beginning to get the shakes, but she found out she was still steady. She was drinking a cup of tea when she saw people running. There was a stir in the house, then the sound of voices, loud voices. She put down her pen and took a closer look out the window. Then she heard, "Barbara, Barbara. They're here with Danny. They have Danny." It was Aunt Martha.

Barbara ran to the kitchen. She saw Uncle Edward going out to the porch. She stopped and put her hands to her face. She was shocked. She did not know what to think. She reached for a chair then looked through the window. The dog team hauling Danny was coming in the yard. People were everywhere. She heard Aunt Martha saying, "My God, my God." She could not see Danny, but then she saw the ropes that were keeping the blankets on the kotamik. She knew Danny was underneath them. "He's hurt," she whispered. She felt sick. It was her willpower that had kept her going and now it told her to get herself under control.

Aunt Martha came in. "Barbara, Danny is not good. Get the spare room ready and the clothes on the bed folded back. We're going to need lots of hot water."

Barbara quickly fixed the bed and came out in the kitchen. The house was in total confusion. She ran to the window. They were taking Danny off the kotamik. The three men that were carrying him were rugged, hairy and dirty, and looking she noticed one man had tobacco juice running down his chin all the way to his shirt collar. She saw no movement in the body they were carrying. She had a job to see because people were everywhere. Then before she could say anything, they brought Danny in the kitchen.

"Oh my, Aunt Martha," said a voice from the dirty blankets. "You got pea soup cooking. It smells good."

Barbara felt relieved. Danny was not dead as she had thought. She stepped a little closer, but the stench made her step back. The three men carried him into the bedroom. Aunt Martha said, "Barbara, you stay here. We're going to take his clothes off." They went to the room and closed the door.

Martha Pittman was a midwife. She had born children in emergencies, but she took care of cuts and dog bites on a regular basis. Barbara went back to the kitchen where Uncle Edward was sitting at the table talking to the Ranger. She could tell by the uniform that he was a very scrubby looking character. He took off his cap when Barbara came near him. His hair stood on end and he nodded as Barbara came near him, but she turned away her head. The kitchen was full of people. Uncle Edward spoke up. "Boys, we got work to do. I think you'll have to go out. We'll keep you informed on what's happening."

The people started to leave immediately. Art came out of the bedroom. "Uncle Ned," he said loudly.

"Well, Art Compton," said Edward Pittman. "How are you?"

Art nodded, then Uncle Edward added, "Art, would you please introduce me to the Ranger."

Art rolled the chew of tobacco and cleared his throat. "This is Ranger Peters," he said ignorantly.

Uncle Ned looked from one to the other, sensing something wrong. "I'm Edward Pittman, Ranger," then held out his hand.

"I'm Ranger Jack Peters of Englee." They shook hands.

Art looked at Barbara with a scowl and rolled his eyes. She received the mesage.

Then the door of the bedroom opened and Ple came out."Peters, I want to talk with you," said Ple.

"Yes, go ahead," said Peters trying now to have a voice of authority.

"Peters, Aunt Martha says that Danny has to be taken to a hospital as quickly as you can get him there. Now what you do is..."

"I know what I'll do," said Peters. Then turned to Uncle Edward. "Have you a wireless station here?"

"Yes, but its three miles away up at South West Bottom."

Ple went back to the bedroom carrying a pan of hot water. He closed the door.

They had put Danny in bed. Aunt Martha had taken his shirt off. She got the scissors and cut the underwear off him. He wore a one-piece combination underwear. It was at one time clean and white, but now it looked like oily rags that had been used to clean a garage floor. The stench was almost unbearable. Danny was now conscious and his mind was alert.

"What's your name sir?" he asked Ple.

"Ple Gillard."

Danny looked him in the eye. "Are you the man that found me?"

"I am one of four that found you."

Aunt Martha started to take off his pants.

"Just a minute, Aunt Martha. I think this is a job for Uncle Ned and Mr. Gillard."

"Call me Ple."

"Okay, Ple. But first I want you to promise me something. Will you stay with me until I get to the hospital?"

"I sure will," said Ple.

The door opened and Peters came in. "I forgot to tell you something, Ple. Come here."

Ple stepped out into the living room.

"I'm leaving Corcoran in your charge. Whatever you do, don't let anybody give him any solid food. It could kill him instantly."

"Don't worry about that Peters. I might not have First Aid, but I got common sense."

"Okay, okay," said Peters, then left.

Ple went back into the bedroom. Danny was talking freely.

"Take it easy, Danny," said Ple.

"I'm starving, Aunt Martha. I want something to eat. I want some of that pea soup."

Aunt Martha went out and the two men started to take off Danny's clothes. It was a horrible task. They had to cut his clothes off, then started to wash him from his knees up. The waste from his bowels was from his waist down to his toes, mixed with rotten flesh and pus. It made the room smell like a fish stage in July. They started taking off his boots. They had to cut them off. His socks were stuck in the sores. He told them how he had sunk through the hard snow on his second day out and drove a stick in his left leg. "What are my feet like, Ple?"

Ple did not know what to say. "Don't worry about your feet. They're alright, but your toes look in bad shape. It's only a matter of getting you to a hospital and you'll be alright."

Danny knew he was lying. "Uncle Edward if I got to lose my legs, I want to die."

Danny knew he was lying. "Uncle Edward, if I got to lose my legs, I want to die."

They got a suit of underwear and put them on him then wrapped his feet in a pillow case. Then Ple went out of the room.

"Uncle Edward, I want to see Barbara," said Danny with a shaky voice.

"Not before we give you a shave," said Uncle Edward. "Hey, Ple."

"Yes," said Ple.

"Come here!"

Ple came in.

"Go out and get my razor. We're going to shave Danny."

"Okay," said Ple. He came back a few minutes later with a straight razor and soap, also a pan of hot water.

The two men gave Danny a shave. It was only then that Uncle Edward realized the frail condition Danny was in. He could hardly believe his eyes, when he saw his face after the beard was off. He almost looked like a human skeleton.

"Ple, Danny wants to see Barbara. Do you think it's alright?"

Ple winked at Danny. "What do you think Uncle Ned?"

"Well, okay," he said. The two men left the bedroom.

"Barbara, Danny wants to see you now, but don't be surprised at what you're going to see when you walk in that room, and don't stay too long in there. You know Barbara he's very weak and too much talk could cause him to go unconscious again."

She lifted her head and said, "Okay, I won't stay too long."

She slowly walked over to the bedroom door and went in, closing it behind her.

Ple Gillard went outside. He needed a wash badly. Outside a crowd was waiting. Noah Pittman was standing near the bridge. "How is he, Ple?"

The crowd moved closer to catch every word.

"Not good. His hands and feet are frozen and it looks like gangrene has set in. He has to get to a hospital immediately. I'd say Noah, they'll have to chop his hands and legs off before it's all over."

Everybody looked at one another. They asked many questions, but Ple ignored them. "Where's Art Compton?" Ple asked.

"He's down by the stage," said Noah.

"I think I'll go down." Ple left then but the crowd followed him. He saw Art near the stage and there was a crowd around him. Art was telling them about their trip on the country.

"Hey, Art, do you want any help with the dogs?"

"No, said Art. "How's Danny?"

"Not good," said Ple. "Have you had anything to eat yet, Art?"

"No," he said, then they talked for about ten minutes. All of a sudden Ple jumped and ran. "Watch out, boys," he said. He ran for the house.

"Hey what's wrong?" asked Art.

"The pea soup," said Ple, as he ran. He reached the house and ran into the kitchen. "Where's Aunt Martha?"

Uncle Edward looked at Ple. "She's in the room Ple, giving Danny some pea soup. He's starved."

"Aunt Martha," said Ple, as he dashed for the bedroom. "My God, you'll kill him," and he grabbed the bowl from her. "Have you given him any yet?"

"No," she said and her voice showed anger.

"Aunt Martha, it will kill him if you give him that."

Danny looked at Ple and said, "I'm hungry, Ple. I want something to eat."

"You'll get something to eat soon Danny."

"I want something to eat now," he said. "Do you realize I haven't eaten for fifteen days?"

"Aunt Martha," said Ple, "skim off a drop of broth from the pot and take a slice of bread and soak it in the broth, will you? And make sure the crust is off the bread and bring it to me. We got to give him light food first."

Aunt Martha took the bowl and left the room.

Barbara sat on the bed. It was obvious she had been crying. Ple walked in the room and said, "The plane should be here by two this afternoon."

"Do you think so?" asked Barbara.

"Yes," said Ple, "and by six he should be in St. John's, even before dark. The plane is in Norris Arm. She can be here in an hour from the time they receive the wireless."

Barbara looked relieved and left the room. "I'll be back in a few minutes," she said.

Aunt Martha came with the bowl of broth. Ple took it from her. "I'll give it to him Aunt Martha."

She was offended. "Why?" Don't you trust me?"

Ple was, and still is, to the point. He wasn't worried if he offended Aunt

Martha. "No, I don't trust you," he said. "For love and mercy, you could kill him, even if you had to do it on the sly."

"Is that so?" said Aunt Martha, turning red. She could smell the stink from Ple from lack of washing for twelve days. "I've got some news for you, Mr. Gillard." She stood with clenched fists.

"Aunt Martha," said Ple, "before you tear my head off, I want to explain something to you. You see Danny hasn't eaten for thirteen or fourteen days, and if one piece of hard food should go the wrong way, he doesn't have the strength to clear it out and he could choke just like that." Ple clicked his fingers. "I'm not mad at you, Aunt Martha. The only thing is I'm not going to see Danny Corcoran die, not after what we went through to find him alive."

"Okay, Ple," she said, "no hard feelings. It's just that I can't bear to see a man hungry.

Ple grinned and said to Danny, "I bet I'm the first one that sassed Aunt Martha Pittman and got away with it." He turned to her and said, "Good enough," as she was walking out the door.

Art walked in. "You know something, Uncle Ned, Ple quarreled all the way from home to Harbour Deep." It was obvious Art was up to one of his games, getting Aunt Martha riled up.

Ple started giving Danny the broth. Danny was grasping after it. Art sat at the table with Uncle Ned. "I wish I had Ple Gillard's nerve and energy," said Uncle Edward.

Art then got up from the table and said, "Noah asked me out."

Ple finished giving Danny the broth as Barbara came in. She noticed that Danny was unable to keep his eyes open. The food made him sleepy.

It was 2:30 p.m. when Peters came back to the small village of Harbour Deep in North East Bottom. He came to the house. He was not in a hurry. "How is Ranger Corcoran, Mr. Pittman?"

Uncle Edward sensed a different type of man, from Danny Corcoran in Ranger Peters. "He is sleeping."

"Good," said Peters. "Where is Ple Gillard?"

Uncle Edward glanced out the window. "He just went over to Stan Randell's to get a shift of underwear. He should be back any minute."

"Very good," said Peters.

"Sir," said Peters, "can I use your living room. I have to write up my report on how we found Danny."

"Yes, you most certainly can," said Edward.

"Thank you," said Peters politely, picking up his pack sack.

"Ranger Peters," said Aunt Martha. "Are you going to be staying here?" He looked at her.

"I mean are you going to be staying in Harbour Deep?"

"Yes," he said.

"Then you better take the spare room."

"Thank you, Mrs. Pittman. You're very kind."

Barbara Gale just stared at him.

"Did Ple tell you about our trip in the country, searching for Danny?"

"No," said Aunt Martha.

"Very well. I would like to have a basin of hot water. I would like to get cleaned up."

"Okay," she said, "I forgot. There are too many things happening at one time."

Peters went to the spare room and closed the door. Uncle Edward looked at Martha and Barbara and said, "I wonder what really did go on amongst them from Englee to Harbour Deep. Maybe some day it will be told, even after I'm dead and gone."

Ple came back to Uncle Edwards house. "Where is Peters?" His eyes were blazing. "Where's Peters?" he asked loudly.

"He's in the spare room," said Uncle Edward.

"Which room?" said Ple.

"That one there," said Uncle Edward pointing to the door.

Ple opened the door and went in.

"What are you doing, Peters?" said Ple very loudly and with his squeaky voice.

"I'm making a few notes. Gentlemen usually knock when they come in a room. What do you want?"

"What time will the plane be here for Danny?" asked Ple.

Peters didn't look up. "I don't know," he replied.

"You don't know. What? You don't know?"

Peters didn't answer.

"Peters," said Ple, "did you wire for the plane?"

Peters looked up.

"No, you didn't." Ple almost jumped on him.

Peters shifted his weight on the chair and acted as if he was going to defend himself. "No, I didn't," he said.

"Why?" asked Ple almost screaming.

"Because there is no need of it."

Ple stood with his hands on his hips. "How do you think we're going to get him to the hospital," he screamed. "Haul him down through the country on dogteam. It would be murder. He wouldn't live to get there."

Peters stood up. "Now take it easy, Ple. Take it easy."

Ple turned red. "Take it easy. My God. You're out of your mind." He stamped his foot on the floor.

"Now you listen here, Ple. I've got things taken care of."

"How?" said Ple.

"I wired Rodrick to come up in the Pioneer after him." (The Pioneer was the United Church Mission boat, 31 feet long made of wood, just a tub on the water).

Ple struck the door. He grinded his teeth. "Peters you're trying to make away with Danny Corcoran. Do you realize he could be in the hospital in St. John's this evening? It's possible he might not live another 24 hours without medical attention. How do you think the Pioneer is going to get up here? There's a solid jam of ice between here and Englee."

Peters didn't answer.

"You are treading on dangerous ground," said Ple. "Now you listen to this."

Peters didn't look up. He realized he had made a mistake.

"If anything happens to Danny Corcoran," said Ple. "I will go straight to the Supreme Court of Newfoundland and I'll stop at nothing."

Peters looked up. He very cooly said, "You are dismissed, Mr. Gillard."

Ple turned and stomped out the door slamming it behind him. He saw Uncle Edward and Barbara standing a few feet from the door. It was obvious they had heard everything. "Is it possible?" They all said at once. They all hung their heads as Ple left.

Peters stayed in his room all evening writing his report. Ple visited Danny several times and went from house to house. Wherever he went a crowd gathered to hear the details of the trip and of how they had found Danny Corcoran. Art chained on his dogs and fed them. Just before dark it got cloudy and dull and about 9:30 P.M., Ple dropped in at Noah Pittman's house to see Nellie. She was sick in bed. She told him about the dream she had about Danny and Ple told her Danny had called to him three times the evening before they found him, when they were camping at the Rocky Stent. "I fear for him," she said.

Ple left then and came out to Edward Pittman's. "Where have you been, Ple?" said Edward.

"Up to Noah's and out to Stan Randell's."

"I guess there was a house full up to Stan's?"

"Yes," said Ple. "The house was blocked full."

Aunt Martha came out of Danny's room. "Danny is not well. He took shivering. My, oh, my. His poor hands. Ranger Peters was in to see him just now and he did the cruelest thing." She looked towards the spare room and said, "Do you know what he put on Danny's feet?"

Ple looked at her wide eyes. "I'd say he put Minard's Liniment on them," said Ple.

"No, not that bad," said Aunt Martha. She wrung her hands and Ple saw tears in her eyes. "He came in the room and pulled back the clothes and hauled on a pair of wool socks on his feet. My, oh my," she said. "He just hauled them on with no mercy at all." She paused. "I've never seen anything done like it before."

"I'm not surprised," said Ple. "Anything is possible."

"Sshhhss," she said, indicating for him to be quiet.

"Where is Art and Jack?" asked Ple.

"They're in the living room. Art is asleep on the couch and Jack is asleep on the day bed."

"Good," said Ple. "They deserve a good nights sleep."

"I don't know Ple where we're going to put you. We got no room."

"Don't worry about me, Aunt Martha. I've spent eight nights sleeping on top of the firewood near the stove, so any place is good enough for me. I intend to stay up with Danny because he's going to need somebody."

"Barbara and Ned are going to stay up. I'll tell you what I'll do. I'll put you on the floor."

"Good," said Ple.

After eight nights sleeping on firewood and nine days hauling and dragging on a komatik, guiding a group through snow and fog, Ple Gillard was given the floor to sleep on, but he didn't complain. He had a roof over his head and for that he was grateful.

Sunday was spent mostly in going around Harbour Deep from house to house telling their story. It was not a good day. The wind was north east. Art was having trouble with his dogs. He kept Uncle Al Hancock's three in the stage alone. He took special care of them now because he knew he had to return to Englee. In the morning Gill Ellsworth came over from the North East Bottom to see Danny. When he came out of the room he shook his head and just walked out of the house. He met Peters and said, "For God's sake, boys, get Danny to a hospital. He's going to die soon."

Peters didn't answer him. It was obvious to everyone that Danny was in great pain and fading fast, but he didn't complain.

Danny told Barbara that he would rather die than lose his legs. She reassured him he wouldn't although she knew otherwise. He also told her things about the country, how he saw a hotel somewhere up there and had run to its door only to find himself running into rocks. He said he had many weird things happen to him during his ordeal on the country.

By Sunday evening he was a very sick man, but nothing could be done. There was no medication available. They found themselves in a hopeless situation as far as medical attention was concerned. During the day, the Pittmans, Barbara and Ple Gillard tried to persuade Ranger Peters that they should put hot presses on Danny Corcoran's legs to help prevent the spread of gangrene, but again he would not agree to have this done. He said he knew First Aid and this wasn't one of the things you should do. On Sunday evening Danny had a slight convulsion and they thought he was going to die.

At approximately 1:15 Saturday, March 27, 1936, a wireless was handed to Rev. Rodrick. He was the young United Church minister at Englee. (He was a close friend of Ranger Peters. They stayed together at Mrs. Annie Fillier's at Englee, except when some important person came in town, Peters moved up to Joe Luther's to make room for them. This was agreed on before Mrs. Fillier took him.) He took the wireless and went into his room-office. He shut the door and took his pocket knife and quickly cut the envelope open. He took the wireless out of the envelope, unfolded it, and began to read its contents. He looked at the bottom first. It was signed Jack Peters, Ranger. He held his breath. It read as follows:

HARBOUR DEEP, MARCH 27, 1936 REV. RODRICK UNITED CHURCH CLERGY ENGLEE, NEWFOUNDLAND. HAVE FOUND CORCORAN HIS CONDITION POOR–STOP–MEDICAL ATTENTION EXTREMELY NEEDED- -STOP-SEND PIONEER TO TRANSPORT PATIENT TO ST. ANTHONY-S-TOP-REQUEST YOU COME IMMEDIATELY. SIGNED JACK PETERS, RANGER

He could hardly believe himself. "Good for you, Jack," he said out loud. He took the wireless and came out into the kitchen. "Aunt Annie, just listen to this," he said. He read the wireless.

"'Tis an answer to prayer," she said.

He went outside and called to one of the young boys, "Eh, son, come here please."

One of the young boys came over. "I want you to go up to Mr. Baxter Gillard's and give him this wireless and tell him to come down to see me immediately. Also get Bob, too."

"Yes, Rev. Rodrick," said the youth.

"Now hurry."

"Yes, Sir." The young boy then ran with the wireless clenched in his fist.

Uncle Bobby Hopkins was out on his bridge and Rodrick called out to him and told him Ranger Peters had found the Ranger that was lost and that he needed him to help get the Pioneer launched to go to Harbour Deep after him. He also asked him to get as many men as possible to help.

"Yes, Sir," he replied.

The word from that started to spread around Englee. Every kitchen was full of the news. Women hung up their cup towels. Kettles boiled uncontrolled on the stoves. Kids stopped their playing. This was big news.

Gus Compton was mending twine when he heard the news and came across the ice to see Rev. Rodrick, who read the wireless to him. "Well, good for Ple and the boys. They found him. I knew they could do it."

The crowd cheered and clapped. Rodrick didn't look pleased. He kept silent.

Baxter Gillard then came to the house. (Baxter Gillard is now Doctor Gillard. He was bestowed this great honour by Memorial University in 1983, for being the Mayor of Englee for 35 years consecutively and for being the layreader of the United Church for all of his adult life.) He then organized the meeting and made plans for a mission of mercy.

He began by saying, "We are taking on a very, very hard task gentlemen. There is a solid jam of heavy ice between here and Harbour Deep and the weather doesn't look good."

He looked down at his hands. "We're going to need all the help and cooperation to get the boat in the water. We have to launch her out over the ice and this is going to be very tricky. I don't know if the ice is strong enough to take the weight of the boat."

Cecil Fillier, the young son of Annie Fillier was at the meeting. He spoke up. "There's no problem there, Mr. Gillard. There's enough people here now to carry that boat almost anywhere."

"Good," said Baxter. "First we'll have to detail different people to do certain jobs. If we could get her in the water fairly quick and the engine checked out, we might be able to get across to Canada Harbour before dark." (Canada Harbour is about three miles across the west side of Canada Bay fro Englee.)

"You're right," said Cecil.

Baxter spoke up then. "We've got to get a crew put together and this will be strictly volunteers. Now my question to you is this. Who will go on the boat? I will volunteer myself," he said.

There was silence.

"I will go," said Rev. Rodrick.

"So will I," said Cecil.

"One more," said Baxter.

Bob Gillard held up his hand.

"No, not you," said Baxter. "We need someone to drive the engine."

Cecil spoke up, "I'll ask Jack Canning. He'll go for sure."

"Okay," said Baxter. "Let's go and get the boat in the water then."

The meeting ended.

Rev. Rodrick looked out the window and said, "There are a lot of men around."

"Good," said Baxter.

It was a very busy evening. The boat had to be launched approximately half a kilometer. It took them a long time to launch her. They had to set out block and tackle with an anchor set in a hole in the ice and about fifty men hauling on the faul. (Faul is the end used to haul on when rigged on a block and tackle.).

Bob was given a job to supply the boat with water. George Brown was given a job to put firewood aboard. John Reeves supplied the food for the trip and soon the boat was in the water. The engine was checked, but it was discovered that it was too late to go anywhere that evening, due to pack ice. Everything was set for an early start Sunday morning and on March

28, 1936, they would have all day in front of them.

Chapter 26
March 28-29, 1936

It was Sunday morning before dawn and the Pioneer was found struggling against rough ice, pushing and grinding, making very little headway. At one point it looked as if the boat would have to return, but they pushed on and at noon they reached Cat Cove. Cat Cove was a little town of four families nestled on the ledge of the open sea. They went ashore to the home of Bill Blanchard, where they were welcomed with open arms. They had lunch. Then someone went up on the hills to check the ice. They saw a break ahead in the pack. Ice was leading up to Red Point but looked a solid jam all the way up to Williamsport. The crew then boarded the Pioneer and started pushing through the ice again. They got to Red Point and had to go into Hooping Harbour for the night.

Almost all the town came on the wharf and greeted them, asking many questions. The crew of the Pioneer was taken to their homes and shown the great Hooping Harbour hospitality. (Hooping Harbour was famous for hospitality and in 1967 the town was resettled to Bide Arm near Englee, where a new town has been started.) In the morning at dawn they left Hooping Harbour, March 29, 1936. The ice had moved off shore a little and their progress was faster, although they had to go through ice all the way. They steamed past Williamsport at noon then got into ice free water and headed for Harbour Deep at full speed.

Ple Gillard, Art Compton and Jack Brown sat down on Noah Pittman's wharf looking across the arm. It was Monday noon. "What a fool we was," said Art, "to come on this trip."

"Why?" asked Jack, looking at Art wide-eyed.

Art rolled a tobacco chew in his jaw then said, "Old man, we found Corcoran alive and now they're letting him die a slow death. 'Tis better if we let him perish in the woods, at least he would have been out of his punishment."

Jack shook his head. "To tell you the truth, boys, I don't understand it. Why in the world is this happening. 'Tis ridiculous. Somebody is going to have to suffer for this some day."

"Yes," said Ple, with a snarl.

A dogteam came around the point. "Eh," said Art. "There's a team coming." The team came near. It was Jim Pollard. He stopped. "Hello, Art."

"Well, Jim, old man. Good to see you."

"Yes," said Jim. "I got a wireless for Ranger Peters. Where is he?"

"In bed," said Ple, "or at the kitchen table up at Uncle Ned's."

"He's up at Uncle Ned's," said Art.

Everyone went up with him. Jim handed the wireless to Peters. He opened it. It was from Rev. Rodrick. It said. "Left Hooping Harbour at dawn. Should be in Harbour Deep this afternoon. Have everything ready to move."

"What date is on it?" asked Art.

Peters looked at it and said "March 29. That's today. They're on their way," he said. He put the wireless in his pocket and sat down to the table.

"Peters," said Ple. Peters almost jumped from the keenness of Ple's voice, then looked up at Ple and said, "Yes?"

"What are your plans, Peters?"

"Plans?" said Peters. "What do you mean, plans?"

"How do you plan to get Danny out to the boat."

"We will haul him out on dog team I suppose, the same way as we got him here."

"Now you listen here, Peters," said Ple. "Danny is much sicker now, then when we brought him here. He's not going to be able to take much beating around."

Peters spoke up, "What else can we do?"

Ple shook his head in disgust and said "Uncle Ned, anyone around here got a coachbox (Coachbox is a closed in sled used for hauling patients on dog team) that we can borrow?"

"Yes, my son," he said.

"Art, you round it up," said Ple.

"Okay," said Art.

"Now, boys, listen," said Ple. "There's no way we can take the twenty seven dogs aboard the Pioneer and we can't leave the dogs here in Harbour Deep, so there's only one thing we can do. We'll have to borrow somebody's boat to put the dogs and komatiks in."

"That shouldn't be any problem," said Uncle Edward. "Nore got a 21 foot motor boat and you'll have no trouble to get that one."

"Good," said Ple. "We've got to start now to get everything under way. Get a crowd and launch her out to the edge of the ice."

Barbara came out of the bedroom where Danny was and sat down at the table. "Is there any news?" she asked.

Peters spoke up, "Yes, my love." Everyone looked away from him. "I had a wireless sure," he said. "It was from Rev. Rodrick. The Pioneer will soon be here to pick up Danny and us. If everything goes well, Danny will be in

St. Anthony early tomorrow."

She looked at him with disgust. "Danny is in very poor condition. I don't think he can last much longer unless he gets medical attention. Today he has a terrible fever and that's a bad sign of a worsening condition. Just now he was delirious and started calling for Uncle Job Randell."

"Who's that?" asked Peters.

Aunt Martha explained "He 's an old saint up in Little Harbour Deep, and I say he couldn't ask for a better man."

Ple spoke up, "There's a nurse at Roddickton, Peters." He looked at Peters. "Maybe you should send a wireless to her and ask her to meet us at Englee to give Danny medical attention when we get there."

Peters knew what Ple was aiming at. "That's a good idea," said Barbara.

"Yes, I think I will," said Peters. He went into his room then and closed the door.

"That man is weird in his ways," said Barbara.

Peters came out a few minutes later. "Mr. Pittman, would you be able to have someone carry this to Gill Ellsworth for me, please?"

"Yes," he replied.

The rest of the afternoon was taken up into getting the motor boat hauled out to the edge of the ice with the dogteams. When this was done, they went back to the house. Ple sat down at the table with Barbara and Aunt Martha to have a cup of tea. "Ple," said Barbara, "Did Danny talk to you very much? I mean between when you found him and here?"

"No," said Ple, "Nothing only foolishness. He was unconscious most of the time, but when we were undressing him he said if he lost his legs he wanted to die."

"Yes," said Barbara. "He told me the same thing. He was telling me last night about when he was lost on the country, he used to see hotels and things. At one time he saw an old woman in a flower garden. I never heard talk of such strange things before. Something about Granny Newman. He must have had an unbelieveable experience." She paused. "Ple," she said, "have you ever seen men with gangrene before?"

"Yes," said Ple.

"Well, you've seen Danny's feet and hands. What do you think is going to happen to them once they get him in the hospital?"

Ple lowered his voice almost to a whisper. "Do you want to know what I think?"

They both nodded.

"If Peters would have sent for the plane and they would have got him in the General Hospital Saturday evening, I'd say there might have been a chance, but taking him to St. Anthony by boat...All they can do down there now is chop off his legs above his knees and chop off his arms around the elbows, and that's what they'll do. They won't have any other choice and even if they got him to St. John's right now, they would have to do the same thing because the gangrene is gone too far."

Barbara put down her head and started to cry.

"Don't cry, Barbara," said Ple. "That don't mean to say he's going to die. He could live to be an old man. The only thing is he won't have no legs or arms."

"What will he do?" said Barbara in a shaky voice.

"I suppose the government will take care of him," said Ple.

"Maybe so," she said.

Aunt Martha spoke up. "I suppose we'll never know the reason why Ranger Peters didn't send for the plane."

"I know the reason," said Ple.

They looked at him.

"'Tis because he was too lazy to travel back over land to Englee so he made that as an excuse to take Danny to St. Anthony, so he could get a boat ride to Englee. He's not worrying whether Corcoran lives or dies. I know what should happen though. Someone should go to the supreme court and have him hung."

The sound of someone yelling outside brought their attention to the outdoors. "Who is that screeching out there?" said Aunt Martha. She got up from the table and went to the door. "What?" she said to the person who was standing in the porch. "The Pioneer is here Ple." She half turned. "The Pioneer is here."

Ple jumped from the table. "Where's Peters?" he said moving towards the door.

"He went down to the store," said somebody.

"Then get him up here," said Ple. "Barbara, you and Aunt Martha, start getting Danny ready."

"Yes," was their reply.

Ple rushed outside and called for Art. "Get your dogs in harness. The Pioneer is here. We got to run out to her."

"Good enough," said Art. "I should be ready in a few minutes."

The town was in a commotion. Everyone who could walk was on the move and headed towards the point to look out the arm at the boat near the edge of the ice. Peters came when Ple and Art were about to leave. "I want a ride, boys," he said, as he jumped on the kotamik.

Neither man spoke. Art unhooked the kotamic and away they went at a fast pace. They arrived at the side of the boat. Art stopped the dogs, then Peters got off the kotamik and walked towards the boat. He was greeted by Rev. Rodrick, who shook his hand. "I knew you could do it, Jack," he said. "I knew you could find Corcoran."

Ple called to Baxter. "Are you ready to leave right now?"

"Whenever you are, we are. The ice is coming in. We got to get on the move as soon as possible."

"Good," said Ple. "Have you got a stretcher on board?"

"Yes," said Baxter.

"All right. We'll go in and bring Corcoran out right now."

They could see the people coming out to the boat.

"When Jack Brown comes out, have some men put that motor boat in the water. We are going to put the dogs and kotamik in here, and Peters."

Cecil Fillier laughed.

Ple and Art left the boat and went back to the town. They went to the house with the stretcher. Danny was awake. He appeared to be very weak. Barbara and Aunt Martha had him wrapped in blankets. Uncle Edward came into the room to give them a hand. Danny spoke up with a frail voice. "I never thought it would ever come to this," he said. "The last time I left this town, I ran out on snowshoes. Now I'm leaving on a stretcher. The last time I left I was to return in four days, but I know this time I'll never return again." He closed his eyes and groaned.

The men took him out of bed and put him on a stretcher. You could smell the stench from his rotten feet. His hands were bandaged, but they were turned black almost to his elbows. Ple and Art carried him out on the bridge, but before they carried him to the coach box, Danny spoke to them and everyone heard his words.

"Turn me around, boys. I want to have a look at those hills on the other side."

They turned him around. He partly sat up. Tears came to his eyes. He knew he would never see those hills again.

"Okay," said Ple, "let's go."

The look on the faces of the people would let one know what was going through his mind. They then put him in the coach box and slowly hauled him out of the yard.

Aunt Martha said, "Just a moment boys. Ranger Peters has left his things in the room. I will get them."

Art quickly spoke up. "Aunt Martha, throw them in the stove."

Then she quickly came with them and put them on the kotamik.

Barbara then leaned over and kissed Danny. "I love you," she said.

He looked at her with sadness in his eyes. This beautiful girl who had been in his dreams. "Goodbye Barbara," he slowly whispered, as the dogs started to move the coach box out of the yard.

Barbara stood there with tears running down her face. "Goodbye Danny. I know I will never see you again."

Then the dogteams quickly moved out of sight carrying the young redheaded Ranger who would never return to Harbour Deep again.

It was on the move for the Pioneer and it slowly moved through the pack ice heading northeast along the rugged coast of the Great Northern Peninsula. The towering cliffs seemed to look down with pity as the small boat appeared to be jolted from stem to stern as it twisted from side to side worming its way steadily onward. The residents of Duggan's Cove came on their bridges to view the small boat as it passed the little town and if Granny Randell thought that the boat she was watching was carrying the redheaded Ranger, she would probably be out in a rowboat to see him. But due to isolation there was no way she could even find out until weeks later.

It is a good thing that man is not permitted to know his future. Can you image just a couple of months earlier Danny Corcoran stood looking out over the same water, listening to a man pray and an old woman playing a piano and singing, and now as the Pioneer wormed its way through the ice, they were unaware of its cargo and even if they knew, there wasn't anything they could do. The boat moved on its way and was within eight miles of Williamsport, when they discovered that something was wrong with the engine. A quick survey was made and it was reported that the shaft was bent. This threw the blades off balance causing severe vibration. They started the engine, but could only run it at half speed. "We will have to go into Williamsport," said Baxter, who was now in charge on the boat. They were making slow progress. It was dark now as they were venturing the fjord leading to Williamsport. They ran out of the ice making a smoother ride.

Ple sat near Danny for quite a while. Danny told him some things that went on in the country. He said that at one time he thought he was walking down Water Street in St. John's and went into a restaurant. He told him many other things that had happened to him while lost.

They were almost in the harbour of Williamsport. Ple said to Danny, "We're going into Williamsport, now Danny. Have you ever been here before?"

"Yes," he said. "I think it was in January. I got a friend who lives here."

"Eh, Ple, come up on deck," said Baxter.

He left Danny and went up on deck. "What do you want?"

"We're going to have to fix the shaft or blades, or whatever is wrong. Do you know anybody here who would give us a hand?"

"Yes," said Ple quickly. "Uncle Sam Brenton. For sure he got stuff to fix it with, but do you know what we're going to have to do. We're going to have to lift the stern of this boat out of the water in order to get at the blades.

"I wonder how far the ice is broke in," said Baxter. "Anyway we'll soon be in."

They could see the lights of the town as they rounded the point. "Look," said Ple. "It's broke into John Reeve's wharf. This is a streak of luck."

They tied the boat up to the wharf. People quickly came down and the news spread around that the lost Ranger, Danny Corcoran, was on board.

They put the boat in on the shore and hauled the stern up out of the water.

Sam Brenton was one of the first men to appear on the wharf. He didn't have to be asked. He wanted to help and upon examining the problem, it was decided that the shaft was not bent, but one of the wings was broken on the blades (propeller).

"You got your blades broke brother. What he gonnna do now?"

"We got a new set," said Baxter.

"Wonderful," said Uncle Sam. He got the new blades and quickly put it on. Then the men pushed the 32 foot boat back into the water. One of the men told them that it would be a wise thing for them to stay at Williamsport until daybreak.

"Eh, you. Eh, you," said a voice loud and clear as a bell. Everyone looked at a tall man who was walking out on the wharf. He had just arrived on the scene. He came straight to Baxter Gillard and said, "Bax, was he doin' yer?"

Baxter knew the voice. "How are you Javis?"

"I just heard Corcoran he's found and ye got em," said Javis Pollard.

"Yes, Javis, we got Danny Corcoran aboard."

"Well I wants to see em." said Javis.

"Well now Javis, there are no visitors allowed. Ranger Corcoran is a sick man. In fact he is in terrible condition."

"Where's he at? I wants to see em."

"We'll have to ask the Ranger in charge."

"Just a minute, Bax," said Ple. "Jave you must be the person that Danny was talking about when we was coming in." Ple motioned to Bax to stay where he was. He knew Peters would not let Javis Pollard visit Danny, especially if it was going to do any good, such as cheer him up. Ple went down in the forecastle. "Danny," he said.

Danny opened his eyes.

"There's a man here to see you. His name is Javis Pollard. Would you like to see him?"

Danny's eyes opened. "Yes, by all means. Show him in."

"Okay," said Ple and motioned for Javis to come down.

Jave came down the steps with his back turned to whomever was in the cabin. He turned around and looked Danny square in the face. Jave smiled at him, then laughed. "Ranger, you're on the broad of your back." He came over to Danny and would have grabbed his hand to shake it, had not Ple stopped him.

"Javis," said Danny. "How are you?"

"I'm vine (fine). It took the Englee crowd to vine you. We said they would vine you." Javis laughed and everyone on the boat heard him.

"I'm grateful, Javis."

"What ye do, Ranger, vreeze ye feet?"

"Yes," said Danny. "The second night I was out I fell in the water and late that night the wind turned northwest and I was lucky I didn't freeze to death."

"Well, you're in good hands now, Ranger. Yes, you're in good hands now. Ple Gillard and Art Compton is the best two men on the coast. If they don't get you to Snanothy (St. Anthony) nobody else is going to."

"I got a feeling you're right," said Danny. "Javis, when I was on the country lost, if I could have got my hands on some of your munge, it would have been honey."

They laughed. "Would you like to have some salt salmon, Ranger? I got some watered."

"Yes, please. Get some quick. I'm starving."

It was then that Peters came into the room and stood in the center of the forecastle. There were no smiles on his face. "I will decide what Ranger Corcoran will eat, sir." He looked at Javis. Peters was trying to look tough.

Ple could sense trouble. He knew what kind of a man Javis Pollard was, hard working, tough and fearless. He could eat Peters and would not take any foolishness from him, (At the age of fifty Javis Pollard was teaming a 2000 pound horse in the winter and the horse got stubborn and would not move. Javis got mad and hit it over its eye with his fist and knocked the animal out. It was said that he came close to killing it.)

Ple got Javis up out of the cabin saying. "Let's you and I now go for the salmon."

"Yes," said Javis and quickly disappeared. It was said later that Peters was a lucky man.

Chapter 27
March 30, 1936

It was just before dawn and the wind was northeast. "Looks like its going to blow," said Art.

"If the wind stays like it is, the ice will trip off from shore," said Baxter.

"Hope you're right," said Art.

There was ice all around but scattered close to the shore. Progress was slow. Jack Brown and Art fed their dogs and cleaned the boat out before they left Williamsport. It was in an awful mess. Some of the dogs got seasick and that combined with refuse and urine made an awful stench.

"Eh, Bax, old man," said Art through the juice that ran down his chin from the tobacco wad, "Uncle Al Hancock's dogs chased us when we left. We tried to drive them back but couldn't so we had to let them come on."

Baxter had to keep from laughing. He knew Art was nervous now he was getting close to Englee. Art was scared of Uncle Al Hancock. "That's not what Uncle Al found out," said Baxter. "My son, there has been an awful uproar since you fellows left home." He winked at Jack Brown. "Uncle Arch Rowsell said he saw you taking his dogs out of the pen the same morning you left. He even told him the color of the harnesses you put on them and Art you might as well prepare yourself. Uncle Al is going to be on the ice when we land in Englee and he's going to be blood thirsty. You know what he's like."

Art blew out the chew of tobacco and cleared some of the scum out of his mouth. "Wait till I gets me hands on Arch Rowsell. I allows I'll turf him over the Tickle Bridge."

Bax started to laugh. "No Art, I'm only joking. When Uncle Al discovered his dogs were gone, first he was a vexed man, but when he found out you were gone to look for Danny Corcoran he quieted down, and when the report came Saturday that you had found him, he's glad his dogs were involved."

This made Art feel better. He took out the black beaver tobacco and bit off a large chew. "Bax old man, you just took a big worry off me, Bax old man!" They laughed.

At 5:30 P.M. the Pioneer was seen pushing her way through rough ice about a mile outside of Englee Harbour and almost everybody in town was out watching its slow progress. It looked to the people at one point that the boat had come to a halt and was stuck, but the thump, thump of the engine slowly pushed the ice pans open and the boat came through. It was approximately 6 P.M. when she stopped at the edge of the ice at Englee back harbour. It was an evening that will not be forgotten by the people that were there, young and old alike. There were dog teams tied to every fishing stage and were barking furiously. Some dogs were running loose through the crowd. The first to get off the boat was Art Compton and Al Hancock was there to greet him. There was a silence as Al reached out his hand to Art. "Good work, Art. We knew you could do it." The powerful frame of Al Hancock looked pleased all over.

Art blew a sigh of relief and said, "Thanks."

Bob Gillard and George Brown came to the side of the Pioneer. Ple spotted them in the crowd. "Eh, Bob, you and George help Art to get their dogs out of the motor boat. Then get the crowd and haul it up."

"We sure will," said Bob.

The crowd of men quickly got organized and literally lifted the boat out of the water with the twenty-seven dogs and two komatiks still in it, and didn't stop until it was up on the shore.

Danny was then taken out of the Pioneer on a stretcher. It was a sad scene. Silence fell over the crowd as he was handed down to the men on the ice. Everyone wanted to help. "The nurse is up at Aunt Annie Fillier's," said Bob. "She said for you to take him up there."

"Good," said Peters.

They carried Danny on the stretcher and everyone followed. It was a moving scene. The kids ran along by the side trying to get a glimpse of the sick Ranger.

"Is he still alive?"

"Is he going to die?"

"How much is he frozen?"

"Will they get him to the hospital?"

"Just look at his hands."

These were some of the questions they were asking as they walked along. They finally reached the house. Nurse Flight was there. She was an English nurse brought over by Sir Wilfred Grenfell and stationed at Roddickton. She covered the district from Little Harbour Deep to Main Brook and took care of the sick. (That is, what the midwives could not handle)

She got Danny into bed first examining his hands, saying, "Oh, chap, you've got two messy looking hands. Have you examined them yourself?"

"Yes, I have," said Danny.

"What happened to your fingers on your left hand? You have them broken."

"I don't remember for sure," said Danny. "I know I froze them, but I think I fell down. It was in the night."

She put some bandages on them, then she rolled up the bed clothes as far as his knees. She could smell the rotten flesh. She saw the grey woolen socks on his feet and noticed dark stains through the socks that was dry and hard. "Ranger Corcoran," she said in her English accent, "What fool put the woolen socks on your feet?"

"Why?" asked Danny.

"They are stuck in the wounds and let me tell you, it's going to be a very painful experience to get them off. Whoever did that must have been insane to do such a thing." She looked mad.

Danny looked at her. He could see pain in her face. "It was Ranger Peters," he said. "He put them on my feet when we got to Harbour Deep."

Nurse Flight paused. "Well," she said, "anyway, it's not much need for me to take them off. We will be in St. Anthony hospital tomorrow morning. They've got better equipment there than I have."

"Nurse," said Danny, "do you think I am going to lose my legs? I mean, how bad are they?"

She could not look at him. "That's not for me to judge. I'm not a doctor you know."

Danny closed his eyes. "Tell Ple to come in when you go out, will you please?"

"Yes," she said. "Okay, young man, you go to sleep now. I'm going to give you a sleeping pill and something for pain."

He lifted his hand. "I don't want anything for pain, nurse. I've got no pain. Haven't had any since...(pause) thinking about Uncle Jobie Randell,...but I will have that sleeping pill."

She could not believe it was gangrene to his knees and elbows. "Impossible," she said out loud. "Okay," she said. She gave him the sleeping pill and went out. She sat down at the table. Everybody was looking at her. "He wants to see Ple Gillard. Where is he?"

"He's gone to his house," said Rev. Rodrick. "I will send someone to get him."

Aunt Annie got the nurse a cup of tea. "How is he?" said Baxter.

The nurse had been with Danny for over two hours. She put sugar and cream in her tea and stirred it and took a sip, then said. "Can we leave for St. Anthony right now?"

All eyes flashed around the table. Peters spoke up. His voice was not steady. "No."

Nurse Flight looked at him.

"Not before daylight. There's too much ice."

"Gentlemen," she said. "I don't think he will last another 24 hours. He can't. He has severe gangrene in both legs and arms and I hate to say this, but the only possible way to save his life now is to amputate both arms and legs, now. I am not a doctor, but it has to be done within the next 24hours. I have never seen a condition so serious as his and still living. What amazes me is he has no pain and not even a fever, but what is going to happen is it's going to grab him all of a sudden."

No one spoke up. She then drank her tea.

Ple arrived and went into the room with Danny. "Ple," he said, "I want you to proceed on to St. Anthony with me if you don't mind. I know what you have gone through so far."

"I don't mind," said Ple. "That's what I want to do."

"Thank you," said Danny and closed his eyes.

"Now you go to sleep," said Ple. He looked at him and noticed Danny was rolling his eyes.

"I'm going to lose my legs. You be careful Danny, you could lose your leg." These were the words that Earl Patey told him and now Danny was repeating them.

Ple saw a tear running down his face. He noticed that Danny was talking in his sleep.

Chapter 28
March 31, 1936

Hours before dawn the lights in the kitchens in the houses in Englee started to come on. Some were Aladdin lamps. More were ordinary wick and chimney lights called bug lights. All were burning kerosene oil. In the kitchen you could smell fish cooking and skin boots drying in ovens. Some men were eating breakfast and their eyes were staring at the burning wicks, but this morning one thing was common. All thoughts were on Danny Corcoran. They had heard the tales last night of the search party of Ple Gillard, Art Compton, Jack Brown and Ranger Peters. The reason they were up early was to be on hand if needed to get the Pioneer on her way, but everyone was wondering if the Ranger had lived through the night.

It was a dull morning. The wind was still northeast but just a light breeze at about five knots and looking from the back harbour you could see the list of rough ice. Ple went out on Lockers Point to get a closer look. He came back and said, "We'd better wait until daylight." He went back to the house and reported the ice conditions.

Nurse Flight went in and examined Danny. She came out into the kitchen. (Ple remarked later that she looked like a crousty old hen.) "Are you ready to go?" she asked.

"No," said Ple flatly.

"Why not?" she asked.

"Nurse," said Ple. "We got to take a look at the ice first. It's not much use moving Corcoran until we can see what we are doing."

"My man," she said, "if we don't soon get on the move, there won't be much need of us going anyway."

"Why not?" asked Fred Fillier. (Fred was one of Annie Fillier's sons.)

"Because Ranger Corcoran is much worse this morning. His temperature is rising and that's a bad sign. I'm afraid he is going into convulsions and could do so any moment."

"Nurse," said Ple. "It's better for him to have convulsions here in this house than out on board that boat stuck in the ice in the middle of White Bay, probably with a twisted propeller."

"Sir," she replied, "I would feel much better if he died on his way to a hospital than die here in this house surrounded by people doing nothing."

Ple stood up. His fist was white. He started to walk toward the nurse. Baxter Gillard stepped in and prevented a serious occurence from taking place. He took the nurse quickly into the living room.

"You're not on the streets of London," said Ple, "but it's better if you were."

The men then went down to the boat and waited for daylight. They thought this was the best thing to do. Just as daylight came, they decided to move. They went up to the house and got everything ready and brought Danny down. All the men of the town came and gave him a hand. Danny was put in the forecastle and the boat got under way. The only men that didn't go, that came from Harbour Deep, were Jack Brown and Art Compton. The only person that was added to the crew was Nurse Flight. Ple sat near Danny as the boat headed out into a field of ice and headed for St. Anthony.

They had gone only a half a mile when they had to search for a channel through the ice. It took them an hour to reach Barbour's Cove about a mile from Englee. After crossing the cove they landed on the eastern point and walked upon the cliffs to have a better look. They discovered that just a half mile from where they were, was all open water. Ple went quickly back to the boat and gave the directions, then keeping close to the shore they got out of the ice and into the open water. The Pioneer was now free from the ice and headed full speed towards Fox Head, fifteen miles northeast of Englee on her way to St. Anthony.

It was a grayish morning and it was not flat calm. The shadows of everything was to be seen reflecting in the water as the Pioneer moved east on her journey. Looking to the south 18 miles out to sea, they coud see the Grey Islands looming up in the cool morning air, but between them and the Island you could see the whiteness of the rough ice that was being moved by the tide.

Danny lay on the stretcher in the forecastle. Ple sat near him. Ple had tried to talk to Danny on a couple of ocassions but could not get any sense out of him. He had a high fever and his breathing was not normal. He had his eyes closed and sometimes he would open them and stare at the cabin ceiling. At one point he looked as if he was having a convulsion. His body started to heave and tremble, but it only lasted for about a minute then he relaxed and lay motionless.

Ple looked out through the cabin window at the rugged shoreline as they moved along the Great Northern Peninsula. They had been steaming for over an hour. The shoreline looked like a rugged ghost shrouded in a white robe and trimmed with the blue streaks of timber that reached like bony fingers, down to the solid granite that was pounded smooth and cracked by the mighty North Atlantic.

As Ple looked through the window at his surroundings, from their position steaming through the briny ocean and thinking about the dying Ranger, he noticed they were off the small fishing village of Conche. (Conche is a small village tucked in around the Rouge Peninsula. It's a thriving fishing village where men work hard, live free, and after death are buried near their church among a forest of headstones. This is where the Roman Catholic priest is stationed and serves the whole peninsula.)

Ple's mind started to operate in a direction that it wasn't accustomed to, and that was thinking about the soul of mankind, and especially about someone of the Roman Catholic religion, although Ple's father always told his boys that they were to respect the faith and beliefs of all denominations, whether Catholic, Protestant or Jew. Now Ple was far from religious. "This is a good way to get Danny to talk." he said out loud. "I'll ask him if he wants to go into Conche to see the priest. Yes," he said, "That's what I'll do."

He sat down again near Danny and put his hand on his shoulder. Danny didn't move. He shook him gently and called, "Danny." No answer. "Eh Danny," he shouted. Danny rolled his eyes. He shook him again. "Danny, can you hear me?"

Danny opened his eyes and said, "Yes," in a voice that was weak and low.

"I want you to listen to me now."

Danny nodded.

"We're off Conche and there's a priest in there. Would you like to go in and see him? It wouldn't take us very long. It's not much out of our way."

Danny's eyes came open. He swallowed. It seemed as if he had been jolted out of unconsciousness. He spoke in a voice as if pleading. "Ple," he said clearly, "I want to go into Conche now. I think I'm going to die and I've got to see the priest as soon as possible. Ple, I can't die without seeing the priest. Please promise you'll take me in."

Ple noticed the look of desperation on his face. He stared with begging eyes and a look that no man could refuse, even if it took risking your life for. "We'll go in right away," said Ple.

"Thank you," he said then lay back with confidence. He had proved in the last few days that if Ple Gillard had said something, it would be done. Ple got up from the locker where he was sitting and went up into the wheel house. Cecil Fillier was at the wheel. He was older than Ple but quite a good humoured man.

"How is Danny?"

"I think he's dying."

"Well," he said as he blew out a long breath of air.

"Cece, haul her in for Conche. Danny wants to go in to see the priest.

They're not like us Protestants. He figures if the priest gives him the rites of the Church, then he can make it all right. So," Ple paused. "Haul her in."

Cecil's eyes moved around the cabin all at once. "Now, Ple, listen. It's not that I don't want to go in. In fact I think we should,, but I got orders from Peters not to alter course for nobody or nothing."

Ple's face turned to a scowl. "Turn her in, Cece."

"Just a moment," said Cecil. "I will get Peters up here."

He opened the stateroom door and called. "Eh, Peters, come up here."

In just a few steps Peters stepped into the wheelhouse. He saw the blackness of Ple and sensed something wrong. "What do you want, Cecil?" said Peters.

Before Cecil could answer, Ple spoke up. "I think Danny is dying. He told me he was. We are off Conche now and Danny wants to go in there."

"What for?" asked Peters.

"He wants to go in to see the priest."

Peters laughed. "Cecil," said Peters (and his voice sounded like a regimental sergeant major giving orders to some buck private whom he had caught on a Friday morning walking the parade square without a hair cut) his voice quivered with authority, "Don't you change this course for one living soul." Peters was almost about ready to go down in the cabin. He half turned.

"Peters," said Ple, and the keenness of his voice almost cut open Peters flesh. "I got something to tell you."

Peters turned around to face him.

"Can you imagine," said Ple with eyes blazing, "what people will say when they pick up the Evening Telegram (provincial paper) and read a dying Ranger gets denied his last request and that is to see his priest? Can you imagine, Peters, what kind of an impact that will have on the whole population of Newfoundland, and what do you think will happen to you, because if Danny Corcoran dies without seeing the priest, I'll go to the newspaper and give them the whole story."

Peters was furious. He shook. He thought for a moment there was no way out of this one. "But wait just a moment," he said. He called out. "Eh, Nurse Flight."

"Will you come up here for a moment?"

She came up quickly. "Yes, gentlemen," she said, looking at the men. "What can I do for you?"

Ple spoke up. "I think Danny is dying. In fact, he told me he was. He wants to go into Conche to see the priest and there's Conche right there," pointing to the shore line.

She looked at him and said, "My man, you said he's dying and it's not hours or minutes, it's moments as far as the life of Ranger Corcoran is concerned. He has to get to St. Anthony hospital immediately and for this reason this boat cannot and will not go into Conche or even alter it's course."

Ple went into a rage and grabbed the wheel and turned the boat towards Conche.

"Now you listen here, Ple," said Peters. "This is what is called an act of mutiny."

"I don't care," said Ple, "what this is called."

"Let me tell you something," said Peters, "if Danny Corcoran dies before we get him to St. Anthony, I will have you hung."

"Good," said Ple.

"The responsibility is all yours," said Peters.

"If that's so," said Ple, "get below."

Peters and the nurse went below and shut the door. Ple checked his position. He was heading towrds Conche. He glanced at Cecil who had a wide grin, but the scowl on Ple's face made him look serious again.

It took the Pioneer 45 minutes to reach the wharf in Conche Harbour. The water was crystal clear. The stages were painted and clean. The people of the little town saw them when they came around the point and a few men were on the wharf. Just before the boat came into the harbour, Nurse Flight went down in the forecastle where Danny was lying semi--conscious. It appeared she was trying to make an impression now on anyone who might come on board the boat in Conche. As soon as the boat touched the wharf, even before it was tied up, Ple jumped out and immediately asked some men where the priest lived. "He's up at the convent," said a man, wide-eyed. "What's the matter?"

Ple who was in a hurry said as he left, "We got a dying man onboard who wants to be annointed for death."

"Come on," said the man. "Sir, I will take you to the Father right now."

Ple and the Conche man left in a hurry. A man on the wharf recognized Baxter Gillard. (Mr. Gillard was well known around the coast. He was a partner in the Northern business of John Reeves Limited, with headquarters at Englee.) "Mr. Gillard, sir," he said. "are you on your way to St. Anthony?"

"Yes, my man, we are," said Baxter.

"Jack Casey is a very sick man. We don't think he will live much longer if we don't get him to a hospital in a hurry. Would you be able to take him? We would pay you."

"We sure will take him," said Baxter. "We've got a nurse aboard too. But he must be brought on board immediately. We can't wait one minute. We've got no time to lose."

The man jumped and ran towards the houses followed by all the men on the wharf calling as he ran, "Get Jack ready."

Ple ran into the yard of the church and tapped with his fist on the parsonage door. It was quickly opened and Ple stood looking at a man in the doorway. This was the elderly priest, Father Williams. He was famous around the coast and everyone knew what this old priest was made of. He had a heart of gold, nerves of steel and a will made of cast iron. He could stand all night in the freezing rain and stand all day in the blazing sun. It made no difference. If someone stepped out of line in Conche or any other part of his parish, watch out. And if anyone spoke to him they did it with courtesy. There were many tall tales told about this man and now Ple Gillard stood in front of him, the man known by all as Father Williams.

Ple said scrambling for the right words, "Sir, excuse me, father. Aw...We need you."

The priest kept silent.

"On board our boat we got a dying Ranger, Danny Corcoran. We found him in the woods. He has his feet and hands frozen and gangrene is killing him."

"Yes, yes," said the priest indicating for Ple to skip the story.

"I think he is dying and wants to see you, sir."

"God bless you, young man," he said.

Ple hardly knew where the voice came from.

"Wait here a moment. I will get my things and be right with you."

"Okay, Father," said Ple more relaxed.

In about two minutes the old priest came out wearing a long robe and carrying his case in his hand. "Let's go," he said.

The man from Conche opened the gate and he stepped out onto the ice in the narrow path. "What's your name, young man?" the priest said.

"Pleman Gillard, Father."

"I know your father well."

They quickly reached the boat. The priest jumped on board. He was greeted by Rev. Rodrick and Baxter Gillard. "Rev. Rodrick," he said, "I'm glad you're travelling with this party."

"Thank you," said Rev. Rodrick and showed the priest down in the forecastle where Danny was, then left immediately.

Nurse Flight sat on the locker near Danny. The priest put down his case and motioned for her to leave. She did not move. "Would you please leave us for a few moments, Nurse," he said kindly. She did not move.

Danny looked at the priest with pity in his eyes and said, "Father."

The priest looked at Danny and said, "Son."

He looked at the nurse again and for the first time since the priest entered the cabin she really looked him in the eyes and what she saw in those eyes would make the most stalwart person jump, and when he opened his mouth, if she had been on the edge of a cliff she would have cast herself into mid air. "Get out," he said and she bolted for the stairway and in one single leap she found herself in the wheelhouse terrified.

Ple and the men from Conche were on the wharf looking in through the window and with the window up, could hear everything.

"I wish he would throw her overboard," said Ple.

"Don't feel too bad yet. He just might," said one of the men from Conche.

The curtains were pulled over and the men from Conche took off their caps as they heard the priest praying and giving Danny Corcoran the last rites of the church annointing him for death. When it was over, the priest came up out of the forecastle and stepped from the boat unto the wharf. He turned to Ple and said, "Did you say you had another Ranger on board?"

"Yes, Father," said Ple, "Ranger Peters."

"Well where is he?"

"He's in the afterroom," said Ple. "Do you want to see him?"

He glanced at the men in the wheelhouse, sensing something wrong. "No, I don't want to see him," he said.

Jack Casey was put on board. The priest gave him a blessing and walked swiftly away.

"Untie her, boys, and push her off," said Ple. As they were leaving the wharf, he looked at his watch. It was 12:30 P.M. "Put the kettle on, Cece," sais Ple. "I want a cup of tea."

The Pioneer was steaming at full speed again. She was not a fast boat, but moved along at an average speed. They crossed Crouse Bight and were steaming close to the shore and moving along very well. They pased by St. Julien's and saw the houses of the small settlement. It was now beginning to blow. The wind was northwest. They proceeded on and had to stay outside of Fishot Islands because ice was blocking the run between the Islands and the mainland. When they went around the Island the wind was much stronger and huge waves were rolling out off Belvy Bay.

"We won't be able to cross the bay in this boat," said Baxter. "She'll swamp and besides that the spray is freezing on."

Nurse Flight came up on deck. "I don't mind risking my life, but 'tis not sensible to drown everyone. We've got to do what's right."

Peters came up on deck. By this time you couldn't see through the window for freezing spray. "Turn her around, boys. Let's wait for a few hours. The wind might drop out."

It was decided then to go back to St. Julien's and wait till the wind dropped. Cecil Fillier was steering the boat. He turned the boat around and in doing so, they came very close to turning the boat over. A huge wave caught the boat when it was side on to the waves and it listed so much that the propeller raced as it came out of the water. Part of the house went down into the water. It finally got turned around and righted itself back to normal. It was obvious Nurse Flight was scared. They then steamed along the coast and went into St. Julien's.

St. Julien's is a small fishing village partly open to the North Atlantic. It is a very picturesque place with its open spaces of rock and barren at the very edge of the tree line. The homes are built close to the shore and the people are very friendly. When they saw the Pioneer come into the harbour, everyone in the little town went to greet them. The story quickly spread through the town they had the lost Ranger on board.

It was 4:30 P.M. when they arrived at St. Julien's. Baxter Gillard told the crew on the boat that it wasn't likely that they would be moving anywhere until morning. "It will take us about an hour to get to Fishot Islands after the wind drops and to cross Belvy Bay in the night would be suicide. It will take two hours to cross and we don't know what the ice conditions are like near Goose Cove. If something would happen in the dark while we're crossing Belvy and this is a place where many accidents have happened, if we broke down, we could drive out into the Atlantic." So he paused. "Gentlemen, the best place is here for the night and move on at daybreak."

Ple agreed. Nurse Flight spoke up. "Is there any chance of going on? Any chance at all?"

Baxter spoke up. "I don't think so. The risk is too great. Do you realize this time of the year the spray freezes on and if that happens, this boat could go bottom up in five minutes."

"But, Mr. Gillard," she said, "I don't think Danny will last until tomorrow morning. He is very serious."

"That's all we can do, nurse. It's not sensible to lose nine lives trying to save one. I am well aware of what's at stake and I have gone through great risk to help people, but this is different. It's like committing suicide."

She did not answer and went below.

"Cece, you get the pot on," said Ple.

"I think I'll put on a pot of soup," said Cece.

"Wonderful," said Ple. "I think I'm going down to have a chat with Danny."

Ple went down into the forecastle. Danny was alert. He had his eyes opened and smiled at Ple. "I owe you a great deal," he said.

"Why?" said Ple "What did I do?"

"Among many things you took me into Conche to see the priest. I am glad. If my mother knew it would make her happy."

Ple patted his shoulder. "That's what we are all supposed to do, help people or at least try."

Danny looked at Ple. "I heard what went on in the wheelhouse before you turned the boat in towards Conche and it amazes me. Ple, I wonder what the problem is?"

"Well," said Ple, "only time will tell that and the real reason might never be known until you and I are dead and gone."

Cecil Fillier was a very nimble young man. As though it was a large ship he moved smartly around the little boat getting the meal ready.

"Danny," said Ple, "are you well enough to talk?"

"Yes," said Danny. "What is it?"

"How far over across the country did you get?"

Danny thought for a moment. "I got out to River of Ponds. I crossed East Bluey Pond and another pond. Outside of that I spent a night near East Bluey Pond and had a terrible time. It was very cold. I went west on those ponds till I came to where a brook emptied out. In the morning I lay down on a big rock. That was where Earl Patey found me. He was good to me. He took me to a camp, started a fire and gave me his lunch. I should have listened to him. He told me to stay until he came back in about two hours. He didn't return, but before he left he told me to steer in a northerly direction and I would get to Hawkes Bay. The only reason I can think of why he didn't come back was when I saw him he was carrying a shot gun and maybe he thought I was going to charge him. He was a good young fellow."

"I started off in the morning. It was raining. I was doing good until I fell in a brook and lost my compass. That was when I decided to come back to Harbour Deep." He paused. "If I had only listened to him. Maybe he had trouble or something. Maybe he fell in the water. I never thought. I saw his tracks where he came back that evening to the camp. I should have followed his tracks. He told me they had a camp further out."

"Well," said Ple. "Danny, I'm going to ask you another question. Why didn't you let someone go with you when you went on the country?"

He closed his eyes. "I was too narrow minded, you know. The people of Harbour Deep are great people. They treated me like my own mother. When I left to go down to Harbour Deep my mother told me I was going amongst the best people in Newfoundland and I proved she was right." He paused and took a deep breath.

"That's okay, Danny. Just stop talking and relax."

"I'm alright," he said weakly. "I was afraid to take a man or two with me because they were all Protestants in Harbour Deep and I was a Catholic. I was afraid to be alone with them at night on the country. So I decided to go alone and do you know something?" he sighed. "That horrible decision probably will cost me my life." He closed his eyes. His hands that were bandaged by his side twitched. "But to prove to you how wrong I have been, all of you people are Protestants and you have risked your lives to find me and are now taking me to a hospital. The only Catholic I have been involved with since last fall was a priest and he has annointed me for death."

Both Ple and Cecil dropped their heads for a moment. Ple had a funny feeling. When he lifted his eyes to look at him he saw tears running down Danny's cheeks. Danny spoke through quivering lips. "If you ever see Earl Patey of River of Ponds, thank him for me." (Earl Patey was always accused of intentionally leading Danny Corcoran astray and it's only now, 50 years later that the truth has been told.)

"I will," said Ple, then left the cabin. It was the last converstion Pleman Gillard had with Danny Corcoran.

The night was spent in conversation. Everybody stayed on the boat. Baxter, Ple, and Cecil stayed up all night with Danny, who lay in the forecastle, sometimes groaning, sometimes crying. He appeared to be conscious all the time.

Chapter 29
April 1, 1936

Just before dawn, they had a cup of tea. They estimated that if nothing went wrong, they would be in St. Anthony before noon. Some men from the town came aboard the Pioneer. It was still dark. One old timer said, "I'd say 'tis blown' a stiff breeze across Belvy now. 'Tis narwes wind up there. You might have to keep in around the bay a bit. Maybe in as far as Spring Island and then go across."

"Yes," said Baxter. "I guess that's what we will do."

Peters spoke up. "I've got a wireless here to send. Would you give it to the wireless operator for me, sir?"

"I sure will," he said.

"Tell him to send it as soon as the office opens. The message is to St. Anthony Hospital telling them we will be in St. Anthony round noon or a little after and have someone meet us when we get in."

Baxter nodded. "Untie the boat and push her off."

In Newfoundland April 1st is called April Fool's Day and many jokes and pranks are played on people, but on April 1, 1936, at the mouth of Belvy Bay, there was no room for jokes. The wind was northwest at about 30 miles per hour and there were about ten foot waves rolling down and it was severely cold. Slob ice was making on the surface of the water. When they went around Fishot Island, they drove a flock of about twenty thousand elder ducks into the air, which took them about five minutes to get off the water.

"What are we going to do, Ple?" said Baxter.

"Point her straight for Goose Cove Cape."

"It's pretty risky. The spray is freezing on," said Baxter.

"I know," said Ple, "but there is only one thing I want now and that is to get to St. Anthony as quickly as possible because I've got a feeling there's another row brewing."

"Okay," said Baxter.

"Give me the wheel, Bax," said Ple, "and I want everybody to go below."

Everybody went below and Ple was the only one in the wheelhouse. The boat started to punch its way across Belvy. After about fifteen minutes the windows were coated over with ice. Nothing could be seen through them. Ple picked up a large wrench and struck one of the wheel house windows a couple blows and smashed it. He could see through now but water and freezing spray came through, making him wet to the skin but the boat steamed on.

After a while he noticed the boat started to list to its side from the ice that was building up from the flying spray. The people in the cabin fell silent. They knew this was how many men went to their deaths leaving not a soul to tell the tale. By now the boat was over halfway across. The waves were only half as high now and not as much spray was going over her. He called to Baxter, "Come up, I want you."

Baxter came up. "What is it?"

"See if you can get out and knock off some of this ice."

"Okay," said Baxter and went to the door, but could not get it open. The deck was covered with six inches of ice.

"I can't even get the door open. There's nothing I can do."

"Okay," said Ple. "We'll have to go on like this and hope for the best."

"We don't have much choice," said Baxter.

Ple grinned. "We should be in near the land in about half an hour. It doesn't look like she's going to ice up anymore."

"Here change your shirt," said Baxter as he threw a dry shirt to Ple.

"No," said Ple. "I might need that later. There's a lot of nurses in St. Anthony." He handed it back.

The boat steamed on and finally came near the shore at Goose Cove Cape. It then proceeded on towards St. Anthony and at 1 p.m. it came around Fishing Point and started into St. Anthony Harbour.

The people of St. Anthony saw the boat as it came around Fishing Point and they rushed to the edge of the ice. The inner harbour was frozen over. They noticed the boat was listing badly to port and was covered with ice resembling an iceberg. It came near the edge of the ice. The engine was slowed for the approach and finally they shut it down completely. The people on the edge of the ice grabbed the boat and held it because no one on the boat could get out of the cabin to even throw the rope as ice preventing the doors from being opened. One of the men on the ice got a dog trace and tied the boat. They then came on board and started chopping the ice away to get the doors open.

After a while one door was freed and Ranger Peters was the first to get out. He had his camera and went out on the ice taking pictures of the boat. This made Ple furious. He pointed to Ranger Peters and said to all on the ice. "Can you imagine, we got a dying man on board here and the Ranger spends his time taking pictures."

Everyone looked at Peters. It did look funny.

Ple turned to Baxter. "As of now," he said, "my job is finished and I never want to lay me eyes on another Ranger as long as I live." He then turned around and kicked the wheel.

The ice was cleaned from the deck and the lines were secured. The doors were opened and Danny Corcoran and Mr. Casey were taken off the Pioneer. A doctor and two nurses were on the ice to meet them. Danny left on an ambulance sled that was pulled by Johnny Stranemore.

Ple looked at him. Danny's eyes were closed. Everybody left then leaving Ple alone on the boat. He went down into the forecastle and sat down on the locker. "What have I just gone through?" he asked himself. He put his elbows on his knees, scratched his beard. He had not yet even had a chance to shave. "It has been the hardest one hundred dollars I have ever earned, but I guess it was worth it. I have gotten to know Danny Corcoran. "Yes," he said out loud, looking out through the window, "I got to know Danny Corcoran just before he died."

Danny was taken to the hospital that afternoon. The medical records say he was in bad shape. His feet and hands were full of gangrene. Both legs were swollen and there was no sensation in both of his legs. His heart was weak, but he was able to eat a small meal. The doctors started to give him treatment immediately trying to stabalize him, nuture him and ward off the dreadful infections. They watched him all night. Because of his extremely bad condition, they gave him drugs for pain and treated his feet and hands.

Chapter 30
April 2-4, 1936

The next day, Danny was a little better but he was watched continually. During the day they brought in Mr. Bill Carpenter. (Mr. Carpenter was interviewed and remembers the event quite well. He is a retired dockworker who worked a lifetime for the Grenfell Mission and is one of St. Anthony's outstanding citizens. During this time he gave, and I quote "Earl, I gave 85 to 90 blood donations to whoever needed my blood. I have international type blood. I was called in to give blood to a Ranger. This was Corcoran.)

He gave blood and they soon gave Danny a blood transfusion. All day and night the nurses and doctors treated his gangrene. That night they held a meeting. The decision was that in order for Danny to live, both arms and legs would have to be amputated. It had taken the rescue party too long to reach the hospital.

That night they started to make preparation to amputate his right leg first. His temperature started to rise and everyone knew that Ranger Corcoran was in for a bad time. The next morning April 4th he complained of a stiff neck and jaw. He looked pale. He was almost unable to control the pain. It was so severe it looked as though the skeleton was going to get up and walk away from the body. Danny had to be strapped to the bed. Every nerve and every cell felt as though it was going to come apart.

The doctors came in with the report and there was no doubt about their diagnosis. Danny Corcoran had tetanus. The doctors immediately gave him 10,000 units of antitoxin. The doctors had a meeting and decided that both his legs had to be amputated at once. The nurses quickly got him ready for the operation. He was then taken into the operating room. The doctors stood almost motionless and looked at the young Ranger with the red hair. Emotions were high. It was an awful thought to have to cut off the legs of someone so young. They glanced at each other and gave a sign of concern. The nurses could hardly look Danny in the eyes.

"Well," said the doctor in charge, Dr. Curtis, "it has to be done in order to save his life."

At 9 a.m. Danny was given ether and very quickly went unconscious. The operation was not considered complicated, but it took all the strength Danny had, because of his very poor condition. The operation gradually weakened him more. Other people were called to give blood, in addition to all of his other medications. He was given more antitoxin through the day, until the hospital supply was exhausted. Then the doctors and the Rangers made arrangements to have more flown in.

Ranger Peters went to the nurses' residence with Nurse Flight. The rest of the crew except Ple (who stayed to take care of the boat and clean off the rest of the ice) went to the annex (a place for visitors to stay when they were travelling with patients). Ranger Peters arranged for sleeping quarters for all the crew except Ple.

In the evening Ple took the boat and pulled it along the edge of the ice to a small fishing stage and with the help of a few residents, they got the boat in along by the wharf and tied it to a flake (flat wooden surface on which cod is dried.) The tide was high so the boat was in near the land. It was almost dark when this work was done and the wind was picking up from the northeast, therefore to leave the boat at the edge of the ice would not be wise. At about 10 p.m. Ple lay down on the locker. He was thinking about the day's happenings and how close they had come to capsizing the boat out in the middle of Belvy Bay. It was more serious than any of the crew knew, but anyway, they had made it to St. Anthony safely.

What hurt Ple most was Peters and Nurse Flight. Can you imagine the two of them out taking pictures and Danny Corcoran dying on board the boat. Those thoughts raced through his mind. He sat up. He felt mad. He went to the stove and put the kettle on. He felt hungry. He looked around for something to eat but all he found was a bun of bread. There was a little butter and sugar. He made a cup of tea and ate the buttered bread. He put the light out and lay back on the locker. It was as if he had just gone to sleep when all of a sudden he was thrown across the cabin. He hit his head on the table. The dishes were flying. The kettle smashed against the wall.

Ple scrambled to his knees and quickly surveyed the situation. "What's happening?" he asked himself. "Where am I?"

He then realized what had happened. The tide had fallen and the boat was on dry land. Suddenly it fell out on its side. He got to his feet and climbed into the wheelhouse and had a look around. Sure enough this is what had happened. There was nothing he could do. It was too dark. He went back down and spent the night partly lying on the sidewalls of the cabin getting very little sleep.

The next morning he discovered the boat was half full of water. When the tide came in a crowd of men came and hauled it in further and discovered a large hole in the wooden hull of the boat. They quickly got to work and repaired it. At about noon Ple was hungry and went up to the local merchant, Mr. Ish Pomeroy, who when he heard Ple's story, could hardly believe his ears. "My son," he said, "here's my store. Take whatever you want: food, tobacco, clothes, or anything, and you don't have to pay me one cent."

"I can't do that, Mr. Pomeroy," said Ple.

Ish Pomeroy looked at him very sternly. "I insist that you do it and furthermore you come straight home with me right now."

"I can't, Mr. Pomeroy. I can't leave the boat. She leaks and she's owned by the United Church. It's our only transportation home and someone has to stay aboard.

The party stayed all that day and night at St. Anthony then left for home the next morning.

Chapter 31
April 5-6, 1936

In the morning Danny had a convulsion. He was now in a very, very worsening condition. He had been too long on the beat before getting to hospital and had to be strapped continually to the bed. What remained of his body was in a trembling condition. He shook as if he were a leaf on a tree. His eyes were rolled over in his head showing only the white of them and looking at him you would think it was just a body in the morgue after being picked up on some beach and stripped bare of flesh by the crows.

In the evening he was sedated again and given pain killers. He then became conscious and rational, but he was in great distress and was deteriorating very fast. That night if either sound was made Danny would go completely to pieces. He had both legs cut off above the knees and it seemed that each time he thought of this he would scream and toss in the bed and would have to be held down. Any little thing would get his attention, even a little squeak such as the door making a little noise, would drive him crazy. At midnight a carpenter had to be called in and oil the door butts to prevent any sound, whatsoever.

On the afternoon of April 5th, an aeroplane arrived from Gander to pick him up, but was unable to land in St. Anthony Harbour because of high winds. It circled the hospital and the sight of an aeroplane drew all the residents of St. Anthony out into the cool evening air. It circled the hospital at low altitude and threw a package out of the window. Somebody picked it up and looked at the address. It was for the Doctor in Charge of the Grenfell Hospital, St. Anthony. The package was quickly taken to Dr. Curtis's office. It was apparent what happened. The small package was wet and soggy and when opened it was learned that the bottle of the drug anti-tetanus toxin was smashed. The doctor lowered his head and groaned. He then quickly wrote off a wireless to the head Ranger telling him what had happened and requesting more. He also wrote a message to the Gander Hospital requesting more. A runner was quickly dispatched to the wireless office and telegrams sent.

On the morning of April 6, 1936, Ranger Danny Corcoran was reported to be in a very poor condition. The doctors and nurses came into his room and dressed his wounds. Danny experienced agony that words would never be able to tell or even attempt to tell. At one point that morning, he screamed and cried as though he was on the country lost and freezing. The scene was so heartbreaking that the nurses had to leave the room completely. It was said that he even looked cold. He was calling Barbara to come near him and warm his feet. He would call his mother to let him put his head in her hands saying, "Mom, please come a little nearer. Please, just a little nearer. I'm dying, mom. Please kiss me." He would cry and say, "Mom, don't you know I'm Danny?" Then he would scream again.

The doctors sedated him and gave him large doses of morphine. His temperature increased and gradually his heart and lungs begain to fail. His body by noon was completely rigid. The pain was so severe he became completely insane. That afternoon more anti-tetanus toxin arrived and this was given to him immediately both intravenously and spinally. There was a slight improvement but again his condition very rapidly slipped. He then became irrational and finally after every ounce of strengh was used up and every cell in his body had collapsed, he lost consciousness.

It was the last time that No. 14, Ranger Danny Corcoran would ever look at and recognize a human being on this earth. He lay motionless and only his breathing made the difference from being alive and being dead. His infection, agony and pain were overwhelming him.

Chapter 32
April 7, 1936

Danny still lay motionless. Only his breathing told the doctors and nurses that he was still alive, but they knew the end was near. The aeroplane had come and gone and Danny could not be moved. It was certain he would die in St. Anthony Hospital. At around noon this young 21 year old Ranger with the red hair and blue eyes, with two legs and two arms missing, had a massive convulsion and died.

The doctor checked his heartbeat and said, "He's gone nurse. He's gone. I've got a feeling this should have never happened if they had got him to a hospital when they found him." He then leaned over and looked at the eyes that were staring out into eternity and very gently closed them for the last time.

On March 27, 1936, the first report in the Evening Telegram said that Ranger Danny Corcoran was missing on the Great Northern Peninsula since March 12. It said that Major Anderton, Commanding Officer of the Newfoundland Rangers received a telegam from Earl Patey of River of Ponds and that Corcoran had his leg injured.

On March 28, the Evening Telegram said, "Missing Ranger Located. Corcoran found after ten days lost."

On April 6, the Evening Telegram reported Ranger Corcoran in serious condition. It said he entered hospital. His condition was considered very serious.

On April 7, the Evening Telegram reported again. "Ranger Daniel Corcoran passed away at St. Anthony Hospital. He died at 1:30 P.M. today. A plane arrived on Monday too late for its mission of mercy. He was a splendid young man.

It was a hazy day around St. John's, warm and very little wind. Danny Corcoran's mother spent most of the day cleaning her house. Every few minutes she would go to the window and look over the city. She had an uneasy feeling. She felt sick all over. There was a pain in her head and her bones ached, but the pain she felt in her heart was the hardest. She had spent most of the last two days crying. She had tried to get more details of Danny's condition but was unable due to poor communications.

It was 4:30 and the elderly woman with the silver hair sat at the kitchen table with her hands to her head as if holding it up. "My, oh my," she sighed. "I wonder what will be the end of this." She thought about Danny when he was a small boy. She could see these little hands and feet of his, how he would sit in the pews of the church with his hands folded and she could see him running smartly with his dog up the grassy lane. But little did she know that Danny had left parts of his fingers and hands along the banks of the Souflett's River. Little did she know that blood and water had dripped from his feet onto the snow turning it a dark red in the moonlight along the Souflett's Riverbank. And it was a good thing that she did not know that just 24 hours earlier the janitor in the Grenfell Hospital at St. Anthony had taken the two legs and two arms contaminated with gangrene, that had been sawed off Danny Corcoran, and was wrapped in white linen, and had thrown them in the incinerator, never again to walk the grass. Never again would those hands smooth the dog. It was a good thing she did not know this, but now she sat at the table wearing a white apron, broken hearted, waiting.....

.....Waiting for something to happen. She had a feeling something was happening. Then a knock. Yes, it was a knock on the door. She got up from the table and very quickly went out into the porch and opened the door. The man that stood in front of her was a messenger, but he wasn't the kind that brought the mail or delivered the paper. This messenger was a middle aged man, wearing a white collar and a long robe. He had a silver cross lying quietly on his chest. Her heart leaped. "Good afternoon, Father."

He looked at this lady, then said, "My child, may I come in?"

She knew by the tone of his voice he was indeed a messenger.

"Excuse me, my dear," he said. He half turned to the man standing a few feet away.

She glanced at him. This man was in uniform. "This is Major Anderton of the Newfoundland Rangers," said the priest.

She did not look up or speak, but turned and walked back into the kitchen and said, "you may come in."

She knew the message she was about to receive was not good. She walked to the table and sat down. The family bible was on the table near her and on it was coiled a set of prayer beads. She picked them up. She looked up at the priest and Major Anderton with tears in her eyes and said "What is it, Father?"

He reached down and took her by the hands and said, "My dear, I'm sorry about what I have to tell you." He searched for the right words, then let go of her hands and she immediately put her fingers in her mouth. Her eyes were wild. She held her breath.

"The news I have is about Danny."

She dropped her head.

"His injuries, my dear, were much worse than first thought." I have to tell her thought the priest, then said. "My dear, Danny passed away early this afternoon at St. Anthony Hospital. I'm sorry."

She groaned, then put her head in her hands. Her body shook. "My God! My God!" she said. 'I'll die."

Major Anderton stepped over near her. He was a sharp looking man, a retired Mounted Policeman, about fifty years old, grey hair showing below his cap. "Mrs. Corcoran," he said in a clear voice, "I'm sorry we did all we could and I want to extend to you our deepest sympathy."

She looked up and said through tears and sobs, "Thank you."

The words hurt Major Anderton. He then turned and walked out the door. As he stepped out on the bridge he stopped, then turned and looked back into the house. He could hear the elderly priest praying as he walked down on the sidewalk. He stood there for a moment and thought about the young Ranger. "I wonder what went wrong," he thought. "Why wasn't he brought to St. John's Hospital?" The noise around him aroused his thoughts. It was the neighbours. They were gathering. He knew they sensed something was terribly wrong. He quickly stepped aboard the car and his driver slowly drove away, leaving the agony to be poured out by loved ones and neighbours.

Barbara Gale, Edward Pittman, and Aunt Martha had finished eating and had gone into the living room. "Someone's coming," said Uncle Ned. "Hello," he called and waited. Then a voice said, "Uncle Ned?"

"Yes?" Why it's Gill Ellsworth. Gill, come in."

Gill came in. He was looking pale.

"What brings you this way, Gill?" said Aunt Martha.

"I got a wireless for Uncle Edward." He reached into his pocket and took out the envelope.

All eyes were on him. Everybody held his breath.

It's a pink message." (A pink message in these days meant bad news.) "This message is for all of you. In fact, it's for everyone in Harbour Deep."

Barbara knew what it was even before it was read. She knew it was about Danny. They had talked about it, then Gill Ellsworth slowly read the wireless.

"WE ARE SORRY TO INFORM YOU DANNY CORCORAN PASSED PEACEFULLY AWAY EARLY THIS AFTERNOON AT ST. ANTHONY HOSPITAL. PLEASE ACCEPT OUR DEEPEST SYMPATHY. MAJOR ANDERTON, NFLD. RANGERS   Barbara got up from the couch and went into the bedroom. Uncle Edward sat in his chair and hung his head.

Epilogue

Pleman Gillard stepped ashore from the small motor boat onto the fishing stage wharf. He had been on the Upper Cloud River with a group of prospectors for six weeks. It was now May 20. The snow was gone except in a few valleys high on the country. He had two packsacks. He took them from the boat and carried them ashore. Once on the road that led around the town of Englee he met Gus Compton.

"Hello, Gus," he said.

"Ple, you're back. Let me carry one of those bags for you."

He handed a packsack to Gus.

"Eh Ple, you got any gold in here?"

They both laughed.

"I suppose you heard about Danny Corcoran, Ple?"

"No," said Ple.

"Sure he died the next day after you left."

Ple dropped the bag he was carrying. Gus looked at him. "Yes, old man. They chopped off both his legs and arms and he didn't recover."

"Well," said Ple. "All that work for nothing."

"It wasn't for nothing, Ple. He should have never died. Maybe somebody will learn a lesson from this."

Ple said nothing.

They reached the house. "Did any mail come for me, father?"

"No, but you got a wireless. It has been here now for two weeks. The operator said it was from the Newfoundland Rangers."

"Where is it at?" asked Ple quickly.

Uncle Noah got the wireless and gave it to him. Ple opened it. There was silence. Both Gus and Uncle Noah looked at him.

"Listen to this." He began to read. "NEWFOUNDLAND RANGER HEADQUARTERS, MAY 5, 1936. REQUEST YOU SEND US BILL FOR WORK DONE WITH RANGER PETERS IN MARCH, 1936. SIGNED PAYC-LERK, NEWFOUNDLAND RANGERS."

Ple growled and sat down at the table. He was mad. "I signed a contract before I went on the country. That was my bill." He paused for a moment. "I wonder what Peters is up to."

Gus spoke up. "Ple, I think you should go down to see him. He's home. I saw him this morning."

Ple tapped his fist on the table. "I certainly am. As soon as I get a shave."

"I can tell you one thing," said Uncle Noah nervously, "there's not much use of you going down to Aunt Annie Filliers' and kick up a racket. All you'll do is get yourself in trouble."

"We'll see about that."

"I got a dirty suspicion," said Gus, "That you'll never see that hundred dollars. Art and Jack got theirs."

"How much did they get?" said Ple.

"They got sixty bucks each."

"Did they send in a bill? Do you know?"

"Yes," said Gus. "The minute you left, Peters got them to send in a bill."

"But listen, Gus. The contract that I signed was my bill."

"Yes, but you see, Ple, Peters only done that just to get you to go. He couldn't do that because if he sent it in he would get himself in trouble."

"Listen, Gus," said Ple, "If I don't get my hundred dollars, Peters will go to the Supreme Court for murdering Danny Corcoran."

"How Ple?"

"Don't do anything foolish," said Uncle Noah.

"Now look here, old man. Peters got money belonging to me and I'm having it."

Nothing more was said. Gus got up and went home.

It was 3:30 p.m. when Ple walked into Aunt Annie's house. She met him at the door. "Ple, my son, how are you? When did you get back?"

"I got home today, Aunt Annie."

Ple was in no mood to carry on any kind of conversation with Annie Fillier and she sensed it. She knew what he was there for. She had overheard a conversation about the one hundred dollars Ple was supposed to get paid, but wasn't going to.

"Where's Peters, Aunt Annie?"

"He's in his room, my son. You can go on in."

Ple went in and shut the door. Aunt Annie quickly moved to the door and put her ear to it to listen.

Peters was sitting at a homemade desk. He quickly looked up when Ple stepped into the room. "Good afternoon, Ple," he said, searching for words.

Ple lightly walked over to the desk, almost like a cat and looked down at him. For a moment all the things that happened while on the country, all the times Peters wanted to go home, why he had not wanted to look for Danny, and why he intentionally made a decision that caused the death of Danny Corcoran were in his thoughts, and as he looked at Peters with eyes blazing, Peters could read them. He rolled the pencil in his fingers, then said chokingly, "What do you want?"

"I want my hundred dollars," said Ple with a squeaky voice.

Peters didn't answer.

Ple took the wireless from his pocket and said, "What does this mean?"

Peters read the wireless then said, "They want your bill, so they can pay you."

"My contract is my bill. Do you remember?" said Ple.

"Yes," said Peters. "I remember."

"I'm sure you do," said Ple. "Then hand it over to me so I can send it in."

Peters was silent. He didn't know what to say.

"Well," said Ple loudly, "hand it over. I want to send it away."

"I can't find it," said Peters, and it was noticeable to Ple that Peters was getting mad.

"I want that contract, Peters."

"You're not getting it."

Ple looked around the desk, then he noticeed a briefcase near Peters. "Maybe it's in there," he thought.

"Give me your bill and get out," said Peters almost screaming.

"I'm not leaving here until I get that contract," said Ple loudly and with this he grabbed the briefcase.

"Put that down. That's government property." Peters was screaming now.

"I will not."

Peters quickly drew his revolver and pointed it at Ple. "Now put down that briefcase or I'll blow..." The door suddenly burst open and Annie Fillier burst into the room. Annie Fillier was only a small woman, who was very kind, but she was like a wildcat when she got mad and now she was mad.

"Ranger Peters, what in the world are you doing? Are you gone mad?" Then she came straight at him. "What are you going to do? Shoot Pleman? Just what are you doing with that gun? Imagine, you're in my home and you've got a gun on a man?"

No one spoke. "Pleman is not a bad boy and none of Noah Gillard's boys are. Now you put that gun away or I'm going to report you."

Peters put his revolver away and sat down at his desk again.

"If I hear another sound, I'm sending for Baxter Gillard." She then went out.

Ple sat down with the briefcase on his lap. He took out a file that said Daniel Corcoran. He looked for the contract and couldn't find it. He saw a letter. It was to Major Anderton. It was a detailed letter and it told about the search for Danny Corcoran. The last paragraph said "Sir, Pleman Gillard, one of our members, only went ahead when we needed a kettle of water or to cut a dry stick of wood for the stove. He stayed behind all the time."

Ple shut the file and put it back into the briefcase, then threw it on the floor. He got up and walked over to the desk and leaned over Peters and said with a low tone of voice that almost cut Peters to the bone, "Peters," he said, "You, Art, Jack Brown and I know what went on in the country and all of us and the people of Harbour Deep know what went on. You would not send for the airplane, but I got news for you. I am going to the Supreme Court. That's it. I can see now what you're up to."

Peters dropped his head and took out his handkerchief. Ple saw tears come to his eyes. "Ple," he said, "my father is dead and my mother and sister live together, and I'm the only support they got. If you go to the Supreme Court, I'll get fired and they'll have to get by on six cents a day. What's done is done."

Ple looked at him with disgust and turned and walked out. He knew he would never get his hundred dollars. A month later when the first mail boat came(The Northern Ranger), he received a cheque for sixty dollars.

The coastal boat, Northern Ranger, blew a loud cloud of steam that made the sound almost like a train. It was a signal to the town of Englee for the people to get ready to help unload mail and supplies. It went to the wharf that was owned by the merchant and fish buyer, John Reeves. After tying up, the crew started to get ready to unload. The famous captain of this fleet of ships was Captain Snow. He was sitting at his desk in the Captain's Office, which was the highest part of the ship. As he sat in this position he could see all parts of the ship by just moving his chair a few feet either way. With the ship docked and the mail put ashore, preparations were made to unload the freight. A light knock came on the door and Captain Snow looked up. "Come in," he said.

The door opened and John Reeves stepped into his office. "John, how are you?" Captain Snow smiled and quickly got up and walked over to greet his old friend.

"I'm fine," said John. They shook hands.

"What kind of winter did you have, John?"

"Very mild. We had a lot of rain."

"Have a seat, please."

John Reeves sat down. The two men had a chat about the Newfoundland economy. Then John stood up to look at the activity on the wharf. He owned most of the freight that was being unloaded. As he was sitting down, his keen eyes caught a glimpse of a box strapped on the upper deck under one of the life boats. John Reeves was a man who used the coastal ships a lot and knew that if a box was carried there it was a corpse. He had seen them there before.

"I see someone has cashed it in," said John.

"Yes," said Captain Snow .

Then John jokingly said, "One more body for the ground."

"I guess," said Captain Snow unconcerned. "Well, to be honest with you, there's only a part of a body in that box."

"What do you mean?" asked John with interest.

Captain Snow looked at John Reeves and said, "You wouldn't guess who is in there, but I'll tell you. In that box is what was left of a young Ranger. His name is Corcoran. They told me in St. Anthony that he was missing two legs and two arms and his frame was just a skeleton. The box is as light as a feather. If we never had it tied down, it would blow away."

John Reeves stared at the box. His mind recalled the story that was related to him by Pleman Gillard.

"Captain Snow," he said. "We know the whole story."

"What happened to him?"

"That's Danny Corcoran you got there. Our men here in Englee found him up on Harbour Deep Brook."

"Tell me more," said Captain Snow.

Then John Reeves slowly told him the whole story. When he finished both men looked out through the window at the box under the lifeboat.

"I am shocked to hear such a story, John. Has there been an investigation?"

"No, not to my knowledge."

"Well, I'll be going to Harbour Deep tomorrow. Do you think I should tell anybody up there that I got Danny Corcoran on board?"

"No," said John. "It might upset the school teacher."

"I guess you're right," said Captain Snow, "but maybe someday somebody will tell the story about the Newfoundland Ranger, of how the Northern Ranger carried him to St. John's, leaving half of him on the Northern Peninsula.

"Maybe so, Captain. Maybe so."

Then John Reeves slowly got up and walked out, leaving Captain Snow looking at the box under the lifeboat.

Barbara Gale looked out through the window from the little school house and saw the Norther Ranger as it came around the point of land looking out Northeast Arm.

"It's the coastal boat!"

There was a lot of excitement.

"It's the Northern Ranger," said one of the pupils.

"It's on its way to St. John's," said Barbara. If it only had been a week later arriving, she would have been joining it to go home. She thought about Danny, how he used to talk about going home this spring. If he had still been here he would be going home to St. John's on this very boat. Her thoughts raced, but instead he was put away somewhere in the ground with his travelling days all over, never to be moved anymore. But then the thought struck her, "I wonder where Danny is buried and I wonder how did they take him to St. John's?" Then she looked at the Northern Ranger. "Yes," she said outloud. "It's funny. I wonder."

Sweat was on her forehead. She looked at her pupils who were standing around. Then she said, "We had a Newfoundland Ranger here this winter, pupils, who is gone. Now we've got the Northern Ranger which is getting ready to leave. But little did she know that the two Rangers were about to leave Harbour Deep right now at the same time and one would never come back again.

Danny was taken to St. John's and is buried in Mount Carmel Cemetery.

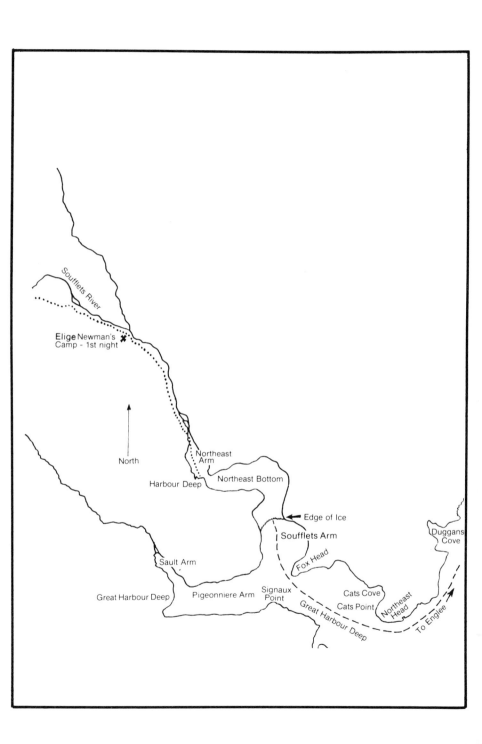

ABOUT THE AUTHOR

Earl Pilgrim started his working career as an Infantry Man in the Canadian Army in the P.P.C.L.I. and while there he became involved in the sport of boxing and eventually became the Canadian Light Heavy Weight Boxing Champion. After a stint in the Forces he took a job with the Newfoundland & Labrador Forestry Dept. as a forest ranger. It was during his time with the Forestry Dept. that he came to recognize the plight of the big game population on the Northern Peninsula. After 9 years as a forest warden he applied for and received a job with the Nfld. Wildlife Service as a Wildlife Protection Officer.

For 12 years now Earl has devoted his life to the conservation and growth of the big game population on the Northern Peninsula and under his surveillance the moose and caribou populations have prospered and grown at an astounding rate. As a game warden and a local story teller he has gained the respect of conservationist and poachers alike. It was during his many hair raising experiences in Northern Nfld. admiration and respect for Danny Corcoran grew.

After many conversations with the late Noah Pittman and Pleman Gillard, he learned of some of the details of Danny Corcoran's attempt at survival in the Northern Nfld. Wilderness and the misery and torture that befell him on what started out to be a routine patrol to protect the wildlife of that area in the Winter of 1936.

Awards: Safari International presented by Provincial Wildlife Div., Gunther Behr award presented by Nfld. & Lab. Wildlife Federation, Achievement Award 'Beyond The Call of Duty" presented by the White Bay Central Dev. Assoc.